Ciel City

Mary Beshay

AOS Publishing, 2025

Copyright © 2025

Mary Beshay

ISBN: 978-1-998662-75-3

Cover Artist: Meredith Lindsay

Visit AOS Publishing's website:

www.aospublishing.com

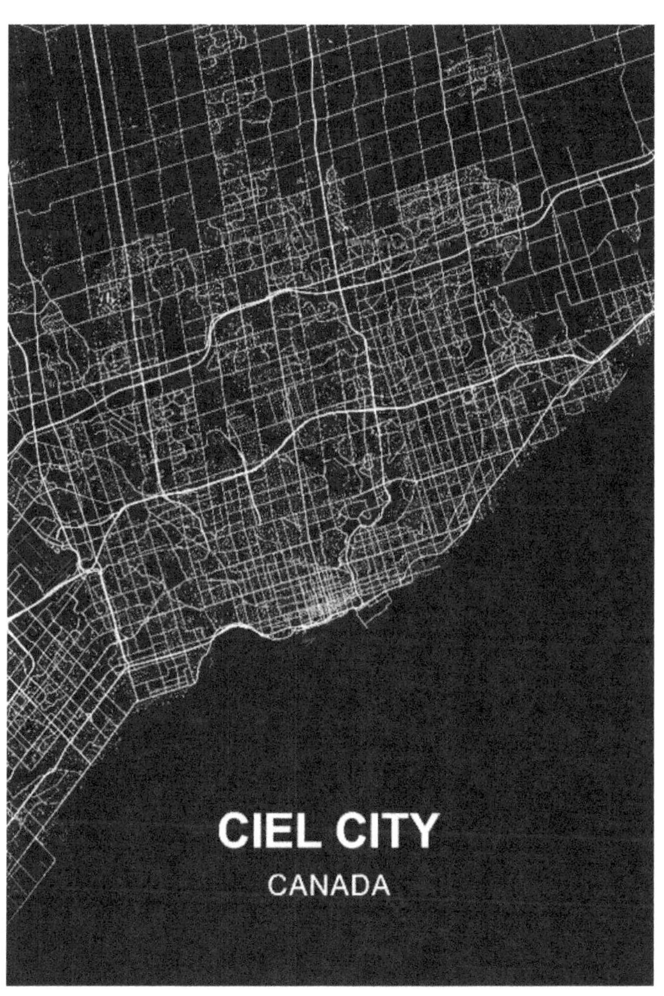

CIEL CITY
CANADA

To all the dreamers and their untold stories.

Author's Note

Overactive imaginations, am I right?

A blessing and a curse. Mostly a curse when you're trying to focus in class and your brain decides to stage a full-blown character death scene in the middle of a lecture on property law.

I used to think writing was just a hobby, something "productive" to do in my spare time. Not a full-blown addiction. And yet, there I was: finishing a full day of classes, clocking out of work, barely alive—and still crawling into bed with my laptop and a playlist that screamed *emotional damage incoming*.

An addict, I tell you.

When people ask me, "What kind of story is this?", I usually just say, *It's the kind of story I like to read.* Which is true. These characters became something more than just names on a page. They became my people— flawed and fragile, brave and broken. I laughed with them. I cried for them. I put them through hell. And still, I rooted for them.

So completing this story, putting in the final touches, and hitting save… that wasn't easy. It felt like saying goodbye to a friend. The kind of goodbye where you promise to see each other again, but deep down, you know life doesn't always make room for that kind of reunion.

All I can hope now is that you'll find something in this story—some part of Ciel City, or maybe some part of yourself—that lingers. That stays with you.

Thanks for giving my novel a chance.

Thanks for reading.

A Word Before You Begin (Content Warning):

This book touches on sensitive materials and potentially triggering topics, including trauma, abuse, grief, violence, and more. I do not write about these themes for shock value, but rather to thoughtfully explore the real struggles people have survived through a fictional lens.

Please take care of yourself while reading.

Contents

The rooftop was unwelcoming.

The sound of the metal door banging shut was like a cannon fire. The city traffic made itself known in an obnoxious display of noise pollution. The sound, mixed with the howling wind, drowned out the echo of footsteps beating against the rooftop.

They continued relentlessly across the hot floor, the sun angrily glaring at the building. There was no hesitation in their march—no pause or second thought.

A school bag flew to the side, skidding across the concrete. The footsteps continued to the ledge of the roof. Once at their destination, they finally stopped at the edge of the building.

Silence followed.

Even the wind decided to quiet down and watch until, finally, their next step was off the edge of the roof.

The wind rushing up, the sun screaming out, the ground greeting.

CHAPTER ONE

Welcome to Ciel

Angela never understood the appeal of going to the big city. The fascination people had with the rush of pedestrians, the towering buildings, and the constant movement. She felt trapped under the unforgiving concrete. Unable to break through the surface to call for help.

Yet here she was, on the bus into Ciel City.

Ciel City, locally known as just Ciel, had a way of drawing in people and changing their destinies. She was proof of that. People would come into the city mistakenly assuming who they were and what they want, but Ciel had already made those choices for them. Coming to the big city for her final year of high school was not what her parents had wanted, but fate had already decided for her.

The bus bounced along as it hit every pothole on the road. Angela rested her head along the window, the bus jolting her around. The skyline was packed with gray buildings rubbing shoulders together, with one needle-like building standing taller than the rest. The sun worked overtime to give life to the dull city. From a distance, the miniature skyscrapers grew into colossal giants as the bus emerged into the heart of the city.

Fidgeting with her ticket, Angela tensely messaged her dad that she would be arriving at the bus station soon. She observed the people on the sidewalk going about their day, imagining the lives they lived: the couple who argued as they walked their dog, the old woman who crossed the road, flipping off a driver, the woman in a leather jacket who twisted through the waves of people while on the phone.

The bus driver announced into the microphone as the bus turned into an overcrowded station, "Ciel City Bus Terminal. Welcome to Ciel!"

The first week of September had bid summer goodbye as students flocked through the station; coming back from visiting their families. Friends greeted one another, while others waved as their loved ones left the metropolis. Angela took her luggage, her eyes scanned the crowd. No one was there to greet her.

Aunty Kim couldn't even wait for me to arrive in Ciel. If it was my sister, she would have cancelled her work trip in an instant, Angela thought bitterly, pushing her way out of the station onto the endless concrete sidewalks of Ciel. Several people wearing black puffer jackets bumped into her. The weather threatened to turn chilly soon despite the sunshine.

The city was an orchestra of cars honking, people chattering, and construction banging from all around. It was a distorted melody she hadn't heard in a while. The last time she was in the city was almost ten years ago, long enough for the sounds of Ciel to be forgotten and then distantly familiar in a far corner of her mind. Even the smell in the air; a mix of lake water and subway exhaust fumes, felt like a second home.

It made Angela nostalgic for a time she could never revisit.

Clenching her purple suitcase tighter, Angela signalled for an orange and teal cab. Instantly, one screeched to a stop in front of her. The trunk popped open dramatically. She hauled her suitcase inside before taking a seat in the back of the cab.

"Where ya heading?" the driver called out, the door not even closing before the cab took off.

"Corner of Michener and 16th in Midtown," Angela answered. She texted her dad another update as the cab jerked her around.

The cab driver nodded as he hit the gas, launching the car into traffic, honking at pedestrians and cyclists; adding another instrument to the melody of Ciel. The meter sped greedily along.

Sleek buildings of glass and stone towered overhead, casting the streets below into a shadow. Angela watched the city flash past her, ignoring the manic driving, ignoring the bitterness that the nostalgia was bringing her, ignoring how tired she was, and not just from the trip to

Ciel—tired of the many arguments and fights she had with her parents about her living on her own, of the months of planning for her trip to Ciel City and transfer to St. Katherine's High School.

Finally being in the city after all that time was overwhelming. Her eyes were not able to keep up with all the different sights the city had to offer: the different subway entrances that littered the corners of intersections, the modern and chic buildings and stores that turned into simple, locally-owned ones the further the car ventured from the bus station.

The variety of people who called this city their home.

Aunty Kim lived in Midtown, a more residential neighbourhood compared to the city's downtown core. Midtown was filled with parks, grocery stores, and schools. It was a place where a family could live and raise children within a bustling city.

The cab came to a stop in front of a brown apartment building. Angela gave the driver a red-coloured bill, thanking him. Once Angela grabbed her suitcase and stepped onto the cracked sidewalk, the cab raced down the street, eagerly searching for another client.

Glancing up at the old building, Angela took a deep breath as she stepped inside. She was greeted with chipped beige paint and the lack of an elevator—another nuisance to deal with. But the building smelled good. The waft of baked goods floated from one of the first-floor apartments. Two kids were kicking a ball back and forth in one of the hallways, their yells of delight vibrated all around. The sound of a T.V. blasting behind one of the doors echoed along with the kids.

It was just how Angela remembered her aunt's place. Angela and her sister used to play in these halls growing up: chasing one another, running up and down the stairs, getting yelled at by the neighbours for making a ruckus. Weekends at Aunty Kim's were the best part of Angela's week.

Angela shook her head, snapping back to the present. The hallway wasn't as wide as it had seemed when she was younger. The lens of childhood had saturated the building with vibrant colours. Now, it was just dull hues.

She gingerly knocked on one of the first-floor apartment doors. A long pause later, an elderly woman dressed in a floral nightgown and silk bonnet answered. Her walker knocked against the door.

"Yes?" the woman asked, a little annoyed.

"Hi, I'm Kim's niece, Angela," Angela greeted her politely with a smile. "She said I can pick up her keys from Mrs. McLaughlin?"

"You're kind of young to be living alone, aren't you?" Mrs. McLaughlin scowled skeptically, her watery eyes scanning Angela's tall form, wrinkly eyes narrowing at her baby face.

"I have my parents' permission, plus I'll be eighteen in January, Ma'am."

"Try to enjoy the last moments of your childhood before life steals your youth away," Mrs. McLaughlin retorted with a deeper scowl.

"May I please have the keys? I've just arrived and I'm pretty tired," Angela tried asking again, keeping her face neutral. Mrs. McLaughlin grumbled as she retrieved the keys, her wrinkly hand gripping the walker tightly.

"You better not cause any trouble for us here. No high school parties or the likes, Missy!" Mrs. McLaughlin warned. Dropping the keys into Angela's waiting hand.

"See you around, Mrs. McLaughlin!" Angela called out over her shoulder as she lugged her luggage up the stairs.

A slammed door was the only reply she got.

Six flights of stairs later, Angela thought, as she wiped her forehead and leaned on the doorway of her unit's apartment. Unlocking the door, a wave of memories washed over her.

The place was exactly as Angela had remembered it. To her right was the small kitchen with the cream-coloured fridge. The 'A' and 'J' magnets were still mounted on their spots, all these years later. Nini's 'J' magnet was annoyingly higher than her 'A'. Straight ahead was the living room with the overly plush armchair that was older than her, the pullout couch that she would share with her sister when they slept over at their aunt's, and the bulky T.V. console from the eighties. The bedroom was right next to the kitchen with the chipped oak wooden furniture set and floral lamps on the nightstands. The pink bathroom was further down the hall; ample sunlight poured inside along with the smell of the citrus cleaner Aunty Kim was obsessed with.

Everything had remained untouched by time.

Well, almost everything. The only new additions were two framed pictures on the T.V. console. Angela inspected them. One was of Aunty Kim at a picnic with her friends. Aunty Kim looked exactly like Angela. A beautiful mane of coily black hair surrounded her round face, stopping just past the shoulders. They had the same chocolate skin and almond eyes.

The only other photo was of Angela riding her sister's shoulder when they were younger. Nini was always ready to play with Angela, despite their ten-year age gap. Their mom always said that they were identical twins who just came out at different times. The sisters were often mistaken for Kim's own children. The resemblance between the three of them was uncanny. Angela held the picture closer, huffing as she saw the wide smile plastered on Nini's face.

Hurriedly, she placed the picture inside the T.V. console's cabinet.

Dragging the suitcase into the bedroom, she began to unpack. Her shoulders were heavier than when she had first entered the humble apartment. There was a bitter taste in her mouth despite not eating.

Her phone vibrated. Angela took in a deep breath as she picked up the call.

"Hey, Dad," Angela answered.

"Hi, Angel, you arrived okay?" her dad asked.

Angela tried to gulp down any of the bitterness that remained in her mouth.

"Y-yes, Aunty Kim's place is spotless," Angela stiffly spoke.

"Living at my sister's place is a big help for us. Rent in Ciel has become wild. Please take good care of it. Kim should be back for Christmas, her contract will end then," he explained.

Angela could hear the distant sound of typing on a keyboard.

Figured he would still be working, Angela thought as she checked the time. *He must be in the reception of the office.*

"We need you to do your very best this school year, Angel. Graduating with top grades from STK will secure you a few scholarships for university," he continued. "Your sister had a full scholarship offered. I want the same for you, Angel."

"Are you still waiting for Mom?" Angela changed topics, picking at the blanket. She heard the lecture a thousand times before. She had to get a scholarship or else her family would be struggling to support her through university. Times have been tough ever since they left Ciel, especially with the constant therapy appointments for her mother.

Her father, ever the patient and stern man, softened his tone.

"Yes, her appointment is almost over. I'm sorry we couldn't come with you, Angel. It's just… your mother needs a consistent schedule. Helping you settle in would have disrupted her weekly sessions."

"I know," Angela mumbled, bits of blanket fluff piled into a little mound by her fingers.

"You're my strong angel, Angie. Please study hard and work hard to make friends. A new school year will be the best place for you to break out of your shell. Like we talked about, try to make at least one friend. I know you won't let us down."

"I'm going to unpack now, Dad, I'll text you before I go to bed," Angela mumbled in a quiet voice.

"Go, Angel. Mom and I are here for you," he reassured her before ending the call.

A heavy fog clouded her thoughts. Her father's words echoing in the back of her mind.

I could go for a run to clear my head, while the sun is still out, Angela contemplated.

Hey Angela, have you arrived yet? – Jaya

Hi, yes! I was just unpacking. We're still on for the city tour tomorrow after orientation, right? I want to see all of Ciel City. – Angela

St. Katherine's High School had organized for another senior called Jaya Sharma to be Angela's orientation buddy. From the few times they messaged over the summer, Angela could already tell that she would be a good person to be friends with. Her positive energy and enthusiasm were a welcomed change to Angela's life. It felt good to message someone who was full of warmth. Hopefully, she could be her one friend in this hectic city.

Yes! Cannot wait to finally meet you and show you how awesome Ciel is! You're going to love it here. – Jaya

Angela sat on the bed, staring at the message. Slowly, her arms wrapped around herself. Unpacking was the last thing she wanted to do. Snooping through Aunty Kim's stuff wasn't even tempting, the same way it was as a child.

Instead, she stared at the phone screen. The sounds of the city faded into the back of her mind; the loud construction from up the block, the chattering neighbours in the hall, the endless people milling about their day just outside her window below. Her throat tightened as she thought back to the picture she hid in the living room.

Angela had mentally prepared herself for coming to Ciel. She thought she was ready for it. She told herself that she wouldn't get overwhelmed—that she could do it.

Her slowly nails dug into her arms as she stared at the message from her new friend, the voice of her father repeating in her mind, rooted to her spot in her new home for the year.

"The next station is *Nomos, Nomos Station,*" the robotic voice of a woman announced through the subway speaker.

A man exited the subway, following the sea of people rushing to resurface onto the abused ground of the city.

The man took notice of the state of the streets but continued his march, stepping carefully around the cracked sidewalks and gum-littered ground. He stopped in front of a neglected building with an exterior gray colour that threatened to suck the life of all who entered its green glass doors.

A broken sign read, 'Ciel City Police Department 97th Division'.

Readying himself, he walked through the sliding glass doors. His trained eyes took in every detail of the building: the spiral staircase in the middle of the lobby, the stained gray carpet, and the overflowing trash cans.

The man walked up to the front desk, his back impossibly straight. He greeted the officer who sat there, obnoxiously chewing her gum. "Good morning, officer. I am here to pick up my badge from Captain Chan."

"You must be the greenie," the officer chuckled as she eyed him up and down. When she saw the look of confusion on his face, she explained.

"'Greenie' is local slang for those new to the CCPD. We don't get a lot of external transfers to the 97th division. Cap will be in his office in room 201." She pulled out a visitor's tag, pausing expectantly at the man.

"Officer Amir Hafiz," he introduced himself.

She jotted his name down, leaned over, and slapped it on his chest with a crooked smile.

"Welcome to the CCPD, Greenie."

Giving his thanks, Amir quickly made his way through the miserable building, taking the stairs to room 201. Pausing to straighten his blue dress shirt, Amir pulled out his gold cross from his shirt. He kissed the crucifix once before tucking it back in again. The gold chain was hidden. He knocked three times on the door.

When he heard a muffled 'come in', Amir entered a quaint office. It was like the rest of the building, in a state of decay. A chipped wooden desk with a pre-historic computer mounted on it, stained beige walls, and an older man sweating in one of the torn leather chairs greeted him. Amir raised an eyebrow at the lack of plaques or awards in the captain's office.

"Officer Amir Hafiz, so nice to finally meet you." the portly man spoke as he shook his hand. "I'm Captain Joel Chan."

"Nice to meet you, Captain." Amir nodded politely. "I am honoured to be a part of your force."

"Oh, you're too kind, my boy! It's not every day a greenie comes in to lead an Anti-Gang Task Force here in Ciel City," Captain Chan exclaimed as he took out an already damp handkerchief to wipe his forehead with.

The office isn't that warm, Amir thought, feeling the AC pump from the vents. Amir took a seat in the other torn leather chair, his head held up high. "I will do my best, Captain."

"Well, I am sure you will. Now, your transfer said you were from Haven Brooke. What's it like out there?" Captain Chan asked, shoving the moist handkerchief into his chest square.

"It's a small municipality, part of the Ciel Greater Area. There I was responsible for investigating drug activity. In this new role, I would like to expand my investigations into disappearances."

"Look at you! A small town bigshot coming to the big city, is that it?" Captain Chan joked, a glint of amusement in his eyes.

Amir folded his hands politely on his knees. "I'm not sure I know what you mean, Captain."

"Now, now, Amir. I can see the gears turning behind those exotic eyes of yours. Let me guess, you're mixed!" Chan commented boisterously.

Amir's jaw clenched at the comment. "I do not believe that that kind of language is professional for the workplace, Captain."

He was used to comments about his appearance, people often

guessing his ethnicity and getting it wrong, assuming he was one thing or another instead of just asking him where his parents were from. His green eyes and short curly black hair were invitations for people to speculate. He had learned to let it go, that people would always have their own biases. Those conversations were expected in his small hometown, not in a city as big and as diverse as Ciel City.

Captain Chan held his hands up in apology, chuckling. "All I am saying is that I just don't want you to invest a lot of time into the Anti-Gang Task Force. There's a reason this force has been dissolved so many times before."

Silence filled the room. Captain Chan grinned at Amir as though he understood the unspoken words.

But Amir did not.

"With all due respect, Captain, I will be putting my best foot forward into the Task Force and into the investigation of the local syndicates," Amir replied slowly.

Perhaps I'm not being clear about my intentions? Amir thought. He had experience with investigating local gangs at his old division in Haven Brooke. He was warned that things in Ciel City worked differently, and that he would have to adjust quickly, but he didn't expect this.

His superior shook his head, still gleeful. "A little career advice, my boy. Do not go looking for trouble. The city issued the Task Force just for show; give it a few months and we will transfer you over to Community Programs."

"But Captain—"

"No 'buts'. Believe me, best not to get involved with them," Chan stated, suddenly serious for the first time since their meeting began.

"It's our duty," Amir responded firmly, irritated by the captain's lax attitude. He knew that the CCPD had a reputation for being slow and complicated. Amir could feel his eye begin to twitch.

Captain Chan sighed deeply. His big round shoulders deflated. He asked in a tired voice, "What do you know of the Syndicates, Greenie?"

Amir took a deep breath to steady himself, to push down his annoyance towards his new captain.

"Although there are many gangs in Ciel City, there are three main ones: the Gates, the Halos, and the Wings, " Amir answered.

"I've read through the CCPD's files, but they were always missing vital information. But from what I could gather, the Gates are the oldest and biggest of the Syndicates in Ciel. They are responsible for organized crimes: money laundering, brothels, and most other unsavoury activities."

Amir recounted the information perfectly. Neither his voice nor his hands shook.

"The Halos are the second oldest, known as the drug dealers of Ciel. Last are the Wings; although newer, their reach of human trafficking spans across Ciel, even into other Canadian cities."

Amir studied the captain's face for any disinterest before continuing.

"They each own many territories and have the manpower to operate in the city with little resistance. Surprisingly, there has never been a gang war between the Big Three. Perhaps they have brokered some sort of agreement. Nevertheless, I believe that the CCPD can put a stop to these criminals. There will be change, Captain," Amir concluded, his heart beating loudly in his ears.

Captain Chan held his eyes for a moment longer before he rummaged through his chipped desk. He placed a folder and badge in front of Amir. His clammy hand lingered on the badge.

"Welcome to the CCPD, Officer Hafiz. Best of luck," Captain Chan sighed, the tiredness from earlier amplified in the way he curled in on himself.

Thanking the captain, Amir took the items and promptly left. His chest tightened the further he went from the office. The meeting with the captain was not at all what he had expected. The words, the *warning*, bounced around in his head.

How did it go? – Helen

Typing his response, he made his way back through the depressing lobby and out the green glass doors.

I have my work cut out for me. – Amir

Believe in yourself and in your cause, I know that I do! – Helen

The heaviness in his chest dissipated slightly, a glimmer of hope sneaking its way in. Leave it to Helen to always message him at the right time with the right words.

Walking through his new city, he took in Ciel: the pleasant breeze that danced in the trees. The families who played at the park. Strangers giving up a bench to a pregnant woman. People rushing to help a college student pick up their groceries after tripping. The smell of a café beckoned him towards the promise of coffee and cinnamon donuts.

Not deterred by the Captain's alarming leniency, Amir was ready to bring change to Ciel.

Saint Katherine's High School, locally known as STK, was known to produce the best graduates in the province. Those graduates were the ones to attend the nation's top universities. The entrance exam was unique only to STK, where all the little grade eights were packed together in the school's gymnasium to take the depressing three-hour exam.

Only a handful of applicants were accepted; much to the dismay of the parents. To attend STK meant that you showed promise as a child; whether it came to fruition or not wasn't STK's concern.

The school uniform of gray, navy blue, and white made it easy to identify the privileged students who attended. Aside from the academic prestige of the school, it remained the same as any other publicly-funded high school in Ciel City. People from all different walks of life were welcomed and encouraged to study at STK.

Saint Katherine's, where the future is yours to claim!

Well, at least that was what the school's website promised. Angela scrolled past the endless pictures of students smiling as they gathered around a laptop or as they played a sport. She rolled her eyes at the pictures.

No one is that happy. Life isn't that kind.

The subway rocked to a stop at Saint Katherine's Station. The station was adorned with imagery of her namesake, Saint Katherine of Alexandria. Broken tiles fashioned into murals of wheels and books decorated the station's walls. Angela stiffly trailed behind the swarm of people back onto the streets of Ciel. Her shoulders hitched up to her ears.

Following the maps on her phone past restaurants and bookstores, she reached a black gate with a grand gothic church behind it. The church took up a full city block. Pointed arches, tall narrow windows, and sharp green copper towers stood proudly beside the plain, modern buildings. It screamed grandiose and foreboding. It demanded the full attention of all those who passed by.

Angela had reached her destination; Saint Katherine's High School.

A swarm of twelfth graders flooded the courtyard just past the black gate, their modern fashion contrasted the twelfth-century gothic architecture.

"Excuse me?" a voice called out behind Angela. She turned around to a girl with beautiful short ebony hair decorated with colourful butterfly clips.

"Hi, I'm Jaya, we've been texting over the summer," Jaya exclaimed excitedly, a wide smile on her petite face. "I'm your Orientation buddy!"

"Nice to finally meet you." Angela smiled back.

"You're a lot taller than I thought, Angela," Jaya said with a giggle as she looked up at her. Angela was nearly a head taller than her.

"Maybe I *should* have worn my high heels today," Jaya contemplated, sticking her tongue out at Angela.

Angela chuckled and the tense muscles she'd been holding tight the past day loosened. It was nice to know at least one person, especially one that was so friendly.

"You can call me Angie."

"Sounds great, Angie." beamed Jaya.

The pair made their way through the black gates of the school and into the stone courtyard. Jaya took the lead as they walked through the busy courtyard into the six-story building.

"The orientation will be in the Assembly Hall," Jaya informed as she waved at a few students making their way into the building as well.

"This used to be a cathedral, you know? But they converted the inside to be more modern. Sorry, but it only looks like Hogwarts on the outside!" Jaya joked.

The girls entered through the impressive gothic doorway. Angela craned her head up to see where the points of the arch met. The school was full of arches, but this one was decorated intricately with flowers and figures holding scrolls. It promised something to those who entered underneath. Inspiration, power, knowledge.

Death.

Angela took a deep breath as they crossed the threshold, her heart beating fast. She stared at the complex arch; it was sharper than before.

Angela had watched Nini disappear into this very school from her mother's car for years, studied the way her sister entered under the arches with a skip in her step. She was always so expressive when she would tell Angela how her day at school went. Now that it was her turn to enter, dread-filled every step as though she was being shackled by weights. Her legs were heavier to lift with every step deeper into the school. She wiped her clammy palms on her pants, hoping that Jaya would not notice her short breaths.

The last thing she wanted was for her new classmate to ask if she was okay. Clearly, she wasn't, but she couldn't tell Jaya that. She would want to know why, and the fewer people who know about Angela and her sister, the better. But Jaya saw her hunched posture from the corner of her eyes. She slowed down.

"We can take the long way around?" Jaya suggested. Worry danced across her petite face.

"Let's just get there quickly," Angela replied, her eyes fixed forward.

The school was beautifully kept, the structure remaining true to its gothic time. The inside was carved out and replaced with modern flooring and outlets. No wonder people wanted to study here, it felt extraordinary.

But Angela was not going to be tricked. This school drained the life out of its students. Sucked the soul out of the youth.

A few teachers were herding the sea of students through grand oak doors; what appeared to be the old sanctuary was converted into the Assembly Hall. The students took a seat on wooden pews which creaked from centuries of use.

It was too loud. Friends greeted one another, teachers tried to settle down a hyper sports team, and the creak of the building was too much.

The pangs of loneliness curled in her chest. Angela knew she was an outsider, as though she was looking at the Hall and her new school from outside one of the ornate stained glass windows. It wasn't lost on Angela that if Jaya wasn't her orientation buddy, she would have sat in the full Hall all alone. If Jaya had decided to get up and leave her, she would have been abandoned in a sea of strangers. Her father's words about making friends replayed loudly in her mind. Coming in her last year, Angela prayed that at least Jaya would want to remain friends with her after orientation. It was hard for Angela to break-out of her stubborn shell. There was a reason she didn't have any friends growing up. Her inability to connect with those around her has been a constant roadblock. But she had decided that here in Ciel City, she would at least try. And Jaya was a good candidate; with her warmth and humour it meant that Angela may finally call someone her friend.

The pair took a seat in the back of the Hall. Angela preferred the aisle seat. Jaya still chatted about the school, all the different clubs to join, and which teachers were cool and which were not.

"Mrs. Foto is an easy 'A' if you can show an interest in her fossil collection!" Jaya wisely advised. Angela made a mental note.

At the front of the Hall, a middle-aged man walked onto the stage. He was the most impressively dressed of the faculty: a full three-piece tailored suit with not a salt-and-pepper hair out of place. In comparison, Angela's old principal wore flannel and jeans to school on a good day.

"That's Principal Patel," Jaya whispered as a hush began to fall on the students. Principal Patel leaned into the microphone at the podium and gave a polite 'ahem'. Immediately everyone settled down, except the rowdy students still laughing and talking in the back.

"Would the volleyball team like to take a seat?" he asked in a calm voice; as though he was speaking with toddlers. Some students giggled as everyone turned to look at the team. They quickly settled down.

The large oak doors closed and Principal Patel had the Assembly's full attention.

"Now, to begin our orientation for our senior class of STK, I am pleased to welcome you all back to another year—."

The sound of the oak doors reopening halted Patel's speech, to his annoyance. A tall boy with fluffy brown hair entered the Hall, wincing at the creak of the door.

"Care to join us, Mr. Grayson?" Principal Patel called out as the student rushed into the Hall.

The boy in question sheepishly waved at the principal as the volleyball team called out, "Tardiness is not permitted, Mr. Grayson!"

The students snickered. Sliding into the space between Angela and the end of the pew, the boy gave her a little nod as he settled himself down. Angela looked over at his trembling hands.

He must be embarrassed, Angela thought as the principal resumed his speech.

"As I was saying," Principal Patel continued, with a slight smile at the antics of the students. "Welcome back to another year with us. I speak on behalf of all the faculty and staff of STK that we have high hopes for our graduating class."

He continued his address with standard school expectations, how hard work is rewarding, and that the school community is a collective body. Angela's hunched shoulders began to drop as she became more accustomed to the dynamic of the school.

Principal Patel paused for a moment; he frowned at his notes. "I was instructed to deliver the same warning to each of our years. As you are all aware, Ciel City is a beautiful city with vibrant people. Just like every city, there are good places and bad places, good people and bad people. I implore everyone here to stay safe and not go venturing off into the night for the sake of fun or teenage antics."

He hesitated, his shaking hands gripped the sides of the podium. He kept his head down as he read his notes.

"The Trustee Board has enacted a new school policy. I would like to instruct all students that if anyone is caught being affiliated with any gang or having any interactions with them, your enrollment at our school will be terminated."

The students broke out into murmurs amongst themselves. Jaya tensed as she looked around the Hall.

"What's the problem?" Angela asked innocently.

Jaya gave her a wild look before she glanced around to make sure no one was listening to them. She leaned into Angela's ear to whisper, "The city is run by the Syndicates, Angie. Patel won't be able to enforce this. This doesn't make any sense."

"Your attention, please!" Principal Patel called out over the commotion.

"Yes. The school is very serious when it comes to gang activities. As gang violence, drug distribution, and disappearances are rising, I entreat you all to look out for one another, to stop misconduct before it happens, and to hold one another accountable."

More murmuring from the students as they were tasked with the impossible.

"He wants us to snitch on each other!" a student whispered from the row in front.

"But the donut shop I work at is in the Gates' territory," another one whispered to Jaya's right.

"Is this because of the junior who was caught dealing last year?" came from the other side of the pew.

"This is a zero-tolerance policy!" Patel's voice boomed across the speakers. "Anyone seen to be interacting with the Gates, the Halos, the Wings, or any low-level gang will be expelled."

That silenced the students.

"I know that these are frightening times, but we can still have a productive and memorable year together. Make good friends, make good choices."

Patel looked at all the students, his eyes resting on Angela for a moment longer than any other student as he scanned the room.

"Remember that only you are in control of your life and decisions," Patel stated hesitantly. Jaya huffed at that. "That concludes our Assembly. I am looking forward to seeing everyone in class on Monday."

Noise erupted as the students got up, most still in disbelief at the principal's address.

"Let's get out of here," Jaya whispered as she nudged Angela out of their row.

Angela bumped into the boy who was late to the Assembly; he was deathly pale in the face until the volleyball team called out for him to join them. Jaya hurried Angela out of the Hall before the sea of bodies exited with them.

"Jaya!" a boy's voice called out behind the pair. Angela slowed down, but Jaya continued tugging her along as they cut through the stone courtyard. Jaya's contagious smile from earlier was gone, replaced with a frown. Her eyebrows were drawn in.

"Come on, let me show you around town instead of STK," Jaya announced in an excited voice, but the pitch was off and too high—she was forcing it. Somehow Patel's warning had shaken Jaya.

Maybe I should ask her what's wrong, Angela wondered as she stared at Jaya's tight hold on her wrist.

"Come on, there's so much to show you," Jaya exclaimed as she pulled Angela through the subway station.

"Jaya, hold up, is everything okay-?"

Jaya interrupted Angela as she dragged her to a map of Ciel. "This area is Midtown, not much action here." She gestured to the middle of the map. "So let's go down to the Entertainment District in the Downtown core. From there we can work our way back up to Midtown and drop you off in time for dinner."

Jaya drew a 'u' with her finger on the map. Angela nodded, still confused by her sudden change in behaviour. But she needed Jaya to like her, to be her friend. She needed to succeed this school year, and having a friend at school would make it happen.

"Lead the way, Jaya."

CHAPTER TWO

The Informant

The last sun of summer gave way to the taunting bite of autumn. The light breeze in the air was pleasant as the girls walked along the waterfront. A light jacket was all the armour needed to brace for Ciel. As they strolled along the Pier, Jaya pointed out the typical tourist attractions around Ciel City: the aquarium, the Port waterfront, and the Stairway Tower. The Stairway Tower was the same needlepoint building that she had seen on the bus ride into Ciel. It crept behind buildings, standing intimidatingly above the city.

Always watchful.

Angela found that Jaya was easy to talk to, as she did most of the talking. She chatted about her favourite boba shop and STK's Halloween party that was fast approaching. Jaya's tone had returned to its upbeat self since they left the assembly. An easy smile replaced her look of shock.

Angela warned Jaya as the pair waited for their bubble tea, "I'm not the most creative when it comes to Halloween." But Jaya had reassured her that she would help her think of a clever costume.

So she still wants to be friends with me, Angela thought with a smile as she held the door open for Jaya. The girls giggled together when Angela failed at stabbing her boba with the straw.

"So, did you move to Ciel City just to attend a senior year at STK?" Jaya asked between sips of her favourite drink.

"That and another thing," Angela answered, more interested in stabbing her drink correctly.

"Ominous, we love it!" Jaya joked, but she pressed further. "But seriously, what else?"

"I want to reconnect with an old family friend, my sister's high school friend," Angela replied, her jaw clenched tight.

"Your sister's friend? Maybe I know her! What's her name?" Jaya asked, smacking her lips.

"There's a ten-year age gap between my sister Nini and I. I doubt you would know her friends from high school," Angela replied, hopeful that Jaya would drop the topic. "Besides, I want to get to know *you* better. Do you have any siblings of your own?"

A follow-up question danced across Jaya's mind, but Angela thanked her lucky stars when Jaya instead spoke about herself.

"I'm the eldest of four kids. All of my siblings are still in elementary school so I kind of do my own thing while my folks take care of them," Jaya recounted as they ventured further from the waterfront and deeper into Ciel.

They arrived at Ciel's Chinatown, a vibrant district with tourists, food spots, and fascinating architecture that contrasted the rest of Ciel's Western-inspired buildings. Eastern-styled buildings with slanted roofs were a sight to see. Even the street signs were a mix of jade and crimson. Angela took notice of the blood-red dragons circling majestic pillars, pillars taller than the surrounding buildings that lined the streets leading to a grand red gate in the distance.

"Chinatown," Jaya groaned, her stance stiff. Her brown eyes darted across the different buildings and people. Her cheerful attitude paused. "Nothing exciting happens here. It's better to check out Koreatown."

Angela noticed Jaya's apprehension and the way her new friend was shifting her weight backwards, subconsciously away from the red gates. But this time, she was not satisfied with that excuse.

"Nothing exciting? Come on, let's take a look around. You did promise to show me *all* of Ciel."

"I don't think that's a good idea, remember Patel's speech?"

"He said to avoid the gangs, nothing about not seeing the different districts," Angela exclaimed as she crossed the street into the district.

If Jaya wants to avoid Chinatown then that's a sign. I need to check every shady corner of Ciel for Nini's friend, Angela thought, continuing her march.

"Angie—Angela, come back!" Jaya yelled. Angela ignored her as she passed the carvings of dragons; continuing down the busy sidewalk. Jaya cursed under her breath and jogged to catch up.

"Angela, let's go. Trust me, you don't want to walk around here," Jaya warned in a low voice, looking over her shoulder.

"And why not?" Angela pressed. She gripped her drink tightly. "I'm just a regular person walking around."

"You are but I'm n—" Jaya stopped dead in her tracks. Angela turned to find the tan colour drained from Jaya's face. Jaya grabbed Angela's upper arm and started dragging her down the street and around a corner.

Their treasured drink fell to the ground as they sped past other civilians, the crowds of tourists and locals beginning to thin. A cold drip of fear dropped into Angela's stomach.

"Jaya?" Angela whispered, alarmed.

"Hey, hey, hey, ladies, slow down!" a deep voice called out from behind them. Jaya tightened her grip as the girls ran down a deserted alley.

"Fuck," Jaya cursed. The group of three men caught up to them, circling around the girls.

The three men all wore a concoction of baggy pants, long sleeves, and bandanas covering their lower faces. They crowded around the girls, pulling their bandanas down to jeer at them with an ugly look. Chains hung out of their pockets.

One of the thugs, who looked the same age as the STK seniors, pulled out a switchblade. Instantly, Angela's bravado from earlier melted. Jaya stepped in front of Angela and her hand pushed Angela back.

"If we didn't know better, we would have thought you were trying to run away," one man sneered into Jaya's face, his ugly yellow teeth bared into a smile. Angela's body turned into lead, refusing to move; her eyes frantically searched for an escape route. Jaya, on the other hand, clenched her fist, her chest puffed out.

"What do you want?" Jaya spat out.

The switchblade inched closer.

"Stop!" Angela exclaimed, throwing her hands up. "We don't have any money!"

The men laughed, their smiles turned uglier.

"Don't worry, doll. We don't want ya money," the leader of the trio gleefully jeered, his yellow eyes looking at Angela hungrily. Jaya spat on him, bringing his attention back on her. The spit landed on his cheek. Angela gasped despite herself, wide-eyed as the man wiped his cheek with a smirk.

"Now you're really asking for it, Jaya—"

The voice of a woman called out, cutting off the yellow-eyed man.

"Why, what do we have here? Long time no see, Billy!" the stranger exclaimed happily, slinging her arm around Jaya's shoulder.

Claiming her.

The men and girls were stunned, not noticing her presence until now. The stranger was a woman in her late twenties, dressed in a black leather jacket.

The woman continued talking as though they were all discussing the weather. "How are you? How's your girl?" she asked.

The thug named Billy was too horrified to speak, taking a step back. He and another man were shaken by the woman's presence, while the third thug holding the switchblade glared at her angrily.

"Who the fuck are you?" he demanded, pointing the switchblade at the strange woman.

The woman smiled calmly at him, a mischievous glint in her dark eyes, as if the whole situation was amusing.

Angela watched the woman, feeling her breathing turn more shallow with every passing second. All of her fears were muted in the back of her mind. The alleyway faded into black as the woman took center stage, a lone spotlight on her. Angela studied the woman in front of her, comparing her to the image in her mind: the tug of her lips, the nonchalant attitude. Her long soft curls and intense dark eyes resembled a painting.

Precise and bold.

"P-Parris…" Billy stuttered, his lips trembling. "Shit, lower that thing, Vince."

Parris never took her eyes off Vince. Her smile was still plastered on.

"The hell is wrong with you two? You're gonna let a bitch intimidate you?" Vince shouted, red in the face. Billy stepped between the two, his eyebrows drawn in.

"Let's go. Now."

"LIKE HELL!" Vince yelled, stabbing towards Parris. Jaya flinched and shrunk away, but Parris did not move. Billy quickly caught the blade in his hand before it came close to Parris.

"You idiot, she's an Untouchable!" Billy roared in agony. Cradling his blood-red hand to his chest.

"Apologize. Now," Billy spat at Vince.

Vince's face drained from all colour, now with the realization of who the woman before him was. He flinched as he muttered an apology. Parris, who had not stopped smiling, spoke.

"Hm, beg."

Billy crumbled to the dirty ground instantly, followed closely by Vince. The third thug fell to the ground for good measure. The three of them begged for forgiveness, foreheads digging into the ground. Jaya and Angela froze at the sight of three men on their knees crying for forgiveness from a woman less than half their size. Parris laughed, an almost cute laugh, and dismissed the men with a wave of her hand.

They rushed out of the alley. Angela watched Parris in disbelief, who hummed as she watched the men scurry around the corner.

Her name is Parris? Angela thought as her knees wobbled. *Could this be her? Long dark brown hair. Late twenties.* A sickening feeling enveloped her, starting from the tips of her fingers, caressing her arms as it reached for her throat, digging its claws into her.

The dark eyed monster from her nightmares had finally materialized before her. Its dark eyes constantly watching her from the corners of her mind her whole life. Angela took a step back, the world tilting, Parris in its center.

This… could be her.

"Well, that was exciting," Parris sang, taking her arm off of Jaya, who was ready to collapse. "Come on, you two," Parris spoke over her shoulder absentmindedly.

The request was a demand.

Jaya followed Parris obediently out of the alley. "Jaya," Angela whispered to her friend, who was uncharacteristically silent. Angela put a hand on her shoulder to stop her.

"Ladies," Parris called out to the pair, and hailed an orange and teal cab for the girls. Angela stopped but Jaya continued towards the older woman. Parris opened the door.

"I'll meet you at *Clueless*. Once you get there, tell my staff that you're my five o'clock," she instructed. Jaya entered the cab, with a reluctant Angela behind her.

A few blocks from Chinatown, in the downtown core of Ciel, was a luxurious glass office building, a sleekly designed building in the heart of the city's Financial District. Financial groups and law offices littered each floor of the building: a place for the professionals of Ciel City to meet their clients, conduct business deals, or simply showcase their wealth. Inside the building was a white marble waiting room, with floor-to-high-ceiling windows that overlooked the city and lake below. The office didn't look lived in; if anything, it resembled a movie set.

Unused and sterile.

A man wearing a well-worn red flannel shirt and paint-covered jeans sat on the leather couch in the waiting room. He impatiently tapped his scuffed shoe against the perfect marble floor, bouncing his knee. Scratching his short scruffy beard as his eyes danced around the waiting room, he ignored the obvious judgemental stares of the secretary who answered the phone.

We all don't own three-piece suits and fancy clown shoes, lady, the man thought bitterly, trying to rub some of the dried paint off of his jeans.

"Mr. O'Brien, Dr. Brown is ready for you," the chic secretary called out from behind the spotless oak desk.

The man made his way through the familiar office, past the pastel watercolour paintings that hung in the long white hallway, to the woman waiting for him by a door. She looked like she belonged in the office with her stylish blue dress suit. Her silver hair was in an updo he could have sworn he saw in one of the magazines he was browsing while in the waiting room.

"So nice to see you again, Logan." Dr. Brown greeted him with a firm handshake and a kind face. "Come in, make yourself comfortable."

He entered the office that he found himself in once every few weeks. Dr. Brown's large glass desk, exotic plants, and numerous awards on the wall always made him feel out of place, especially the ridiculously comfy couch, which would cover his rent for the next few years. But the most impressive part of her office was the view of Ciel from the floor-to-ceiling windows. The Stairway Tower was front and center, not as intimidating at this height. He should feel like he was king of the world looking at the city from above, but he never ventured too close to the windows.

"How have you been since the last time we saw each other, Logan?" Dr. Brown asked as she placed a glass of water next to him.

"Okay."

This wasn't a regular clinic. Dr. Brown was more interested in research and writing. But she had taken Logan on as one of her very select few private clients, an exclusive patient of sorts. Logan kept an eye on her publications, in case any of their sessions made their way into her latest theory or findings.

"Anything new?" she pressed cautiously, she settled down in her own armchair, clipboard in hand.

"Got another job actually," he spoke to the floor.

"That's wonderful news! I am so proud of you, Logan. I know that it isn't easy for you to put yourself out there." She beamed at him as she jotted down a quick note. "And you're still bartending?

His cheeks burned a little at the praise. "Yeah, still at the *Loose Screw*. But it's nothing special, just a delivery driver."

"Logan, be kind to yourself," Dr. Brown reprimanded gently, the way a grandmother would. He was about to say something back, along the lines that people like him don't deserve kindness—that the world made sure he knew his worth. But Logan thought better of it. Dr. Brown smiled as she put her pen down.

"Anything else new?" she asked. Logan did not respond. "Alright, how are we with our new anger management tactics?"

He snorted as he looked out of the window, bouncing his knee again. "I can't remember the person I used to be before I was always angry."

Dr. Brown looked at him expectedly, waiting for him to continue.

"I think I was more mild-mannered, but… but that's not the case anymore." His face fell to the floor again, crossing his arms in a pseudo-hug.

"Losing someone dear to you is difficult to heal from. We can talk about what happened to her and how that is still impacting you," Dr. Brown suggested.

"She's out of my life now. Gone like I didn't matter. Like everything we did, all the time spent together wasn't worth a thing to her in the end.

I'm not going to waste my breath talking about *her*."

"Of course, Logan." Dr. Brown wrote something down with a deep sigh.

The pair sat in silence as Logan refused to look at the doctor, staring at the scuff marks on his shoe instead.

"When do you start your new job?" she pivoted the conversation, discarding the clipboard to focus solely on him.

"Tomorrow."

Smiling, Dr. Brown suggested, "Well, why don't we end early today so you can go home, take a nice hot bath, and get a good night's rest for your first day tomorrow? I know how rare it is for you to have a night off from the bar."

Logan nodded in agreement as he said his goodbye and made his way to the door.

"Oh, and Logan," Dr. Brown called out as she took a seat behind her glass desk. "You've been approved for more sessions, so I've booked you for once a week now."

He left without a look back, walking past the pastel watercolour paintings, through the white marble waiting room, past the pretentious secretary, and back onto the concrete ground of Ciel.

The cab zoomed through the streets of Ciel, identical to the one Angela rode in yesterday. The city's rush hour did little to slow down the speeding orange and teal car.

Angela didn't fully understand what had just happened, but she knew enough to be afraid and realize just how stupid she was. She should have trusted Jaya when she said not to go into Chinatown. Her curiosity almost got them hurt. Angela pulled bits of fluff from the seat cushion of the cab. Her fingers fidgeted endlessly since entering the car. She tried to regroup her thoughts, to understand what had happened, how close the switchblade had gotten to her, the way the blood looked.

"Breathe," Jaya whispered. Jaya was staring at the back of the driver's headrest, her eyes wandering to the rearview mirror once every so often.

Filling her lungs with air, Angela held her breath. Repeating the action helped.

And yet, it wasn't all for nothing. Angela might have found out something important, or rather, someone important, and they were headed to her now.

How the hell did she scare them like that? Is Parris a gangster? But they called her an 'Untouchable', whatever that is. How the hell did she find us to begin with?

"Who was that?" whispered Angela.

"Jaya?" she asked again, getting the attention of her friend. Jaya broke from her trance. Her reply was brief and cold.

"Her name is Parris. That's all you need to know," she murmured back, her brown eyes narrowed skeptically at the driver. Angela caught the cab driver's wandering eyes in the rearview mirror. He quickly broke contact.

He reacted to her name. Parris... Angela thought, digging her nails into her palms. *I need another close look at her. I want to hear the way she speaks. I need to be certain it's her.*

Silence fell on the pair until the cab came to a halt in front of a plain building in the Entertainment District. The building was black sans for the neon sign that read *Clueless* across it.

A nightclub, Angela guessed as they exited the cab, the fare paid in advance. For a moment the girls lingered outside on the sidewalk.

"We can just leave, you know," Angela suggested. She needed Jaya to believe that she wasn't interested in this Parris person. "We're underaged, we won't even be let in."

Jaya scoffed at her as she made her way to the side of the building, down a small alleyway with trash and recycling bins. A steel door stood out against the black building.

"If you have an appointment with Parris, there is no cancelling it. That's not how this works," Jaya sighed as she approached the side door as though she'd done it before, her forehead shiny from sweat.

"Jaya, what are you not telling me?" Angela asked, noting every piece of information and hesitation from her new friend.

"Shit…" Jaya muttered as she raised a fist to knock, but stopped. "Listen, Angela. Once we're inside don't talk. Don't look at her. Don't let her take an interest in you."

"But who is she? What's an Untouchable? How did those guys know you—?"

"Please, Angie!" Jaya pleaded, her brown eyes begging desperately at her. "For your safety and mine, just listen to me and then I'll explain once we're out of this mess."

"Okay." Angela backed down.

Jaya knocked on the club door. A few moments later, a young man, only a few years older than the high school seniors, opened the door, eyeing the pair. His serious face was mismatched on his young body.

"We're her five o'clock," Jaya stated.

Without saying a word, the man let the girls in.

The outside of the building betrayed just how chic and elegant it was on the inside. The side entrance opened right into the belly of the building. Angela was right, it was a nightclub, and a fancy one at that. To their left was a large bar spanning the entire body of the club, the black marble running from wall to wall. Black velvet-covered stools stood at the ready by the bar, ready for mixing and mingling. Black velvet booths were built into the wall across from the side entrance. A doorway, which presumably led to the front door, was hidden between the booths. Inconspicuous was the theme of *Clueless*. In the centre of the club was an expansive dance floor. The club was dark, with warm lights glowing down on the dance floor. Angela could imagine hundreds of people dancing and drinking while music echoed into the night. The only thing that seemed out of place was a staircase to the right of the side entrance, leading up to a white door.

There was no one inside the club aside from the young man. He directed the girls towards the bar.

"What would you ladies like to drink?" he asked, taking his place behind the shiny marble.

"Two vodka cranberries," Jaya replied instantly like she'd ordered alcohol while underage before. Angela quirked an eyebrow at her.

"Two cranberry juices," the man countered, quickly pouring the juice into glass cups.

"Good man, Lorenzo," Parris called out as she entered through the side door. Jaya choked a little on her juice. Angela slowly drank hers, studying Parris with narrow eyes.

The woman smiled at the girls before motioning to the staircase with her head. Both girls moved from their stools towards the out-of-place staircase.

"Not you, just Jaya," Parris corrected. Her eyes lingered for a moment on Angela's.

Parris and Jaya ascended the staircase. Angela knit her eyebrows together, her muscles tensing the further Jaya went with Parris. Once inside the door, the entire upstairs portion of the club lit up. An office appeared behind glass windows.

"When she turns on the transparency, that means she wants you to watch," Lorenzo informed as he cleaned some glasses.

Angela turned her attention to the scene she was apparently meant to watch. Jaya was stiff and unmoving while Parris leaned casually against a white marble desk like nothing in the world was wrong. Angela had no idea what the conversation was about, but she was certain that whatever it was, it wasn't good for Jaya.

Once finished with her drink, Angela turned her attention to the bartender. His head was pointed down, stray black hair covered his eyes, concentrated on the glass he was polishing. Angela studied the slight hunch of his shoulders.

"Your name is Lorenzo?" Angela returned the glass with a small thanks.

"Yes." His answer was curt.

"Lorenzo, can I ask you a question?"

"Depends on the question."

"What is an Untouchable?"

Lorenzo stopped what he was doing, giving his full attention to Angela. "Why do you want to know?"

"I heard someone call Parris that. I want to know what it means."

"Ms. Parris... an Untouchable is a person, place, or thing that is deemed just that, to not be touched by anyone. They are protected by the Syndicates."

Angela leaned forward against the marble counter. "Who gets to decide that?" she pressed, thrilled she was finally getting answers.

"The Gates of the Big Three syndicates decides."

"How does one become an Untouchable?"

Lorenzo huffed as he put away his final dish. "Asking too many questions in Ciel City will get you in trouble, kid. You should know that."

"I'm new in town."

"It shows."

"So?"

Lorenzo's indifferent mask lifted for a moment; sadness peeked through. "No one knows how someone or thing can become an Untouchable. Only three Untouchables have ever been declared in Ciel. Ms. Parris is one of them."

"And... and is Parris a member of the Big Three? What's her last name?" Angela pried deeper, pressing her luck.

Lorenzo gave her a confused look before the sound of Jaya marching down the stairs cut their conversation short. Jaya was more flustered than before, and Parris was just as happy. Jaya caught Angela's eyes, tilting her head towards the side door.

"Did you make a new friend, Lorenzo?" Parris called out.

"No," Lorenzo answered in passing, focused on his tasks.

Parris laughed and opened the door for the girls. Angela spared one last look back at Lorenzo before exiting *Clueless*.

"Now, I want you girls to get home right away. It's getting dark soon," Parris requested as she guided the girls to the curb, and gave each one a brown bill.

Angela took the bill, memorizing the woman, still unsure if she was the person she was looking for. Parris looked at her with curious eyes, as though she were doing the same thing.

"And what's your name?" asked Parris.

"She's a nobody," Jaya answered first.

"Hm, even a nobody has a name." Parris chuckled. She looked expectingly at Angela.

She doesn't recognize me either. If I tell her, that might just confirm her suspicions of me…

"Angela," she answered after a beat.

"Cute name! Can I call you Angie?" Parris asked with a smirk, a knowing look in her dark eyes.

Fucker! Angela cursed.

"Only my friends and family call me that," Angela bit back, a deep scowl on her young face. Jaya glanced between the two, drawn to Angela's stiffness.

"My name is Parris, so now we're friends, Angie." Parris tilted her head, her dark eyes locked onto Angela's.

The pair stared at one another, each one refusing to look away first.

"We should get home, then—goodbye," Jaya said, breaking the duel as she grabbed Angela and walked towards the road. Parris waved at the two enthusiastically as they got into a cab and sped off into Ciel.

Once out of sight, Parris put her hands into her leather jacket and looked at a man standing just a few meters away, staring at her with electric blue eyes.

"It's rude to follow people, Tony, " she reprimanded as she walked back to the side door, "You should know better."

The man was in his mid-thirties, pale, and skinny. He was also dressed in a leather jacket. He followed Parris in silently, limping.

"You know not to come here without an appointment, " she sang as she walked up to the bar. Lorenzo handed her a coffee. He tensed when Tony followed Parris to the bar and stood too close to her.

"We have a shipment leaving tonight," Tony announced as he took a glass of whiskey from Lorenzo without taking his eyes off her.

Parris smiled into her coffee. "Is that so?"

"Just thought I would inform you myself." Tony inched closer to her, but she finished her cup and took a step back.

"You thought to inform me? The Informant?" she asked in an amused tone. Parris giggled and made her way to the staircase leading to the office. She called out over her shoulder.

"I've known about this shipment for the past month! I've already told Marcel that I would be buying."

Tony's nostril twitched into a snare. "Really?" he asked.

"Really," Parris responded with a smile that was all teeth before closing the white office door.

The sun bowed to the towering skyscrapers of Ciel, casting the city into twilight. The cab arrived in front of Angela's building. Jaya paid the driver with the money Parris gave as Angela fumbled with the keys. The girls hurried past the children playing in the hall and up the stairs. They had decided to wait until they were in private before talking about what had happened.

Entering the apartment, Jaya kicked off her shoes and flopped on the couch with a heavy sigh. Angela settled down in the overly plush armchair, a tinge of embarrassment running through her as she regretted not cleaning up her aunt's place before leaving for orientation. But Jaya didn't mind the scattered grocery bags and clothes.

The events of today replayed like a movie in Angela's mind.

"Those guys are part of the Halos," mumbled Jaya.

Angela watched Jaya stare at the ceiling, speaking with a blank expression. "The Halos are known as the drug dealers of Ciel. If it's drug-related, they're probably behind it."

Halos equal drugs... but why were they after her?

A million more questions buzzed in Angela's head.

"I knew someone who was involved with the Halos. That's how those jerks knew me,"

Jaya continued. "Don't worry, Angie. I'm safe now. That's why I didn't want to go to Chinatown, it's one of their territories. They wear chains hanging from their pockets, that's their tell."

"I'm sorry. I was reckless, I should've listened," Angela apologized meekly, her head dropping, a few coils covering her face. Jaya waved her off as she pinched the bridge of her nose, fighting off a headache.

"You don't think we'll get in trouble for being seen with gang members, right?" Angela wondered, thinking of Principal Patel's warning just earlier that day.

"No, I don't think anyone saw us," Jaya reasoned as she checked her phone. The light bounced off her face, Angela just now noticing the eye bags on her tanned face.

They sat in silence as the night sky claimed Ciel. The city lights came to life in a flicker of warm yellow.

"And Parris?" Angela hesitantly asked.

"If I asked you to let it go, would you?" Jaya responded wearily.

"What did she talk to you about? How did she know where we were? Was she following you or me—" Angela bit her tongue to stop herself but it was too late.

"Why would Parris have been following you?" Jaya asked, her eyebrows scrunched together.

Angela did not respond. Jaya sighed as she stood up, making her way to the door. Letting Angela's comment go, her mind was too preoccupied with the conversation with Parris and the Halos.

"I'm sorry your first day in Ciel ended like this, Angie. But if we keep our heads down, it should be smooth sailing until graduation, " promised Jaya. Angela stood there awkwardly, unsure of what to do.

Do I hug her goodbye? Should I apologize again? Angela thought as she watched Jaya lace her shoes. *Does she still want to be my friend after I messed things up? I've never been good at making friends, let alone keeping them. Nini could make friends so easily.*

"At least tell me which territories belong to whom so I stay away," Angela decided to say, to break the silence.

Jaya looked around the living room; spotting a hung map of Ciel City, she grabbed a dry-erase marker from the cream fridge, next to the 'A' and 'J' magnets.

"Chinatown belongs to the Halos, obviously, along with Eaton. They wear chains in their pockets. While Port Front West and Weston belong to the Wings. They all wear black rings on their pinky fingers. Fucking bastards are known to groom and traffic children," Jaya explained as she circled all the named districts of Ciel City with the red marker. "Finally, the Gates are more concentrated in the East end, with some places in the Financial District and Old Town in their possession. They're not interested in a pissing contest with the other gangs. They prefer to slip under the radar. No chains or rings for them. They'll mostly be dressed in suits."

"And what do the Gates do?" Angela asked quietly.

"They are responsible for most organized crime in Ciel. The brothels, underground casinos, you name it… but Midtown is generally safe, given that STK is such a big deal. So I wouldn't worry too much about your safety here, Angie," Jaya reasoned, watching Angela study the markings on the map.

Jaya gently touched Angela's arm, a thin smile on her tanned face. "I'm going to head out before it gets too late. You said your folks and STK are okay with you living by yourself, but… you're going to be okay on your own, right?"

"Thanks, Jaya. I actually prefer being alone."

"No one likes being alone, Angie. At least, not really."

Angie paused and looked out at the night lights of Ciel, trying to find the right words to tell her new friend.

"Well…it's better than always putting on a show. Better than always taking care of everyone."

Jaya tilted her head to the side with a frown. She opened her mouth to ask something and then thought better of it. Enough excitement and secrets for one day.

"See you later, Angie,"

The girl with butterfly clips waved as she left. Angela made her way to the window, watching her new friend flag a taxi down as she zoomed down the street. Angela grabbed her purse from the living room and threw it across her bedroom floor before she collapsed on the bed.

Streetlights shone warmly onto the sidewalk, shooing the darkness away. The STK volleyball team emerged onto the beaten sidewalks of Ciel, roughhousing and making a ruckus as they left the school's gym. Deciding on a last-minute game to warm up for the upcoming season after the assembly, the team left school later than expected.

"Hope you get captain, Theo!" a boy called out, waving at the team as he got into a car. "Sorry, Patel grilled you like that."

"Thanks, Nathan!" Theo called back, hiking his backpack higher on his shoulder. "Don't worry about it, I came late to the Assembly, I deserved it."

A smaller group of the team headed to the subway together. While joking with a teammate, Theo's phone beeped at him. He stopped in his tracks.

"I forgot something, don't wait up," Theo called out as he made his way back to the school.

His teammates called out goodbye as he rounded the corner. Theo continued walking past the school until a luxurious black foreign car with tinted windows pulled up beside him.

Theo opened the door, entering the dark car.

Sitting in the back was a giant man dressed in a tailored suit. The maroon suit was snug against the man, highlighting his large frame. Theo whispered a quiet hello as he buckled up, the car rejoining traffic in a smooth motion. The car was silent; even the engine did not dare make a sound. The man smelled good, like wood or vanilla, something expensive. Theo stared at the seat in front of him, hands clasped tightly. The man was reading something on his phone. Theo risked a glance at him. The light reflected on his defined features, slicked-back silver hair, and a white goatee.

"When does school start?"

Theo jumped a little at the man's deep voice.

"Monday, sir," Theo sheepishly answered.

"Do you play a sport?" the man asked, continuing to look at his phone.

Theo's heart pounded in his chest, not knowing what to expect from the older man.

"Yes, I play volleyball."

The man smirked and put away his phone, giving Theo his full attention.

"Train both the body and the mind. Smart boy."

"Thank you, sir."

The car turned onto one of the highways, away from Downtown. Theo bit his lip as he looked out the window. The man reached into his jacket and pulled out an envelope, holding it out for Theo.

"This should be enough for you, *Cucciolo*."

Theo went to take the envelope, but the man did not let go. His chestnut eyes held onto Theo's green ones.

"I am not doing this out of the kindness of my heart," he explained. "I am expecting payment."

"But I don't have anything…" Theo began, but the man's laugh cut him off.

"It's not about money, *Cucciolo*. How about you join me for dinner next week? We can discuss it then, " he suggested, his chestnut eyes leaving no room for objections. Silently, Theo nodded obediently.

The man let go of the envelope.

The car slowed down in a suburban neighbourhood, rolling to a stop in front of one of the houses. Theo's eyes widened.

"How do you know where I live?" he asked the man, hating that his voice sounded small.

The man chuckled deeply. "Looking forward to seeing you again, *Cucciolo*."

With that, Theo left the black foreign car with the large smartly-dressed man, jogging to his front door.

Envelope secured.

Night had fully set in Ciel City. The everyday person was back in the safety of their homes, double-checking their locks, while the city's underground came to life.

"Hurry up! Hurry up!" Parris called out from the back seat of the car. The driver sped to Port Front West. Parris tapped away on her phone until the car came to a stop in front of a warehouse on the port front.

Exiting the car, she entered the warehouse with a song. "Oh, Marcel, I'm here!" she sang as she walked up to a group of men around a shipping container. Each one wore a black ring on their pinky finger.

The Wings.

"Parris." A man who was built like an athlete but dressed like a banker greeted her. Parris smiled at him, eyes drawn to the container.

"How is today's shipment looking, Marcel?" she asked, not paying the men with guns any heed.

"Our latest catch was a bit dry," Marcel replied, going to open the container. "Once the school year starts again, we should be catching better fish."

The shriek of the metal door dragging across the warehouse floor was deafening. Marcel shone a flashlight into the metal prison and the light bounced off of the faces of young girls, all bound and gagged.

"You weren't kidding," Parris commented as she stepped into the metal box.

Inside were seven girls, all of different sizes and ethnic groups. They huddled together, frightened. One was hysterically shaking her head while the others looked at Parris with tear-filled eyes. They were no older than high school kids. Parris smiled as she inspected the products.

"How much for the lot?"

Marcel laughed as he shook his head. "I don't know what you do with them, but I can't sell them all to you again. I need to satisfy the Wings' orders."

Parris pouted as she turned her attention to Marcel, batting her eyelashes at him.

"Not even this one?" she whined as she pointed to a young Indigenous girl, no older than thirteen. Marcel paused, scratching the side of his buzz cut, as though considering it.

Parris pressed him. "I'll pay ten thousand dollars now and you won't have to bother with her."

Marcel shook his head with a grin. "I don't care if you eat them or use them, but you pay a fair price."

He laughed, along with a few of the gun-wielding men. Parris smiled as she motioned for the girl to follow her.

The other bound children yelled from behind their gags, begging for her to take them too. But Parris paid them no heed as Marcel handed her the girl's folder. She gave him the money in an envelope in return. The little girl struggled, refusing to leave the container, but the armed men grabbed her and pushed her into Parris's car. Parris flipped through the folder boredly.

"This will be our last open sale for the season," Marcel explained as he walked Parris to her car. "From now on we'll be focusing on our orders and preparing for the Re-Pavement Project."

"The Re-Pavement Project... you expecting a lot of business?" Parris asked with a pleasant hum.

"A shit ton! The Gates will need labour at a cheap cost and foreigners just so happen to be the cheapest." laughed Marcel.

"Thank you for tonight's dinner, Marcel!" she called out as she entered the black car. Marcel winked at her as he closed the door behind her.

The car rushed back to the streets. The bound girl screamed and thrashed about as Parris removed her gag.

"Twelve times more likely," Parris stated casually. She worked on untying the little girl's hands. "That's how much more likely Indigenous women will go missing or murdered compared to non-Indigenous women."

The girl looked at Parris with confused eyes.

"Tonight you are returning to your First Nation," Parris declared, her smile no longer present. "Lorenzo up there will make sure you get on your flight alright."

The little girl did not speak but the tears continued, too many emotions displayed on her little face. Parris resumed playing on her phone. Her dark eyes focused solely on the screen.

The car slowed to a stop in front of *Clueless*. Parris left the car without a second glance at the little girl she just saved. The car just as quickly sped away as Parris disappeared through the side entrance.

Just as she entered the club, Amir took a photo of her from his car. Hearing a buzz from his phone, he looked down to find a message from Helen.

Are you still working? – Helen

Yes, I think I found a thread to pull on. – Amir

Which one? – Helen

Amir typed back quickly, looking at the photo of Parris.

One they're not expecting. – Amir

CHAPTER THREE

The Big Three

"**B**reaking News!" the television cried out into the apartment. Angela stood in the pink bathroom brushing her teeth, preparing for the first day of school.

"Suspected gang activity related to two explosions in Old Town today. No official statement has been released by the CCPD as of yet, but security cameras spotted two individuals placing what seem to be homemade bombs under two cars parked outside of the Ciel Construction Company. More as this story develops… In other news, bids for the Ciel Re-Pavement Project are now open—"

Angela turned off the television, ready to head out the door. Her fingers were in a state of ruin, as she had picked at them last night, a bad habit she couldn't quit. She looked over her blue and gray uniform one last time, catching her sunken eyes in the mirror before she grabbed her school bag and headed out the door.

Did you see the news? – Angela

So scary, good thing no one got hurt! – Jaya

Angela walked past the corner grocer and record stores towards the subway. Noticing everyone glancing over their shoulders, suspicious of one another, she followed the crowd's lead and did not stand near the edge of the platform. Angela rested her back against the tiled wall of the subway.

Do you think Parris was involved? – Angela typed, but quickly erased the message, thinking better than to ask Jaya about the woman again.

The platform collectively groaned when the train was announced as delayed due to the ongoing investigation in Old Town. Angela glanced at the people waiting on the platform, catching a few people staring at her, their eyes drawn to her uniform, as though it was a neon sign advertising the city's most prestigious school. She fought the urge to bite the skin of her fingers as she followed the crowd onto the train, squished between the door and a baby's stroller.

Her mind wandered as the train raced to the next station. The weekend was uneventful, as she listened to Jaya's warnings and remained in Midtown. She had gone on runs in Midtown, and her feet beating against the concrete street brought some clarity to her thoughts of the Informant and the gangs. She tried to look up Parris and Lorenzo on social media, but without a last name, her search did not yield results. Even *Clueless* did not have pictures of the pair, fronting as a normal nightclub.

I'll go on a run by Clueless *this weekend, maybe I can take a picture of her.*

Marching to the gothic church-turned-school, she joined the flood of blue, white, and gray. The air was electric as the first day of school came into full swing; the students greeted one another while rushing to their homerooms. Angela tugged on her gray skirt as she walked through the crowded halls, feeling invisible.

Good luck. Remember to work hard. – Dad

She ran up the stairs, finding her room with ease. English was her first-period class. She entered the fully renovated room, the vaulted ceiling a vast contrast to the modern curved desks. She found her name card on a desk close to the pointed window. The stone courtyard and black gate were in clear view. The teacher leaned on his desk, speaking with the group of students sitting at the front.

Find your room okay? – Jaya

Yes, let's meet for lunch? – Angela

Hell yeah! – Jaya

"You're new, aren't you?" a voice to her right asked. The voice belonged to a boy with familiar fluffy brown hair and green eyes. She remembered him as the boy who was late to the assembly.

"Yeah, I am," replied Angela.

"I didn't think I recognized you at the assembly. My name is Theo, it's nice to meet you," he welcomed her with a warm smile.

"I'm Angela," she responded politely.

"I can't imagine how hard it is to go to a new school in your senior year." His smile remained. "Especially STK! Speaking of, how did you get in for senior year?"

"My transfer was greenlit since my sister had an almost perfect academic record here," Angela answered quickly.

"Oh cool, who's your sister?" he wondered, his upbeat nature reminded her of Jaya.

"She graduated a long time ago. We would have still been in elementary school," Angela replied, busying herself with opening her own notebook.

"So she's an alumnus… Well, if you need any help around STK, let me know," Theo kindly offered.

Angela was about to thank him but another boy approached Theo with a call before slugging his arm around Theo's shoulder. The boy excitedly talked about a party that was coming up, not aware he cut their conversation off.

Theo smiled sympathetically at Angela. He held out his phone, a new contact page open. Sheepishly taking the phone, she added her name and number. His overt friendliness continued as he greeted another classmate who sat in front of him.

"Alright, settle down!" the teacher called out, mostly directed to Theo's friend. Theo took the phone and gave her a thumbs up. Angela's phone lit up with a message.

Hey, this is Theo! Send me your schedule. – Theo

Angela saw Theo paying attention to the teacher, jotting down notes quickly. Her fingers hovered above the keyboard for a moment. Could she commit to letting another person into her life? One was enough. She had fulfilled her father's quota of one friend. But a quick glance back at Theo and his warm presence reminded her that Jaya could drop her at any time. Having more than one friend was the right choice to make. Angela replied.

"Everyone stand for the national anthem!" the teacher instructed as the school day began.

Not a square inch of Ciel's sidewalks or roads were left uncovered by cars or pedestrians. The constant sound of cars honking in the Downtown Core added to the rush hour chaos. Swarms of people all dressed for different occasions and responsibilities ran between the cars stuck in traffic. Racing the clock to get to where they needed to be, the threat of tardiness loomed overhead.

Inside *Clueless*, Lorenzo held a team meeting with the staff. Pleasant conversation flowed between the workers. They were all in their early twenties, and Lorenzo blended in easily with them. Coffee and bagels decorated the black bar as the team of seven sat on the black velvet stools.

A rough knock from the side door made the easy atmosphere instantly disappear. The staff stiffened as Lorenzo quickly made his way to the door. Opening it, a group of men rushed into the club, armed to the teeth with guns.

"Her office is closed!" Lorenzo called out as the armed men poured in. In their centre was a large man dressed in a tailored suit. Lorenzo froze once he saw the man. The man ignored Lorenzo as he made his way up the stairs, pushing the white door open.

"Closed!" Parris shouted from behind a white marble desk, her eyes focused on a laptop screen. The sound of footsteps filled the checkerboard office, along with the clicking of guns. "I said that I am closed…" Parris repeated.

A flash of annoyance before her saccharine smile graced her face as soon as she saw who it was invading her office. The smell of his wood and vanilla cologne invaded her senses. She beamed at him.

"Boss!" she exclaimed, closing the laptop with a snap, "I thought you stopped making house calls—"

"*Bella*, this is quite the office," the man spoke, cutting her off, hand sliding against the white marble desk. The man was tall and aging, with silver hair and lightly wrinkled skin. Yet he held himself with authority, his shoulders pushed back and muscular arms that could snap a neck hidden beneath his suit. He strolled in as though it were his office.

"Clearly you have done well for yourself since my last visit," he continued, stalking his way to her side. Parris remained seated. His silver hair was still a little damp, as though he were in a hurry to get to her. His chestnut eyes remained alert.

The armed men took up more than half of the office, each one ready to pounce at a moment's notice.

"Aw, thanks, Boss!" Parris gushed at the older man. He reached for a lock of her curly hair, slowly playing with it. He remained silent, his fingers intertwining with thick strands of her hair.

"I want you to find out who placed the bombs."

"Hm, would love to, but as I said, I'm closed right now."

The hand playing in her hair stilled. The men held their breaths.

"I wasn't asking."

Parris sighed as she stood up, his hand still in her hair. She looked up at him; he was a full head taller. The top of her head barely reached his shoulders.

"I'm not taking on appointments or jobs right now, Boss. But! If you leave a name and number, I will be sure to return your call in five to six business—"

He yanked her head down by the lock of hair.

"*Bella*," he growled deeply, "now isn't the time to play."

Parris chuckled through the stinging in her scalp, looking up at him. "Even you are spooked, eh?"

A knock on the door stole their attention. Lorenzo entered the office with a tray of drinks for the unwelcome man, keeping a neutral expression when he saw Parris in the man's grasp.

The man looked at Lorenzo and then back to Parris, smirking. He continued to play with her hair, "Now, I know that pain doesn't motivate you, but what about your own people's lives—"

A gunshot rang in the room.

Lorenzo dropped the tray, glass breaking on the checkered floor. The smell of coffee flooded the office. Lorenzo's fingers twitched as he looked down at his chest, at the pool of blood forming quickly. He looked back up at his boss, a choked sound all he could muster before crumbling to the floor.

The men all cleared away from the body, readying their own guns and pointing them at Parris. Parris held her gun steady, looking at the dead Lorenzo with indifferent eyes. The man's hand remained in her hair.

She picked up the phone on her polished desk. "Clean up on aisle one!"

A group of the club's staff quickly entered the office, picking up the dead body and dragging it down the stairs, wiping the blood and coffee from the floor until the office looked just as pristine as ever.

They left without a word. Parris finally returned her gaze to the man, still smiling.

"Sorry, Boss! I couldn't hear you over the ringing in my ears," she whined.

The man fixed his eyes on her, studying that persistent smile that he loved. He broke out into a hearty laugh and waved at his men to leave the room.

He sized Parris, looking at her up and down. Slowly the hand unwrapped around her hair and lowered to her waist. Parris immediately placed the gun under her chin.

"After all this time, you still have trouble understanding the word 'no'," she whispered, intense eyes locked onto his.

The man chuckled as he held his hands up in front of him, in false surrender.

"You really are special, aren't you," he whispered. He took a seat in her chair. "Even the mafia can't get you under our thumb, *Bella*."

Parris shrugged as she leaned against the white desk, a smirk on her lips, the gun discarded on the desk.

"Kneel," he commanded, his eyes leaving no room for disagreement. Parris slowly dropped to the floor, perching her cheek on his knee. His hand returned to her hair, petting it like a cat. She closed her eyes with a hum.

"I trust you to find out which band of children placed those bombs."

"Hm, you want me to investigate the Wings and the Halos?"

"Yes, find out which one of those sons of bitches thought that they can hit the Gates."

She remained silent for a moment. "Thirty thousand dollars," she sang, almost dreamily.

"In your dreams, *Bella*!" The man barked out a cold laugh.

"Thirty thousand dollars. The Wings and Halos are also clients of mine. You're asking me to risk my life, Boss!"

They held each other's gaze, both refusing to break contact first. The man finally smirked and patted her head before standing up.

"You'll be the death of me, Parris."

"Wouldn't that be fun, Giovanni?"

"You'll get the money the usual way," he spoke as he left through the white door. Parris followed him. "Once you know, I expect you to come personally to deliver the news," he continued as the pair went down the stairs and out the side entrance.

"I know, I know," she whined as she followed him outside, the sun glared angrily at them.

"Where are you going?" Giovanni asked as the door to the black car was opened by the driver. Parris planted a kiss on both of his cheeks.

"In the mood for donuts!" she exclaimed as she waved goodbye to the mafia boss.

Giovanni watched her leave, happily skipping to a song that only she was listening to, a song she refused to share with anyone. Her leather jacket hid her disappearing form from him. With a final longing look at her, he entered the car and left *Clueless*.

The shutter of a camera echoed in Amir's car. He knew that staking out at the club would yield results. He quickly started his engine, his eyes fixed on the form of Parris skipping down the street.

Good morning, how are you, Amir? – Helen

About to make my first arrest. – Amir

Amir tailed Parris down the block, around the corner, until she entered an empty coffee shop. His heart was beating too loud for his liking, his usually composed self nowhere to be seen since he followed the Informant.

You were right, she did go to Jim's. – Amir

Then now is your chance, Amir! – Helen

Amir shut the engine. She responded quickly.

Be careful, she is cunning but I know you can catch her. – Helen

The store door chimed as Amir entered the coffee shop. The deep musk of beans roasting flooded his nose. His eyes were trained on Parris, as she casually spoke with the barista.

Average height. Late twenties. Long dark curly hair. Latte tanned skin. Leather jacket. This is her, Amir thought. *Now or never.*

The coffee shop was quiet, the morning rush over. Only a lone barista manned the station.

"I have a dozen mixed and a Ciel latte for a Parris," the barista called out.

"That's me," Parris sang as she grabbed the brown bag and latte.

"Parris," Amir spoke from behind her, his fingers shaking despite his best efforts. "That's a unique name."

Parris turned to look at him with an easy grin. "Thanks, stranger."

Butterflies flurried in his stomach; he was dealing with a dangerous woman. Possibly the Head of one of the Big Three. He had to keep it cool. Grateful he had decided to not wear his uniform today.

"I don't think I've had a Ciel latte before," Amir chatted. "Would you suggest it?"

Parris looked thoughtfully between her drink and Amir, as though she was comparing the two. "It's rather strong, with deep earth notes and a bitter bite," she explained. "I wouldn't recommend it for the average Joe."

"And you wouldn't consider yourself average?" Amir asked, swallowing around nothing.

Her grin widened. "No."

Amir chuckled nervously. *Keep it together,* he reprimanded himself. *She hasn't done anything.*

"You haven't asked me for my name, you know," Amir attempted to keep the conversation going.

Parris took a long sip of her drink, leaning calmly against the counter. Amir shifted his weight between his feet, his hold on the conversation slipping from his grasp and into hers.

"Do you want me to know your name, Officer Amir Hafiz?" she asked with a pout. Amir's posture hardened.

How did she know my name? My transfer to the CCPD was done internally so that my name would not be leaked to the public should I need to go undercover.

"Well, answer, Officer Hafiz," Parris sang. "What's so special about your name that I should ask for it?" Her eyes sparkled as she finished her latte, settling it down on the counter. She hummed as she gave him one last look before turning to leave.

Amir grabbed her wrist, his hand wrapped around her. "You are under arrest for suspected connections with organized crime groups. You have the right to remain silent and to retain and be instructed by counsel…"

Fireworks went off in her dark eyes as Amir took out his handcuffs and continued reciting her rights. Excitement exuded from her. A small spark of hope ignited in his chest.

"Right," he huffed, a little breathless, "let's get you down to the station."

Amir led her out of the café, guiding her head into the back seat of his car. The bag of donuts lay discarded on the coffee shop counter.

Jaya would be lying if she said she was well-rested for the first day of senior year. She rubbed her eyes, trying to rub the dark circles away. Ever since her incident with the Halos and the Informant, she hadn't had a moment of peace. Just when she thought she had left that life behind…

"Why aren't you eating?" Angela asked her.

Jaya snapped back to the present, her spoon pushing her dal and rice around. They were seated in the cafeteria, large oak tables running from wall to wall to accommodate the mass of students at STK. The rib vaults of the ceiling echoed the chaos and stress of lunch around the cafeteria. Some students were shoving food into their mouths while doing schoolwork at the same time. Others forsook food altogether, their nose buried deep in textbooks thicker than bricks.

"Sorry," Jaya mumbled, shoving her spoon into her mouth. Her throat was too dry to swallow.

"You're still thinking about what happened, aren't you?" Angela asked, taking a bite of her pear. Her mature eyes focused on Jaya.

She's as perceptive as ever, Jaya thought as she shook her head with a soft smile. "No, I'm just tired from babysitting my sister and brothers this weekend. Enough about me, how's your first day so far?"

"Pretty solid." Angela shrugged. "The workload is more than my previous school, which was to be expected."

Jaya chuckled as she chugged her water. "Just wait until exam season, the student council hands out full tissue boxes!"

Angela groaned as she checked her phone. Jaya snatched it out of her hand.

"Hey!"

"Oh, come on, you've been on it since we sat down!" she joked with Angela as she handed it back.

"That's because he's being too nice," Angela complained.

"He?" repeated Jaya, a sly smile on her face. "Just two periods in and you've already scored a number. Who's the lucky guy?"

"Hey!" Theo greeted as he took a seat next to Jaya. The girls greeted him, Jaya sneaking a wink at Angela and mouthing, 'He's single'.

"I noticed that we also have third and fourth together, Angela. I thought that we could head out together," Theo offered as he dug into his sandwich.

"Sounds good," Angela shyly responded.

His face lit up. He turned to Jaya. "How're ya, Jaya? Last I saw you was in sophomore year."

"I was here for junior too, Theo," Jaya grumbled as Angela held out a container full of cookies. Jaya softened as she took one and bit into the chewy goodness.

"Yeah, but I didn't see much of you around last year," Theo replied, thanking Angela with a light blush on his cheeks. Angela studied Jaya's face as she spoke with him.

"Anyway, there's a party this weekend at Kevin's place," exclaimed

Theo. "He said to invite whoever I wanted, I think it'll be a good place to introduce Angela to our class."

"Kevin?" Jaya asked.

"Yeah, Kevin Wong. He lives near Flushington Station. His parents bought him a condo when they moved out of the city."

"That's in Chinatown…"

"Is that a problem?" asked Theo, tilting his head.

"No!" Angela responded quickly, startling her new friends. "Jaya was just saying how she had to babysit this weekend. But I would love to go, Theo."

Jaya mouthed 'Thank you' at her.

The bell rang, and a flurry of students rushed out of the cafeteria.

"I'll see you tomorrow, Jaya," called Angela as she followed Theo to their next class. Jaya watched Theo excitedly speak with Angela as they left the cafeteria together.

Maybe I should start wearing heels around them. Stupid tall giants.

In the calm after the storm of lunch, Jaya put her head down on the table, having a spare period.

Resting.

Reflecting.

"What do you want?" Jaya grumbled through clenched teeth as she entered the Informant's office. The checkered tiles reminded her of a chessboard.

"The question that needs asking is what the hell were you doing back in Chinatown?" Parris asked as she leaned on her white marble desk.

"I…" Jaya started but stopped. She didn't want to draw attention to Angela. She didn't want to involve an innocent, not like how she was swept in.

"I took a wrong turn."

Parris howled in laughter, "You, Jaya Sharma, wandering into Chinatown accidentally. Rich!"

"Stop laughing." Jaya snarled, "Why am I here?"

Parris calmed down, wiping an imaginary tear from her eye. "Have you already forgotten what I did for you back in May?"

"No," Jaya answered, refusing to make eye contact.

"How I convinced the Halos that you were just being used by that thing you called a boyfriend? That I allowed you to live another day so long as you followed a few rules?"

"Don't remind me!" Jaya pleaded. She didn't want to cry in front of her. Not with Angela watching from below.

"Then tell me why I had to save you from the Halos again?" Parris pressed. Jaya remained silent. Parris sighed, checking her phone. "Let's add a few new rules to your conditions."

"But—!"

"Number one!" Parris spoke over her, "You will report to me any news of gang activity, specifically in relation to the new drug called 'Cloud 9' in STK."

Jaya opened her mouth to protest but Parris cut her off again. "Number two! Do not go into Chinatown ever again, or I will hand you over to the Halos myself."

Parris paused, considering another term. Her dark eyes quickly darted to Angela down at the bar before returning her attention to Jaya.

"Is that it?" Jaya asked with a wince. Parris took a step forward, so that Jaya had to look up at her.

"You know that I don't care for you, for any of you. So start caring about each other. That's all you have in the end." Finished, Parris opened the white door.

The loud ruckus of the seniors on spare woke Jaya up.

Rubbing her eyes, she made her way towards her fourth-period class.

Purposely walking in the music hallway, her eyes darted to the faces she knew, the people she used to deal to. Spotting another senior up ahead, she ran up to her. They chatted about the new school year and made other small talk until Jaya finally asked:

"So, what do you know about Cloud 9?"

Amir escorted Parris through the soul-sucking doors into the lobby of the CCPD. She announced their arrival with a loud yell: "Make way, peasants!"

All personnel froze as they saw her, handcuffed, marching through the station. "Don't cause a scene," Amir reprimanded as he guided her to an interrogation room. He ignored the distraught stares from his colleagues.

Parris, on the other hand, was a child in a candy store. She had remained quiet the entire car ride over, resting her head on the window. But now she was energetic, wildly looking around the station while oh-ing and ah-ing.

"Is that where the murderers go? And is that where you keep the confiscated drugs? And—"

"Enough!" Amir snapped, tired of her antics, his eye twitching. "I will conduct a pat-down search now, would you feel more comfortable with a female officer?"

Parris shrugged. "I don't care."

Amir nodded as he felt along her arms and legs. No concealed weapons, no wallet, no phone. Nothing on her person.

How did she pay at the café, then? Amir wondered. His flicker of hope from earlier started to dim as he hooked the handcuffs to the metal table.

"Have you thought any of this through, Amir?" she mused, looking up at him through her eyelashes from her seat at the table.

"You will address me as Officer Hafiz," responded Amir curtly.

Parris laughed at him. It sounded like a real laugh, which unsettled him. He could not afford to be undermined here. He had to take charge.

"Do you want to call a lawyer? If you do not have one, we can assign one to you–"

"No thanks," she interrupted him, inspecting her nails. "I would rather get all of this over with. I have things to do, you know."

His eye twitched again. He needed to keep her focused, he needed to assert authority.

"This will end when I say so," he spat back as he took a seat in front of her. He opened the file on the table and pulled out a few photographs. "Why don't we start with why you often leave your club at night and return early in the mornings?"

He threw down pictures of Parris leaving through the side door of *Clueless*, entering different vehicles or walking. Parris never looked down at the pictures, instead staring at Amir.

"It's not a crime to go out."

"It's not, but when shady individuals show up often at your business, that raises a few red flags," Amir quickly countered as he produced two more photos. It was a picture of Tony and her outside her club and her kissing Giovanni goodbye earlier that morning.

"Quick little fox," Parris praised him with a smirk.

The spark began to grow inside Amir's chest again. He could do this. Get to the heart of all the crime in Ciel City through her. Helen's information was right.

"Well then?" he pushed. "Do you know these individuals?"

"Do you like watching T.V., Amir?" Parris asked instead.

"Answer the question, Parris. Do you know—"

"I love watching T.V.!" she answered her own question enthusiastically. The handcuff rattled as she spoke with her hands.

Shit, Amir thought, slowly losing hold again. "How do you know

Giovanni Moretti and Tony Moretti? How are you connected to them?" Amir quickly demanded, but it was too late, Parris had shifted the focus, speaking over him.

"I love watching mystery shows: finding leads, watching out for red herrings, and the spectacular chase scene in the end! Thrilling! But the ending is always the same." She captivated him. "They unveil the monster and the person underneath is always someone they trusted. Someone they overlooked."

He took a deep breath, his mind trying to read between the lines. *Overlooked? But I've already arrested her. Unless there's meaning behind her words? Or is she just spouting nonsense?*

"Are you trying to say," Amir spoke slowly, unsure of his words, "that when I unmask this city's monster, I will find you underneath?"

Parris held his green eyes in her dark ones.

The interrogation room door slammed open. Amir jumped from his trance. Captain Chan yelled at the top of his voice:

"OFFICER HAFIZ! HAVE YOU LOST YOUR GODDAMN MIND?" His eyes were ready to pop out of their sockets.

"Zoinks!" commented Parris.

"Captain Chan, I can show you concrete evidence that this woman is involved with the Big Three." Amir held the photos but Captain Chan pushed past him.

"I am so incredibly sorry for my subordinate's behaviour, Ma'am," he apologized as he uncuffed Parris from the table, not making eye contact with her, his head bowed.

"Captain!" Amir called out in disbelief. "I lawfully arrested her! What are you doing?"

"Shred those pictures."

"Excuse me?"

Captain Chan turned frantically around, a look of horror on his pudgy face. "You heard me! Shred them and all records of this incident, *now*."

The flicker of hope in Amir's chest was extinguished under a police boot.

"NOW!" Captain Chan repeated, the colour drained from his face.

"Now, now, boys," sang Parris as she rubbed her wrists, standing up. "No need to be so upset."

"You knew," Amir accused her in a low voice. She adjusted her leather jacket, not making eye contact. Amir marched up to the Informant, looking down his nose in disgust at her.

"You knew about me since the start. That he… all of them wouldn't help. That they would try to stop me. You hold them in your hands, that's why they're afraid of you," he spat.

His chest heaved against the police boot.

"You are a monster," Amir concluded. Parris chuckled, finally meeting his green eyes.

"I've been called worse," she whispered as she walked past Amir. Captain Chan pressed up against the wall. "Oh, and stop by *Clueless* for a free bottle, it's on me!" she called out as she walked through the door.

All commotion in the lobby was silenced when the officers saw her, taking multiple steps back as she made her way out of the station.

"Captain—"

A sharp slap echoed in the empty room. Amir held his cheek, more from the surprise than the pain.

"Count your blessings, Greenie. She usually isn't the kind to let things go so easily," warned Captain Chan. His look of horror was replaced with one of frustration as he gathered the evidence, slamming the door behind him. Amir slumped into the metal chair, trying to process everything.

The sun was beginning its descent for the day. A mix of purple and pink painted across the Pier, the lake reflecting what little light was left in a shimmer across its water. Parris stood in the middle of an abandoned warehouse. Her hands were in her leather jacket, she closed her eyes as she waited calmly. The slight crash of the waves from the lake filled the silence of the building. The inside was hollowed out, only the walls and support beams were left. Flickering lights did their best to brighten the dark warehouse, but years of neglect worked against them.

Eventually, three cars rolled into the warehouse. Four figures exited the cars, coming to stand in front of the Informant in a semi-circle.

"I asked to be informed personally, not with an audience," declared Giovanni. His men poured in from one of the entrances.

"Oh, is someone disappointed?" Tony sneered. "Good."

Giovanni ignored his son's remark, solely focused on the Informant.

Marcel placed a hand on Tony's shoulder to reign him in. "Take it easy, man." Their men were behind them by a few feet.

"I'm not here for a pissing contest," the fourth person huffed, popping her gum loudly. Her high pigtails swung dramatically. "Parris, tell us why you gathered us all here today. Our meeting is not scheduled until October." Her people lingered by the car, their guns showing in their waistbands.

"Can't I see my best friends earlier than that, Huifen?" pouted Parris as she stepped closer to the gangsters.

"I said you can use my English name, Tiffany," Huifen huffed. Parris shrugged as she pulled two photographs from her pocket.

"I know you were all so anxious about that little boom in Old Town today," Parris started, the gangsters giving her their full attention. "You'll all be happy to know that I found out who placed those bombs!"

Giovanni glared at Marcel. Marcel looked at Huifen with narrowed eyes. Huifen raised an eyebrow at the Informant.

"Well?" yelled Tony impatiently.

"It wasn't the Gates or the Halos or the Wings," Parris exclaimed happily. She showed them the pictures of two men being arrested by the CCPD.

"Turns out to be low-level thugs who wanted to make a name for themselves. Whelp, too late now." She giggled as she handed a picture to Giovanni and Tony.

"They have connections?" Giovanni asked, murder in his chestnut eyes.

"Nope!" Parris answered as she snapped the pictures from them to give to the remaining two. "They operated by themselves. They don't even have family that you can go after."

"Well, isn't that convenient," Giovanni commented.

Parris's smile widened. "Isn't it!"

Marcel inspected the photos with interest. "And how did you come by this information?"

"You cannot ask for her sources, Wing," Huifen snarled. "You should know better, but I should have expected less from such a new syndicate."

"The fuck you said to my executive, crack-dealing bitch?" Tony growled, inching towards her. The armed men readied themselves for a fight.

"You heard me, *Cucciolo,*" she mocked him with a cruel grin.

Tony's face contorted in pain, but he could not say anything back. Marcel swore at the Head of the Halos, vile curses thrown without hesitation at the woman. Huifen laughed at them, along with her men. The Gates' goons smirked at Tony's lack of response. Giovanni ignored them and crept towards Parris, handing her an envelope.

"Your services are as flawless as ever," he whispered. Parris watched the exchange unfold between the Halos and Wings, but gripped the envelope tighter. Giovanni leaned down to whisper hotly in her ear.

"I would love to thank you personally, *Bella—*"

"Payment is sufficient," Parris announced loudly, drawing the attention of the other gangsters.

Tony cursed at how close his father stood to the Informant. "Are you certain it wasn't just the Gates trying to set the rest of us up? Just when the Wings have a big order to fill!" he exclaimed as he limped up to his father. Giovanni barely paid mind to his son, a bored look on his older features.

To the unknowing eye, the two of them barely looked related. Giovanni towered over all of them with his muscular frame, while Tony was a small child in comparison. The pair stared at each other, so many unspoken words filling the warehouse. Huifen and Marcel remained rooted, not daring to interrupt the family.

Parris sighed loudly as she stood between the two. "I am, Tony. Are you trying to say that you're not satisfied with my service?"

Tony turned away first, his chest heaving with shallow breaths.

"One last order of business," Giovanni declared. His gaze turned to Huifen, who scowled at him, the second most senior member of the Big Three. Huifen, the Head of the Halos, huffed as she nodded at her men. The car door opened and out came the same Halo from the alleyway in Chinatown—the same one that followed Jaya and Angela, the one who tried to stab Parris with a switchblade.

"What is this?" Marcel demanded, pulling Tony to the side and out of Giovanni's reach.

Vince was thrown onto the concrete floor of the warehouse, bound and gagged, frantically looking around trying to catch Huifen's eye, screams muffled by the gag.

"A very naughty Halo tried to stab my Untouchable the other day," Giovanni announced to the warehouse. Marcel's eyes widened. Tony went rigid in his hold. Parris tapped her cheek, trying to remember what happened the other day.

"How old is he, Tiffany?" Giovanni asked. He leisurely strolled to Vince's side, looking down at him with a smirk.

"Sixteen," Huifen replied through ground teeth. Her pale face was red with humiliation.

"Sixteen," Giovanni repeated, his shiny dress shoe turned Vince's face, to focus solely on him. "A little young to be dealing drugs for the Halos, aren't you?"

Everyone turned into a statue as they watched Giovanni. Vince nodded, tears streaming down his face.

"Do you know what happens when you touch an Untouchable?" Giovanni asked. His words had jagged edges of concern and possessiveness. Vince didn't react. Giovanni pushed his shoe's heel deeper into his cheek.

"No one *touches* my Untouchables. Especially not my Informant. No one hurts her. Hell, no one can even fuck her."

Muffled pleas of mercy fell on deaf ears.

"Even I abide by this rule. It's the simplest term of our agreement."

A gun was pulled from Giovanni's tailored waistband. Vince tried to worm away. Giovanni pulled the trigger and the sound of the bullet echoed in the warehouse. Vince wailed as his leg sprayed blood across the floor.

"Did that hurt?" Giovanni asked with a pleased hum. "Imagine my pain when I was told someone tried to hurt her."

Another squeeze of the trigger, another screech of pain.

"You don't want to hurt me, do you?" Giovanni pressed.

Another bullet. This one between Vince's eyes.

"Do you, Tiffany?" Giovanni asked again, his grin directed at Huifen. She could only ball her hands into fists as she shook her head.

"How about the Wings?" Giovanni asked in Marcel's direction. Tony snapped his head away, trembling in Marcel's hold.

"No," Marcel choked.

"Good. Good." Giovanni returned the gun to its place. His chestnut eyes swept across the warehouse, a delighted look on his aged face.

"What about you, *Bella*?" He returned to Parris's side. "What do you say?"

"Thank you, Boss!" Parris jumped up and down, eyes full of adoration. Giovanni chuckled at her enthusiasm.

"Until our next meeting," he concluded as he departed for his car.

Once the Gates had left the warehouse, Marcel led Tony back into their car in a rush, sparing one last look at the Informant. Parris winked at him as she skipped up to Huifen, who stared at the dead body on the floor.

"Can you give me a lift to *Jim's*? You have an extra seat now!"

Ciel's city lights finally came to life as Logan went for his final delivery for the day. His new job was exactly as he expected, boring and repetitive. Just how he wanted it. He hated excitement. He wanted something dependable and stable. It was the perfect job to do during the day before he had to bartend at night.

The white truck slowed down as Logan approached a black building with a neon sign that read *Clueless*, his last stop. Logan glared at the sign, knowing he had to make the delivery to the club at some point on his route. He took a few deep breaths, just like how Dr. Brown taught him, and counted to ten.

"Fuck," he groaned, the blood still pulsing loudly in his ears. He slammed the door shut behind him as he grabbed the final bin for the day.

"Stupid fucking lemons for this stupid fucking…" he mumbled as he checked his clipboard.

"I would appreciate it if you weren't so hostile in front of my place of business," a voice mocked him from behind. Logan turned around, ready for a fight. He froze when he saw her.

Parris stood there holding a donut bag, that same *damned* smile on her face. When Logan didn't reply, she walked past him to the side entrance.

"You!" Logan spat, his hands shaking. Parris ignored him as she opened the door.

"You fucking Parrasite!" he yelled.

That caught her attention. Parris marched up to Logan. He held his breath as she snatched his clipboard.

"If you knew the day I just had, you would know better than to call me that," she warned him, signing the paper. She slammed it on top of the lemons, a cruel grin on her face. "But who are you to be kept in the loop?"

Logan wanted to yell at her, to curse her, to make her smile break, even for just an instant, but he could not stop shaking.

"Oh, and tell your boss that I only want the fruit," Parris called out over her shoulder as she entered her club without a second glance at Logan.

"Fuck!" Logan shouted into the night, dreading his next deliveries to *Clueless*.

Parris finally entered her nightclub after a day that did not want to end. The staff of *Clueless* frantically cleaned the club, preparing for opening later that night. She swung her donut bag as she descended a set of stairs hidden behind the black bar. A cozy lounge with couches, beds, and computers hidden in the basement of *Clueless*. On one of the couches was Lorenzo's body.

"Oi, Lorenzo, how you feeling?" Parris asked as she crouched near his head. Lorenzo groaned as he was awakened.

"Like I've been shot," he answered, deadpan.

"I think you're exaggerating," Parris replied with a smirk. She dropped the bag of donuts on his belly. Lorenzo eyed the contents of the bag carefully before an innocent look came across his face.

"You bought my favourites."

"Are they? Hm, lucky pick," Parris responded.

"Thank you, Ms. Parris. I owe you my life," Lorenzo admitted meekly.

"I've seen it and I don't want it," Parris retorted as she straightened up. "I'm just glad the blood bags and bulletproof vest worked."

"I didn't think Giovanni would come himself to ask about the bombs," mumbled Lorenzo between bites of a chocolate donut. "What did you tell him?"

Parris winked at Lorenzo. "It pays to have a few loose lips on the payroll."

She looked down at her phone, her eyebrows drawn in. "We're about to open, so I'll have the others take care of you. I need to head out again." She rested her hand on his shoulder, her face finally showing a genuine emotion. "Thank you, Lorenzo." Lorenzo flushed at the statement, mouth full of donut.

Heading up the stairs and out the side door, Parris disappeared back into the night.

CHAPTER FOUR

Spiderwebs

The soft glow from the T.V. on the floor brightened the empty, dim apartment. Amir sank deeper into his couch, not able to focus on the Saturday night news properly. He hadn't been able to enjoy his first night off since he started at the CCPD. The T.V. was surrounded by cardboard boxes that begged to be unpacked, to make the apartment into a home. A single framed photo of a young girl with similar green eyes rested on the windowsill. She wore the same gold cross Amir was currently wearing around her neck.

The picture was the only personal touch the apartment had.

The news anchor was discussing the Ciel Re-Pavement Project with Mayor Gordon Robert. The Mayor, an older man with skittish eyes and thin gray hair, was recounting all the benefits the Re-Pavement Project would bring to Ciel, discussing the absurd budget the city was putting towards the Project.

"The Re-Pavement Project will focus on the Downtown Core. This will include the Entertainment District, parts of the Financial District, and the Pier and Harbour Front," Mayor Robert explained, bouncing his knee. "Of course, the city expects the Ciel Construction Company to submit a bid for the Project. Although the city has a long history with the CCC, we invite any construction companies to tender a bid."

Amir rubbed his dry eyes with a yawn. He didn't understand the political jargon or the significance of the CCC's bid.

Amir hadn't felt this defeated in years. Not since his sister…

No, don't go down that path. He caught himself before he was consumed with those dark thoughts. His mind replayed the arrest again: Captain Chan's reaction to her in handcuffs, Parris's teasing declaration of mysteries and monsters.

She had them all in her hand. Maybe that's why they had an out-of-town transfer lead the Task Force. They just needed me to fill the spot.

His phone beeped.

Amir, talk to me. What happened? – Helen

He didn't feel like talking to her. He didn't want to relive that feeling of failure.

Please, I am the only one who can understand what you're going through. – Helen

Amir knew she was right. Helen was always right. She knew that he should stakeout *Clueless* for leads. She knew Parris would go to *Jim's*. It made sense that the former head of the Anti-Gang Task Force would know how the city truly functioned. He was lucky she reached out to him when she knew about his transfer before her dismissal.

At first, Amir was skeptical of a random woman claiming that she was the old lead of the Force. But when Amir's request for files from the CCPD on the Big Three was 'lost' or 'incomplete,' Helen graciously gave him the files, the information that the CCPD had worked so hard to keep from him. After Chan's actions with the Informant, Amir's faith in Helen had been cemented. She was a trustworthy source, a bigger help than his own colleagues.

I am sorry, I thought I could catch her. – Amir

Don't be. I've tried going after her for years. She is slippery. It also doesn't help that she's an Untouchable. Nobody would help me investigate her. They were all afraid of the consequences. Especially from the Gates. Listen, what you've accomplished in your first week, gathering evidence, confronting Parris, I couldn't even do in my first year as lead of the task force. I'm proud of you, Amir. – Helen

At that moment, the pangs of loneliness pinched his chest. It made him miss his home, his parents, and his friends. Moving to a new city in his early thirties was a big change, especially with his surprising difficulties in building social connections within the force. He missed having a village support him. But he had come to Ciel City on a mission, to do his job and to keep an eye out for runaways.

His eyes wandered back to the photo on the windowsill. He had promised himself that he wouldn't let what happened to her happen to others, to stop the disappearance of young girls.

The loneliness of moving to a new city did not heal as time passed. His own officers in blue avoided him like the plague now. Each one turned the other way when they spotted him in the division. Helen was all he had left.

If you are comfortable with it, do you mind if we meet? – Amir

He asked, already knowing the answer. Helen had made it explicit that they were to never meet in person. Since her dismissal from the CCPD, she had wanted to help Amir in fighting the gangs, but she would only be available over text. Helen told him how she was forced out of the CCPD and into hiding for gathering evidence against the Big Three.

Helen stopped replying.

Regret filled his veins as he sank deeper into his couch, waiting for a response that wouldn't come.

The nightlife in the city began to awaken as the last trickle of sunset made its departure for the day. The bells chimed as more patrons entered the *Loose Screw*. Logan glanced at a large group of construction workers who entered.

The bar was filled with patrons, mostly men who tried desperately to hold on to their twenties by flirting with barely-legal girls. The sticky nylon floors and walls covered in sports jerseys were designed to attract their male clientele, while the cheap drinks and the motel across the street drew in a different kind of customer. The motel's suite doors were in clear view from the large window adjacent to the bar. The cheers of middle-aged men playing darts filled the crowded bar, along with music and the chatter of failed flirtations.

"Another round!" a patron called out, throwing down a wad of green bills onto the wooden countertop that was covered in watermarks. Logan nodded as he popped the caps off of green glass bottles, throwing the empty ones into the bin under the counter.

"I'm cutting you off if you finish this one in less than ten minutes again, Raj," Logan shouted over the music.

The patron took the drinks with a yell over their shoulder. "You're a good man, Lo!"

Logan kept moving behind the bar, dancing through his routine, wiping up a spilled cocktail, cashing out old Benny, and stepping in to break up the fight by the pool table.

Just another night at the *Loose Screw*.

"Come on!" came a squeal from a girl pressed against the bar. "Look over here, Mister."

Her low top left nothing to the imagination. Logan scowled as he approached her. A group of girls behind her, dressed in a similar fashion, giggled as he finally paid them attention, not like they needed any. The male patrons watched them enter the bar in a herd, hungrily eyeing which one they would claim as theirs for the night.

"What?" Logan demanded, drying his hand on the tea towel over his waist.

"Six vodka sodas!" the leader of the herd exclaimed, pushing a red bill across the sticky counter.

Logan raised an eyebrow. The girl played with a lock of her blonde hair, batting her gloopy mascara at him.

"Six vodka sodas when I see six IDs," Logan countered. The girls murmured amongst themselves in disappointment.

"I told you this wouldn't work," a girl from the back of the group whispered.

"Shut up, it will!" the leader spat back. "What if I show you a good time in the back?" she whispered, an attempted sultry look on her young face.

Logan's scowl deepened. Her hand reached for his. Logan stepped back.

"Either you six leave now, or I'll call the cops. Your choice, kids," Logan stated, pulling out his phone.

"Wait!" the leader shouted, her mask of confidence dropping instantly. "We're sorry, we'll leave."

"What's going on here?" a man in a black dress shirt appeared. His shiny bald head shone under the spotlights. "No sad faces in my bar!"

The group of girls perked up at his words.

"You ladies want something to drink? No problem! Logan, go refill the ice, would ya?" he directed, his eyes drawn to the low shirts of the girls, not hiding his obvious stare.

"Mike, they don't have IDs," Logan leaned down to whisper into his boss's ear. Mike waved him off as he popped the tops off of six beers.

"We'll cover their bill, Mike!" a patron behind the girls called out. The girls squealed as they grabbed the beers from Mike. The patron introduced himself with a cheeky smile, pointing to a group of men crowded around one of the standing tables. They all wore black rings on their pinky fingers. The girls followed his lead to the table, away from the bar.

"Mike," Logan repeated more forcefully. Mike made himself busy with counting bills.

"They're not nineteen," Logan stated.

"Really? I couldn't tell."

"Boss."

"Logan, refill the fucking ice already," Mike spat. Logan spared one last glance at the girls, each one already claimed by a man with a sneaky hand around their shoulders or waist.

Just another night at the *Loose Screw*.

"First party in the big city, eh?" Theo asked as Angela left her building. He leaned on a parked car, his blue and white varsity jacket stood out under the warm streetlights.

"It's a milestone, for sure," Angela replied as she joined him, heading to the station together.

"A few of my other friends will meet us at Flushington Station," Theo informed, pocketing his phone and giving Angela his full attention.

"Sounds good," Angela replied. She tugged on the sleeves of her denim jacket. Butterflies filled her stomach; this was going to be her first-ever high school party. Since Jaya wasn't with her as her social buffer, the butterflies were caught in a tornado.

Jaya had video-called her to make sure her outfit was cute enough—her words, not Angie's. Black jeans, a white tank top, and a black denim jacket were the safest options that Jaya had approved on.

Theo was nice enough to go with her, which she was eternally grateful for, even if Jaya made kissy faces at her during the video call.

Over the first week of school, they had grown close; having most of their classes together helped form the friendship. Theo was constantly asking her questions and trying to make her laugh. Angela couldn't remember the last time she laughed so much in such a short period of time. Jaya was also a victim of his jokes, the three of them spending the lunch period giggling and sharing whatever baked goods Angela had decided to make the night before.

"You're totally a Hufflepuff! Although, you could pass for a Ravenclaw," Angela affirmed. The pair rocked with the subway as it launched from station to station.

"No way." Theo shoved her shoulder gently, "I'm totally a Gryffindor. Have you seen this luscious mane?" He pushed his hair back in a dramatic swoop.

Angela rolled her eyes with a smile. "You're a hard worker and way too nice. You've managed to read ahead and share the notes with our entire class!"

"I was brave enough to venture into the unknown pages of our textbooks. *Such* a Gryffindor move!"

"Maybe you are a Gryffindor," Angela thought aloud with a finger on her chin. "Arrogance is one of their traits." Theo placed a hand over his heart in false hurt. Angela snorted loudly, quickly covering her face in embarrassment. Theo laughed, his cheeks turning a little pink. She shoved him again, not immune to his infectious laughter.

But Angela really thought Theo was too nice. Someone was always trying to talk with him or get his attention, be it a teammate or classmate who tried to talk with him during their lunches or on the way to the station. Although, Angela noticed he was brushing people off. When she had reassured Theo that he could eat lunch with his other friends, and that she wouldn't mind, he had insisted that he enjoyed hanging out with Angela, and by extension Jaya.

"I like how there are no expectations when we hang out," he replied earnestly.

"Nothing weird is going to happen, right?" Angela asked, following Theo up the station stairs. In retrospect, she should have asked that question sooner.

"If you mean drugs and alcohol, hopefully not. That stuff ruins people's lives and those around them," Theo answered.

The cold night air was refreshing as they resurfaced in Chinatown. The recent memory of the thugs was at the forefront of Angela's mind. Subconsciously wandering closer to Theo, she was on high alert for any men with scars or chains hanging from their pockets.

"Over here!" a girl called out as Angela and Theo joined a larger group of STK students who were crowded on the sidewalk. They looked like normal kids without the blue, gray, and white neon signs of STK's uniform.

"Hey, guys," Theo greeted as he introduced Angela to his friends. Another volleyball player with braided hair named Nathan complimented Angela's jacket. Angela's ears burned at the compliment. Theo's glare at Nathan went unnoticed by Angela.

"Let's go, let's go!" someone yelled as they walked down the dragon-lined streets. The group chatted with one another, but Angela remained quiet.

"I told you to shut up about that," Theo scolded one of the boys.

Angela followed closely behind, drinking in the glowing lights of the street. She was still unsure of the whole party, but her parents had endlessly lectured her that she had to make friends while in Ciel City. A party seemed like a good place to start.

Out with a new friend tonight, Dad. I'll message you when I'm home. – Angela

After a short walk, the rowdy group stopped in front of a building complex. Angela's anxiety eased as they arrived at Kevin's place. His building was a stark contrast to Angela's, his being a new build with endless windows and a sleek design. An apartment was glowing with strobe lights, the sound of muffled music flooding onto the street.

This place must have cost a fortune.

Ready for her coming-of-age movie moment, she turned to Theo with a nervous smile. Theo, on the other hand, was looking at his phone in distress.

"Is everything alright?" Angela asked quietly. Their group already headed up to the loud party, leaving the pair behind.

"Huh?" Theo's eyes were glued to his phone.

"Theo, is everything alright—?"

Angela caught a glimpse of a woman behind Theo. She wore a leather jacket and was skipping down the street. She stared with a slack jaw.

Theo had a look of concentration as his eyebrows narrowed at his phone. "Angela, I am so sorry, but I need to go," Theo uttered, a little breathless. But when he looked up, Angela had jogged down the sidewalk.

"I saw someone I know, don't wait up!" she called out over her shoulder.

"Wait, Angie!"

She disappeared around the corner. He didn't have time to chase after her.

"Shit," he muttered as he looked at his phone again.

Go to Town Hall Station. – G

Theo looked between the party and where Angela had disappeared. But his choice was already made for him. He quickly typed a message as he sprinted towards the subway again.

Sorry, Angie. I had to dip, something came up. Let me know who you're with, where you went, and when you get home! – Theo

He hit the send button just as the train arrived.

Parris took every turn and alleyway to her destination. Angela struggled to keep up. A few times she had to duck behind a dumpster to keep out of sight, as though Parris knew she was being followed.

"Damn," muttered Angela, feeling too warm in her denim jacket and regretting wearing it, labouring for air as adrenaline coursed through her veins.

This is more important than some party. I need to know if it's her. She reasoned with herself, *if it's really her, then maybe I can corner her. Finally ask her what happened.*

Panting, Angela peeked around the corner, catching Parris finally entering a restaurant called *The Golden Duckling*.

The adrenaline that Angela was still high on gave her the confidence to enter as well. All common sense was left at the door as the bell chimed dully.

The establishment was grim inside, with dimmed lights that blinked every so often, refusing to die out of sheer determination. A place like this should have been deserted, but it was packed full of loud college students. The restaurant smelled divine, with rows of hanging barbecued meats behind a window, plastic-covered tables, and constant steam rolling from the kitchen.

A woman yelled at her from the back of the dining area, "One?"

Angela nodded as she was pointed to a rickety table in the far corner. She pushed the laminated menu away. Looking around, she spotted a leather jacket disappear behind a red door with a sign that said 'Keep Out.' Her phone buzzed with messages from Jaya and Theo. Angela ignored them, the Informant consuming her thoughts entirely.

I can't lose sight of her.

Her curiosity encouraged her. She noticed that none of the staff entered or left through the red door, only going through the kitchen.

Now or never. I won't get this opportunity again.

Angela walked quickly to the red door, looking constantly over her shoulder. The staff were busy pushing out steaming plates. Crouching down behind a cart full of dirty dishes, she turned the doorknob slowly and as quietly as she could, hoping that the chatter of the customers drowned out the small creak of the door as she wedged it open.

Crawling through the door on the grubby floor, Angela found an empty hallway with a lone lightbulb shining. She crept along the walls, still hunched until she saw a door ajar down the hall. Light flooded into the depressing hallway.

Creeping closer, she heard a few people speaking. Women. With a cold sweat beading down her face, Angela peeked into the room.

"Now?" Logan grumbled into the phone. The loudness of the bar found its way into the phone call. His boss on the other line yelled at him.

"Yes, now!" she yelled. "Get your ass in the car and drive there, NOW!"

"Alright!" Logan shouted back, hanging up.

Who the hell needs an emergency delivery of green onions at night?

Logan stepped out of the walk-in, and back to his position behind the sticky bar. Mike was busy chatting with a few regulars. He checked the table the girls had gone to a few hours ago; he was keeping an eye on them between serving drinks and breaking up bar fights.

All six girls were gone.

Along with the men they were with, they had left the *Loose Screw* when he went to the back to take the phone call. He looked out the window to the motel across the street; his eyes searched for blonde hair. He caught a glimpse of the blonde girl entering a room with a man who was much older than her.

The door shut.

"Hey Mike," Logan called. "Listen, I gotta run out… I'll be back right away. Can you cover for me?"

"That your delivery job?" Mike asked between bites of bar peanuts.

"Yeah, I need to run a quick job."

"We can cover ya. Grab a pack of smokes on your way back, O'Brien!" Mike waved him off.

The inner room of *The Golden Duckling* was big, with people sitting around a large circular table. They were in their forties, all dressed casually as they ate their dinner. Angela spotted a few chains hanging out of some of the men's pant pockets. The Informant stood in the middle of the room, her back to the door, speaking directly at a woman.

The woman who sat facing the Informant seemed to be the leader. She had high pigtails and wore trendy clothing. She was dressed more like an influencer than a potentially dangerous criminal.

Angela did not recognize the people. They weren't on the city's watch list that Angela so often found herself looking at throughout the week. The one thing she did know was that she had wandered into the Halos.

"You felt brave after that? Did bombing the Gates get your rocks off?" Parris spat at the other woman. "You thought you could cover your tracks and use nameless thugs? It was sloppy work at best, Huifen. If you wanted to test his control and the Gates' influence, acting like a Looney Tunes character doesn't cut it."

"Then why didn't you expose us to the old man?" the woman named Huifen sneered at the Informant, readjusting her glasses as they steamed from the food. "You shouldn't complain, you got paid for lying. It must come easy to you."

"Easy?" Parris laughed. "You're funny, Huifen. You should stop engineering drugs and pursue clown school."

"Bitch," Huifen spat at her.

"Thank you," snarked Parris. "Now, about your stupid new drug—"

Angela was abruptly yanked back from the conversation by her hair. A hand slapped across her mouth, silencing her scream before it could come out.

A cold sweat dripped down the back of her neck.

"Looks like we got a pest problem," a man whispered hotly into her ear. Angela was pulled from the ajar door and back into the depressing hallway. Multiple hands were on her, grabbing and dragging her through the building: away from the inner room, away from the bustle of the restaurant, away from people who could help.

Her feet uselessly struggled to dig into the floor but the arms were too strong. She tried to scream for help, for anyone, but she was too deep in. The hand that covered her mouth silenced any yells. No one could hear her. No one would care.

Fuck, I didn't even tell anyone I'm here, Angela lamented to herself as she was thrown onto the dirty floor of the backroom. She scurried away, trying to sit up, to get her bearings. But the room was dark and her eyes refused to readjust.

"Who sent ya, little mouse?" a man with yellow eyes appeared in front of her, inches from her nose.

Angela tried to back up, but she hit the legs of another. She looked around to find herself surrounded by men with ugly looks of hunger in their eyes, chains hanging out of their pockets.

"No one!" Angela answered, her voice shaking. The same plunge of cold fear found its way back into her body. "I got lost. I was trying to get back to the restaurant."

Her arms were seized by two men, restraining her on the floor. The yellow-eyed man grabbed her face, his nails digging into her cheeks.

"Oh, we can get ya to squeak, isn't that right, boys?" he smirked, his eyes feasting on her. The other men cheered. Her denim jacket was skinned off in a frantic rush. Angela screamed, trying to free her hands. The men howled at her sad attempt to fight them off. Hands pulled at her coily hair, tugging her in different directions.

When they continued laughing at her, tears finally left her eyes. She couldn't regret every decision she made: moving back to Ciel, following the Informant. She had made all of those choices. Angela had to know who Parris was.

"There you are!"

A familiar voice called out, cutting the violence in half. "Sorry, lads, I left my staff in the restaurant to grab my takeout," Parris explained easily as she cut through the center of the circle.

"She must have separation anxiety, poor baby." Parris pulled Angela from the clutches of the men. Angela's chest heaved in relief. She held on to the leather jacket for dear life, her knees refusing to re-solidify from jelly.

Strangely, Parris allowed it.

"We found her snooping around. She could be Gates or Wings!" the yellow-eyed man exclaimed after the initial shock disappeared. Parris gave him a sharp look.

"I said she's mine."

He backed off, cowering at the possessive look in the Untouchable's eyes. She looked down at the discarded denim jacket, and one of the goons rushed to give it to her.

"Come on," Parris grabbed Angela's upper arm, still supporting her. "Let's get out of this shithole."

The duo went out the back door as the men fumed in their spots, but there was nothing they could do. Not to an Untouchable.

The world was moving too fast for Angela's mind or body to catch up. Her feet refused to move on their own, entirely dependent on the Informant. She followed her lead to the shipment dock outside of the restaurant. The Informant was uncharacteristically silent, but her grip grew tighter. A white truck was parked outside; a man spoke from behind the wheel.

"Take the bin so I can get back to work…" he trailed off, catching a glimpse of the Informant. The staff hurried inside with the green onions upon seeing the Untouchable.

"Logan!" Parris greeted as she slammed Angela into the side of the truck by the driver's seat. Angela gave a yell as her shoulder smashed into the metal frame. Parris still held her in her death grip. Her talons refused to budge.

"Be a useful shit and take this lovely lady home."

"I'm not your taxi driver," Logan's eyes faced forward, refusing to look at her.

"Oh, I have a feeling you are," she sang as Angela finally pulled herself from the Informant's grip and snapped out of her daze.

"The fuck is wrong with you!" Angela screamed, rubbing her shoulder.

Parris slapped her across the face so hard that her head banged into the car. Grabbing Angela by her hair, Parris brought her face close.

"What's wrong with me?" Parris repeated venomously. Angela's heart dropped into her stomach. The pain in her shoulder and head paled in comparison to the dread she faced.

"What the hell were you doing following me? Are you just a crazy thrill-seeker? Do you think that this is some game?" Parris hissed, her eyes wide with madness and an anger that simmered just below the surface. "This is the second time I've saved you from the Halos. Do you know what they would have done to you if I wasn't there?"

Angela tried looking away but Parris tugged harder, forcing her to look.

"Answer."

"Just let go of me already!" Angela shouted. She was sick of the fear, sick of the anger that was threatening to resurface, of the way she wanted to wrap her hands around Parris's neck.

"You're not angry with me, you're angry you got caught," Parris said knowingly, to Angela's dismay.

How could she tell?

Angela couldn't break eye contact with the Informant. Her face still had a childlike glee. It hasn't changed after all these years.

"I'll report this to the police," Angela threatened after a moment of silence. Parris jerked her head into an awkward position. Angela whimpered in pain.

"Go ahead. But since you don't learn the easy way, let me tell you what's going to happen the next time I find out that you've been putting your nose where it doesn't belong," Parris lowered her voice, her intense eyes like an endless void for Angela to peer into.

"I will personally deliver you to the Halos for a playdate. Hell! I might sell you to the Wings, they would pay a pretty dime for a little thing like you. Don't think you're of sentimental value to me, Angela Williams."

Hot tears sped down Angela's face. The woman's words cut deeper than Angela had expected.

"Do you understand?"

"Yes."

Angela's chest deflated. Parris finally released her. Angela leaned heavily against the car, her mind trying to keep up. She took deep breaths to fight the onslaught of emotions that threatened to control her. Logan remained quiet, staring at Angela and Parris through the side-view mirror with a permanent scowl on his face.

"Take her home," Parris instructed as she threw Angela's denim jacket at her, leaving without a second look. She marched back into the restaurant, slamming the door shut.

Angela looked up at Logan through the car's side mirror, not wanting to get inside. He didn't seem the friendliest with his deep scowl. But his sad blue eyes softened his rough appearance.

"I don't have all night," he grumbled as he started the engine up. She entered the truck.

"Where am I going?" he asked.

"Corner of Michener and 16th."

He reached into the glove box suddenly, spooking Angela.

"Calm down." He pulled out a first aid box, tossing it at her. "You're bleeding, kid," he spoke softly.

Angela looked in the mirror and saw the cut on the right side of her temple, where the Informant had slammed her into the truck. Angela mumbled her thanks as she cleaned the wound.

The truck sped through the city. The pair sat in awkward silence. She was grateful for the buzz from her phone, opening a plethora of messages from Jaya and Theo.

"Give me your phone," Logan instructed as he held his hand out expectingly. Angela jumped a little at the roughness of his voice.

"Why?"

"Just give it."

At a red light, Logan took her phone and added his contact information, calling his cell phone for good measure. He returned it with a grumble.

"If you ever find yourself in trouble again, give me a call. I have a car."

She gasped when she saw his name; her hands shaking. Logan O'Brien.

It can't be him!

"Logan?" she asked, trying to read his expression, but his dark hair got in the way. "Do you remember me?"

Fate was toying with Angela.

"I do," Logan huffed, his eyes trained forward.

"Logan…" Angela said in disbelief. He remained quiet.

"Logan, about Nini—"

"I already told your parents and the police everything I know," Logan cut her off roughly. Angela snapped her mouth shut, her eyes beginning to sting.

"I'm sorry… that was harsh. Stay away from that Parrasite, she's nothing but trouble."

"Parrasite? You mean Parris?" Angela asked, rubbing her eyes aggressively.

He didn't respond. He didn't have to, as they stopped in front of her building.

"Um—I guess, thank you," Angela whispered as she fumbled for her keys. Logan stayed silent, glaring at the road, as though waiting for it to open up and consume him. Angela hurried out of the truck, wanting the night to come to an end.

"Kid!" Logan called out before she shut the door.

"Stay away from her," he repeated, looking Angela in the eye. "She's bad news. A Parrasite is someone who continuously takes and never gives back. They are selfish, devious, and most importantly, they suck the life from all around them. She'll make your life a miserable hell, or worse, you'll end up dead," he explained with a sad look on his otherwise handsome features, as he resumed his staring contest with the road.

Angela couldn't find her voice; instead, she shut the door and stood there for a moment.

"Logan—"

"Stay safe, Angie."

The white truck sped away. She watched the disappearing tail lights.

You'll end up dead

"You know he's right," a voice called out sharply behind her. Angela snapped her head towards a man wearing a leather jacket, who leaned casually against his red sports car.

"She is nothing but bad news," he remarked, his gaze heavy with implication.

CHAPTER FIVE

The Morettis

"The next station is *Town Hall, Town Hall Station*," the robotic voice chimed through the subway car.

She didn't respond to my texts yet, Theo thought as he took the stairs two at a time. Pushing his way through the station's barriers, he messaged Jaya to let him know if Angela contacted her in the meantime.

Whipping his head around, he searched frantically for the black car. *He said something about dinner last time, but why meet here? What does he want me to do? Am I late?*

Town Hall, technically in the Downtown area, had less traffic and fewer locals during the nighttime. People preferred the nightlife of the Downtown core.

Theo breathed deeply through his nose and out through his mouth several times. He didn't want to have another panic attack in public. Not when he had to meet with Giovanni.

Get it together.

Finally, the black car slowly rolled to a stop in front of him. There was no overpowering smell of vanilla or wood when Theo entered the car this time. He was alone.

"Excuse me?" he called out to the driver through the dark divider. The divider slowly rolled down soundlessly as the car sped.

"Sorry, but where is he? And where are we going?" he asked, hating how his voice shook. The driver looked at him through the rear-view mirror.

"Would it make a difference if you knew?"

The divider rolled back up before he could reply. Theo tried to recognize where in Ciel City he was. They were driving east along the waterfront, but that was all he knew. He hadn't been to this side of town, which was not easily accessible by subway or buses. The uncertainty of where the driver was taking him doused his nerves with gasoline. The smallest spark would set him off.

The streetlights sped past in blurs of yellow. He leaned his head against the cool window. His Saturday night plans had been derailed: leaving the party early, Angela disappearing.

His dad…

The sound of the T.V. was deafening as Theo descended the stairs of his home. He crinkled his nose at the overwhelming musk of beer and smoke, but not regular cigarette smoke. Something harsher, unfamiliar. He entered the living room to see his dad slumped into the armchair with a random woman sprawled in his lap. Theo sighed, speeding to the kitchen. He hadn't had dinner since his dad and the random woman were… busy downstairs.

"You didn't say you had such a handsome boy, Roger!" the lady cooed, her makeup running down her face. Theo hunched his shoulders.

"Yeah," Roger scoffed, still focused on the movie playing. "He's a looker alright."

"He gets it from you, gorgeous!" She batted her thickly-covered eyelashes at Roger.

Theo tried his hardest not to gag at the sight. The Graysons looked nothing alike. Roger was a balding blonde with a prominent beer belly.

They only shared a last name.

Theo busied himself with his search through the cupboards for a snack, ready to head out to pick up Angela. Long fingernails glided up his neck. A shudder ran through him.

"Is that the only thing you got from your daddy," Clair whispered, the fingers making their way down his back. "Or is there more?"

"Cool it, Clair!" Roger yelled as he kicked the woman off his son.

She giggled as she held her hip, swaying as she got off the floor, too high to feel any pain. She returned to the armchair, smoking something from a pipe.

Theo grabbed his snack, ready to dash through the front door, but his dad trapped him against the counter. The smell of beer and the weird smoke filled Theo's space.

"How's school, son? I feel like I haven't seen you all week! You haven't been avoiding me, right?" Roger grabbed Theo's chin.

"School's fine," Theo mumbled despite the death grip, keeping his eyes down.

"I never did thank you for the bail money, did I, son?" mocked Roger.

Whenever Roger would 'thank' him for something, it would result in a colour palette of bruises he would have to hide the next day.

"You don't have to," Theo responded, eyes locked on the sneer on his father's face.

"Oh, but I think I should." Roger yelled back to the woman. "What do you think, Clair?"

She didn't respond; she kept inhaling the smoke, her face turned a deep shade of red. Roger looked back at her, letting go of Theo as he rushed to her side.

"Don't be a hog, you bitch!" he yelled as he tried to smoke what little was left.

Theo seized the opportunity and ran through the front door and out of the house. Taking deep breaths to fight the oncoming panic attack, he made his way into the city.

Theo's eyes refocused as the car finally turned into a low building on the waterfront, stopping right in front of the entrance.

Lumière Lounge—the name of the place shone against the night sky in cursive. It was a roaring factory back in the day, but now it served another purpose with its lakefront real estate. Patrons pulled up in their antique cars, valets stood at the ready.

The divider slid down again. "We're here."

Taking that as an indication to get the hell out, Theo left the car and stood in front of the entrance.

"Sir," a waiter in a black uniform called out, ushering him into the *Lounge*. "This way."

The inside was covered in hardwood floors that led deep into the *Lounge*, exposed red bricks of the factory walls, and dangling crystal chandeliers. Theo passed little booths adorned with velvet and champagne bottles. He blushed a little as he heard the obnoxious giggles of women. A jazz singer's voice echoed from deeper within the *Lounge*.

Theo was severely underdressed and out of place. Spotting the linen and silk suits of the other patrons, he anxiously pulled at the sleeves of his varsity jacket. He was shown to a table at the back of the lounge. The booth was so tall that it essentially made the table into a private room, with a brilliant view of Ciel's skyline shimmering in the distance. Theo couldn't help but gasp.

Ciel City was beautiful. The night lights of the city danced across the lake's dark surface. Soaring skyscrapers competed with one another, trying to touch the moon up above. The Stairway Tower won, standing proudly amongst the rest, its lights fading between red and blue.

In the private booth sat Giovanni, who fit right in with the aesthetic of the *Lounge*. His midnight blue suit complemented the dark wine he sipped, like a king upon his throne.

"*Cucciolo*," Giovanni acknowledged.

"Sir," Theo greeted back.

Giovanni pointed to the spot next to him with his glass. A curtain was pulled, separating the booth from the rest of the Lounge, plunging it into silence. Theo sat with his hands folded on his lap, staring at the table.

How come I wasn't I.D.-ed at the entrance? I don't think I can be here.

Theo shifted in his seat; he wasn't comfortable with how tiny the booth was. How he was squished in place. How he was too close to the older man, feeling unusually small next to him. Theo was used to his height being a defining characteristic of his, but Giovanni was massive in comparison. His personal space was nonexistent. The overwhelming smell of vanilla and wood flooded his senses, as well as the wine.

"How was your first week back?" Giovanni asked, barely looking at him, reading the wine bottle.

"It was good. Got back into the swing of things, Sir."

"And volleyball?" Giovanni poured himself another glass.

"I made captain."

"Congratulations." Giovanni lifted his chestnut eyes to look warmly at the young boy. "I'm proud of you, Theo."

Theo held his breath. *Proud of me?*

Giovanni smiled. "Nothing like taking charge of a team, it shows good character qualities after all—"

"What is this all about?" Theo interrupted, a surge of courage coming from within.

"Whatever do you mean, *Cucciolo*?"

"I mean this!" proclaimed Theo, his voice shaking. "I mean why am I here? Why haven't you, I don't know, kidnapped me to take my kidneys?"

Giovanni barked out a hearty laugh. Theo backed down, not meaning to make himself smaller, but with Giovanni, he had no option. The man's presence, his words, his mass, demanded to be cowered before.

"Oh, *Cucciolo*! You need to stop watching T.V.," Giovanni answered. "I'm not going to steal your kidneys or your eyeballs. I just thought you were under a lot of stress and could use a relaxing evening."

"But why me?" Theo pressed.

Sighing, Giovanni finally turned towards the boy, giving him his undivided attention. "Because you asked for my help. You came to my company asking for the Gates, begging for money."

Theo turned away, his eyes beginning to prick at the recent memory.

"When you needed the money, I delivered. All I ask for is your company."

"But *why?*" Theo repeated, trying his hardest to stop his shoulders from trembling, to not cry in front of the terrifying man. A heavy hand rested on the side of Theo's neck, lifting his head.

"Because you remind me of my son," Giovanni admitted softly, his eyes searching Theo's face for someone else. "Because I lost my boy so many years ago and you remind me of him."

Hot tears sped down Theo's face. Giovanni's paternal voice hit a delicate nerve within him.

"I'm sorry," Giovanni wiped the tears from Theo's face with his maroon handkerchief. "It was selfish of me to want to spend time with you for such a foolish reason."

"It's not foolish," Theo mumbled back as he took the cloth and wiped his eyes aggressively.

A warm hand rested on Theo's upper back; he flinched immediately. More gasoline was being added to his nerves. But once Giovanni started rubbing his back in a soothing motion, Theo couldn't help but lean into the touch, not used to the comforting affection.

"What happened to your son?" Theo asked, trying to get a hold of himself.

"He died a long time ago," Giovanni replied, a bitter bite to his words. A hard look settled on his face, the memory replaying in his head. Giovanni's aura morphed for a moment, and next to all the intimidation and power was the tenderness of a father.

They sat in silence as Theo tried to even out his breathing; the comforting hand continued.

"If you would be open to it, could we meet again?" Giovanni

removed his hand from Theo's back. Theo subconsciously tried to follow the warmth of the hand.

"Would this be my way of paying off my debt?" Theo wondered, holding out the handkerchief. Giovanni laid his hand over Theo's, pushing the item towards the younger man.

"In a way."

Theo nodded as he held on to the cloth, clenching his gift tightly. Giovanni poured him a glass of water, which he promptly chugged.

"I think it's time you went home, *Cucciolo,*" he murmured in a gentle tone, the same tone a parent would use to remind a sleepy child about bedtime. He rang the bell on the table.

The waiter from earlier materialized instantly as he pulled the curtain back. The sound of the *Lounge* flooded back into Theo's ears. The giggles and chatter and jazz conquered the silence of the booth.

"When is our next meeting?' Theo asked as he stood up.

Giovanni picked up his wine glass, a kind look in his eyes.

"I'll call you."

Theo clenched the maroon handkerchief as he bid his goodbye. He went out through the buzzing *Lounge* and back under the night sky of Ciel.

Even the warm glow of the streetlight didn't dampen the sense of danger that the night brought. Angela shifted her weight between her feet, torn between running up to her apartment and listening to the stranger.

A voice inside her begged her to make a run for the apartment. It reminded her that night in Ciel was dangerous, regardless of being in Midtown, however close to STK she was. There were only a handful of people on the street, but they were too far along the sidewalk to see her or hear their conversation.

"She is nothing but bad news," the stranger announced confidently from his relaxed position against the red sports car.

"And how do you know that?" asked Angela. The man chuckled as he took a step towards her with a limp.

"Stay back!" Angela yelled. Her fist wrapped around her keys in defence. The man held his hands up before him, taking a big step back, intimidated by the keys in his face.

"Hey, hey!" he said, "I'm not here to hurt you. I saw what she did to you in Chinatown, you must have a splitting headache."

He saw what happened... Was he following her, too?

"You saw?" Angela's fist was still raised.

"Yeah, I did," he answered. He returned to his spot leaning against his car. "I was following her, you see. I think she may be involved with the Halos."

Angela's eyes widened. "You do?"

"Just a suspicion," he shrugged. Angela took a hesitant step forward, lowering her fist.

"Who are you?"

"The name's Tony," he answered. "Yours, sweetheart?"

"Angela."

"I also happen to know that you were at *Clueless* recently with a small brown girl. Why is that, Angela? You're not in trouble, are you?" Tony lit a cigarette; he held one out for Angela, but she declined.

"Or maybe you're looking for trouble?" he chuckled.

He's not wrong. Angela shook her head, almost childishly. Tony took a long drag of his cigarette, watching her intently.

This may be an opportunity to get to know more about Parris, understand who the woman was, and bring Angela one step closer to confronting her.

"Parris… what do you know about her?" Angela inquired.

"Parris is a bad woman. She finds ways to get her claws into you and she doesn't let go," Tony easily answered; the smoke danced through the air when he spoke with his hands. Angela held on to every word.

"And now that she has her eyes set on you, you're not safe."

"I don't think she has her eyes set on me. If anything, she's trying to avoid me."

Tony laughed sharply, frightening Angela.

"That's what she wants you to think!" He threw his cigarette butt on the ground. "Believe both me and that guy who dropped you off. You'll end up dead before you know it."

Tony was rough around the edges, with his unfocused electric blue eyes and sharp grin, but he knew Parris, an advantage Angela needed.

"Who is she?" Angela pressed.

"Parris is an Informant," Tony lit a second cigarette. "She gathers information and sells it to the highest bidder. I happen to know that she first appeared to the Gates and then to the rest. Since she's an Untouchable, she jumps from client to client, trying to dig up dirt that turns her a fortune. She says she's a free agent, but I think she's working with the Halos, and tonight proves it."

The wealth of information Tony was sharing with her was useful.

But how does he know all of this? Angela thought, the seeds of fear began to bloom in her chest. *Is he... is he involved with the gangs?*

"How do you know what an Untouchable is, Tony?" Angela's breaths were growing more shallow.

Tony gave her a wink. "She's got her claws in me, too, sweetheart."

Angela's phone vibrated, Jaya was calling again. Five missed calls and several texts from both her and Theo. A message from her parents as well. Knots formed in Angela's stomach.

"Listen, I need to go," she started. Tony smirked as he threw the second butt on the ground.

"Well, before you go, I need to ask you something," he took a step closer, Angela mirrored him.

"Yes?"

"Do you have protection, sweetheart?"

"I don't know what you mean."

"I mean this," Tony pulled back his leather jacket to show the handle of a gun poking from his waistband. Angela gaped at the weapon, stunned to see one in the flesh. Guns weren't a daily sight in Canada, even in a city as rough as Ciel. Ice-cold fear coursed through her veins. Tony continued as though they were discussing the weather.

"You need one of these if Parris has her sights on you."

"But you just said she's an Untouchable," Angela responded breathlessly. "What am I going to do with a gun, shoot her?"

This was nothing like the switchblade. This world was real, the world of crime lords and drug mules and trafficking. Ciel City was real.

Death and Parris were real.

Tony's sly smile grew, his greasy hair shone under the warm streetlights, casting his face in shadows. Angela's lips trembled. Her palms turned clammy. He hadn't dismissed her yet. She couldn't leave the conversation, not when he could pull the gun on her.

"Tell you what," Tony grabbed Angela by her upper arms and slammed her into the side of his car.

"STOP—!"

A hand over her mouth silenced her scream.

"Shh," Tony shushed her as he pushed against her, one hand grabbing the gun from his waistband. Angela struggled harder against his grip, her nostrils flaring. He continued to shush her as he placed the gun into the waistband of her jeans.

"There," Tony whispered into her ear, pushing a few coils aside. "Now you have protection."

Angela shoved him off her.

"And what do you get out of all of this?" Angela wiped her mouth with the back of her hand.

"I get the knowledge that I helped out a young girl from a cruel fate," he declared.

Tony smirked as he made his way to the driver's side of the car.

"Now go home, it's not safe for pretty little girls this time of night," Tony advised with a wink.

Angela ran into her building, the unfamiliar weight in her waistband a tether to what had just happened. She ran up to her Aunt's apartment, locking the door and triple-checking.

Her phone was screaming at her again. She finally answered Jaya, yelling at her from the other end.

"What the hell, Angie? Theo said you ran off in Chinatown by yourself. What the fuck?"

Looking at herself in the mirror with a sigh, Angela replied, "I know, sorry for not answering earlier."

"What were you thinking?" Jaya reprimanded. "Why did you leave the party? Is everything okay?"

Angela placed the gun on the bathroom counter, contemplating whether she should tell Jaya the truth.

"I recognized someone I knew outside of Kevin's," Angela answered truthfully this time. "We caught up together. Sorry, I should have checked my phone earlier."

Jaya was silent.

"Have you heard from Theo?" Angela changed the subject.

"Yeah," Jaya responded. "He's heading home now."

"That's good."

"Angie… if something did happen, you would tell me, right?" Jaya pressed.

She couldn't tell Jaya the truth. She couldn't tell her about Parris and Logan, or about Tony. Jaya was involved in her own mess, she couldn't handle Angela's world, too.

This path she had to walk alone.

"I'm pretty tired right now, I'm heading to bed," Angela avoided the question. "I'll message you tomorrow, Jaya."

Jaya wished her a good night and hung up. Angela breathed out a sigh of relief, taking her first deep breath of the night. She prodded the cut on her forehead. She would have to come up with an excuse for when Jaya and Theo saw it at school.

Angela carried the gun into the bedroom, drawing the curtains closed as she inspected it. Her blood ran cold when her finger traced the barrel of the gun. She hid it under the bed, where all monsters should go. Counting her blessings she had survived the night somehow.

Blessings like Parris? The only reason I'm still alive is because of her. Having the gall to say that she saved me and then hit me! The way she treated me like a child! she thought to herself with a sour look on her face, she hugged her pillow tightly.

Logan looked so different from the yearbook pictures. He was more youthful then, his eyes full of hope. Nini always said he was going to do great things in his life. Ciel has been cruel to him. I wouldn't have recognized him in the car tonight if he hadn't added his contact.

Angela pulled the comforter over her head, a little part of her hoping it would suffocate her.

The red sports car slowed down as it entered a dim parking lot. Tony parked next to a blue sports car. The rest of the parking lot was filled with vans and trucks.

Tony entered an old factory building with a whistle, the sound echoing off the dark walls.

The factory floor was gutted of the production machines, and replaced with shipping containers and several forklifts. Tony nodded towards a few Wings, thin black rings adorned on their pinky fingers as they held guns. They nodded back at their boss, kicking the shipping containers to quiet them. Tony smirked as he caught a glance of a group of men chained in a container before it was slammed shut.

We did have a labour order due sometime soon.

Their current base was growing smaller and the shipping containers were filled quickly. Orders out west to farms and to the Gates' brothels were always in high demand. The Wings would have to expand their operations or relocate sooner than Tony thought.

He continued his whistling as he made his way to the upstairs main office. Marcel was sitting behind the desk, reading over files and punching away at numbers.

"Hey, man," Marcel greeted as he reached for another folder.

"Hey," Tony replied, lurking by the door, lighting a cigarette. "Guess who went to dinner with the Halos again?"

Marcel sighed, looking at his friend over the folder. "Tony, we talked about this, you can't keep following her—"

"That's the second time this month!" Tony exclaimed.

Marcel closed the folder, giving Tony a pointed look. "Man, listen, you need to be here for the Wings. You can't spend your free time trailing Parris. It'll be bad for business."

"They're up to something! Parris doesn't buy drugs from the Halos, so why the fuck is she in Chinatown?" Tony leaned on the folders that scattered across the desk. His electric blue eyes pierced at Marcel's tired brown ones.

"Plus she's been talking to these girls."

"What girls?" Marcel asked, exacerbated.

"She's been talking to these two girls in high school," A smirk pulled at the corner of his lip. "One of them was chased by the Halos but Parris stepped in. Then today, she was roughing up the other one for following her.”

“Bro, do you hear yourself? You’re becoming obsessed with her!” Marcel shouted at Tony. His finger jabbed at Tony’s chest. “Don’t think that I wouldn’t notice you dressing like her, too, with that leather jacket.”

“You don’t know shit, Marce… Besides, she doesn’t want these girls to be near her, pushing them away,” Tony continued, a crazed look in his piercing blue eyes. “Especially the one I just met.”

“Wait, you talked to one of them?”

“Yeah,” A sleazy smile pulled on his pale face. “I got to talking to her, pretty little thing, even gave her a gun. Little kid wasn’t right in the head, she was following Parris around. The informant didn’t like that, so she fucking did a number on the kid. I figured she might use the damn thing on her. Shoot her and the kid can take the heat from the Gates for us.”

Marcel grabbed Tony by the collar of his shirt, his nostrils flared with anger, “Why the *fuck* would you do that? Why are you trying to compromise yourself and the Wings?”

“Parris cares about her, you should’ve seen the way she was yelling at her. Almost like a big sister.” Tony laughed in his face “If she didn’t have an interest in her, she wouldn’t have cared if the kid got home safe. If the kid is a soft spot for the Informant we should use it. Leverage is important.”

“We don’t need leverage!” Marcel’s grip tighten. “We don’t need a lead, we don’t need shit from the Informant! What we do need is more product. We need to gain more territory. Not fucking around with teenagers! Haven’t you learned your lesson, man?”

Tony shoved Marcel off him. “Shut the fuck up, Marce.”

“No!” Marcel yelled pointing at him. “Because you did this exact thing before and look at what it cost you. You lost your position and your dad fucked you over for it!”

Tony roared, “Don’t call him that!” but that didn’t stop Marcel.

"Fine, Giovanni fucked you over for messing with that STK girl!" Marcel thundered back.

Tony looked anywhere but at his friend.

"You cannot mess with Untouchables, Tony. You have a firsthand experience of what happens when you do. Your status doesn't matter to him. Moretti or Untouchable, it doesn't matter to Giovanni. The Wings cannot take any more heat from the Gates or even from the shitty Halos." Marcel lowered his voice, trying to calm the situation. "Please, think of what we started."

The Head and Executive stood in their office, their spat over but the consequences lingered. Tony moved first.

"I need to fuck something," he slammed the door behind him.

Marcel punched the desk.

Taking his seat, he scowled. He remembered the first time he met Tony. When their friendship... brotherhood started. Marcel's uncle went to the Gates for money, he remembered following him into the red brick building in Old Town. He remembered meeting Tony outside of Giovanni's office door, and how excited Tony was to finally see a kid his age in the building. The two of them ran through the halls, playing cops and robbers.

He remembered the way Giovanni smiled down at him when he left his office with Marcel's uncle, the way he patted his head when Marcel claimed he wanted to be a businessman one day when he was older. The words "you have the mind for it" would repeat in Marcel's mind, pleased that Giovanni thought so highly of him. He was excited when Giovanni invited him to come back to the office building to play with Tony again the next day.

Marcel rubbed his temple.

That was a lifetime ago. Time changes everything and everyone.

Theo awkwardly thanked the driver as the car stopped outside his home for a second time. The divider remained up in response. His hunched shoulders lowered the instant he left the car but a cold sweat dripped down the back of his neck when he approached his front door. With the handkerchief tucked away in his pocket, Theo unlocked the door.

Ready to bolt up to his room.

And bolt he did, taking the steps two at a time and locking his door. He was grateful that he installed a lock when his dad was under police custody. His dad and Clair were too preoccupied to notice him.

Taking deep breaths to hold off the anxious tightening of his chest whenever he was home, he grabbed his phone to help ground him. He saw that Angela had finally replied to his messages, and he responded.

Just got home, I'm sorry the night didn't go as planned. – Theo

He changed into his pyjamas, trying to drown out the sounds coming from the living room. Clair's obnoxious moans made the hair on the back of his neck stand. His phone buzzed.

Not a problem, Cucciolo, *I enjoyed our time together nonetheless.* – G

Shit, Theo thought as he sent the message instead to Giovanni.

I trust the ride back was pleasant. – G

He nervously chewed on his lip as he stared at his phone. Was this a part of him repaying his debt? Was he expected to text the Head of the Gates? Deciding to play it safe, he responded to the older man.

Yes, the car is pretty cool. – Theo

I will let you drive it next time. You have a license, correct? – G

You would let me drive your car? – Theo

Of course. Is there a reason that I should not let you drive? You would not be spinning donuts with it I imagine. – G

Theo laughed a little. His nerves began to settle the more they messaged.

No, I am a really good driver! I just have never driven an expensive car before, my dad only lets me use his car if he's in a good mood. – Theo

In a good mood? Why should his behaviour impact you? – G

New sounds emerged from the living room, making his chest tighten.

His everything impacts me… – Theo.

Tell me. – G

CHAPTER SIX

Cloud 9

Time moved differently in the city, as though the sands of the hourglass were slipping through Angela's fingers. She desperately tried to slow down time, to make the hours stretch just a bit longer, to hold on to the daylight before the moon conquered the sky. But the sand was too fine for her to grasp.

Angela had spent the remainder of the weekend going on long runs to help settle the wave of anxiety that arose from finally finding Parris. Purposely slowing down in front of *Clueless* during her runs through the city, her eyes and phone at the ready for any sight of her. The club remained stubbornly closed during the day with no signs of a black leather jacket emerging from its side door.

Going at night was out of the question.

The incident with the Halos played on repeat in her mind: the feeling of being tossed around like a ragdoll, of being utterly helpless, her voice and power robbed from her. The cut on her forehead still stung when she dabbed it with rubbing alcohol. She was angry that she was afraid of shadows and figures hiding in the dark.

She wouldn't go out at night by herself again.

By the time the first-period bell rang, Angela was seated next to Theo. He greeted her warmly as he sat down, pulling out his notebook filled to the brim with notes and questions for the teacher. Angela adjusted her hair to cover the bandage on the side of her temple. Theo appeared satisfied with her excuse for ditching him at the party. They had texted a little over the weekend, mostly Theo making sure she got home alright.

Not that Angela would share how her night really went. Theo didn't need to be involved with the Syndicates.

He has so much going for him, she thought as Theo answered the teacher's question with ease.

"Claudius is the power-hungry uncle of Hamlet. His character is obsessed with gaining and maintaining power, his incestuous-like relationship, and killing his nephew," Theo gracefully answered.

Soon enough, Angela was seated in front of a disappointed Jaya at lunch. The cafeteria rattled with students eating and others quizzing one another on content they barely understood.

"How was your weekend?" Jaya asked from across the table.

Angela feigned innocence. "Pretty boring, how was yours?"

Jaya grumbled words of worry about how phone calls are meant to be answered and texts replied to as she twisted the lid of her thermos. Angela smiled at her friend's antics as she dug into her lunch.

It's nice to have someone care about you, Angela thought as they discussed the upcoming week. Angela spotted Theo enter the cafeteria, praying that he wouldn't say anything about her ditching him in Chinatown. Jaya would only use that as ammunition.

"My chemistry assignment is kicking my ass," Jaya complained.

"I've been meaning to ask," Theo slid into the seat next to Jaya. "What happened to your face?"

Horrified, Angela began to mumble, "S-something fell from a cupboard and hit me."

Jaya took a judgemental bite of her food, not satisfied by her answer. Theo's phone buzzed and he quickly glanced down at it, a ghost of a smile pulled at his lips.

"That sucks!" he exclaimed, and brought his attention back to Angela. Another buzz. Theo smiled at his phone, quickly typing out a reply.

"Anyway," said Jaya. "I heard things got crazy at Kevin's."

That had caught Theo's attention. He snapped away from his phone, his brows scrunched together.

"What do you mean?" he asked.

"I heard that someone brought Cloud 9," Jaya's tone was accusatory towards Theo. "If you had known, would you have still taken Angie?"

Theo's phone buzzed again but his focus stayed on Jaya.

"I swear, Jaya, I didn't know," Theo admitted. "I am so sorry, I should've asked those guys whether they would do something stupid like that before inviting her." A brief look of anger flashed over Theo's face. "Idiots! Didn't they hear Patel's warning? And with university applications coming up, why would they risk it?"

Another buzz.

"You good?" Jaya tried to peek a glance at his phone.

Theo stood up, bag in his hand. "All good, thanks for telling me, Jaya. I'll have a word with those guys… Angie, I'm sorry about Saturday. I noticed you were struggling with answering in English today, maybe we can do a study session?"

"Of course," Angela replied. "Hard to pass up an offer from the smartest student in our year."

Theo grinned, his ears a little pink. Jaya rolled her eyes playfully at him. She couldn't disagree with Angela. Everyone in STK was smart, obviously, but Theo really was exceptional.

"You know that's not true, Angie!" Theo called out as he weaved through the crowd and out of the cafeteria, his phone glued to his face.

"Cloud 9?" Angela turned her attention to Jaya. Jaya, however, was more interested in finishing her lunch.

Is that the drug Parris was talking about? Angela thought.

"Jaya?"

"I don't know why you're keeping secrets."

Angela bit her tongue. She couldn't tell Jaya everything, she had decided that over the weekend.

But she could tell her…

"Remember my sister's friend that I was looking for?" Angela asked, putting her trash into a little pile on the table.

"I remember," Jaya answered, her hard shell cracked. A softer look peeked through.

"I found them," Angela confessed with a neutral face.

"Oh, that's awesome, Angie," Jaya congratulated, happy that she was sharing the news with her.

The lunch bell rang loudly.

"I'll see you tomorrow, Jaya," Angela called out.

The vaulted hallways quieted down as the herd of students raced into their third-period class. The echoes of chatter and footsteps died as the final classroom door closed. The silence that followed was eerie. Jaya walked through the quiet music hall, the faint sounds of a band practicing behind stone and oak coming from a distance. She waited patiently outside of a practice room.

Maybe she ran into her sister's friend while in Chinatown, that would explain her ditching the party. I wish she had just said so.

Jaya sighed as she leaned against the stone wall, frustrated with her friend.

She doesn't know that friends make you strong. I had to cut off so many from my circle since that incident. Angela probably didn't have many friends growing up. That would explain why she's so reserved. I wish I could show her that I'm here to help. Theo, too. There's no need to have her guard up all the time.

"Waiting on me?" a voice cut through her thoughts. Jaya rolled her eyes as she followed a boy into a music practice room. His snow-white sneakers walked along the carpeted floor, not a single crease in them. He pushed back his straight black hair from his face.

"Shut up, Kevin," Jaya snapped. Kevin laughed as he took a seat on the piano bench, and the padded walls bounced the sound around the room. He was too tall, with long lanky legs that seemed disproportionate to the rest of his body. He played alongside Theo on the volleyball team, which was his only redeeming quality.

"What's up?" he searched his bag for his sheet music. His notebooks were carelessly tossed inside along with black credit cards.

Jaya cut straight to the point. "Where did you get the Cloud 9?"

Kevin raised a black eyebrow with a cocky grin. "Are you scoping out the competition?"

"I don't deal."

"You mean," Kevin corrected her, he stood up, towering over Jaya. "You don't deal *anymore*."

Craning her neck upwards, Jaya tried to meet his stare, but she barely reached his shoulders.

"Who gave it to you?" she asked again, a hard look settled on her petite face.

"What do I get if I tell you?" he asked, taking a step closer to her. She cursed herself for taking a step back involuntarily.

"This is a transaction," Kevin explained, another foot closer. "You get something and I get something."

"You get to still see Petra on the weekends, without Selena ever knowing," Jaya spat at him. His cocky expression dropped immediately.

"How the fuck did you—?"

"Where did you get the Cloud 9, Kevin?"

He backed off, sitting with a huff on the piano bench. "Some juniors got a hold of some from this supermarket in Chinatown, they brought it to the party."

Jaya marched up to the piano, more confident now that they were at eye level.

"Which supermarket?"

"How the fuck should I know?"

"Does Coach know you hosted a party where even the freshmen were doing Cloud 9 and other shit?"

"*Fresh To Go*!" Kevin rushed to answer. She left without a look back at him, her phone in her hand.

"You won't snitch, right?" Kevin called out. "My mom will kill me if I get expelled!"

The door slammed shut behind her.

One source of Cloud 9 in STK is a Chinatown supermarket called Fresh To Go. – Jaya.

Jaya stomped through the school towards the library. Pulling out her cursed chemistry textbook, she sat at a table. She was ready to sit there until she finally understood what the hell was happening in that class. Her phone buzzed at her.

Any dealers? – P

I don't know. – Jaya

Find out ;) – P

Jaya stared at the command. Her anxiety shot through the roof.

Amir would be lying if he said his weekend was restful. He spent most of it lamenting his decision to arrest Parris and with Helen… Helen.

She still hasn't responded.

Amir took a deep swig of his extra-large coffee as he slugged through the green glass doors of the CCPD. His chest caved a little as a group of officers turned to look at him, whispering among themselves. He continued his march through the lobby, nodding politely at the secretary, but she turned the other way.

He climbed the stairs to the third floor. The once-white walls of the hallway were now a shade of beige. He didn't have any neighbours, his office was tucked away in the furthest corner of the division.

Unlocking the shoebox room, he turned on the lights with a sigh as it flickered to life. The walls were more grubby than the ones in the hallway, as though they were colour-matched with vomit. The desk had to have come from a crime scene, dark spots blotched all over the wood and a foul odour suspiciously coming from one of the drawers. Amir sat down heavily in the desk chair; it rocked back and forth, missing a few wheels.

Trying not to be discouraged, he went through his emails on the prehistoric laptop provided to him. The most recent one from his Captain successfully ruined his mood.

The Anti-Gang Task Force has three weeks to produce results on the investigation of Ciel's criminal organizations. Fellow officer support is entirely voluntary. – Captain Chan

He clenched his jaw as he reread the email. Without the compliance of the other officers and no leads, it looked like he would be transferred to Community Education sooner than he thought.

He did warn me...

A chime rang in the office. Amir grabbed the phone like a lifeline.

Sorry, I was busy. – Helen

Amir sighed deeply, relief flooding his veins. His heavy arms felt lighter. Maybe his day could be saved.

I was looking through my files and found an interesting piece of information. I interviewed a Wing member once, he mentioned that there were three Untouchables in Ciel. The first is Parris the Informant. The second is a school in Midtown, St. Katherine's. Do you know of it? – Helen

Yes, the school for exceptional students? It's one of Ciel's best-

selling points. Plus, the area by the school hardly receives any reports of crime. It's one of our safest areas. – Amir

There's a reason for that. An Untouchable means that that thing, person, or place is off-limits to every Syndicate, and by extension to everyone who has knowledge of it. No one is to mess with it or touch it. – Helen

So why didn't you warn me before I arrested Parris? – Amir

He stared at his phone, waiting for a good reason from Helen.

One, to prove to you that my information is reliable and that you can trust me, Amir. I told you about the Informant and my information was correct. Second, because people needed to see your drive. That the current hierarchy is meaningless in front of the law. That the Syndicates do not have immunity. That good people will oppose them. That their empire will eventually crumble. – Helen

That same feeling of hope started to bubble in his chest again.

Because we will bring justice to Ciel City. – Helen

The sparks of change whistling in his heart, Amir could not help but ask.

We? – Amir

Yes, we will tear them down. Together. I suggest you look into the school to get a better understanding of the way the Syndicates run. How they move their operations around STK. – Helen

And what about the third Untouchable? – Amir

The Wing didn't want to say, but the third Untouchable is a person. An untouchable status would be well-known throughout the gangs and Big Three. The everyday person wouldn't be aware. But I wouldn't be surprised if it was Tony Moretti. Listen, I have to go. I will message you if I find new information for you. – Helen

Amir was about to respond when he heard a light knock on his door.

"Yes?" he called out. A younger officer opened the door, a pile of paper in her arms.

"I was asked to bring these to you," she said in a small voice. She was a young recruit with auburn hair pulled into a tight bun and brown eyes that wandered around his run-down office.

Amir smiled through the exhaustion. "Thank you, Officer…?"

"Kristina Sanchez."

"Thank you, Officer Sanchez," Amir flipped through the paperwork, forms that needed to be read, things to drain his time. He couldn't blame her for bringing the work. He dismissed her with a nod of his head, but she did not move from her spot next to the foul-smelling desk. Amir looked up to find her staring at him, her lip quivering.

"Yes?" He tilted his head in confusion.

"Officer Hafiz, I just wanted to commend your bravery, sir. I have been with the CCPD for five years since graduation and never has anyone tried to arrest an Untouchable. Thank you for your service, sir!" she announced with a salute.

Amir shot up out of his seat, unsure of what was happening. She continued her salute of him, as though he were a war hero.

"It wasn't bravery, Officer Sanchez. I was reprimanded for it."

"You did the right thing, Officer Hafiz. Many of the recruits also think so!"

"Really?" he asked in disbelief. She checked over her shoulder, shutting the door. Her mousey eyes scanned over the room, searching for something. Seeming content with her investigation, Officer Sanchez replied.

"Yes, sir. Just because we cannot support you in front of the more senior members does not mean we do not support your cause."

The bubble of hope in his chest inflated bigger and bigger. The idea of having a colleague he could grab a coffee with or invite out for lunch snuck into his heart, a colleague who would help him bring change to Ciel.

"Officer Sanchez, I appreciate your words… and I understand that you cannot be singled out for siding with me," he admitted in a bitter tone. "But can I ask for your help with something?"

"Yes, sir."

"STK, the school in Midtown, what do you know of it? Anything about that school that would warrant the Syndicates deeming it an Untouchable?" he asked as he took a seat, gesturing to an empty chair across from him.

"You're not from Ciel, are you?" Officer Sanchez sank into the deflated chair, her eyebrows scrunched in thought.

Amir shook his head in response; she continued. "Aside from it being in an academic league of its own, the school doesn't stand out. The students keep their heads down. No obvious use of drugs by the students or teachers. No gang involvement with the school. The students don't disappear. They seem clean…" she drifted off.

"But?" Amir pressed, praying for something, anything that could help him.

"But there was an incident a couple of years back when I was attending high school myself. A girl jumped from the roof… but there were rumours that it wasn't a normal suicide."

Officer Sanchez stopped, looking at the red blotches on the desk as she raked her memory.

"I would have to find the file but I remembered that there was a possible suspect. Another female student was suspected of having pushed her off of the roof. That same night, there were reports of a female student missing. At first, the CCPD considered that she had something to do with the suicide but then dropped the investigation when the principal reassured that there was no missing student."

Amir's ears felt like they were bleeding from how loud his heart was beating.

"Eventually the CCPD announced it as a suicide even though there was no suicide note. Crime in Midtown dropped almost overnight. I think that was when STK was reaffirmed as an Untouchable by the Gates."

All Untouchables are made by Giovanni Moretti. Maybe there is a connection between all of them?

Amir stood up, Officer Sanchez followed his lead. He extended his arm out for her to take. She shook his hand in a firm grip. She nodded at his look, at the flame of determination in his green eyes.

"Tell your fellow recruits that I will bring down the Syndicates."

The cloudy autumn sky darkened dramatically around noon, threatening to flood the city. Chinatown disappeared through the window as a sleek black car sped through Ciel.

Huifen, the Head of the Halos, sat in the back, re-tying her pigtails back into place. She was a huge fan of the hairstyle. It kept hair out of her face and it made men more docile to her words. With her forties slipping away from her, Huifen held on to whatever youthful charm she could, especially when dealing with the Gates.

The vibrant streets of her turf turned into concrete gray highways, endless billboards of criminal lawyers advertised like a forest of trees.

She had learned from watching her mom mix powders and chemicals, selling them out of their dry clean shop over twenty years ago. She remembered the way Giovanni walked in with his expensive suits, asking when the shipment would be ready. She remembered meeting with the older man when she had shot her mother. How his hand clapped her shoulder, congratulating her on the promotion to Head of the Halos. The sense of pride coursed through her when she destroyed the other smaller gangs, consolidating the Halos' influence. She remembered the toast the older man gave to her success.

The way the man had stopped looking at her once she had gotten older.

She popped her gum loudly as the car exited the highway. The buildings of the West End run down from neglect and the rise of the cost of living. The sleek car came to a stop next to a blue sports car in an abandoned plaza parking lot. Huifen spat out the gum in her mouth before throwing a new piece in.

The car door opened and a man slipped in. He wore circle glasses and a tight suit that made him look like he belonged in the Financial District. He leaned over and planted a kiss on her cherry-red lips.

"Hey, beautiful," Marcel whispered as Huifen held onto his face as she kissed him.

"Hey, baby," she breathed, the smell of mint filling both of their senses. She looked at his cuff with a scowl. "Grease again?"

"Yeah, I was working on my cars this morning. It helps me de-stress."

"Drop them off later, the shop will make them good as new."

Huifen's delicate fingers glided up the Executive's arm. He was the second-in-command of the Wings, the brains behind Tony Moretti's gang. Huifen traced the muscle hidden under the thin fabric.

"Speaking of de-stressing…"

Her hands began to wander, but Marcel held them in a firm grip, leaning away from her embrace.

"Always business before pleasure, I see," she huffed at him impatiently.

"I don't have much time today." Marcel placed a kiss on her inner wrist before releasing her hands.

"You're a slave to the Wings, baby," her gaze lingered on his lips for a moment longer before she opened her purse and produced a small clear bag with green crystals inside. Marcel's eyes widened as he took the bag from her, holding it with care.

"Cloud 9 in the flesh," Huifen announced as she leaned on his chest. He inspected the green crystals. "It was a bitch to engineer but I think it was worth it. After just one use, the user will do anything to get that rush again."

"We have a large labour order that we'll need to start catching for the Gates. The Re-Pavement Project is going to bring in a lot of business. More labour demands means more products to catch," Marcel recounted, giving back the clear bag to her. "Are you sure you have enough supply to satisfy demand? My Wings are stressing a little."

"Supply is starting to go down since demand is beginning to increase, but I'm not pressed. My Halos will be able to make more Cloud 9 and distribute it. *Fresh To Go* is acting as a stash while we plan redistribution," she drew shapes on his thigh. "Speaking of satisfying…"

Marcel's phone rang loudly, to both their annoyance. Marcel groaned when he saw the caller ID, bringing a finger to his lip. He put the phone on speaker.

"What's up, Tony?" Marcel answered with an upbeat voice. Huifen rolled her eyes. She could hear the Head's slimy voice coming from the phone.

"She's in Chinatown again!"

"What do you want me to do about it? Maybe she likes eating Asian food?" Marcel responded sharply, trying to reason with him, trying to hide his irritation.

"Since when does she grocery shop in Chinatown, she usually gets delivery—"

Marcel cut Tony off.

"Bro, we spoke about this, leave her alone. The Gates will grill us if they find out the Wings are messing with an Untouchable."

"The way she walks, it feels familiar. Like I've seen someone walk like that before…" Tony spoke mostly to himself. Huifen gave Marcel a pointed look.

"Listen, I need to go," Marcel said. "When I get back to base your ass better be there too. We need to go over orders. A new shipment is leaving tonight. We're selling to the Gates' stores, your favourite type of shipment. I might let you keep one of the girls this time!"

Tony hung up the phone on him. Marcel pinched the bridge of his nose in frustration, squeezing his eyes shut. Huifen's hand crept along Marcel's leg.

"He's such a bitch," Huifen exclaimed.

Marcel leaned his head back. "He's just used to having things his way. I wish Giovanni had beat that lesson into him harder."

The pair sat in silence, the mood shifted at the mention of the Head of the Gates.

"We need to get rid of him; you do know that, right, Marcel?" Huifen pulled away from the Wing.

"Tony or Giovanni?" Marcel joked half-heartedly.

"The old man isn't the problem right now. Tony keeps derailing the Wings. His constant need to be babysat by you has been bad for business. You can't keep covering for his ass and fulfill orders at the same time." She returned the Cloud 9 to her purse.

"Tiffany, as annoying as he is, he's still my friend."

Huifen huffed and crossed her arms. "Friends come and go, baby. But business is forever. Isn't that why we decided on this little arrangement? We're both not satisfied eating the crumbs that fall off of Giovanni's table. I want more. I want more business. I want more power. And so do you."

"And pleasure?" Marcel asked, finally looking at her. She blushed as she straddled his lap.

Although he was new to running a Syndicate, his ambition drew Huifen in. She could appreciate a drive for more, an insatiable hunger like hers.

"I thought you didn't have time."

Marcel placed his hands on her waist, looking up at the Head of the Halos.

"Tony can wait."

CHAPTER SEVEN

Service!

The blinding glare from the laptop illuminated the crowded bedroom. Angela hugged her knee to her chest as she read the endless information from a local city forum. The bulky old wooden furniture made the room smaller than it was. The only other light was from the floral lampshade on the nightstand.

Angela briefly looked over at her English textbook which lay neglected to the side. Cursing under her breath, she remembered her assignment that was due on Monday.

Jaya wasn't joking about the workload; I can't keep up. I need a high average to get at least an entry scholarship.

Angela glanced at the clock over the door: just past midnight. Scrolling through another news article about gang activity, she yawned loudly as her back begged to be stretched. The old desk chair groaned in protest. She should have been working on her assignments, but she was busy researching Cloud 9 and the increasing disappearances among young girls and male foreigners.

Could there be a connection between the drug and the disappearances? Are the users being trafficked? Is Parris in on it, getting a cut?

At the thought of the Informant, Angela's eyes wandered to the small shoebox tucked under her bed. She didn't know what to do with the gun. Aside from hiding it, she did not feel safer having it.

Is Logan also connected to her? I couldn't find him on social media. He did listen to her after all. But... he called her a Parrasite. No way they're friends anymore.

"Ugh." Angela groaned, rubbing her eyes.

Cloud 9. Disappearances. Untouchables. The Gangs. The gun... If I pull on the loose threat, the whole tapestry unfolds. I don't want to get involved with any of that. I just want to talk with Parris. Ask her about Nini. That's it. Should I just go up to the side door of Clueless *and ask to speak with her? Is it that easy?*

Sighing, she got up to grab a snack from the kitchen. The 'A' and 'J' magnets were still in their places on the cream-coloured fridge. She had meant to go on more runs, but the workload was becoming unmanageable. The teachers must have thought that the students must have had more than twenty-four hours in a day with the volume of assignments they were throwing their way. Even her parents had reminded her to go on runs to help her relax from the school work.

Another all-nighter it is.

Her phone rang as she returned with a bag of ketchup chips.

"'Ello?" she mumbled as she chomped on the chips.

"Bad time?" Theo's voice came through the speaker.

"No, just starting our English reflections," Angela replied as she lay down in bed, licking the red dust from her fingertips.

"Finished mine last night."

"Once again, I have no idea how you work that fast, Theo Grayson."

"If I don't work, then I'll crash and burn, Angela Williams," he responded as though it were a joke, but there was a hint of truth there. Angela frowned, about to pry into his words, but Theo pushed the conversation along.

"Anyways, I'm sorry for the late call but I wanted to invite you to my game tomorrow. STK versus BA."

"A game on a Sunday?" Angela resumed her munching.

"Yeah, STK schedules most games on the weekends. Something about not disturbing the school day's 'rhythmic cycles' or something. But events like Halloween and Homecoming will be on a weeknight."

She could picture the goofy look on his face. She snickered, enjoying their phone calls. He was always a ball of energy, drawing her into his words, easily lifting the constant weight on her chest.

He had successfully wormed his way into her life.

"Maybe we can hit up the Ciel City Museum after?" Theo tempted. "Students are free on Sundays!"

"How can I say no to that? I'll be at the game tomorrow with my 'rhythmic energy'," Angela decided. "I'll bring Jaya along, too."

"Over here, Jaya." Angela pulled Jaya by her hand to get a spot on the edge of the first row of the bleachers by the gymnasium doors.

The school was busy for a Sunday. The gymnasium was full of students from STK and BA. Blessed Andre was a school from the Greater Ciel Area; far away from the ruff tides of Ciel City. Even some faculty joined the students on the bleachers. Principal Patel was easy to spot in his perfectly-tailored suit as he stood by the changing room door, greeting spectators as they made their way in.

"I haven't attended a game in so long," Jaya recounted as the pair settled down. "My last time was probably in sophomore year."

"I didn't think volleyball was so big!" Angela thought out loud, "I thought football or hockey would be more popular."

"We're a city school, there's no space for a backfield, let alone a whole football field," Jaya explained. "Our gym makes do. I think the girls team is still looking for a setter if you're interested!"

"I don't have good hand-eye coordination. Besides, I ran track at my old school," Angela answered. Missing the lush green tracks of her old school, the nostalgia disappeared once the gym doors closed.

A loud cheer erupted from the crowd as the STK team emerged from the changing room, their uniform a royal blue with gold accents. The other team, BA, wore a white and red uniform.

A group of seniors behind the girls were barking at the team, the girls laughed at their shenanigans. Nathan and Kevin looked over, pointing finger guns at their classmates, huge grins plastered on their faces. The girls clapped and cheered when they spotted Theo. He had a determined look on his face as he led the team huddle.

"Let's go, Royals!" Jaya screamed.

Both teams began to warm up, hitting volleyballs back and forth over the net. The ricocheting sound of the balls sailing through the air ignited the gym with electricity.

The energy made Angela feel alive. All of Angela's worries, all of her obsession with Parris, researching Ciel's underbelly, university and scholarships, were quieted in the back of her mind.

Did Nini attend games back in her high school days? I wonder if she preferred watching volleyball or basketball. I can see Logan and her attending, Angela thought with a warm smile.

"Woo! Let's go, Theo!" Angela yelled.

"You're a friend of his?" a man asked Angela. He stood by the end of the stand, one hand in his pocket, the other holding his coat. Angela hesitated to answer, Jaya leaned over to see.

"Yeah," Angela finally said. He took the seat next to Angela, the smell of vanilla and wood filled her senses. Jaya scooted over to make more space for the large man.

The crowd calmed down once the whistle blew and the game began.

"Are you his dad?" Angela whispered, trying to fill the silence. Theo jumped high into the air as he spiked the ball, earning a point for STK.

The crowd erupted in an explosion of cheers and howls, but the man clapped calmly in contrast.

"I'm his family," he responded with a dazzling smile.

"I'm Angela and she's Jaya," she introduced them, happy to have met Theo's family. The man politely nodded at Jaya, the smaller girl waved at him.

The game continued, both teams playing neck and neck. The sound of the ball being hit echoed off the gymnasium's walls. The teams calling out 'help' or 'mine' was the only noise they made as they battled for victory.

"He's been training for a while. I'm surprised he has time for this and to read ahead in all of our classes," Angela exclaimed, clapping loudly as Theo served an ace.

"Practice makes perfect," the older man responded.

When the final whistle blew, Theo yelled as his team successfully blocked the ball at the net, earning the winning point. The gymnasium exploded in incoherent screams as the team celebrated their first win of the season. The BA students tried to boo but that only added to the chaos. Jaya and Angela rose to their feet, shouting alongside their school.

"GO ROYALS!"

Even Principal Patel celebrated, his dress shirt out of place as he congratulated the coach and team. Angela felt a heavy hand on her shoulder, bringing her attention back to Theo's dad.

"Tell him to meet me out back, I'll bring the car around for him," he spoke with a kind look.

"Sure thing!" Angela replied, excitement pumping through her veins, as though she was the one playing.

The cheering eventually died down when the teams disappeared into the changing rooms. The gymnasium cleared out shortly after. Angela and Jaya remained behind to congratulate Theo. The pair chatted about the intense game.

"What a win!" Nathan yelled as he jumped on Theo. The boys left the changing room with their duffle bags, their hair damp.

"Those plays paid off," Theo pushed his friend, a huge smile plastered on his face.

"You sure you won't come to the party? I promise they won't say anything about your dad's arrest—" Nathan said, but the girls cut him off as they rushed Theo.

"Congratulations!"

Theo hugged the both of them, his eyes sparkling. "Thanks for making it, you two. I knew we wouldn't embarrass ourselves in front of you!" His ears were a little pink.

They laughed as they made their way out, waving goodbye to Nathan.

"By the way," Angela spoke as the trio walked through the deserted hallways. "Your dad said he would wait for you out back with the car."

Theo stopped in his tracks. His smile disappeared instantly.

"My dad?"

Jaya looked between Theo and Angela, confused by his reaction. "Yeah, your dad. He sat next to us."

"*My* dad?" Theo repeated, the colour drained from his face.

"Theo, is something wrong?" Angela asked, familiar spikes of anxiety piercing her lungs. Theo didn't answer; instead, he ran through the halls.

"Hey!" Jaya yelled as she took off after him, Angela followed. Theo ran fast, disappearing through the back doors. But Angela was also fast, beating Jaya. She slammed the back door open. Jaya emerging behind her after a few seconds.

Huffing, they were met with Theo looking up at the man in the smart suit in shock. His eyebrows disappeared into his hair. An expensive black car was parked on the street.

"You came to my game, Giovanni?" Theo panted.

"Was I not supposed to, *Cucciolo*?" the man responded, his thumb brushing Theo's cheek. He jerked back at the touch.

"I could get expelled! You know that—"

Theo bit his tongue once he saw his friends. Panic flashed across his face; his eyes darted between Giovanni and his friends. Giovanni looked over at the girls, his chestnut eyes gleaming.

"Angela. Jaya. How nice to see you girls again so soon," Giovanni spoke in a convincingly friendly tone.

Theo... he's not comfortable with him, Angela thought, seeing the hunched shoulders of her friend, his happy smile just moments earlier gone, replaced with a look of panic.

"Theo and I were just about to leave, weren't we, *Cucciolo*?" Giovanni's hand rested on the back of Theo's neck. He looked anywhere but at his friends, nodding his head in silence.

Angela took a step forward, but Jaya's hand shot out to grab the back of her shirt. Jaya stared at the man with narrow eyes.

We need to get him out of here, Angela thought. She tried to speak but her voice caught in her throat.

"I thought we were getting boba, Theo?" Jaya called out, her hand still gripping Angela's shirt.

"I..." Theo trailed off, he began to shake.

"There you are!" Principal Patel exclaimed as he approached the group, "I thought I recognized you sitting in the crowd, Giovanni."

"Krish," Giovanni shook the other man's hand. Giovanni towered over Patel. "How have you been?"

"Not bad, Giovanni, not bad at all!" Patel replied. His suit was back to its pristine state after the game. Principal Patel looked between Theo and Giovanni; his face remained neutral at Giovanni's possessive hand on his student.

"Good work today, Mr. Grayson, your performance was extraordinary," Patel congratulated.

Theo stared at the ground; he mumbled a small thanks. Giovanni clapped his hand on Theo's shoulder.

"Go wait in the car, son. I need to speak with your principal...

Ladies, a pleasure meeting you," Giovanni declared with an air of finality. Theo entered the black car without a glance back at his friends. The girls reluctantly went back inside, Angela not closing the door fully as she placed her ear by the crack, trying to listen to their conversation.

"Angela, now isn't the time…" Jaya trailed off. A boy standing in the hallway derailed her train of thought.

"Heya, Jaya!" he greeted with a crooked smile. The dimples on his face did little to soften his rugged appearance.

"Shh!" Angela shushed him as she craned her head, trying to listen.

A hard look settled on Jaya's face as she marched down the hall. She grabbed a fistful of the boy's shirt, tugging him along after her.

They disappeared around the corner.

I'll ask her about him later, Angela reasoned as she listened through the crack in the door.

"… and STK is still protected?" Patel's voice shook.

"An Untouchable will always be just that, Patel," Giovanni responded, almost annoyed. "Untouchable."

Angela's eyes widened. *Untouchable? Like the Informant? STK is an Untouchable? It would make sense…*

"Right, but you see, Cloud 9 has made its appearance in our student body and I was assured that drugs wouldn't be dealt to our students."

"The Halos don't deal with STK students, the same way the Wings don't take them. If your students are trying to hide their identities to access our services, that is your own fault," Giovanni growled at the man.

"You're not questioning the Gates' capabilities, are you Patel?

Goosebumps rose on Angela's arms.

"No—no!" Patel stuttered. "Never, sir. But once the drugs start, then so do the disappearances. Two BA students have been reported missing just last week. And you just attended a school event! I should expel Mr. Grayson just for being seen with you."

Silence hung over the pair.

"Theo is mine," Giovanni ordered. "So treat him like an Untouchable."

Is Giovanni in one of the Syndicates? Did he just say Theo is an Untouchable?

The snap of a car door closing was the last thing Angela could hear. The back door pulled open suddenly, causing her to fall over.

"Ms. Jo—… Ms. Williams," Principal Patel reprimanded. Angela scrambled to her feet, the door slammed shut behind him. She pressed her back against the lockers.

"Ms. Williams," Principal Patel repeated as he approached her, his eye twitching. "I've been meaning to speak with you since the start of the term."

"About what, sir?" Angela hated that she cowered away, her back flush against the lockers.

"I hope you understand just how lucky you are. No one *ever* transfers to STK, let alone during their senior year… but we made an exception for you, against my better judgment," Patel slowly inched closer to her. He was Angela's height, but at that moment he was bigger. More intimidating.

"I understand, sir."

"So I trust you won't ruin this one-in-a-million opportunity, correct?" Patel pressed. His shoulders were tense, as though he might lash out at any moment.

"Yes, sir," Angela responded.

"Out of respect for your sister, we made the transfer happen, but I will not hesitate to dismiss you from our school if you keep this behaviour up. Your sister wouldn't have acted in this disgraceful manner," he concluded as he held her eyes. "Am I understood?"

Leave Nini out of this. The claws of dread and pain closed around her chest, making it difficult to breathe.

"Yes, Principal Patel."

She flinched when he petted her head.

"Good girl," he straightened out his perfect suit that reminded her a little too much of Giovanni's as he marched down the hallway.

Leaving her alone without her only friends in a city that constantly took.

Jaya pulled the boy along into an empty science classroom. She looked out in the hall, making sure they were alone before shutting the door.

"Why the rush, babe?" the boy jeered.

"Why are you here, Rafael?" she crossed her arms.

He gave her a lopsided smile, pushing his chocolate hair out of his eyes. "Would you believe me if I said I missed you?"

She scoffed. "If you don't give me a real answer then I'm leaving."

"Always in a rush!" he shouted, causing her to jump. He sneered, stepping into her personal space, "I truly did miss you, babe."

"I'm not your babe anymore, Raef," Jaya looked away.

"Are you seeing someone else?" he pressed. She stared at the wall just past him, clenching her jaw.

"Then you're still mine," he reasoned. He landed a kiss on her cheek. Jaya winced, tears stinging in her eyes. "Good to see you taking care of yourself, God knows your parents don't do shit for you."

"You disappeared and left me for the Halos," she cried.

Despite the horrors he put her through last year, the drug dealing, the unsavoury places he made her go to, the dangerous Halos who got to know her by name, a part of her was relieved he was here, that he was still alive somehow.

"Babe, I knew that they wouldn't hurt you. They were on my ass and

I had to run," Rafael brushed away the tears that betrayed Jaya.

Jaya gasped at the gentle gesture. "But Parris—" she started.

"Parris sold me out!" Rafael yelled, cradling Jaya's head. She flinched again, his touch a bittersweet memory.

A painful reality.

He shushed Jaya as she sobbed. "Oh, babe, it's okay. I was never angry at you. You didn't know any better. You just got caught in the crossfire." He rocked her back and forth, but the action did not comfort Jaya.

He might just be saying that, Jaya thought.

"What do you want from me?" she finally asked shakily, looking up with teary eyes.

"I need your help, babe," Rafael whispered in her ear; she tried to pull away but he didn't budge.

Jaya hated the way he held her, like she was his possession. But she hated the way a small part of her enjoyed it. Before the incident, they were a happy couple still in their honeymoon phase. Being the eldest daughter meant that she was the last concern of her parents. Her younger siblings were more important. She understood the natural order of things. Her siblings needed more time and attention, something her parents couldn't give her anymore. Jaya knew that she was loved, but Raef made sure she *felt* loved. Going on dates, taking classes together, whispering sweet nothings in the back seat of his car. But all of that changed, from the few times he told her to wait in the car, then to giving her packages to drop off inside sketchy pawn shops and park benches. She knew they couldn't go back to those days. The Raef that she knew and loved was gone, replaced with *him*.

"I need to start dealing again; I owe the Gates and they're knocking."

She looked up through damp lashes. "The Gates?"

Rafael chuckled. "Yeah, the Gates, babe. You were just speaking with the Head."

She gasped; this time she successfully shoved Rafael off her.

"No… he's not the Head. I thought maybe an executive when I saw the car, but not the Head himself."

Rafael quickly snaked his arms around her waist, trapping her. "Giovanni Moretti is the Head of the Gates, fuck knows what Theo Grayson was doing with him."

"I need to go!" Jaya yelled. Both her mind and her heart were racing.

I need to make sure Theo's okay, and Angela! I need to tell them. Fuck, Patel saw us talking with him.

"Hey!" Rafael yelled loudly in her ear. "I need to know where I can get some Cloud 9 before the supply goes down."

Jaya shook her head, trying to get him off her. Raef finally let her go, taking a big step back. Without the press of his warm body, Jaya returned to the present moment.

"Fine then," Rafael held the handle of the door. "I'll just ask that friend of yours. Angela, was it?"

He'll hurt her… he'll hurt me, too.

"Stop. I'll tell you. Just leave her out of this."

"Hm, what was that?" Rafael brought his hand up to his ear, feigning that he couldn't hear.

"*Fresh To Go*. That's where you can get a stash." Jaya wiped the tear stains from her cheeks.

"After you, babe," Raef smirked as he held the door open. Jaya stepped out with him, as though nothing had changed since May.

"Give me your phone," Giovanni requested gently as he entered the car. The driver immediately joined traffic as soon as the door was closed. Theo stared forward, hands clasped tightly on his knees.

The excitement and joy he felt from the game was gone. He could only feel an immense worry for himself, for what his friends thought of him, if he was expelled for being seen with the older man. Patel had easily recognized him, speaking like old friends. He listened to their conversation, confident that his principal knew Giovanni was the Head of the Gates.

"*Cucciolo,*" Giovanni pressed.

"Huh?" Theo snapped from his thoughts, his eyes unfocused.

"Lie down, you must be tired after your game," Giovanni offered kindly, hand patting his thigh. Theo looked down at the invitation and back up at the older man. He didn't want to, but when he saw the hard look in his chestnut eyes, Theo lowered his head to rest on Giovanni. Large hands immediately went to play with his damp hair, the way a parent would soothe their distraught child.

"Give me your phone, *Cucciolo.*"

Theo wordlessly retrieved the device and handed it to Giovanni. The older man took the phone and turned it off. Putting it in his pocket, his hand returned to the damp hair.

"You showered?" Giovanni asked, even though he knew the answer. Theo mumbled a small 'yes', trying not to squirm from the intimate action. His feet hit the door; he was too tall to lie down comfortably.

"Would you like to go home to drop off your belongings before we continue the day?" Giovanni noticed the way Theo tensed at the mention of his home, how his back stiffened.

"Ah. Your father must be home now, correct?"

The high schooler stayed quiet, which answered Giovanni's question. Theo measured out his next words carefully.

"Why did you come to my game today?" he tried to look up at the man, but Giovanni's hand kept him in place, facing forward, with the slightest hint of force.

"It was your first game of the season, I did not want to miss it. You are upset that I attended?"

Dad never came to any of my games before…

"Or, perhaps you are upset that I spoke to those girls?" Giovanni continued. "They were nice. Angela especially was very polite to me. She's very pretty."

Theo tried to sit up at the mention of Angie, but Giovanni pressed his hand deeper into Theo's neck. The pressure on his neck was uncomfortable; he could not move from the awkward position. Theo's heart started racing, grabbing the hand holding him down.

"Cucciolo."

That was the only warning Theo needed. He clasped his hands together. Giovanni smiled down at him, noticing the deep breaths he was taking.

"I'm not hurting you, Theo. I just asked a simple question."

He's not hurting me…

"I was upset that you didn't tell me," Theo confessed, relieved that the hand returned to playing with his hair. The pressure on his neck was gone. "I was upset that you didn't tell me that you were coming. I would have wanted to know. I've never had someone attend my games before," he finally turned to look up at the older man.

Giovanni smiled at the boy. "I apologize, then, I will be sure to inform you next time."

Theo's eyes widened, he couldn't believe he had gotten an apology from the older man.

"Am I someone important to you, then, Theo?"

He gave me the money when I asked. He messages me throughout the day, making sure I'm alright and taking care of myself. He always drops me off at home after we meet. He does care about me… not like Dad.

"Yes, you are… also… Principal Patel should expel me."

"Patel will do nothing to you."

Theo finally sat up, moving back to his seat, looking at the man eye-to-eye. "Why? Because I should be treated as an 'Untouchable'?"

Giovanni barked out a laugh. Theo was incredibly small again.

"Do you know what an Untouchable is?" Giovanni pulled out his phone, responding to a text. Theo remained silent, fuming at his own ignorance. When he did not respond, Giovanni looked out the window as the car parked next to the entrance of a hotel.

"Come now, *Cucciolo*. I want to celebrate your first win of the season as captain. The restaurant here is rather impressive."

"Giovanni!" Theo called out as Giovanni held the door handle.

"Yes?"

"You're not going to hurt me, right?" his voice shook. Giovanni sighed as he released the door handle.

"Is it so hard to believe that someone wants to do something nice for you?"

When Theo did not respond, Giovanni left the car. He followed behind him.

———————————————————

Giovanni was right, the food at the restaurant was impressive. Giovanni did not even look at the menu when he ordered for the both of them.

Their table was stationed by the window, offering a beautiful view of Ciel.

The needle building peeked around the corner of the Financial District. The Stairway Tower was more stunning the higher up the view was. Other glass buildings reflected the sun, making the city shimmer. Theo's eyes scanned the city below from his seat, not used to seeing his home from this angle.

It made him feel like a king.

In comparison, Giovanni was a king, with his fancy clothing and the way he dabbed the corners of his mouth between bites. Theo fiddled with the edge of his shirt, noticing he was underdressed again.

"I need to start wearing a dress shirt when we meet up," Theo said between bites of his steak.

"I apologize for not telling you ahead of time, *Cucciolo!*" Giovanni laughed boisterously. "Next time I will buy you a few pieces that you can wear."

The conversation came easily between the pair; Giovanni asked questions and Theo responded enthusiastically. Safe questions about school and volleyball, topics Theo felt comfortable sharing with the other man.

"Have you thought about post-graduation plans?" Giovanni asked between bites. Theo nodded excitedly.

"I'm hoping to do pre-med at the University of Ciel."

"You want to be a doctor?" Giovanni inquired with a raised brow.

"That's the plan!" Theo felt pleased with himself when Giovanni smiled warmly at him.

"You're going to have a great future, *Cucciolo.*"

The sun started to set in a blaze of red across the city. The glass buildings turned into red pillars.

"Any plans for Thanksgiving? I can't imagine you would want to spend it at home," Giovanni asked.

Theo polished off his plate, chewing on the last piece of potato.

"Not yet, but I was thinking of asking Angie if she wanted to spend it together since she's not heading home for the long weekend."

Giovanni didn't comment. Instead, he hummed as he motioned for the bill. Theo tried mimicking the gesture under the tablecloth.

"I am aware that you have school tomorrow morning, but would you be interested in joining me for a little while longer?" Giovanni asked.

"What did you have in mind?" Theo replied as Giovanni led the way to the elevator. An attendant pushed the button for the ground floor.

"This old man needs a nightcap," Giovanni chuckled as they made way for the black car.

"Like a bar?" Theo wondered.

"Like a lounge," Giovanni corrected.

"I've never been to a lounge before…" Theo recounted tentatively, not sure if he could count the *Lumiere Lounge* since he went to see the Head.

Giovanni rested his hand on the back of Theo's neck. "Not to worry, you're safe with me."

Theo smiled as he agreed. He was arguably the safest he'd ever been when next to the most powerful man in the city.

The car sped through the downtown core as night arrived in Ciel. The streetlights and neon signs came to life. The car stopped in front of a black building that read *Clueless*. Theo left the car, his eyes wandering across the front of the building.

There was a long lineup to enter *Clueless*. Women in high heels and short dresses crowded together for warmth, as the night brought a chill in the air. Theo was grateful for his blue and white varsity jacket. He raised an eyebrow at the men, who wore some concoction of business, casual, and preppy attire. They clearly didn't coordinate like the women.

Unsure of where to go, Theo made his way to the back of the line, but Giovanni grabbed him by the hand.

"I don't wait in line," the older man led the way to the alley next to the building, stopping in front of a side entrance. Knocking on the door, a bouncer opened up. Upon seeing Giovanni, he stepped to the side quietly.

"They're letting me in? But I'm underaged," Theo whispered.

Giovanni winked at him as they entered the body of the club. House music blasted on the speakers, bodies dancing, drinks being made. Theo looked around wide-eyed.

"Sir," a waitress greeted the pair immediately. "Please follow me."

She walked them to a black velvet booth tucked in a corner, close to the spotless bar. It was dark inside but warm lights shone down on the dancefloor. Theo spotted the staircase that led to a white door, wondering what was behind it. They took a seat, the plush velvet comfortable.

"What do you think, *Cucciolo*?" Giovanni asked as he made a hand gesture that the waitress understood.

"It's amazing! Do you own this place?" The music made his heart beat louder. Giovanni winked at him.

The waitress promptly returned with two glasses of whiskey.

"Anything else, sir?" the waitress avoided Giovanni's eyes. He gave her a bill, which she took and left in a hurry. Theo stared at the glass. Giovanni picked his up, smelling it.

"I'm not—"

"Cheers to a game well played, *Cucciolo*!" Giovanni announced, Theo rushed to pick up his glass, clinking it with the other. The older man took a deep sip of his. Theo hesitated but did the same, making a face when the liquid burned his throat. Giovanni found that amusing.

"You'll learn to love it, *Cucciolo*."

"I'm not a fan." A woman wearing a leather jacket interrupted the pair. Theo jumped a little as he didn't see her approach the booth.

"It's like a bitter pill," Giovanni spoke to her, his chestnut eyes turned hungry. "You just have to swallow it."

She hummed as she glanced at Theo. "May I recommend a different drink from the bar? One that's non-alcoholic?"

Giovanni read Theo's thoughts. "You're not in trouble. Go on," he took another sip, eyeing the woman.

"Okay," Theo responded as he left the pair alone.

Parris stared at Giovanni who finished his drink, moving to take Theo's abandoned one.

"Is he a minor?"

Giovanni ignored her question as he swirled the brown liquid around. Taking another sip, he took a deep breath.

"You're not jealous, are you, *Bella*?"

Her infamous smile dropped immediately, replaced with a frown. Giovanni smirked into his glass.

"Don't look so upset, *Bella*. He's a young man."

"Is he working?" her eyebrows knitted together. Giovanni turned to hold her chin, pulling her closer. Parris let him.

"No, he's not a whore," Giovanni reassured. "He's a companion."

Glancing at Theo to see him still looking at the drink menu, Giovanni pulled Parris closer.

"However, a man has needs…"

Parris pulled out of his grip, her eyes burning, but her smile resumed.

"Oh, how the urges of men have led them astray."

Giovanni held her eyes as he reached for his phone. He quickly read the screen over and over again, his face rapidly turned red. Theo returned to the booth holding an abnormally shaped glass full of cranberry juice.

"What's wrong?" Theo asked.

Giovanni glared at Parris, his chestnut eyes holding onto her dark ones.

"Did you know about the construction deal?" he accused.

"Which one?" Parris answered with a shrug.

Giovanni stood up, pushing the booth's round table aside forcefully, looking down at Parris. The two whiskey glasses fell and shattered on the floor. Theo took a step back, never seeing Giovanni act so aggressively before. It scared him. It reminded him of his dad.

Seeing the way Theo flinched, Giovanni straightened his jacket.

"The Re-Pavement Project fell through," he snarled through closed teeth. "My CCC lost the bid."

"Sucks," Parris groaned.

"Have one of your men drive him home," Giovanni instructed as he made towards the side entrance. Theo abandoned his drink as he followed the pair.

The quietness of the outside world was deafening.

"Wait—Giovanni!" Theo called out, but Parris held her hand out, stopping him.

"Get him home and then come to my office in the CCC, we need to discuss your insurance," Giovanni ordered as the black car pulled up. He opened the car door. Finally looking at Theo, he reached into his pocket, returning the boy's phone.

"Apologies, *Cucciolo*."

The door shut and the car zoomed into the night. Theo stood there dumbfounded, gripping his phone so tightly that his knuckles were white.

"'*Cucciolo*'?" Parris repeated, her eyebrows drawn in. "Why did he call you that?"

Theo ignored the woman, trying to understand why he felt abandoned. It felt like when his dad didn't show up for after-school pickup. He didn't want to compare Giovanni to his dad, since Giovanni had been nothing but kind, dare he think, a better father than Roger could ever hope to be. But only one word echoed in his mind.

Unwanted.

When he didn't answer, Parris sighed as she made a phone call. Not long after, another black car pulled up, and she held the door open for him. Theo turned his phone back on once inside the car.

"Where's home?" Parris sat next to him. The black car drove through the downtown core silently.

"In Castlebrooke," Theo replied. He went through the infinite amount of messages he received, stopping at a message from his dad.

Poker night tonight. – Dad

Panic dug like barbed wire into his chest. He knew that the woman was watching him. He couldn't go home when his father hosted poker nights, he wasn't safe. He could handle being alone with his dad at home. But with him and his friends plus substances, it was just a recipe for disaster and bruises. Hitting the call button, he tried to calm himself down.

She lives alone, she won't mind, he thought as the ringer continued.

"Theo!" Angela exclaimed as soon as the phone connected. He winced, he could hear how worried she was.

"Hey," Theo whispered, glancing at the woman. "I can't explain but can I please crash at your place tonight?"

"Of course," came the reassuring answer.

I'll do your history homework for the rest of the semester, Williams, Theo promised.

"See you soon." Theo hung up the phone. "Sorry, but can you take me to the corner of Michener and 16th instead?" his voice small. Parris nodded, her eyes flickered to the rear-view mirror, meeting the driver's.

The car merged off of the highway, heading into Midtown.

"Sorry about that, Miss…?" Theo asked.

Parris smiled. "Do you have a name aside from *Cucciolo*?"

"Theo Grayson."

"Theo," Parris repeated. "Giovanni likes you, right?"

"I think so. He said I reminded him of his son."

She hummed as she studied him. Theo fidgeted under the intense stare. Giovanni barely paid him any mind once she appeared. And the way he looked at her…

Giovanni must really like her, Theo thought.

"Am I in trouble?" Theo finally asked her, shattering the tense silence.

"You haven't the faintest idea," she replied, her hand rubbing her left side.

The car came to a stop in front of the apartment building. Theo thanked her, rushing out of the car. Angela greeted him in the lobby. Parris watched the pair hug one another. Angela scowled at the car trying to make out who was inside. Parris was grateful for the tinted windows.

"Lorenzo," Parris called out, sadness dancing behind her dark eyes, "take me to the Ciel Construction Company."

CHAPTER EIGHT

Yearbook

The pull-out couch snapped into place, just the way Aunty Kim had done for Angela and Nini all those years ago. The springs were visible under the thin fabric, well used during their childhood. Nini in particular enjoyed jumping on the couch when Aunty Kim hid the T.V. remote from them.

Angela tucked a floral bedsheet into place, making a mental note to buy Aunty Kim some new ones for Christmas.

Theo was taking a while in the bathroom, rushing in as soon as they entered the humble apartment. She knocked gently on the door. "Everything alright?"

"Be out in a second," his voice muffled back through the door.

Angela retreated to the bedroom, making sure the shoebox under her bed was still hidden.

I couldn't see into that black car. Giovanni knows where I live now… add this to the list of worries.

Her phone buzzed.

I won't be at school tomorrow, feeling sick :/ – Jaya

Sorry to hear, Jaya. Are you still with that guy from earlier? – Angela

Since Principal Patel's demeaning warning, Angela wasn't able to reach either Theo or Jaya. Jaya had disappeared with the guy from the hallway. Since then, Angela had been messaging her every hour, asking about her, making sure she was alright. Jaya stubbornly hadn't answered her messages about the mysterious boy.

Maybe this is karma for not telling her about following Parris in

Chinatown, Angela thought bitterly.

Theo knocked gently, standing awkwardly in the doorway. He fiddled with the end of his shirt. His eyes were red, as though he was asking permission to cry.

To let the walls come tumbling down.

"Thanks again for letting me crash here, Angie."

"No problem," Angela replied, taking a seat on the bed, she gestured to the desk chair. He took a seat, rubbing his eyes as he leaned back.

"Theo—"

"I'm sorry."

Angela hugged her knees to her chest. She wasn't good at comforting people, especially people who were her friends. She didn't have any practice growing up. Comforting her mom when she would cry was different than this. Whenever her mom would get into a mood, Angela just held her and whispered words of comfort to her. Eventually, her dad would swoop in to pick up the pieces.

Nini would know what to say, what to do. She would have gotten Theo smiling and forgetting about his worries in an instant.

But Nini wasn't here. Angela had to make do now. Theo also looked uncomfortable; he played with his shirt sleeves.

"The man you were with?" Angela decided to ask.

"He's not my dad," Theo admitted, his eyes focused on the floral lampshades. "I'm scared. I'm scared that if I tell you, you might get involved."

Angela sighed, an amused look on her face. "I think we're both involved somehow."

"What do you mean?" Theo asked, puzzled.

"I've been caught by the Halos twice since I arrived. Not to mention the oddballs here and there…"

"We're both fucked, aren't we?" Theo laughed despite himself as he rubbed his face. Angela could not help but smile.

"I've somehow landed the Head of the Gates as a… friend," Theo admitted.

"The Head?"

"The man who came to my game. He's the leader of the Gates. The boss."

"Shit," Angela muttered, remembering that Patel saw him with the gangster. "Are you… are you expelled?"

"No," Theo responded, "Giovanni said that Patel won't expel me. Something about being treated as an 'Untouchable.'"

"You?" Angela gasped loudly. "You're the third Untouchable?"

"I'm the what?" Theo tilted head to the side.

"Listen, Theo," Angela exclaimed as she sat up straight.

The dots of mystery in her mind were now connected with a red string. It made sense. The pieces fell so perfectly into place.

"I was taken to a club called *Clueless* where I was told that there were three Untouchables in Ciel City. An Untouchable is protected by the Syndicates. One is an Informant called Parris. The second is our school, STK. Which means that you must be the third. The last Untouchable."

If he is the last Untouchable, I could have him come with me to Clueless. *She would have to speak to me then!* Angela plotted, hope bubbling in her chest.

Theo stood up, shocked by Angela's words. Angela mirrored his action, jumping up.

"I just came from *Clueless,*" he confessed.

"Who drove you here?" Angela grabbed his arm. Theo looked down, her grip tight, and back up at his friend.

"Angela…"

"Who?" she asked again, excited.

"A lady, she was wearing a leather jacket."

Angela lit up. "That's Parris!"

She started pacing her room. Theo remained in his spot, unsure what any of it meant.

I can do this! I can ask Theo to escort me to Parris. Since he's an Untouchable, she can't kick us out without causing a problem. Theo can help me confront her. Nini. I'm so close!

"So, I'm not fucked?" Theo asked.

"No!" Angela faced him with a sparkle in her eye. "Don't you understand? No one can mess with you, you're essentially a get-out-of-jail-free card. This is great!"

"So no one can hurt me?"

Angela stopped dead in her tracks, suddenly seeing Theo in a new light. He wasn't the tall popular boy she knew. He looked small and fragile, as though it would only take a gust of wind to bring him tumbling down.

"Why do you ask that?" she asked, all the excitement gone. All the glory of epiphany disappeared, dimmed by dread. Theo sat on the bed heavily, tears finally speeding down his face. His breath hitched as his shoulders shook. Angela sat next to him, laying a gentle hand on his knee, but pulled back once she saw how he flinched.

"I'm sorry…" he mumbled as his shoulders shook violently. "I've been using our friendship to hide away. You weren't here when my dad got arrested. I've been trying to avoid it, avoid my friends and their stupid comments, so I clung to you, the new girl who didn't know me. Going to Kevin's, during lunch, during class. You were an excuse to be busy… to be away. I'm sorry."

Angela didn't say anything.

"I needed money for his bail. I panicked and remembered someone saying that Ciel Construction Company gives out loans to kids if they ask, so I went. I didn't think he would be the Head of the Gates. How could I have known? I just wanted my dad back, I didn't think he would care for me."

"Care for you?" Angela pressed, her mouth dry.

"He's so nice to me, Angie!" Theo divulged, finally looking at her, his eyes bloodshot. "I swear I didn't do anything, he's just been talking to me and making sure I'm okay. He likes talking to me and asking about me. I thought he was going to be sketchy but he cares about me. I feel safe when I'm with him. He promised he wouldn't hurt me, not like my dad."

Lead dropped into her stomach. She had to ask. It's what a good friend would do. It's what Nini would do.

"Like your dad?"

Theo rubbed his knee as he hesitated, but decided that he had already come this far.

"He… he's not a bad guy, my dad. He… he just gets angry," Theo confessed.

"Oh, Theo," Angela rested her hand atop his.

"I'm sorry, Angie. I'm sorry for using our friendship like this," Theo mumbled as the hot tears continued.

The pair hugged. Theo's face pressed into her shoulder, wetting her shirt. But that didn't matter. The only thing that mattered was that Theo was safe with her now.

"You're not using our friendship, Theo," she assured him, "I didn't have a lot of friends growing up, so you and Jaya are very precious to me. I'm just sorry you had to be strong on your own for so long."

Somehow, her aunt's apartment shielded them from the outside world. No one could get to them while they were inside. It truly was their only safe space.

"I'm here," Angela whispered, Theo continued crying, years of hurt coming to the surface. She could wait to talk to Parris. She'd waited ten years. Angela tightened her hold on Theo.

"I'm here, Theo."

"Don't we love early mornings!" Parris announced as she entered the same abandoned warehouse on Port Front Central, holding a Ciel latte from *Jim's*.

A collective groan was heard from Marcel and Huifen, each leaning against their car, arms crossed. Tony was next to Marcel, greasy-looking in his leather jacket. His electric blue eyes locked on to Parris.

The warehouse was bare sans for the three black cars and the Heads. There were no bodyguards or executives today, except for Marcel. The Informant skipped next to Huifen, standing beside her. Parris's hand rested on her left side, and she hid a wince behind a sip of her Ciel latte. The other woman rolled her eyes, popping her gum loudly.

Giovanni stood in the middle of the half-circle, dressed as though he had just come from a business meeting.

However, his chestnut eyes were darker than normal.

"Although it is not our scheduled semi-annual meeting time, I do believe we have some business we need to take care of," Giovanni announced as he grabbed the lot's attention.

"I appreciate the work the Halos have done in moderating their distribution of Cloud 9. Too much of a good thing at once would crumble our current system." He nodded towards Huifen.

"The Wings on the other hand are lacking in product," he turned his attention towards Marcel. "Which is not surprising."

Tony snarled his teeth at his father; Marcel sighed at his antics.

"More products will come soon," Marcel announced. "Only if someone would hurry up and make more Cloud 9."

Marcel looked at Huifen with murder in his eyes. Huifen met his eyes with the same hatred and intensity. Parris sipped her coffee loudly.

"The reason I called this meeting, however, has nothing to do with Cloud 9 or the less-than-satisfactory performance," Giovanni continued. "We are here because an out-of-town company has just won the bid for the Re-Pavement Project."

That shocked the gangsters into giving Giovanni their full attention. Parris tipped the cup all the way back, pouting at the finished coffee.

"How?" Huifen asked. "How did the CCC lose—?"

Giovanni spoke over her. "They are a new company; somehow the City gave them the Project as opposed to the Ciel Construction Company… Now, since my company doesn't have the Project to work on, I'll no longer be needing the Wings' products, since there is no extra labour."

"Wait a goddamn minute—" Marcel called out.

"And I most certainly will not be allowing the Halos free movement into the many territories I own."

"You old fuck!" Huifen yelled, her face red.

He's losing his hold on the City Council so he's taking it out on us! Marcel thought.

"Then what *do* you want instead of the Re-Pavement Project?" Parris asked, licking the lid of her cup for every last drop of coffee.

Everyone watched Giovanni intently. He looked at his Informant with knowing eyes; she already knew what he would ask for. His creation was so clever after all.

"I want a new Untouchable."

Uproar amongst the gangsters. Marcel and Huifen yelled at Giovanni, spitting vile curses and complaints. Tony paid them no heed, not even joining in on bad-mouthing his father. He was focused instead on the Informant, his stare locked on her.

"How are we supposed to operate if you keep making Untouchables, Giovanni?" Marcel demanded.

"Are three not enough?" Huifen exclaimed, "I can't even get my product into that damn school. Those kids would pay top dollar for my stuff."

"Oh, it's in STK already," Parris called out.

All eyes landed on her.

How the fuck does she know that? Marcel thought. *How is she always ten steps ahead of us?*

"What?" Huifen huffed.

"Someone is not keeping tabs on their dealers. STK is not being treated as it should be." Parris met Giovanni's stare, challenging him.

"It's not being treated as an Untouchable," Parris declared.

"What else do you know?" Giovanni asked; he was a bull ready to charge at the Informant's taunting red flag. Marcel and Huifen resumed their yelling.

"At this rate, you'll run business out of the city," Marcel complained loudly. He wasn't used to yelling at the older man like this, but since Tony couldn't, he had to step up.

Huifen shouted, her face as red as her cherry lips. "I'll be damned if we let you make another Untouchable just so we can use your turf, Giovanni. The Halos should have free rein to deal wherever in Ciel without your permission!"

"What would your Untouchable be?" Tony finally broke his silence. Marcel worriedly looked between Tony and Giovanni.

Giovanni finally turned to look at his son with a stoic expression.

"A person."

Tony's eyes turned livid as he limped up to Parris, his demeanour coldly calm.

"I don't think people should be Untouchables; I mean, I can touch her just fine." Tony grabbed Parris's curly hair in a fist, pulling at the crown of her head. Huifen gasped, eyes popping from their socket. Marcel cursed and rushed to Tony, grabbing at his wrist.

"Let go of her!" Marcel panicked. "Please let go, Tony!"

"Help!" Parris yelled, not fighting back. "Pervert! Fire! Geezer! Help!" Tony's eyes lit up in recognition; his sneer turned ugly.

"You," he whispered.

The clearing sound of a gun clicking snapped him back to reality. Giovanni pressed the barrel into the back of Tony's skull. Marcel and Huifen took a step back.

"Do not touch her," Giovanni ordered calmly. Tony's hand left her hair, his eyes showed genuine fear. Parris took a step back, throwing her empty coffee cup at him with a face. Slowly, Tony lifted both hands, the gun still in its place.

He might do it. He might actually kill Tony this time! Marcel bit his lip.

"When I deem something Untouchable, then it's not to be goddamn touched," Giovanni growled at Tony. "I made you into an Untouchable all those years ago. It is only through my power and grace that you get to act like a complete imbecile and still *live*. A disappointment is what you are. Acting like a child, throwing a tantrum, for a *sliver* of my attention."

Tony gulped around cotton. His father was always crueller with his words than with his knives.

"Anyone else want to try touching an Untouchable?" Giovanni challenged in a loud voice.

Everyone remained silent; even Parris was not being obnoxious. Nobody dared to move. Giovanni's chestnut eyes scanned the group, resting on the Informant. The gun was removed. He rolled his shoulders back, recomposing himself. He spoke as he made his way to his car.

"We will discuss this at a later time. Until then, honour what we have agreed on."

With a sharp snap of the car door, he left the warehouse promptly. Tony's face was a mixture of emotions, ranging from shock, hurt, and happiness. Marcel grabbed Tony by the nape of his neck and pushed him into the back of their car, leaving without a word.

Leaving only Huifen and Parris in the empty warehouse, Parris went to pick up her coffee cup, muttering to herself about littering.

"You're more trouble than you're worth," Huifen snarked as she blew a piece of gum. "Maybe you and Tony should kill one another. Be down to one Untouchable in Ciel."

Parris smiled at the other woman, handing her the empty coffee cup without the lid. Huifen took the trash, her eyes narrowed. Looking into the cup, she pulled out a small square foil with a kissy face on it. She eyed the Informant, holding the condom.

"For Marcel," Parris winked. She skipped out of the warehouse.

Leaving the Head of the Halos fuming.

"What the fuck is wrong with you?!" Marcel yelled at Tony as the car sped through traffic, mirroring the Executive's rage.

"Why did you do that?" his brown eyes blown wide.

Giovanni was going to kill him this time! Why does he always risk everything for his attention? Marcel thought, his nostrils flared. Tony stared at his hands, ignoring his friend.

"Fuck!" Marcel shouted in frustration.

"Take me to STK," Tony mumbled to the driver.

"No," Marcel yelled. "You're not going to mess with two Untouchables today."

"STOP TELLING ME WHAT TO DO!" Tony retaliated. "You forget that I'm the boss! Not you. The fucking Untouchable! Just because those two can walk all over me does not mean you can as well." Tony's face was red from the rage and humiliation.

The Executive knew that was the only reason his friend was still alive, the only reason they were able to form the Wings to begin with: the promise of an organization led by Giovanni's first Untouchable, his very own son, Tony Moretti. That they owed their lives and business to Giovanni's influence.

The silence stretched on.

The car screeched to a halt outside of the gothic church-turned-school. Tony finally turned to Marcel, venom in his voice. "You deal with the product and I will secure our position as a gang."

He left the car without a second glance at Marcel, slamming the door shut behind him. Tony pulled his leather jacket into shape as he limped towards the gothic building.

"Where to, sir?" the driver asked Marcel hesitantly. Marcel watched his friend disappear, his chest tightening.

"Chinatown."

A security guard nodded towards Tony as he entered the school.

Do they call this security? Tony thought, as he asked where the main office was. *It would only take a few men with guns to have this entire fucking Untouchable on lockdown.*

He walked through the barren vaulted halls towards the main office. The school was eerily quiet during class time, no signs of life in the hallways.

"Hi there!" a warm voice called out to him, signalling him to the secretary's desk. Tony marched up to her, putting on a charming smile.

Just how Giovanni taught him.

"Hey there..." He glanced at her name plaque. "Linda." She batted her eyelashes at him.

"I was wondering if I could have access to a past yearbook?" He leaned on her desk. "You see, it's my sister's birthday in a few days and I would love to surprise her by getting a few of her pictures photocopied."

"Aw, that's so sweet of you," she gushed at him. "What year did your sister graduate?"

Tony told her and she rushed off to grab it. When she returned with the yearbook, he gave her a wink.

"I just need a name and phone number so we can lend it out to you," Linda instructed as she gathered a pen and paper.

Tony leaned over, writing the name 'Marcel' and his phone number on the paper. His hand rested on hers as he pushed the paperback. She blushed at his boldness.

"I would love to be reminded personally about the yearbook, lovely Linda," Tony flirted.

The lunch bell rang loudly, interrupting their conversation.

"You better leave before the lunch rush. The kids will stampede down these halls!" Linda warned over the bell.

The halls were full of footsteps and rumbling as the students evacuated from their classes. Tony weaved through the river of students, flipping through the yearbook urgently. He pushed his way back to the grand doors and onto the stone courtyard.

"Tony?" Angela asked, waiting outside the main doors of STK in the courtyard.

Tony looked over at the security guard and back at the girl. She looked worried, as though she would get in trouble.

"Hey, sweetheart," he greeted as he ducked to the side of the doors, away from the view of the guard. "How's school?"

"I don't think I should talk to you here," Angela stated, turning away from him.

"Hey, hey, it's all okay. Come on." He motioned towards the street. "You were heading out for lunch, right?"

Angela ignored him, marching to the black gates silently. Tony couldn't help the hungry smile as he followed her.

She's nervous, that's cute. If she wasn't an STK student, I would keep her chained in my safehouse. Maybe I can get her alone for a bit.

"Come on, let me treat you to lunch, sweetheart," Tony whispered behind her.

"Why are you here?" Angela asked sharply, turning to face him, anxious that he was speaking to her on school property, especially since she didn't know who he was.

Tony held up the yearbook, his charming smile still equipped.

"Doing some research. How have ya been? Been keeping out of trouble? Or in trouble, I suppose." He winked at her. He tilted his head in confusion at the shocked expression on her young face, her eyes wide.

Nini's graduating year? Angela wondered as she reread the year on the yearbook cover. *Why would he have that?*

"Hey Angie," Theo greeted, jogging up to her side. "Sorry for making you wait... who's your friend?"

Tony scowled at the boy, wanting the girl alone. He was strangely possessive over Angela, despite this only being their second meeting.

It must be the way her coils framed her face. Or her full lips. She's my type, Tony thought.

"Come on," Tony called out, leading the way with a limp, one hand wrapped around Angela's wrist, the other holding on to the yearbook. Tony tugged Angela onto the concrete sidewalk just outside of the school's gate.

"Hey! Don't touch her," Theo protested.

Tony let her go, taking a step closer to Angela.

"Did she hit you again?" Tony demanded, catching her off-guard. Angela stiffened, her mouth zipped shut.

"Who hit you?" Theo asked, his eyes hardened at the man. Angela didn't answer Theo, staring at Tony instead.

"Listen, sweetheart," Tony continued, "you need to be careful, things are starting to get heated. Especially with the low supplies of Cloud 9, it's not safe out in Ciel."

"Who is this guy?" Theo's hand landed on Angela's shoulder. Tony glared at his hand, a roar of possessiveness echoing in his mind.

Angela didn't reply to anyone, her mind reeling at the sight of the yearbook. She knew that yearbook well. She had studied it. It was in her bedroom at home.

Why does he have it? Angela thought.

"If you know something, anything at all, you have to let me know. You owe it to me, sweetheart. I'll take *good* care of you," Tony pressed.

"Let's go, Angie," Theo pulled Angela away from Tony. Tony instinctively grabbed Theo by the collar, pushing him into the black gate that surrounded the school, pinning him by driving his elbow into Theo's collarbone.

"Hey!" Angela shouted, awoken from her trance. "Leave him alone!"

"You think you're a man, punk?" Tony growled at Theo, pushing him into the gate. "I wasn't done talking to her."

Theo struggled to pry him off; Tony spat on his face.

"He's an Untouchable!" Angela threatened.

That was the wrong thing to say. Tony throttled Theo into the gate harder.

"The fuck she called you?" Tony demanded with wide eyes. Angela grabbed Tony's arm, pulling with all her strength.

"He's an Untouchable! So don't you dare touch him," Angela warned.

Tony barked out a cold laugh, his electric blue eyes devoid of any mirth.

"He's not an Untouchable, sweetheart. What kind of bullshit are you on?" He pushed Theo aside, grabbing Angela by her arm, dragging her closer. "There are only three Untouchables. One is that shitty Informant and another is this school."

It was like the night in Chinatown all over again. Angela tried to pull out of his grip, but it didn't budge.

"Who called this shit an Untouchable?" Tony's face was too close to Angela's.

She froze in place and the hair on the back of her neck stood up. She had been so sure Theo was safe, that Giovanni and Patel's conversation meant that he was the third Untouchable, that she would have an opportunity to talk to Parris.

The pedestrians on the sidewalk began to look at the trio. They scurried past them, a few stopping to look at the conflict. Some students on lunch pointed in their direction.

"Let go of her!" Theo hollered, recovered enough to push Tony off.

Stumbling back, Tony swung at Theo with the yearbook, and the spine caught him by his eye. Theo held his face as he staggered back.

"Who said it?!" Tony grabbed Angela by the neck, and spit flew onto her face. She trembled in his hold, frozen by the realization that she couldn't break free, that Tony was stronger than her.

"Giovanni Moretti!" shouted Theo from the ground, his face bruised from the impact. Tony looked at the boy deadpan, releasing his grip on Angela.

The next moment Tony was on Theo, hands wrapped around his throat, the yearbook on the ground.

"YOU?!" Tony shrieked. Theo grabbed onto Tony's arms, trying to break free. "WHY YOU?!"

Angela wrapped her arm around Tony's neck from behind, trying to pry him off.

"WHAT MAKES YOU SO GODDAMN SPECIAL?!" Tony

continued shrieking at Theo, spit flying everywhere, choking in Angela's hold.

"Get off him!" Angela cried. Theo's face was pale, blue spots forming from the lack of oxygen.

"What is happening here?!" a voice demanded.

A police officer glared down at Tony. Reluctantly, Tony released Theo. The boy crumpled to the ground in a coughing heap. Angela rushed to his side.

"Nothing here, Officer," Tony answered. Reclaiming the fallen yearbook. Angela looked up at the officer. She read the name on his badge.

A. Hafiz.

"Looks like Tony Moretti was choking a high schooler," Amir accused. His chest puffed out, looking directly into Tony's eyes.

"Moretti… like Giovanni?" Theo choked out, his voice scratchy. Tony looked back at the kid with rage at the mention of his father.

"I should arrest you for assaulting a minor, Mr. Moretti," Amir brought Tony's attention back to him.

"You won't do shit," Tony spat, looking up at Amir. "You wouldn't dare arrest a Head."

"So you admit to being the Head of the Wings, a known criminal organization?" Amir locked eyes with him.

Tony gave Amir a sleazy smile, brushing imaginary dust from his broad shoulders.

"You can stop here, Greenie. You've saved the day. Anything more than this and you're just asking for trouble. You know better than to arrest an Untouchable. And I would hate to see our City's finest dead in a ditch."

He's the third Untouchable? Angela began to shake. Theo pulled her into him as they got off the ground.

Amir did not react, his composure calm despite the threat from the

Head of the Wings.

"As for you, I better not see you again." Tony turned to Theo. Theo stiffened, his grip on Angela tightened.

"I'll see you around, sweetheart. Don't forget about the gift I gave you!" Tony called out as he stepped past Amir, gripping the yearbook with white knuckles.

Angela shook violently, trying to understand what had happened. They were just going out for lunch. Everything had happened so quickly.

The sounds of Ciel were muted for once. Angela couldn't hear anything, not the construction from up the block, not the group of juniors whispering and pointing at her. She couldn't hear the officer and Theo speaking. She could only hear her thoughts and pulse.

He's a Head and an Untouchable? Why did he give me the gun that night? The yearbook! Why did he have that yearbook? That was Nini's graduating year!

"You kids alright?" asked Amir.

"We're alive," Theo groaned as he rubbed his neck, red from the assault.

Amir inspected the bruise by Theo's eye, noticing the way Theo stiffened when Amir stood close. He shifted his attention to Angela. She was trembling and hyperventilating. Her nails dug into her palms.

"Hey, it's okay, he's gone," Amir reassured. "Deep breaths, come on. Breathe," Angela gasped in short breaths, trying to bring herself to the present moment.

"Are you well enough to move?" Amir asked her. Angela nodded shakily, her mouth too dry to speak. Angela held onto Amir's forearm, his presence grounding her.

"Let's go inside," Amir instructed.

Some of the students stared at Theo's injuries and Angela holding on to the police officer. Theo led the way to the office; the secretary jumped up once she saw the blue-clad officer.

"Oh dear, what's happened?" Linda asked as Amir sat Angela down.

"I need to speak to your principal," Amir ordered. Amir stood tall, his expression hard, a slight furrow to his brow. Linda rushed to grab Patel.

"Hey," Theo whispered, his voice scratchy, he sat next to Angela. "How does that thug know you? What gift was he talking about?"

Angela took in a shaky breath. She owed Theo an answer. He got hurt by Tony for her.

"He's the third Untouchable… I was wrong. I was so wrong, Theo. I'm sorry."

Principal Patel emerged from his office in a hurry, and his stunned expression at seeing a police officer in the school morphed into suspicion once his eyes landed on Theo and Angela.

"I'm Principal Krish Patel. How can I help you, Officer?" he asked politely as he approached Amir.

"My name is Officer Amir Hafiz, I'm with the CCPD's Anti-Gang Special Task Force," Amir informed. "As I approached your school today, I saw a man attacking your students. He was choking this young man."

Patel looked at Theo with worried eyes as he saw the bruises around his throat and eyes.

"Did you arrest the man?!"

"No, I did not," Amir answered. "The individual was Tony Moretti, a known gangster. I have yet to question your students as to why Mr. Moretti was attacking them, given the state of shock they are in. I thought it best to inform you before I question them."

Patel stood there dumbfounded, unsure of what to do.

"Would it be possible to excuse them from the remainder of their classes for the day?" Amir asked.

"You said Tony Moretti?"

"Yes."

"You need to leave."

"Excuse me?"

"You need to leave," Patel repeated, sweat rolled down his forehead. "I will speak to these students privately. I'm sure this entire incident was a misunderstanding."

Amir marched up to Patel, looking down at him. "I just saw two of your students fight against the Head of the Wings and you want me to leave?" he demanded in a loud voice, disbelief written across his tanned face.

Patel looked Amir back in the eye, suddenly brave.

"I want you off of my school's property. Or I will report this to Captain Chan," Patel replied back just as loudly.

"But Principal Patel—!" Theo started.

"Not now, Mr. Grayson!" Patel yelled, panic settling on his face. Angela slapped her palms over her ears. The main office was too loud and bright. She couldn't breathe properly, and panic hugged her chest with spikes, refusing to let go.

"May I ask for an appointment with you then, Principal?"

Patel calmed down with a reasonable request. "Yes, you may, Officer. Kindly speak to Linda at the front, she will set the appointment time. As for this incident, I will deal with it personally, rest assured."

Amir gave his back to Patel as he went to Theo and Angela, pulling out a business card.

"You will want ice for that bruise on your head, kid," Amir slipped the card into Theo's hand. Theo crumpled the card and pushed it deep into his pocket. Amir did the same with Angela.

"And you may want a less stimulating environment than a school to help with your panic attack." His green eyes lingered on her, pity filled them briefly.

Everyone waited for Amir to finish setting the appointment up with

Linda. With a nod at Patel, Amir left the office.

"Sir!" Theo started at Patel, but the Principal had a deadly look in his eyes.

"My office. *Now!*"

CHAPTER NINE

Guilty

The chairs in Patel's office were extremely uncomfortable. Perhaps it was his strategy to have students confess to cheating faster if the chairs were hard to sit in. Angela and Theo sat in those uncomfortable chairs in silence. Their gazes were fixed on different things. Angela looked at the paper clips as though they were the most interesting thing in the world. Theo was fascinated with a scuff mark on the wall.

"I won't ask again," Patel stated forcefully, his eyes narrowed at his students. "What happened?"

Patel stood behind his bland desk. There were no photos of kids smiling, or any other personal items, as though he wanted to hide away his loved ones from his job. Only the bare essentials littered the desk: a computer, stapler, and a 'World's Best Principal' mug. Theo looked at the stapler with an absorbed look.

"Mr. Grayson? Ms. Williams?"

The pair remained silent. They had shared a look before entering the office. They both understood what it meant, or their academic careers would come to a grinding halt.

Stay quiet.

"Well, one of you will have to talk," Patel crossed his arms. "Ms. Williams, is there a reason Mr. Grayson was being choked by a mafioso?"

Angela looked at the floor stubbornly.

"I will not let this slide, Ms. Williams. Don't think that I wouldn't notice your grades are not up to STK standards," Patel threatened. Theo's ears perked, risking a glance at his friend. Angela clenched her fists, staring at her lap.

"Your teachers tell me that you have been struggling in every class. I knew letting in a student during senior year was a mistake. You're not up to par with STK. Do you even intend to go to university, Ms. Williams? Especially after everything STK has done for you out of respect for your family."

Angela bit her lip, the skin threatening to break.

"You're dishonouring your sister, failing to even amount to a fraction of the care she put into her studies. She was top of her classes, the hardest worker I have ever seen. Your actions at our school have been a disgrace, Ms. Williams. Unfocused is what you are."

The skin of her lip split at the mention of her sister. The taste of copper spread in her mouth.

Patel huffed, now focusing his attention on Theo.

"And you, Mr. Grayson. Perhaps I should call your 'father'. Have him come to pick you up."

Theo looked up at his principal; his eyes flashed with momentary fear before a cold look took over.

"Actually, Principal Patel, that's a great idea. Have my father take time out of his *very* busy schedule to come and deal with you. You can explain why you let the man who assaulted his son walk away without a police report," Theo threatened, the words flowing from a dark place within.

The flow of power shifted from Patel to Theo. Even Angela looked at her friend, surprised at his sudden change.

"As you know, my father is very protective of other people touching me."

Patel cleared his throat, taken aback by the sudden viciousness of the boy. As though he was dealing with *her*. The same dark look clouded Theo's eyes. Patel fiddled with his tie.

"He would want to know that you are safe—" Patel started.

"And a text from me is enough, Principal Patel," Theo stood up. The chair made an ugly scratching sound.

"Come on, Angie. We're done here." Theo headed out of the door.

"Mr. Grayson!"

Theo looked over his shoulder, showing more confidence than he actually felt. Gears turning in his eyes.

"Treat me like an Untouchable, was it?"

Patel seethed. Angela scuttled out behind Theo, sparing one last look at her principal. Patel slammed the door shut after them, phone in his hand. Not believing her friend's gusto, Angela caught up to him.

"Theo?" she asked. Theo walked out of the building and through the stone courtyard. The bruise on his face and neck developed into a dark shade of red.

"He lied to me, Angie," Theo finally spoke. His eyes were downcast as they made their way towards the subway. "Giovanni said his son died a long time ago. But that creep has to be his son, the same last name, the fact he is an Untouchable…Why would he lie to me?"

"Where are you going?" Angela swiped her metro card, following Theo through the station. He finally turned to her, looking hurt, not just from the bruises; he looked betrayed. It was a pain she hadn't seen on him before.

"I need time alone to think. I'm going to message Giovanni to tell him what happened with that Tony guy. I think you should go home and rest… that was a little disturbing."

Angela hadn't noticed her hand was still shaking until Theo held her. He scowled as he saw the toll the assault had on her. She wasn't used to physical pain and fear the way he was. Her guards were still up, even with him. He hugged her. Angela hugged back, squeezing tightly.

"I wanted to ask what Patel meant about respect for your family," Theo murmured as he held her. "You never talk about your sister, Angie. Can you talk to her about any of this?"

Angela shook her head. He didn't want to push her to share

something personal.

"Be safe," Angela whispered into his shoulder.

"I'll try," he replied, pulling away.

His smile returned but it was a little dimmer. He made his way towards the uptown train.

Angela watched her friend descend the stairs before heading to the Midtown train. She messaged Jaya that she needed to talk.

Parris… Only Parris can clear any of this up. She would know why Tony had that yearbook. I need to confront her. Since Theo's not an Untouchable, I'll need to think of a different way.

Hearing the ding of the train she entered. Sitting down, she inspected the crumbled business card of the officer.

Something happened at STK today. I saw Tony Moretti attacking a few students. The principal didn't want me talking to the kids at all… You're right, Tony Moretti is the third Untouchable. I need more information. – Amir

Amir thanked Officer Sanchez as she brought in more files. She asked him if she could be of any help as he entered the CCPD in a storm after leaving STK. Amir jumped at the opportunity to ask her about the Morettis and why there was no substantial information on the family.

"I think you know why, Officer Hafiz," Sanchez closed his office door after her. "Captain Chan makes sure that no one gets too close to the Moretti Family, especially not Giovanni's Untouchables."

"That's why he acted the way he did when I arrested the Informant," Amir thought aloud. "He's not being paid off by the Gates, is he?" Amir prayed that there was at least a sliver of integrity left on the force. But Officer Sanchez looking at the floor answered his question.

I need help, Helen. – Amir

Helen still did not reply. Amir set his phone down on the pile of documents: news clippings of STK's opening, a photo of Giovanni Moretti congratulating Mayor Robert, the report of the suicide, and Tony Moretti's file.

Running his fingers through his curly hair, Amir sighed deeply. Sanchez left to go look in records for more files.

There's an undercurrent in Ciel, he thought as he picked up a highlighter, getting to work. *I just need to bring it to the surface.*

Tony took a long drag of his cigarette. The smoke twirled along in a pattern until it dispersed on the ceiling. His room was dark, the only light coming from a lamp by the armchair he was slouched in.

He flipped through the yearbook leisurely. His finger pressed on the pretty faces of young girls smiling at the camera with their silly graduation quotes under them. He looked through until he found the name.

The graduation picture was poorly photoshopped, with a tacky black cap placed on a picture of a young girl beaming at the camera. He continued flipping through the book. He stopped at a picture of two girls smiling widely. Their eyes were crinkled with laughter. Another with the same girls and a boy at their homecoming. He remembered buying that silver dress, how it had hugged her body so well. His eyes grew hungry as he flipped back to the first page of the yearbook.

In Loving Memory of Janine Johnston.

Janine was beautiful. Tony felt himself longing for her, to cup her face, to play with her coily hair. He loved playing with her hair. She had enjoyed it, too.

He flipped back to the picture of Janine with the other girl, the girl with dark intimidating eyes.

Taking a longer drag of the cigarette, his eyes danced with dark thoughts as he came up with a plan.

I need to talk to you about something important, Giovanni. Please call me. – Theo

Theo paced his bedroom as he waited for Giovanni to reply. He had hurried home to change, grateful for having a spare uniform in his locker.

His dad had only raised an eyebrow when he saw Theo rush up the stairs during school hours, more interested in reaching for another beer than asking his son why he was missing classes.

What else is new?

Theo had done a good job going over what he would tell Giovanni and how he would ask why he was dishonest with him. His phone chimed back at him, and Theo rushed to read the message.

Apologies, Cucciolo, *but I am busy with work at the moment. We can meet sometime next week if school does not prevent you. –* Giovanni

Anger overtook Theo, hitting the call button before his mind caught up.

"Yes," Giovanni answered, a slight annoyance in his deep voice.

"What happens when I don't survive 'till next week?" Theo spat out, his anger spiking. The bruise around his neck had darkened, along with the one near his eye. Giovanni stayed silent.

"I didn't know the dead could walk, Giovanni! Imagine my surprise when a 'Tony Moretti' started assaulting me outside of school today."

"What?" Giovanni growled. Theo felt vindicated, that he deserved to be angry, that he deserved to be protected, that he was worth something.

"Your dead son, Tony, hit me and choked me. Unless you had another son that you didn't tell me about, then you lied to—"

"Are you home now?"

"Yes, but I don't want to see you—"

"The car will pick you up. Be ready."

The phone call ended. Theo yelled in frustration, throwing his phone towards his bed. He curled into a ball, heaving. The feeling of vindication dissipated as quickly as it came. Instead, feelings of uneasiness filled his chest. His heartbeat was too loud in his ears, his eyes were burning, but he refused to break down.

The honking of a car horn brought him back to reality. He stood up, his legs protesting the action.

How long was I on the floor?

He put on his jacket as he descended the stairs, slowing down as he saw his dad looking out the window.

"I'm heading out now," Theo put on his shoes, popping the collar of his coat to cover the bruises from his father.

Roger made a noise as he narrowed his eyes at the black car.

"That car's been here a few times now," Roger said suspiciously, turning his attention to his son as he left through the front door, watching him disappear into the backseat of the car.

The sunset dipped over Ciel's horizon, the day's excitement coming to a close just as the nightlife would soon begin. Logan slammed the brakes as a group of university students crossed the road in the middle of traffic.

Logan fumed as he drove towards *Clueless* for his final delivery. He saw Parris skipping back to her club on the sidewalk, head in the clouds. Logan narrowed his eyes at her as he stopped at the lights, distaste in his mouth.

Of course, she would be easy to spot; her obnoxious personality could be detected from space.

His eyes darted to a man also wearing a leather jacket following behind her by a few paces. The light turned green and he resumed his drive to the nightclub, thinking nothing of it. He arrived first at the club, knocking loudly on the side door.

"Delivery!" yelled Logan.

"Cutting it close, Logan!" Lorenzo answered the door, propping it open. The club was empty, with only Lorenzo to help carry the delivery in.

"When every client complains about the produce, it puts you behind," Logan responded as he started carrying the bins of fruit inside, setting the lemons down on the polished black marble counter.

The delivery job was going well but it was making him late for work at the *Loose Screw*. Mike had insisted that he could come a little later; he thought delivering produce was more important than bartending. Logan, on the other hand, liked to be punctual.

"Welcome back, Ms. Parris!" Lorenzo called out warmly.

The Informant entered through the side door. Logan remained at the bar, his back turned, breathing a sigh of relief when she didn't acknowledge him, rushing up to her office instead.

"I don't have any appointments tonight, Lorenzo!" she called out before the white door shut with a snap.

Almost subconsciously, Logan glanced up at her as she entered through the white door. He watched her walk through her office behind the glass, shedding her leather jacket before throwing it on the red couch. He usually never crossed paths with her when he delivered to the club. Either the glass was opaque or she was out.

It was strange seeing her in person. Logan had to push down the emotions and memories that always threatened to resurface.

As though she felt like she was being watched, Parris met Logan's eyes. They held the contact briefly before she turned off the transparency of the glass.

Cutting Logan off.

"We've been busy lately. We've even had to hire some new kids," Lorenzo rambled as he set a crate of oranges next to Logan, snapping Logan from his trance. "I shouldn't be working the bar anymore but we're training the new hires on where the extra—"

"I don't care," Logan cut him off, glaring at the bar. He saw his reflection in the black marble. He took a deep breath to relax his face, his scowl slowly disappearing. Lorenzo sighed as he went to retrieve the rest of the delivery.

"Where is she?" a slimy voice called out.

Logan saw the way Lorenzo visibly tensed as he looked at the man standing at the side door. It was the same man dressed in a leather jacket limping behind the Informant.

"She's not taking any appointments tonight, Sir," Lorenzo informed, his hands balled into tight fists.

"So she's in her office."

The man rushed up the stairs. Lorenzo called out for him to stop, but he entered the white door and slammed it with a bang.

"Shit," Lorenzo cursed, calling someone on his phone. "Tony's here again!"

I should leave, Logan reasoned as he watched how frantic Lorenzo became. It wasn't his business why an angry man was looking for Parris. It wasn't his business that it was the same man trailing behind her for more than two city blocks. It wasn't his business what the Parrasite got into.

But he couldn't move from his spot. He was rooted next to the bar, looking up at the white door. He chewed his lip, Lorenzo's conversation fading in his ears as he watched.

The black car stopped outside of the Ciel Construction Company, a tall brick building in Old Town. A guard in a suit ushered Theo into the building silently.

Theo walked through the lobby, the same route he had only a few weeks ago when he asked Giovanni for the bail money for his dad. He passed the reception desk to the elevators.

The Ciel Construction Company was Ciel's City Council's go-to for construction projects. The floor directory contained real departments and real workers. But it was also the front to the Gates' operation. Organized crime, protection money, brothels, and so many more vices Theo couldn't wrap his head around. He took the elevator up to the top floor, to Giovanni's office.

The large polished door was opened for Theo as he stepped into the office once again. Dark mahogany floors, a sharp black desk, and floor-to-ceiling windows reminded Theo of just how powerful Giovanni was. A fireplace crackled to Theo's left.

The Head was seated at his desk, looking over a mountain of papers and folders with a scowl on his face, his reading glasses on. Once he looked up to Theo, he dismissed the guard with a nod.

Shutting the heavy polished door behind him, the pair were alone in the office. Theo normally felt small in Giovanni's presence, but today he was angry. He pushed his chest out as he stood in the middle of the office, claiming the space around him as his own. Giovanni pointed to the couch for Theo to take a seat, but he remained standing in the middle of the room. His eyes narrowed at the older man.

"You lied to me."

Giovanni sighed as he removed his glasses, pinching the bridge of his nose.

"*Cucciolo*—"

"No!" Theo shouted, his throat still hurting. "Don't call me that. Not when you lied about your son. Not when Angie and I were attacked!"

Giovanni rose, making his way to the boy. Theo shook, his eyes pricking. He looked up at Giovanni, the man casting a shadow over him as he stood close. Giovanni looked down at his neck, seeing the bruises. He caught Theo's chin in a gentle hold, tilting his head to look at the mark next to his eye.

"I'm sorry you were hurt, Theo."

Theo grabbed Giovanni's wrist, tears flowing down his face. The rush of vindication flooded through his veins. It felt good. It felt good to be recognized.

To be cared for.

"Tell me everything," Giovanni whispered, anger brewing behind his chestnut eyes.

"Tell me everything, son."

The white door slammed shut, trapping the two Untouchables together. Parris stood in front of her white marble desk, her back towards Tony, going through her mail.

"I'm not open, Tony," Parris called over her shoulder, not bothering to look at him.

Tony crept up behind her, delighted in the way she stiffened. He rested his chin on her shoulder, throwing an envelope on the desk.

"Open it," he whispered hotly into her ear.

The smell of tobacco flooded Parris's senses. She crinkled her nose as she leaned forward, away from him.

"Back off," Parris spat. "After your stunt at the meeting, I don't have the patience for your shit today."

"Open it," he commanded again.

"What is this?" Parris huffed as she grabbed the envelope. She tore the seal open, dumping the contents on her marble desk.

Photos fell out, littering the surface—photos of young girls smiling, photos of Janine Johnston.

Parris froze.

Looking down at her bare arms, Tony cherished how the goosebumps rose on her, delighted that she took off her leather jacket, that he was in the presence of Parris, not the Informant. She was softer around the edges, no longer hard and rough. He snaked his arms around her front in a pseudo-hug, Parris too stunned to yell at him.

"Where did you get these?" Parris picked up a picture, holding it up in a shaky hand.

Enjoying the power of controlling the conversation for once, Tony hummed, tucking his face into her neck.

"I remembered you," he sang into her ear. "Help. Fire. Geezer. Help."

Parris shook violently. She set the photo down on the desk hunching over, as though she was going to be sick.

"I couldn't find your name in the yearbook, or your graduation picture... but I still found you." Tony picked up a photo of Parris and Janine, smirking into her neck.

"You pushed her, didn't you?" demanded Tony.

"Leave." Parris shuddered.

"You pushed her from the roof. She wouldn't have jumped on her own."

"Shut up."

"She was your friend and you killed her. I loved her."

"SHUT UP!" Parris tried to turn towards Tony. He pinned her hips to the desk, pushing her head down onto the photos. Parris screamed, her hands searching for anything as Tony leaned in, his other hand grabbing at her body. He laughed maniacally, adrenaline pumped through his veins. He had finally caught his prey.

Finally touching an Untouchable.

"I own you now, Parris. You're just a little girl trying to make up for the wrong she did!" he shouted, the expression on his face wild. "And now that I know your little secret, you're going to do everything I say. You're going to tell me why you've been in Chinatown so often, why STK kids were following you. And then, I'll make *him* see that you're just a knockoff of the original Untouchable!"

Parris's fingers found the phone on the desk; she grabbed it and slammed it into Tony's head. He stumbled back, holding his eye with a shout. Parris picked herself up from the desk, shrieking.

"Get out!"

"Pledge allegiance to the Wings and I promise to not hurt you!" Tony lunged at her again, making a grab for her, but she stepped back. She grabbed the lamp from her desk, hitting him across the face with it like a baseball bat. Tony spat out blood, his eyes still wild.

"NOW!" she screamed.

Tony pulled out his gun, pointing it at her.

"Tell me why he replaced me!" Tony demanded, the gun shaking violently. His mouth was full of blood; a trail dripped down his chin.

They stared at one another, panting heavily.

"There's no purpose for a soiled tissue. Once blown into, it's discarded immediately," Parris spat cruelly at him.

Looking at the photos scattered around the Informant, Tony put the gun away. Parris was still armed with the lamp. They were both still Untouchables. Killing one another would be a guaranteed death sentence.

"A 'soiled tissue', eh? You do know what this new Untouchable means."

"I'm sick of hearing your fucking voice."

"He'll just replace you," Tony spat at her. "He's not going to allow for four Untouchables in his city and you know that. What deal did you make with him? I'll be safe, but you… what deal did you make with that devil, Parris?"

Parris glared at Tony. For all his idiocy, he was still a Moretti, still cunning and smart when he tried, all according to Giovanni's design. Tony chuckled, wiping his chin as he moved towards the white door.

"So that's it, then. Your status as an Untouchable will be revoked once this punk becomes one. Your days are numbered and you'll be mine soon enough, Parris. You owe me that much for Janine." Tony slammed the door shut behind him, limping down the stairs and out the side door.

Logan watched Tony leave. Lorenzo stopped his conversation on the phone as the side door slammed shut behind the Wing, looking up at the office with wide eyes.

Seeing the blood on Tony's face, Logan's body moved on its own. He ran up the stairs and entered the office. Lorenzo shouted behind him, "Stop! She'll want to be alone!"

Logan entered the office, slamming the white door open. His eyes landed on Parris, who was on the floor in front of the desk. Photographs were scattered around her. She was heaving, her hair was messy and her shirt untucked. Logan's anger flared at the man who left.

Taking a step closer to the Informant, he stopped as he stepped on a photo. He picked it up. Senior year of high school flashed across his mind as he saw himself in the picture. It was a picture of him at homecoming with two girls.

With Parris and Janine.

"What the fuck are these?" Logan spat.

Parris ignored him as she picked herself off the floor. Logan grabbed her by the hair, bringing her face inches from his.

"Why the fuck are those pictures here?" Logan growled, grip tightening in her hair.

"Leave me alone, you fucking brute!" Parris winced as he pulled her neck into an awkward position. Logan pushed her to the floor, seeing only red.

"Tell me why those pictures are here!"

Parris laughed, her face a mix of glee and pain.

"TELL ME!" Logan yelled again. "What did he do to you? Just let me in this once! Why is our homecoming picture here? Why did you disappear?!"

Tears streamed down her face, shocking Logan. He hadn't seen her cry in nearly ten years. The last time she cried in front of him was the same night they had gone their separate ways.

"Leave me alone," Parris whispered as she cradled herself.

Logan calmly rose, his upper lip pulled into a snare. "You really are a Parrasite. You poison everyone around you. You only care about yourself. Always have and always will."

He spared one last look at the pictures of Janine and Parris before leaving through the white door.

Leaving Parris on the floor, tears no longer falling.

CHAPTER TEN

Listen to My Voice

The autumn sun sleepily awakened in Ciel. Marcel exhaled smoke slowly from his nose. He sat by the window in a plush gray armchair, a sheer white curtain filtered in the early morning light. He was fidgeting with the condom package in his hand.

Huifen shuffled under her thick duvet. Her plain beige room did not reflect her profession or personality at all. One look around the showroom-like bedroom and no one would ever guess it belonged to the Head of the Halos, the chemical engineer herself.

"Time?" Huifen mumbled from her nest under the covers, her cheek squished against the plush pillow.

"Six a.m.," Marcel answered, taking a longer drag of the cigarette.

"Too early," she grumbled as she sat up, yawning. Marcel threw the condom on top of the bed, eyebrows scrunched together. He looked like a dragon with the smoke rolling around him.

"How did she know, Tiff?"

Huifen stretched as she reached for her glasses. "I would rather not talk about the Informant in my bedroom."

Walking to the window, she pulled back the curtain, letting in the early light. She sighed as she turned back to him, finding a hard look on his face.

"She won't care about us, so long as she doesn't feel threatened. We need to get rid of Tony. He's the problem. No syndicate can ever reach its full potential if its Head is unfocused."

Marcel snuffed out the butt of the cigarette. Huifen took a seat on his lap; her fingers danced across the back of his neck.

"You do know that, don't you, Marcel?"

"But Parris—"

"She doesn't matter!" Huifen snapped. "We need to focus on gaining turf and getting rid of Tony! The Gates still own everything. They have the most men. They have the most territory, the most weapons. But the Halos and the Wings could be so much more if we could just *focus*."

Marcel couldn't meet her eyes, opting to look out the window.

"He's still my friend, Tiff," Marcel whispered. Huifen sighed as she got off him, heading to the bathroom. She paused at the door, turning to look at the Wing.

"Friendships in this business make you weak. You should know better by now, Marcel. Tony is bad for business. Bad for you."

"I should know better, and yet," he responded, a smirk on his lips. "You let me into your life."

Huifen looked at Marcel, her eyes dancing with ambition.

"If you get in my way, Marcel, then you should know what I'll do to you."

"You would kill me, Tiffany?" Marcel asked, his heart in his throat.

"Don't be foolish, of course not." Huifen waved the thought off. "You also want more business. More power. We're too alike, baby. We both want to eat at the table."

She opened the door to the bathroom, throwing Marcel a sly look over her shoulder.

"I'm hopping in the shower. Care to come?"

Amir stretched on his yoga mat, pulling at the strained muscles, hearing the satisfying crack of his back. He continued his routine, enjoying the early morning light that shone into his battered apartment.

He had finally started to make the place into his home. A map of Ciel hung over his couch. A few plants were stationed on the windowsill, drinking in the sunlight that entered his place. He even added a few pictures on his T.V. console: one of him with his parents at Niagara Falls, one of him on his graduation day from the academy. The last one was of the young girl with the same green eyes as him, courtesy of his father.

He had received several reports of girls disappearing at night. The parents had sworn up and down that the girls wouldn't have run away on their own. He had to investigate a local bar, the last known location of the girls. But it was impossible to investigate every gang-related activity alone.

His phone beeped, disturbing his peaceful moment. He rushed to look at the message. *I'm getting addicted to this thing.* He read over the message from Helen, his first message from her for a while.

Fresh To Go. *Distributing Cloud 9.* – Helen

His heart raced. This was Helen's first lead on Cloud 9, the horrific drug that ran rampant in Ciel.

How do you know? – Amir

She responded right away.

Hurry. – Helen

Amir rushed into his bedroom, grabbing his uniform from his ironing board. Jumping into his pants, he heard another beep. He read the message with knots forming in his stomach.

A package was just delivered to your office from the courthouse. – Officer Sanchez

---

"*Flushington, Flushington Station,*" the automated voice announced as the subway came to a stop. Jaya yawned as she stepped off the train, pocketing her phone.

Rubbing her eyes as she made her way to the surface, she pulled her blue hood down to cover her face. Blood-red pillars of crawling dragons adorned the streets.

Chinatown.

"Good morning." Raef greeted her with a kiss on her cheek. She tried to pull away futilely. He was also wearing a blue hoodie that hid his medium-length brown hair. He pulled up his medical face mask to hide his features. Only his eyes peered out into the world.

"Morning," Jaya grumbled as he tugged her along the sidewalk. "I'm missing school today again, my teachers are going to get suspicious…"

"I just need a little bit of cash to keep me afloat, so we need a little Cloud 9 to resell when supply goes down."

"But why am I here?" Jaya hissed. The recent memory of being chased in Chinatown with Angela was still fresh in her mind. She scanned the streets for men with chains hanging from their pockets.

"Because I need my lookout, of course!"

She stopped in her tracks, pulling her arm free from him. Her shoulders stiffened.

"Lookout? What the hell are you planning to do?" Jaya asked.

Raef pulled out a medical mask, handing it to her. She took it with uncertain hands.

"Put it on and don't ask stupid questions, Jaya," Raef responded coldly. "You're smarter than that."

They continued further into Chinatown, the streets still busy even after the morning rush. Jaya looked over her shoulder the whole way, dragging her feet to the small grocer. A peeling white sign hung over the shop.

Fresh To Go.

Stalls of food littered on the sidewalk, all with prices written on cardboard. It was beatdown, but sure enough, university students were raiding their shelves for affordable produce.

"Stay out here," Raef whispered as he entered *Fresh to Go*. Jaya watched him disappear as he ventured deeper into the store. She stood on the sidewalk, trying to look busy with her phone, her eyes scanning the road.

Raef had taken her to his hideout yesterday, a dirty apartment on the outskirts of town where trouble lurked. He had her take inventory of the different drugs he had stashed, while he went out to deal. He was in debt to the Gates, and everyone knew that if you couldn't pay, they would make you find a way.

Good morning, Jaya, how are you feeling today? Did you want me to ask your teachers for your classwork? – Angela

Jaya didn't have the heart to respond.

I baked some cookies last night (it helps me de-stress) I added extra chocolate for you! – Angela

I can't tell her what's going on, it'll just put her on edge.

Jaya narrowed her eyes at a CCPD vehicle that came to a stop in front of the store. A few customers looked at the two officers who left the vehicle.

A man and a woman.

Shit, Jaya thought as they made their way towards *Fresh To Go.* She ducked inside the grocery store, frantically looking around for a blue hoodie. The store was tight with narrow shelves and rows of produce. She spotted Raef at the cashier all the way in the back of the store, arguing with a man with wispy white hair.

"I'm saying to give me the lot," Raef argued through closed teeth.

"No, I told you already. I'm not selling anymore until I get my next delivery!" the man responded sternly, gripping a cardboard box.

"You old fuck, I'll light you up!" Raef spat back. One of his hands flew to his waistband. Jaya heard the shuffle of customers clearing as the police officers headed inside, towards the cashier.

"Babe!" she grabbed Raef's attention. He turned back at her, eyes narrowed.

"We have to go. Now!" Jaya whispered, the icy drops of fear coursing through her veins.

"Excuse me!" the male officer called out. He held out a piece of paper, walking down the aisle. "We have a warrant to search this premise. Are you the owner?"

The old man turned pale, his grip lax enough for Raef to snatch the box from him with a yell.

"Run!" Raef shouted.

Raef and Jaya ran down the produce aisle.

"Officer Sanchez, pursue them!" the officer with the warrant called out.

The pair ran out of *Fresh To Go*, the woman officer hot on their tails.

"Freeze!" Sanchez called out.

Raef knocked over a stall of apples, blocking the officer's path. He pulled Jaya along with him, running onto the road. Cars came to a screeching stop, others cursing at them with words and their horns. The officer had a harder time crossing through the speeding cars. Jaya panted as she followed Raef into a streetcar, the doors closing just barely after them.

The passengers cleared the area around the pair. Raef laughed as he held the box tighter, a plain cardboard box with the words 'green onions' printed in black. Jaya held her stomach as she tried to regain her breath.

"I got it," Raef whispered as he stepped off the streetcar, a few stops from Chinatown. Jaya followed him obediently.

"Let's get this home, babe!" Raef beamed gleefully.

Officer Sanchez returned to *Fresh To Go* in a pant, her face red from running. Amir stood with the owner, notebook equipped in hand.

"Who were those kids?" Amir questioned.

"How should I know? I just got robbed while you had your thumb in your ass!" the old man yelled, spit flying everywhere. Amir's eye twitched at the rude comment.

"What did they steal?"

"… Green onions."

Amir looked up from his notebook, eyebrows drawn in. "Green onions?"

"Yes, green onions, scallions, spring onions. Take your pick, asshole!"

Amir took a deep breath. Officer Sanchez took the warrant from her superior.

"They got away; I will include it in my report once we return to the division. I can conduct a search of the store now, Officer Hafiz."

Amir nodded, the man still yelling at him about the green onions. A single vein popped on Amir's tanned forehead.

Officer Sanchez cleared the store, locking the front door. Some of the workers stopped what they were doing as she explained the warrant, instructing them to wait by the owner at the cash register. Once alone in the back, she pulled on plastic gloves and began her search. She looked through the refrigerators, pausing at several boxes labelled 'green onions'.

"Find anything?" Amir asked behind her, also gloved.

"Nothing yet."

Amir nodded stiffly; he had a lot riding on this search. Captain Chan's words about being transferred to Community Education taunted him. He still had to investigate the disappearance of the girls.

"Officer Hafiz, may I ask you something?" Sanchez asked as she dug through a box of green onions.

"You may," Amir replied, looking through another box.

"How did you know to search this store? Follow-up, how did the judge sign the warrant so quickly? Usually, it takes a few days, since the application is filed for a response. But it was hand-delivered to your desk this morning. Why was that?"

Amir paused his search, but quickly resumed pushing green onions aside to search the box with vigour.

"I told you things would change, Officer Sanchez," he answered. "And hard, honest work will always be rewarded." He pulled out a small plastic bag of green crystals.

Thank you, Helen, Amir thought with a triumphant smirk. He held the small Ziploc bag as he returned to the old man.

"Mr. Carl Li, you are under arrest for carrying and trafficking drugs, namely Cloud 9, or in your case 'green onions'. You have the right to remain silent and retain and be instructed by counsel."

"Fuck..." groaned the shop owner under his breath as Amir handcuffed him.

The feeling of victory fueled the candle of hope in Amir's chest.

Angela sent Jaya another message, asking how she felt today.

Poor thing, Angela thought as she sat alone at lunch, eating her pasta in silence. She didn't have the appetite for the baked goods, plus she had made too many cookies for her to eat all by herself. They were meant to be shared with Jaya and Theo. She missed Jaya and her snarky comments. She couldn't see Theo in the cafeteria, or he would have made his way to their spot by now.

Hey, want to eat lunch together? – Angela

She messaged him again. He looked drained in the first period, heavy bags under his eyes. When she asked if he had spoken to Giovanni, he didn't respond, instead focusing on taking intensive notes.

With the volleyball team. Head to third without me. – Theo

Angela frowned at her phone.

Why was he being so distant? Maybe being vulnerable made him uncomfortable?

She followed the crowd of students when the bell rang, going through the motions, her day dimmer without her only two friends. She entered her history class, taking her seat by the front. She turned around looking for Theo, finding him laughing with Nathan as they sat in the back.

The teacher called for everyone's attention, dimming the lights as the projector lit the screen.

Are you avoiding me? Angela typed, but quickly deleted it. She would ask him after class, as they made their way together to their fourth period.

She couldn't resist turning to look at him one last time, catching him staring at her. He turned his head sharply as he mumbled something to Nathan, the both of them snickering.

An ugly weight settled on Angela's chest.

"Alright, anyone know who wrote the *Iliad*?" the teacher called out, the class silent as the lesson began. Theo immediately raised his hand.

"Mr. Grayson?"

"Homer wrote the epic poem," Theo answered.

"Correct as always!" the teacher praised, flipping through their PowerPoint. Theo's hand raced across his notebook. He looked back up at Angela, his friend also racing to write everything their teacher was saying.

His chest felt like a black car was parked on it.

"That's when we left Patel's office," Theo sniffed as he sat on the leather couch in Giovanni's office. Giovanni sat next to him, rubbing soothing circles into his back.

"And the girl?" Giovanni asked.

"We went our separate ways. Angie was really disturbed after

everything that had happened."

"She suffered because you chose to tell her about my conversation with Patel."

"I didn't think anything would happen!"

"No, but you both said you were an Untouchable without thinking of the consequences when you barely know what an Untouchable is."

Theo knew that Giovanni was right. He knew that he shouldn't have betrayed Giovanni's trust, that he was the one who endangered Angela by naming the Head.

"I'm sorry, Giovanni," Theo said in a small voice. Giovanni leaned back, his arm draped across the back of the couch. He smirked when he saw Theo lean closer to him, trying to chase his warm comforting hand.

"Theo, I want you to look at me."

The boy obediently turned to him, eyes red and puffy from crying.

"You need to distance yourself from this friend. You've seen what happens when people know that you are mine."

"But I'm—" Theo started, but Giovanni spoke over him.

"You're mine until you've paid your debt."

That silenced the high schooler.

"You need to distance yourself from your friends. You've seen what trouble it can cause. Instead, be cold. Be cruel. Be distant so you can protect them," Giovanni commanded, noticing the way Theo hugged himself.

"I don't think I can do that."

Giovanni tapped his lap. Theo looked at him before lowering his head. He glanced up at the ceiling, the position making it hard to breathe with his runny nose. Giovanni's other hand started playing with his hair.

"You can and you will, Cucciolo. If you are seen with her again, it might encourage others to hurt me by getting to you. Your friends are an

extension of you, son. I would hate for Angela to be caught in any more violence and pain because of you. Telling her you were an Untouchable, putting thoughts in her head. Her life depends on it. Am I right to assume you have feelings for her?"

Theo squeezed his eyes shut, trying to control his emotions.

"Tony?" Theo asked instead.

Giovanni sighed as he continued petting his hair. "Tony is my son. But he's been dead to me for a very long time."

"What happened?"

"He crossed a line. He did something that shamed the Gates, the Morettis, and me. He touched an Untouchable. Maybe it's because his mother died early on in his life and I couldn't fill that hole. Maybe it was because of the company he kept. But the fact that he had disobeyed my most sacred agreement had killed him in my eyes." Giovanni's hand stopped. "I couldn't kill my only son, but I had to make an example of what happens when you touch an Untouchable."

Theo shuddered, thinking of what the man was implying. His mind imagined different types of torture, remembering how Tony had walked with a slight limp. Theo had to remind himself that Giovanni wouldn't hurt him, not when he was comforting him in that instant.

"Cucciolo, I want you to promise me that you will stay away from that girl."

Theo tried sitting up, but Giovanni's hand pushed his forehead down.

"Stay away from others for a little while, just until I deal with Tony."

He gave up trying to push against the hand.

"For their safety."

"Yes, Sir."

Giovanni cupped his cheek. "You're doing so well, Cucciolo. This will blow over soon. Until then, I want you to spend your evenings here. You may continue playing volleyball, as I enjoy watching the sport. A car will pick you up after school and then drop you off at your home by bedtime."

"You want me to come to your office every day?" Theo asked; the idea didn't sound so bad.

"Yes, Cucciolo. Does that sound good to you?" Giovanni asked softly.

"Yeah," Theo responded, enjoying the attention Giovanni gave, enjoying how he was so concerned for his safety.

"That sounds good."

"Theo!" Angela called out for the third time, a few students turned to look at her as she rushed out the front doors of STK.

Theo had slipped out of third period faster than Angela could notice. All of fourth he spent discussing his assignment with the teacher during their study time. By the time she packed her bag, the tall boy was speeding through the vaulted hallway. She kept calling out for him, but she was certain of it, he was ignoring her. She ran through the stone courtyard, a few paces behind him.

"Theo Grayson!"

He stopped in front of a black car, his shoulders tensed together. Angela panted as she caught up, panic flaring in her chest.

"Why are you avoiding me?" she asked. The back of the car was empty; Theo tossed his bag in. "I'm talking to you, Theo! What's wrong?"

He took a seat, his eyes downcast.

"Did something happen with—"

"You need to learn to take a hint, Williams."

Angela opened her mouth in shock. She had never heard Theo speak with venom before, at least not towards her. He slammed the door shut, and the car sped off into Ciel. Angela stood dumbfounded, not sure if she should be angry at her friend or if she should cry.

"Hey, it's Angela, right?" a voice asked behind her. A tall lanky boy came into sight. She'd seen him around school and at the volleyball game. He wore creaseless white sneakers.

"Right, hi, I'm Kevin. Weird question, but do you know where Jaya is? She hasn't been around these past couple of days," he asked, his lanky body cast a shadow on Angela.

Angela finally found her voice. "What do you want Jaya for?"

He pulled out his phone, a news page open. "Have you seen the news? They found Cloud 9 at a Chinatown store. It says that the police were chasing two people."

She looked at the headline and back at Kevin.

"And?"

Kevin glanced over his shoulder before leaning down to whisper, "And if Jaya is caught up with the Halos again, or worse, the cops, she might snitch on the rest of us. I can't afford to get kicked out of STK for blazing on the weekends."

"You're worried about your own ass? What about Jaya?" Angela took a step back, into the light.

"It's every man for himself," Kevin sneered. "Don't act like you're a saint."

The boy left in a huff. Angela hit the call button on Jaya's contact instantly.

The phone rang but was sent to voicemail.

Angela's commute home was a blur as she continued messaging both Jaya and Theo. Neither answered her. Angela entered her apartment in a daze. She didn't know what to do.

Are they in trouble? Why did they just leave me all of a sudden?

She found the crumpled card on her desk, and called the number. The phone rang and rang and rang.

"This is Officer Amir Hafiz."

Angela wasn't able to talk.

"Hello?" Officer Hafiz repeated. "Hello, is anyone there?"

Angela hung up.

My friends left me.

She called her father, her fingers numb as she held her phone to her ear. She hugged her knees to her chest.

"Angie?" her father answered. "Angel, are you alright? "

"H-hey dad…" Angela choked a little. "Just wanted to hear a familiar voice."

"What happened, Angel?"

"Dad… I listened to you and Mom. I made friends. I made two wonderful friends but they left me," she whispered into the phone. "I actually made friends and they left me. My heart hurts. My heart hurts so much! Why does everyone leave me? Everyone I love leaves me."

Angela wiped the tears that escaped, angry that they were able to break through.

"It's better to be alone, that way I don't have to worry about anyone. It's better to be alone…"

"No, Angel," her father said, a sternness in his tender voice. "It is not better to be alone. Friends sometimes hurt you when you let them in, it's just a growing pain. Friends make you stronger."

"I've had enough pain!" Angela cried.

Her father did not respond right away. She could hear her mother crying in the back. Angela could picture her face welling with tears. That's why she called her father, he was always more level-headed than her mother. He could take bad news, pain, and grief and still stand upright. Her father finally spoke.

"Do you want to come home, Angie?"

Should I? Angela thought as she bit her trembling lip. *Should I just abandon this cesspool and go home to them? But if I do, I'll never get what I want. I'll never be able to confront Parris.*

"No… no, I still have something on my mind. I'm not done with Ciel yet. I'm going to hang up now, Dad."

"We love you, Angie. Mom and I both love you—"

Angela cut the line.

Confront Parris.

The thought echoed in her mind: her goal for coming to Ciel City, the reason for all of this. Theo and Jaya fell to the back of her mind for the first time in days. She ripped her uniform off in a frenzy. Pulling her jeans and denim jacket on, she marched through the front door. Angela passed the children playing in the hallway. Mrs. McLaughlin yelled at her about something but she couldn't hear anything, just the same two words on repeat. She pushed through the building doors and stomped onto Ciel's concrete sidewalk.

Ciel was muted for a second time. The downtown train's commotion didn't puncture through her bubble of focus. Only one thought was on her mind.

Confront Parris.

One foot in front of the other, her feet delivered her to her destination.

Clueless was still a fortress during the day. But Angela wasn't going to linger on the other side of the street as she always had. This time, she marched down the side alley, past the dumpster and recycling bins and trash bags. She glared at the side door. Raising her fist, just as Jaya had. Consequences be damned.

Confront Parris.

She knocked loudly. A moment passed. She knocked again, harder this time.

"Open up, Lorenzo!" Angela demanded.

Immediately, the side door opened. Lorenzo raised an eyebrow at her; he blocked her view of the club inside. Angela panted, stunned that it had worked.

"I need to speak with her."

"Do you have an appointment?" Lorenzo asked politely.

"No—"

"Then you cannot speak with her," Lorenzo said, closing the door. Angela stuck her foot in.

"Tell her that it's me!" Angela pleaded. Her foot was being squished; she pushed her body against the door.

"Doesn't matter," Lorenzo replied coldly. He pushed back, but his eyes betrayed his stoic exterior. Angela saw pity in them.

Pity for her.

"Lorenzo, please!" Angela begged, pushing back against him with all her might. "Just tell her it's Angela Williams." She could see the dancefloor of the club but not the upstairs office. She was so close!

"I said no."

The door was closing. Lorenzo was stronger than Angela.

"PARRIS!" Angela shrieked. "PARRIS, COME DOWN HERE AND TALK TO ME! YOU OWE ME!"

"Enough!" Lorenzo yelled back, his stoic mask cracking. The door was almost closed. Her reason for coming to Ciel. Her one chance was about to slam shut in her face.

"YOU OWE ME FOR J—!"

The door swung open.

Angela fell onto all fours with a yip. Lorenzo stepped back, eyes wide. Angela peered up from her spot on the black marble floor. A leather jacket and dark eyes filled her vision.

Parris looked down her nose at Angela. There was no air of

eccentricity and mischief around her, no smile, just distaste. Angela couldn't get up, her body rooted in the ground. Parris's presence kept her there, kneeling before her like a beggar.

"You have thirty seconds of my time," Parris stated coldly.

"I—!" Angela choked.

It wasn't fair. Thirty seconds wasn't enough time to ask every question that burned Angela for years. To be told the story. The *full* story.

"Twenty seconds."

"I want to know—."

"Eighteen seconds."

"STOP COUNTING!" Angela howled, tears raining down on the black marble floor.

"You don't get to treat me like an animal. I deserve to know *everything*! My world is shattered. My friends are gone. Everyone who loves me is gone and I'm here begging you for more than thirty fucking seconds of your time! It's not fair!"

"Zero."

A broken cry rang through *Clueless*. Angela screamed, her chest pushing every last bit of air out. Lorenzo stared, wide-eyed. He agreed with her. It wasn't fair. None of this was.

Parris grabbed a fistful of Angela's coily hair, dragging her back outside into the alley. Angela kicked out, scratching the sleeves of the leather jacket. She didn't know if she was yelling coherent words or just sounds of anger and resentment.

A black garbage bag cushioned her as Parris threw her into a pile of trash. The clinking of bottles and the stench of vomit floated around her.

"Knock on my door again and there will be hell to face, Williams."

Parris marched back into her club, slamming the side door shut without a glance back at Angela.

Angela cried loudly, her chest heaving violently against the concrete. Feelings of loneliness and worthlessness ate at her as she sat with the garbage in a city that consumed everyone.

CHAPTER ELEVEN

Helen

The senior English class took a seat after the national anthem, the sound of chairs scraping against the floor filling the air. The students distracted themselves as they waited for their lesson while the morning announcements rang into the classroom. Some students were on their phones while others were frantically finishing their assigned readings in the few minutes they had left before the start of class.

"Congratulations to our boys' volleyball team for their fourth win of the season!" The morning announcements echoed into the classroom.

Angela peered out the window, not paying attention. Her eyes refused to focus on anything in particular, her chin rested in her hand.

"Did you go to the game on Sunday?" the girl to her right asked in a hushed voice. Lucy was her new seat partner in the first period. Theo had switched places with her, asking the teacher the day after Angela ran after him.

"No, I didn't," Angela responded monotonously. Lucy was too friendly to her, to the point that it irked Angela a little. She was the personification of a golden retriever. Nothing wrong with that; Angela thought she was nice, but she wasn't Jaya or Theo. The more Lucy spoke, the more Angela missed her friends, if she could still call them her friends.

"It was so good! Kevin jumped like so high up! And Nathan did this cool dive! And—"

Angela tuned her out, looking out the window at the trees. The school term was well into October. A few trees peeked above the black gate of STK. Red, brown, orange, and yellow leaves littered the stone courtyard. She watched longingly at a few seniors on spare throwing the colourful leaves at one another. They laughed gleefully with one another. A lone janitor raked the leaves into bags, shaking his fist at students. Angela pictured it was Theo, Jaya, and her fooling around down there instead.

Angela had tried to get in contact with Theo after that day but it was futile. He even avoided her in person, slipping out the door of any room Angela was in, always looking past her. Angela gave up when her messages stopped sending.

Jaya was another story. Her friend had finally returned to school, but she was just like Theo, avoiding her like the plague. It didn't help that they didn't have any classes together. She never saw her around STK. Their saving grace lunch hour was taken from her, as Jaya always ate off-campus with some guy.

Angela had stopped baking. If there was no Jaya and Theo to share her cookies with, then there was no point. She instead filled her time going on longer runs before the weather dipped below zero, running from her apartment in Midtown all the way down to the Harbourfront Piers, purposely running in front of *Clueless*. Angela hadn't spoken to anyone about her attempt to speak to Parris. She had her chance to finally ask what had happened all those years ago. Thirty seconds of her time, and she blew it. But Angela wasn't going to give up. She couldn't give up, not after so long.

I could mail her again. Ask for an appointment this time. But the post just returned my letter... maybe I'll address it to Lorenzo instead.

"Are you going to the upcoming Halloween Party?" Lucy asked, pulling Angela from her thoughts.

"I'm not sure, Lucy."

"Well, it'll be like *the* party of the year! Besides our homecoming, of course."

"Really?" Angela asked, disinterested.

"Really!" she squealed.

Lucy lowered her voice into a whisper, leaning closer to Angela. "My younger brother is a freshman, and his entire year is super excited for the Halloween party. They think that they can find the lost suicide note in the chemistry lab. There's some superstition that the note will only appear during the night, the same one that's been missing for ten years!"

Angela snapped her head at the bubbly girl, an angry look settled on her face. Lucy was taken aback.

"Did I say something—?"

"Ladies!" their English teacher called out, reprimanding the pair. The class snickered, turning to look at the girls. Theo didn't look back.

That's not something to joke about! Angela dug her pen into her notebook, not paying attention to her teacher. *There is no suicide note. There never fucking was.*

A security guard in a suit held the office door open for Theo, closing it behind the boy with a quiet noise.

"*Cucciolo!*" Giovanni welcomed from behind his desk as Theo entered his ornate office, tossing his bag by the coffee table.

"Hello, Sir," Theo greeted back, kissing Giovanni's left and then right cheek. Having learned the man's preferred reception, Giovanni returned the greeting.

"I take it the class was exciting after your win this past weekend? I must say it was your best game yet. I thoroughly enjoyed it."

Theo plopped on the couch facing the fireplace, his preferred seat in the office. He responded flatly.

"It was fine."

The older man hummed as he resumed his work on the computer. Theo took out his homework, spreading his history assignment on the coffee table.

Ever since Theo's second visit to the red brick building, this had become their routine. Theo would come to the office every day after school. Sometimes Giovanni would be there, sometimes they would eat together, sometimes he would take Theo shopping, or sometimes Theo stayed by himself for hours. Giovanni sometimes ate dinner with city officials or was at business meetings for both the CCC and the Gates. But one thing was guaranteed, and that was the car waiting downstairs at eight p.m. to drop him back home. He was lucky that Giovanni was in the office today, missing his company a little.

Theo looked at his assignment with a scowl. He also missed Angela, and by extension Jaya. He felt guilty for the way that he'd been acting towards her.

She doesn't deserve it… I wish I could tell her why, but Giovanni is right, it would just put her at risk.

He instead spent his time with the volleyball team, but he was growing sick of their immaturity. Along with Kevin's constant comments and jokes about his dad's arrest, Theo might blow up at him soon. Nathan had been good at keeping the peace and Kevin in line, but he was only one voice among many others.

"Boss," Theo called out.

"Yes, *Cucciolo*?"

"How much longer until Tony's off my tail?" Theo asked. "It's been a while."

Giovanni chuckled as he typed on his computer. "Is someone sick of this old man?"

"No, Sir," Theo responded with a smile, "but seriously… I miss my friends. I want to apologize for being so cold to them."

The older man hummed as though he was lost in thought. "It should be soon, son. My plan has been working in the background, Tony should almost be off your trail. Please see it through 'till the end."

Theo nodded, focused again on his assignment, his highlighter dashing across the instructions in a flurry of yellow.

Theo's hunched posture over his work reminded Giovanni of just how hard of a worker he was. It also reminded him of another boy—the same way Tony had sat in his office doing his own schoolwork many many years ago.

"It's your birthday next week, isn't it, *Cucciolo*?" Giovanni rested his chin in his hands as he watched Theo work.

"Yes, Sir!" Theo replied, a wide smile on his face as he looked up.

"And what does Mr. Theo Grayson want?"

"I don't want anything, Sir." Theo chuckled, "You've already done so much for me. I still can't thank you enough for all the new clothes and watches."

"If you won't choose then I have an idea," Giovanni suggested, his eyes dark. Theo looked on innocently. "Have an overnight bag packed, the car will pick you up late the night before your birthday."

"Are we going somewhere?"

"It's a surprise, *Cucciolo*."

"It's not a cottage trip, is it?" Theo asked with a raised eyebrow. Giovanni laughed softly.

The sound of Giovanni's phone ringing stole the older man from their conversation. The easy smile on his face disappeared instantly, instead replaced with a scowl.

"Did you find information on the company?" Giovanni answered. Theo tried to distract himself with his assignment, but he couldn't help but overhear the conversation on the phone.

"It's been weeks. I want to know how they got the bid for the Ciel Re-Pavement Project over my company. I'll be damned if I lose any more business. I pay the city council a hefty amount for this exact reason."

Giovanni quieted when he saw Theo staring.

"No, I will not ask Parris for something you should know as secretary of the mayor! Either Robert makes a meeting with me or I will drop by his office. And we both know I will *not* be a pleasant guest to have."

The person on the phone was speaking quicker.

"I want answers soon."

With that, Giovanni hung up the phone with a sigh.

"Is there a problem, Sir?" Theo asked in a quiet voice, unsure if he should have left. Giovanni pinched the bridge of his nose, his chestnut eyes closed.

"I'm about to lose a lot of money. And money equals power, Theo." Giovanni motioned for Theo to join him by his desk. The boy got up and made his way to the sharp black desk. Giovanni gestured to his computer screen and desktop. A litter of inventory, receipts, and financial statements covered the surface.

"Should I be seeing this?" Theo stood next to the Head.

"Knowledge is power, *Cucciolo*."

Theo looked at a statement; it detailed monthly payments to the Ciel Construction Company. The high schooler picked up the statement, recognizing the shop.

"Why is a local donut shop paying the CCC monthly?" Theo questioned. He faced Giovanni, finding the older man grinning.

"Why do you think, *Cucciolo*?"

His heart sank a little when he realized. He whispered the answer.

"Protection money."

Giovanni clapped a hand on his shoulder as he stood up, towering over the high schooler.

"Well done, *Cucciolo*! Now, what should I do to cover the cost of the new equipment I bought for the Re-Pavement Project?"

Theo knew the answer, but he didn't want to say it. He couldn't. Giovanni pulled him closer, hand resting on the back of Theo's neck, the other one pointing at the invoice for services that never happened.

"I know you know," Giovanni whispered. Theo gulped; the hand was heavier the longer it took him to reply. He answered with a dry mouth.

"Increase the cost of protection."

Giovanni gave a loud laugh as he ruffled Theo's hair. "You are an STK student alright. As bright as the sun, you are, *Cucciolo*!"

Theo felt conflicted with the praise.

"But what about the people? What if they can't afford the new rate?" A wave of worry washing over Theo for strangers. Giovanni took his seat, looking at the high schooler with curious eyes.

"You tell me, Theo. What should happen?"

Theo opened his mouth but Giovanni cut him off.

"Remember that it was their protection money that paid for your father's bail. Without the Gates, your father would still be in police custody."

Theo clamped his mouth shut immediately. Giovanni smirked at his antic, taking his hand and placing a kiss on the back of it.

"Go finish your assignment, *Cucciolo*. I'll deal with this. After all, I've been the Head of the Gates for over thirty-five years."

The couch in Amir's apartment offered him some comfort after a long day's work. Amir groaned as he sank deeper into the worn cushions. Since the seizure of Cloud 9 at *Fresh To Go*, he'd been worked to the bone every day.

It was hard work tracking down the store's produce suppliers. They were all like rats, frantically running in every direction. Too many for Amir and Sanchez to chase on their own.

Captain Chan congratulated him at the lunch social the 97th division held for him and Officer Sanchez, but the Captain's eyes were full of warning. And Amir had understood the warning all too well.

Don't get too excited.

Once the media calmed down and the final interview was finished, Amir messaged Helen to thank her for all of her help, but she didn't answer. Their investigation into Cloud 9's distribution was underway.

I still have to investigate that bar concerning the disappearing girls…

With the arrest of *Fresh To Go*'s owners, the drug activity had calmed down. The CCPD had seized twenty kilos of Cloud 9. Although an impressive amount, it did not address the root of the problem.

The Halos.

One beast at a time, Amir thought as he closed his eyes. Images of the past few weeks flashed across his eyes: the snares of his coworkers, how Officer Sanchez hesitated before she admitted to helping him to the squad. His phone chimed, disturbing his moment of peace.

Congratulations, big shot. I just watched your interview with Channel 24. You photograph well. – Helen

Amir smiled at his phone, quickly typing out a response.

Very funny. But I couldn't have done it without you or your intel. – Amir

I wish I could be of more help. – Helen

More help? I owe you my career for all of your help, Helen. I am so blessed to have you on my side. By now I would have been transferred to Community Education. – Amir

She stopped responding, but Amir had grown accustomed to her ways. Helen never told him what she did for work now that she left the force. Amir chose to respect her privacy, not willing to risk their working relationship. But he suspected she was a journalist of sorts, since she had a vast information network.

Amir, I think we should meet. – Helen

He sat up instantly, rereading the message over and over again to make sure he had read it right. She must have read his mind.

Yes, I'm serious. – Helen

Are you sure? I know that you've made it explicit that you would never meet in person. I don't want to cross any boundaries. – Amir

He held his breath as he read her reply.

I'm sure. I want to meet you in person, Amir. – Helen

Where and when? – Amir

Tomorrow night, at Clueless. – Helen

Clueless*? But that's the Informant's place. Can't we meet somewhere else? –* Amir

I'll see you there, Amir Hafiz :) – Helen

Marcel parked his blue sports car in the abandoned parking lot. The only other car there was Tony's. The Executive made his way into the dull building towards the upstairs office.

Business had slowed down since the police's investigation into Cloud 9. *Fresh To Go* had the largest stash of the new drug. With fewer drugs in circulation, there were fewer addicts for the Wings to prey upon. It had put a dent in the Wings' trafficking, to Marcel's dismay.

The warehouse was quiet. No shipment containers filled the empty floor, no cries of young girls or pleas of men.

No product to be sold.

He better not have fucked up again, Marcel thought as he turned the doorknob, entering the shabby office.

"There's my favourite Exec!" Tony hollered as he greeted Marcel with a hug. Marcel returned the hug with a smile, his mind racing with questions.

"Someone's in a good mood, it looks good on you, man!" Marcel patted his back, taking a seat across from Tony at the desk.

Tony bubbled with energy as he sat across from Marcel, his cigarette left abandoned on the tray. The smoke twirled in streams towards the ceiling.

"I've good reason to be in a good mood," Tony explained as he leaned forward. "The Wings are about to get an upgrade."

Marcel lit a cigarette of his own, raising an eyebrow. "How so?"

"We're going to take over the Gates."

The good energy in the room was replaced by a tense feeling of dread. Marcel looked at his friend; he left his cigarette in the tray alongside Tony's, seeing the crazy look in his electric blue eyes.

"Tony…"

"I've been planning for the past few weeks! The Wings will own the Informant. We'll use her to get information on the Gates to bring them down. She knows where their weapon warehouses are. If we equip the Wings with assault rifles and raid the Gates' brothels, casinos, and shell corporations, we could seize their assets! Of course, we need more men, but the Informant also knows where the smaller gangs hide; we could have them join us," Tony plotted, his eyes dancing with ambition.

"Man, we talked about this!" Marcel exclaimed, disappointed in his friend.

"LISTEN TO ME!" Tony bellowed, catching Marcel off-guard. Marcel held his hands up in surrender.

"The Informant is mine; she will give us information on the Gates. I'll have her sell out the old man. We will kill the current Head and then I will lead them. They won't care who leads the Gates; so long as it is a Moretti, the Wings have a chance."

"What makes you say you have the Informant? She's an Untouchable. Protecting the Gates is in her best interests. Without the power and influence of the Gates, she's not an Untouchable. She wouldn't be safe."

Tony chuckled, dark and creepy. "I have her. She's nearing an expiration date and she'll need my protection soon. Trust me, Marce."

"Since when do you want to take over the Gates, Tony?" Marcel asked, his cigarette also lying forgotten. Smoke danced across the ceiling.

"It's the Head of the Gates who makes the Untouchables," Tony explained. "We only agree to his Untouchables or else we can't have access to his territories. If we take the Informant, the school, and his assets from him, it'll show everyone that the Gates are weak. That Giovanni no longer has control."

Tony bared his teeth when he said his father's name, but his words rang in Marcel's head.

"You know that there is no loyalty in the Gates. He prefers to rule by fear rather than love."

"You want to kill Giovanni and take his place?"

"I want to take everything from him." Tony declared.

"Tony, are you sure this isn't your jealousy talking right now? I was there when he kicked you out of the Gates. I've seen how you still try to prove yourself to him. We formed the Wings together but you had made the Wings to impress him. But when he announced Parris as the third Untouchable, I saw how that broke you. You no longer had the motivation to lead or to grow the Wings. Not only were you cast aside, but replaced. Getting revenge on Giovanni won't make up for the horrors you had to endure."

That quieted Tony a bit. His electric blue eyes turned sober for a moment. Marcel changed the topic, seeing the way his lips began to tremble.

"And the Halos?"

Tony shrugged as he leaned back into the office chair, picking up the cigarette.

"I don't give a shit so long as they don't fuck with my plan."

The only reason I've been cooperating with Tiffany was because I wanted to expand the Wings. I want to believe Tony, that he, too, is serious about gaining more business. More power.

Marcel studied Tony's face: the dark eye bags, his chapped lips, the unfocused look in his eyes.

"Do you want to lead the Gates, Tony? Or is this just a ploy for revenge?"

Tony's eyes pierced into Marcel. Marcel tried his hardest not to squirm under the stare.

"This is more than revenge, Marce," Tony spoke, sitting straighter. "This is about my birthright as a Moretti. This is about recovering lost property with interest from the Informant. This is about teaching the old bastard a lesson. The current order is about to change and I want you by my side." Tony stood up, Marcel following suit.

"What do you say, Marcel? Want to rule Ciel City together? Make a shit ton of money and become the strongest syndicate in Ciel history?"

Tony held his hand out for Marcel. Marcel looked between the hand and his eyes, remembering his friend before he was ostracized from the Gates: the Tony that was charming, the Tony that always got his way, the Tony that was moulded by *the* Giovanni Moretti. Marcel clapped Tony's hand in a firm handshake, grinning at his friend with bright eyes.

"About time, Tony!" Marcel exclaimed, feelings of eagerness beginning to creep into his mind. Tony laughed.

"We need to thank the Informant! She reminded me of exactly what I've been missing. My fucking purpose."

"I don't pity the bitch!" Marcel responded, "What did you have in mind, boss?"

Tony grinned at his friend, lighting a new cigarette.

"I say we have a nice long conversation with her, really show her her new place in our Ciel."

The lunch bell rang loudly, dismissing the twelfth-graders from their second-period class. Angela followed the stream of students through the front doors of STK, deciding to treat herself to lunch from across the street and mail her letter to Lorenzo. Lucy had invited Angela to eat with her and her friends, but she declined.

It didn't feel right to let anyone else into her life. She had learned from the pain Theo and Jaya gave her.

People just end up distracting me. I'm glad I don't have to deal with anyone anymore, Angela thought depressingly as she stepped past the sharp gothic arches of the school onto the city's sidewalk. She wrapped herself tighter in her denim jacket, the weather teetering between warm and chilly.

Typical of autumn in Ciel.

"Why didn't you tell me?" a familiar snarky voice yelled into the phone. Angela spotted Jaya on the sidewalk.

A smile tugged on Angela's face for the first time in weeks. Her negative thoughts were pushed to the back of her mind as she ran to Jaya's side. A small voice whispered in her mind that she hadn't meant any of that, that seeing Jaya now, with her butterfly clips, inflated her heart.

Her friend was right there!

"Jaya!" Angela cried. Jaya stared at her with wide eyes, holding her arm out to stop her from coming any closer. Angela stopped just a few feet from the girl.

"No, Raef! Next time just message me instead. I can't miss any more classes and you know that. University applications are next month!"

Who's Raef?

"Fine! I'll be there after school."

With that, Jaya hung up the phone in a fury. Angela stood there awkwardly, unsure of what to say. Jaya seemed to be having the same inner monologue as she fidgeted with her phone. Angela had thought of this moment for the past few weeks, the moment she would finally see Jaya again, but now that she was here, she was speechless. Angela bit her lip, hating the way she froze up in front of someone again.

Parris's glare flashed across her mind.

"Want to grab jerk chicken?" Angela suggested after the silence had reached a peak. Jaya huffed as she started down the sidewalk.

"You know I love jerk chicken."

The girls fell into a comfortable silence as they bought their lunch, deciding to eat in the nearby park instead of the crowded STK cafeteria. They ate in silence, only commenting on how delicious the food was.

A chill sailed through the air, the leaves blowing in the wind around them in a flurry of red, yellow, and orange. Jaya wrapped herself tighter in her cardigan.

"Jaya…" Angela started.

"I'm sorry, Angela," Jaya interrupted, wrapping herself tighter in the cloth, so tight it looked like it was cutting the circulation in her arm. "I'm sorry, but I'm caught up in something and I can't get out."

"Who's Raef?" Angela asked, hating the way Jaya stiffened at the name, her heart steeped in worry.

"Remember when I told you that I was caught up with the Halos? That my ex roped me into dealing with him?" Jaya began to play with the wrapper of her drink.

"That's Rafael. He stole some dope from the Halos and disappeared for a few months. The Halos were going to pin it on me since I was helping him deal." Jaya's hands began to shake. "I was so scared, Angela! I thought they were going to shoot my hands off or sell me to the Wings to get trafficked!"

"What happened after?" Angela asked softly.

"Parris happened!" Jaya laughed.

Angela's eyes widened. "What did she do?"

"She convinced Tiffany, the Head, that I wasn't involved, that only Raef defected… She gave away the location of a smaller gang's safehouse in exchange for my life."

Parris… she saved Jaya? But why? She's self-centred. Even Logan called her selfish! Why would she do something good? Angela thought. A spike of anger flared in Angela's heart.

So that Parrasite is capable of saving someone!

"Why would she help you, Jaya?" Angela asked. She noticed the redness of Jaya's eyes. Jaya looked away in an effort to stop the tears from spilling. But she was unsuccessful.

"She wanted an informant inside STK. If she saved me, I would be indebted to her. That's how she gets some of her information. I wouldn't be surprised if she had someone in every organization."

Angela stared at the park bench, pondering what her friend was confessing to.

I told her that I wouldn't do it. But like I said, you can't really say no to her. I couldn't tell my parents either. They would just freak out. Plus my siblings are still young, I didn't want to ruin their lives with a huge move or gang involvement," Jaya explained as she wiped the tears with her sleeve.

"Did you ever speak about me?" Angela asked quietly. Jaya looked at her funny before responding.

"No, why would I? The only thing she said was that we needed to look out for one another. What would she want to know about you?"

Angela shrugged her shoulders. Jaya continued.

"Besides, I only tell her about Cloud 9 and other gang activity in STK," Jaya said. "Then Raef came along. Fucking bastard!"

The tears ran down her face. Angela handed her the napkin that came with her food, but it wasn't enough. "He acts like I'm his, that I don't have a life outside of him. I don't want to steal shit! I don't want to deal, but he yells at me if I don't and he… he..."

"Jaya," Angela probed carefully, "is Raef hurting you?"

Jaya pursed her lips; she couldn't say it, couldn't admit it aloud. Angela's heart fell into her stomach.

"Oh, Jaya," Angela whispered as she hugged her. Jaya held onto her, weeping openly now.

The autumn chill cooled her hot tears. Angela held onto her, gently rocking her. Jaya's nails gripped into Angela's denim jacket.

The weeks of abuse from Raef finally came to the surface.

"How do I get away?" Jaya mumbled as she pulled away from Angela, her face red. Angela rubbed circles on her back, her mind racing with different ideas.

"I might," she started, "I might have an idea, Jaya. On how to get rid of Raef and keep you safe."

Jaya looked up at her with wide eyes, flickers of hope dancing.

"I have a police officer's number. He is in charge of the Anti-Gang Task Force… he helped me and Theo when we were attacked by the Head of the Wings." Jaya gasped, Angela continued. "He seems like a good guy… We can talk to him, see if you can get immunity for giving up Raef. Maybe the best thing to do is to turn him over."

Jaya thought about her idea, to lock Raef up and be done with it.

"That… that could work." Jaya's frantic heart began to settle, hope taking the place of panic.

"Wait, why did the Head of the Wings attack you and Theo? Speaking of Theo, what happened since he went with the Head of the Gates?" Jaya asked, guilty for neglecting Angela when so much was going on.

"Jaya… I'm worried about Theo. Something's happening with him."

Jaya placed a reassuring hand on Angela's shoulder, looking her friend in the eye.

"Tell me, I'm here now."

Angela told her everything since the volleyball game, happy to have Jaya back, happy that Angela wasn't actually abandoned by her like she thought, that she still had a friend in this vicious city. Angela didn't tell

Jaya the full story of Tony, the gun, or her second visit to *Clueless*.

Jaya didn't need to know about Nini. She couldn't help Angela when it came to that.

Those walls stubbornly would not come down.

The Harbourfront Pier was chilly; seagulls screamed overhead. The lake reminded the people of Ciel that the frigid cold was close.

"Come on, boss!" Logan groaned into the phone. He was seated by the harbour with a coffee from *Jim's*. He'd been laid off from work for the past few weeks; ever since one of their buyers got caught selling Cloud 9, his boss had stopped all deliveries.

The *Loose Screw* wasn't enough to keep him afloat. His rent was increasing, along with the price of everything else in the city, and he couldn't make do.

"I don't understand why there's no more work now. I need this job!"

"Not my problem, Logan!" his boss yelled into the phone. Logan could hear other people talking in the background.

"I won't deliver anything until we know we are safe!"

"Safe from what?!" Logan yelled back, failing to keep his temper under control.

His boss, a short woman with a shorter temper yelled at someone in another language. "You idiot, you know exactly why! Until I say so, no more work!" With that, she cut the line.

Logan cursed under his breath. The relaxing waves of the lake did little to settle his rage.

Deep breaths. Count to ten like Dr. Brown taught me.

He watched people walk along the pier. Couples, families, friends— all things he didn't have.

He opened his old wallet, he stared at the fading picture of his high school homecoming. He stared at Janine, wondering what she would say to him at this moment.

Probably to keep my head up and keep trying my best.

His eyes darted to the other girl in the picture. She still had the same dark eyes. If you looked into them long enough, you could see gears turning. He closed his wallet with a snap, needing to distract himself.

He looked through his phone's contact list, which was rather short. His finger hovered atop Dr. Brown's contact. He scrolled up instead.

He passed Angela's contact. He had wanted to message her since the night he dropped her off, to tell her to bundle up, to stay warm, to eat her fruits and veggies, to offer her a ride if she needed one from a party if she found herself drinking. But that wasn't his role to play with her.

She probably hated that she even saw me after all this time. Poor kid had probably wanted to forget all about me and the Parrasite. We just made her remember all of the pain.

He stopped at the contact that read *Clueless*. It was usually Lorenzo who would call him, asking where he was with their delivery.

Their delivery, Logan thought.

"Tell your boss that she isn't sending us the fresh stuff!" the shopkeeper of *Fresh To Go* had yelled at him.

"Oh, and tell your boss that I only want the fruit," he remembered the Parrasite had told him. His stomach churned, and not from the strong coffee.

No, no, no. He called his boss again. She answered on the third ring.

"What now?" she snapped.

"You were having me deliver drugs, weren't you?" Logan accused. His usually chatty boss remained quiet.

"You were hiding drugs in the produce, that's why there's no work now. You don't want to get caught!" he yelled into the phone, and a few pedestrians looked over.

"You were having me deliver drugs!" he repeated, his voice betraying his panic. He panted as his blood pounded in his veins.

"You're fired," his boss said in a quiet voice, Logan strained to hear.

"I hired you as a favour to her, but you're too much trouble!"

"Fuck you!" Logan cursed. "I'll tell the police everything!"

"Do that and the Halos will shoot your hands."

That silenced him. The Halos' *modus operandi* was to shoot the hands of those who betrayed them or wronged them. The hand would be damaged, the nerves frayed, the appendage rendered useless. Sometimes, the Halos would shoot the hands and then kill the person, to send a stronger message.

"We'll be keeping an eye on you, Logan O'Brien."

His boss hung up on him a second time. His eyes focused on a spot on the Pier before he threw his coffee at it with a yell. Some seagulls fluttered away. People who were seated on a nearby bench got up and left in a hurry.

He swayed to the cup, picking up his trash. His legs remained like noodles, refusing to resolidify. Scared for the first time in years, he remained crouched on the Pier, taking deep, shuddering breaths.

Amir anxiously tugged on his sleeve as he waited in line for *Clueless*. He felt naked out of his uniform, deciding to wear a deep navy chino and a black turtleneck, the gold chain tucked under his shirt. Amir blended well with the young crowd, a rowdy bunch waiting for the bouncers to let them into the nightclub. He was easily ten years older than the other patrons. He checked over Helen's message again.

I'm by the bar when you come in. – Helen

"Next," a gruff voice called out to him. Amir waited patiently for the huge man to pat him down before tilting his head towards the door. He entered through the black front doors, the sound level of the music was concerning. He could feel his heartbeat pounding loudly in his ears.

He followed the music through a hall and into the belly of the beast. He looked around, impressed by the pristine club. Black marble twinkled under the lights. Bodies moved to the music in some sort of summoning ritual. His eyes swept over the club, taking in every exit point, noticing the out-of-place stairway and white door that led to an upstairs portion.

Maybe a VIP area, Amir thought as he approached the bar hesitantly. Keeping an eye out for the Informant, Amir looked for any women sitting alone. He spotted a redhead by herself at the far side of the bar. Amir felt his heart leap when he looked at her. She caught his eyes in an enticing smile. Amir smiled back and made his way to her.

"Hey, stranger," she sang as she sipped her colourful drink.

"Hello, it's so nice to finally meet you," Amir held his hand out. The woman raised an eyebrow, shaking his hand elegantly.

"You've waited a long time, eh?" she responded, her eyes full of mirth.

Amir took a seat next to her, his heart beating loudly, but he couldn't tell if it was from the music or the fact that Helen was here in front of him!

"I'm so glad we're meeting tonight, Helen," Amir ranted, his smile infectious, but it dropped as soon as he saw her face twist in disgust.

"Helen? At least ask my name before you get it wrong!" she yelled, leaving in a fury.

"What did I say?" Amir asked, turning to watch her leave. His eyes landed on the stool next to him, a familiar woman wearing a leather jacket.

"Hey, Handsome!" Parris greeted with a grin. Amir looked away, his face hot with embarrassment. He could picture her smile, mocking him.

"Oi, Lorenzo!" she called out to the bartender. "Get this fine man a drink!"

The man named Lorenzo appeared instantly, hands at the ready. Amir looked around the bar for any woman sitting alone. But there were none.

"Your poison?" Parris temptingly asked.

"I'm not here to talk to you," Amir spat at her.

Where are you? – Amir

Did she leave when she saw the Informant next to me? He thought, dread gripped his chest. *Was she even going to come?*

His phone vibrated; his eyes read over the message in horror. He slowly turned to the Informant as she waved her phone at him, her screen displaying the same message that Helen had sent.

Hey, Handsome! – Helen

Parris leaned in close to him, Amir too dumbfounded to move, to run for the hills, to ask the earth to cover him. His heart shattered as she laughed a little, her dark eyes shimmered.

"About that free drink, I owe you!" Parris grinned. "Let's take it upstairs in my office, Officer Amir Hafiz."

CHAPTER TWELVE

Clueless

*O*f *course, it would have been too good to be true.* Amir kicked himself for being so naïve to accept Helen at face value.

In retrospect, he was a fool for being so swayed by convenient emails and a few weeks of texting. Amir was easy to play, and Parris played him like an elementary school recorder.

At the end of the day, he only had himself to blame.

Amir begrudgingly followed the Informant up the ominous stairs and through the white door. Once inside, his eyebrows shot up in surprise at the hidden office.

The checkered floor, a bold low red couch, and the white marbled desk suited the Informant. She shed her leather jacket, throwing it across the desk. Amir noticed a few bruises that littered Parris's upper arm. She didn't try to hide them, wearing a black tank top and jeans, leaning against her desk. He followed behind her. Shame, anger, and humiliation ate at his heart.

"Take a seat." She pointed to the couch. He remained rooted in the middle of the room, his hands balled into fists. Parris sighed dramatically.

The white door opened; Lorenzo entered carrying a vast array of drinks on a tray, setting it down on the low coffee table in front of the red couch. He left without a word.

Parris walked past Amir, helping herself to a coffee and adding milk until it matched the colour of her skin.

"Why?" Amir finally growled through closed teeth, his eyes tracking her movements.

"Be more specific, Handsome." She sipped her coffee loudly.

"Why help me?"

Parris took a seat on the couch, gesturing with her cup towards the other end. Amir refused to move. She rolled her eyes tiredly.

"You'll want to take a seat, it's a long story."

Instead, he grabbed the office chair from behind her marble desk, taking a seat directly in front of the Informant with a scowl. His green eyes narrowed at her.

"Talk."

"Help yourself to something first; I am a good host, after all."

Amir grabbed a bottle of beer, eyeing it suspiciously. Parris sighed again; she grabbed the bottle from him and took a swig. She made a face as she returned the bottle to him. Amir was surprised by the human reaction to the alcohol, as though the Informant was capable of being a normal human being and not just an Untouchable.

"I hate the taste of alcohol," Parris mumbled as she drank more of her coffee to chase the flavour. "I never understood the desire to relinquish one's control over themselves."

"I'm not here to be your drinking buddy, Parris," Amir commented. "I want answers. Now. Why did you pretend to be Helen?"

She leaned back into the plush red couch, her eyes dancing with secrets. "I was Helen because I needed a link to you, Amir."

"Why?" Amir growled, finally taking a swig of the beer. "What do you want from me?"

"Do you know about Ciel's Re-Pavement Project?" Parris leaned forward, smirking. "It's a huge construction deal to re-pave the entirety of Ciel's downtown core, all the way to the docks. It's the biggest job Ciel's construction industry has ever seen. Millions upon millions of dollars are poured into the Project, ripe for the Syndicates to grab a chunk. But the Gates' shell corporation, the Ciel Construction Company, lost the bid for the Project."

"What does this have to do with me or Helen?" Amir interrupted.

"Everything!" She beamed at him. "If the CCC won the bid, they would have bought labour from the Wings, which would fuel the city's underground markets and auctions."

Amir nodded, albeit taken aback by the cheery attitude she had when discussing such horrible things.

"The Halos also rolled out their latest creation, Cloud 9. Cloud 9 makes the user dependent after only a few uses, which leads the user to become desperate, since supply is so low. The more users dependent on the drug, the easier it would be for the Wings to get supply for the Gates' orders by trafficking more people…"

Parris smirked, never breaking eye contact with him.

"Do you understand, Amir? Everything and everyone in Ciel City are connected."

"But the CCC lost the bid," Amir remembered. He gripped his beer tighter, trying to understand the puzzle. She winked at him.

"They did. So where does that leave us? Come now, Amir. Think."

Amir searched his brain for an answer. The checkered floor that reminded him too much of a chessboard mocked him.

"The current order is in jeopardy."

By the Informant's reaction, he was right. A smile came his way, but this time there was a shine in her eyes.

"The current order is in jeopardy," she repeated.

"The current order that Giovanni Moretti designed is nearing a cliff. Giovanni's influence goes down without the Re-Pavement Project. The Wings and the Halos are getting angsty, pushing their luck, and treading on the Gates' turf, seeing if Giovanni still has the power to push back. If he can't keep the current order running, he'll be removed, and a war will ensue from the power vacuum."

Tony Moretti visited STK and attacked the students, Amir remembered.

"We're seeing it now with the Untouchables. Giovanni is losing his grip on keeping the Untouchables protected. If Giovanni can't keep the Untouchables protected, then he can't control the city. You've experienced it firsthand, Amir: Tony Moretti attacking STK students, *Fresh To Go* dealing *Cloud 9* to STK students."

"And you?" Amir asked, his gaze returning to her bruises. "I thought you were supposed to be Untouchable as well."

Parris set her empty mug on the table with a pout. "Aw, is someone worried about me?"

"No," Amir responded too quickly, "but if you're a stumbling block for the collapse of the Syndicates, then I need to utilize that."

She hummed as she leaned back against the couch, her smile no longer full of mirth.

Does she have someone who worries about her? Amir wondered. A tiny thorn of guilt pierced his lung. But he plucked it away quickly.

"Is that why you had me arrest you?" Amir continued, beginning to understand the puzzle. "To inspire others that you're not really Untouchable? That the Gates, Giovanni, were losing control?"

"Did you inspire others, though?" Parris asked mockingly.

"Yes!" Amir huffed. "I'll have you know some of the junior officers support me privately. One of them even helped me when investigating *Fresh To Go*."

The pair stared at one another.

"I wouldn't trust a soul in that division, Officer Amir Hafiz," Parris cautioned, her eyes refusing to depart from his. Amir broke eye contact first, taking a deep sip from the bottle.

Does that include Officer Sanchez? Amir thought depressingly, hating the way she made him second-guess himself so easily.

"I contacted you because you are an important piece, Amir," Parris praised; her face had a childlike glee with the way she vibrated with excitement. Amir sat upright, straighter from her demeanour.

"Just my luck that an out-of-town transfer would lead the Anti-Gang Task Force! Someone not bought out yet by any Syndicate, Officer Amir Hafiz, graduated top of his class at the academy—a perfect academic record, involved in the community, enjoys teaching kids self-defence on the weekends." Parris detailed his life.

"In top athletic shape, your favourite sport is volleyball. You enjoy quality time as a form of love. You must've been a heartthrob!"

"How do you know all of this—?"

"But it was your personal statement to the academy that convinced me that you would be the perfect fit for the role." Parris leaned forward.

"You wrote something along the lines of your younger sister disappearing when you were young. Your family, the whole town really, all went to look for her, but they never found her. Local law enforcement was too slow, not taking the issue seriously."

Amir's tanned face paled.

"Young Nour Hafiz was deemed missing at age eight. The town was unable to find a body, so the police deemed that she had run away of her own volition."

"Enough." Amir's chest shook. Parris stood up suddenly, causing Amir to flinch.

"But we both know that's not what happened," Parris continued. She poured herself another cup of coffee, adding milk to the black liquid.

"Havenbrooke is a boring town. Really, it's a miracle the teens haven't burned the town down in a blaze of fun!"

Amir watched her recount the horrific events as though they were discussing what to have for dinner.

"No, we know better. We know that sometimes kids would hop on the train into Ciel, hoping for something, whatever that something was. Or they were invited to Ciel, their bus tickets paid for by online strangers in private chat rooms. That's why you took the transfer, Handsome, keeping an eye out for girls with the same gorgeous eyes as you?"

Amir grabbed Parris by her wrist. His hand wrapped around her wrist completely. The coffee mug shook. She raised her gaze to his green eyes.

"Careful, now."

"Do you—" Amir's voice caught in his throat, but he spoke over the lump of cotton. Amir's grip did not loosen, but he didn't hurt her.

"Do you know where Nour is?"

"I'm sorry, Amir," Parris answered, "I looked for her, but I couldn't find Nour. It happened too long ago, before my time. But if she did come to Ciel, then I can guarantee that she was a victim of grooming and trafficking. I don't know where she is now, if she's even alive."

His grip tightened.

"Are you going to hit me now?" Parris asked instinctively, not trying to escape from his wrath. Amir released her instantly.

"You've been hurt enough, Parris."

He sat in his chair with a puff, chugging the rest of his beer, a defeated expression resting on his face. His little spark of hope for Nour extinguished before it could even dance to life.

What was the point in taking the transfer then? Was coming to Ciel pointless in the end?

"Why look for Nour?"

Parris handed him another beer, and he took it silently. She returned to her spot on the couch.

"I know what it's like to lose someone without closure." Parris held her mug out. Amir leaned forward, clinking the green glass with the mug.

"To those who we've lost."

The pair sat in silence, drinking their preferred beverages. There was no need to fill the silence. Amir was comfortable sitting there and mourning for Nour with Parris. Nour's cross sat heavily around his neck.

The music from the club did not reach into the office. Rather, the checkered space was its own bubble, one that the outside world could not touch.

"You've still not answered my question," Amir said after finishing his second bottle. "Why are you doing all this? What do you get out of this?"

Parris gave him a sharp look, as though he wasn't ready for what he was about to hear. She indulged him with an answer.

"I get to have revenge for someone dear to me, Amir. I get the pleasure of dousing this shithole in gas and then lighting it myself. I get the peace of avenging a childhood stolen from an innocent girl. I will achieve justice, that's what I get out of this."

"Justice and vengeance are not the same thing, Parris," Amir wisely advised.

Parris smiled, a brief sadness dancing across her dark eyes, as though she knew he was right but she was too far gone to think anything different.

"Next question, Handsome!"

Amir set the empty bottle on the table, his mind raced with questions. Which should he ask?

Should I ask her about the suicide at STK? Or maybe I should ask about how all the Untouchables were made?

"Parris…"

She hummed.

"Are you still going to help me as Helen, or whatever I should call you? Are you still going to help me bring down the Syndicates?"

A few moments passed. Amir was going to take her silence as an answer that tonight would be the last time they ever spoke, that after tonight, Amir would truly be on his own.

"I will work on my own plan," her words measured carefully, standing up. "I will give you instructions when the time comes."

"No," Amir followed her, "I won't be a pawn for you to play with. I want an honest answer. I still need your help. If I can't save Nour then I can still save others."

Parris laughed aloud, her eyes squeezing shut as she fought the fit of laughter. Amir narrowed his eyebrows.

"Oh, you're not a pawn, Amir!" she exclaimed as her laughter subsided. "No, no, you're my Queen! After all, it all depends on you."

Marcel's dark blue sports car sped through Ciel, music blasting through the speakers. The city's nightlife vibrated in the Downtown Core. Young women in revealing clothing flocked together for warmth as they waited in line for the clubs. Men smoked, not hiding their hungry stares at the women. A bridal party surrounded a woman wearing all white as she emptied the contents of her stomach onto the sidewalk.

All was well and good.

Tony whistled as they slowed down near the black building, looking at the feast just waiting to enter the club.

Clueless.

"I don't know man," Tony drooled over the women. "Maybe I'll take one or two home with me after our meeting."

Marcel laughed as he parked the car, also enjoying the sights. He nudged his friend. "Ready?" A devious glint in Tony's eyes was the only answer Marcel needed.

"You know you're my only ally in this city, don't you?" Tony lit a cigarette gingerly. Marcel spared Tony a look, crossing the street towards the club.

"Yeah, man…"

"My only friend in this hell?"

"Tony?" Marcel asked.

"Thanks for looking out for me, Marce," Tony stomped out the butt and led the way to the front of the line.

"We could catch a lot of product here," Tony commented, changing the subject.

Marcel hummed in agreement. "Slip a little something in their drink, take them to the motel, sell them to the Gates' stores, make a profit."

They stopped in front of a giant bouncer. He easily towered over the pair of already tall men.

"There's the line," the bouncer huffed, irritated.

"Tell your boss that the Wings are here," Marcel instructed, slipping the intimidating man a brown bill. The bouncer threw the money away.

"She's not seeing any Wings," he responded, pointing at Tony. "Especially this one."

"Listen here—" Tony started, but Marcel stepped between them.

"I understand that we're here without a meeting, but the issue is urgent," Marcel spoke diplomatically. "Ask her if we could come in. Out of respect for your place of work, we wanted to walk in through the front door." Marcel took a step closer. "We could have easily entered through the side door and caused a scene. But here we are. So ask her if we can come in."

The bouncer looked surprised at the reasonable attitude Marcel adopted. He signalled for the doorman to take his spot, leaving the Wings as he made a phone call.

"How dare he…" Tony glared at the man.

"It's okay," Marcel reassured. "Remember to keep your cool. At least until we're inside."

A few moments later, the bouncer returned, lifting the rope up, allowing the Wings entrance. Marcel smirked as they stepped through the metal detector, beeping dramatically as both he and Tony crossed the threshold.

"Please follow me, sirs," a man wearing a bartender outfit greeted them, a stoic expression on his young face.

The pair followed him through the hallway and into the club, Tony's usual temptations no longer distracting him as he saw the white door. Marcel's eyes darted over the staff of *Clueless*. He couldn't help but smirk with realization.

The bartender knocked on the white door before holding it open for the Wings to enter. Parris sat behind her desk, wearing her leather jacket, typing away on her laptop.

"The Wings, Ms. Parris."

She continued typing, completely ignoring Marcel and Tony. She wasn't alone in the room. Two men, both beefy and tall, stood at each end of the marble desk.

"Thank you, Lorenzo," she called out, her focus still on her computer. Lorenzo did a little bow, turning to leave, but Marcel clapped a hand on his shoulder.

"Oh, Lorenzo, I remember now!" Marcel exclaimed, his grin widened when he saw Parris look up at him.

Bingo, Marcel thought.

"We sold you this one, right? He was the first buy you made from us." Marcel felt the way Lorenzo stiffened under his hand. Tony took a seat on the red couch, ready for the show.

"You taught him English and everything, Parris. Impressive! I was ready to sell him out west to a farm for labour."

Lorenzo began to shake under Marcel's grip.

"And here I thought you were a cannibal, given how frequently you bought from us. Guess I shouldn't be surprised, given that I counted seven of your staff being products the Wings sold you." Marcel continued.

Needing a reaction from her.

"So, Lorenzo, tell us what the infamous Informant has you do for her since you're the oldest product she has."

We need to get under her skin first, Marcel strategized. *We need to beat her to the mind games.*

Lorenzo stayed silent, staring at the floor in an effort to control his emotions, his stoic mask slipping.

Parris stared at Marcel blankly.

"Does she ask you to cook all the little kiddies she buys? Or, maybe she eats you? Is that it? Are you her boy toy for all those lonely nights? Is she the kinky type? Answer Lo—"

"If you came here to harass my staff and to bore me, then you can take your leave now," Parris called out, bored.

The sound of typing resumed. Marcel scoffed, pushing Lorenzo away, approaching the desk. The Wings had agreed that Marcel was to do all of the talking while Tony enjoyed the show.

"Why the extra muscle, Parris?" he asked, looking at the beefcakes. "Is someone afraid of something?"

Parris closed her laptop shut with a snap, finally giving the Wing her attention. A forced smile graced her features. Marcel could see her irritation.

"If you're hoping for a power trip, you won't get it here, Marcel."

Tony howled out a laugh, startling Lorenzo, who was still frozen. He called out from his place on the couch.

"She's afraid to be alone with us, Marce! Poor baby's worried that something might happen!"

Snickering, Marcel leaned on the marble desk. "Is that true? We very well can't have a private conversation with these men in the room, wouldn't you agree? As an Informant, you must value secrecy and privacy above all else."

"If she needs someone to be her support animal," Tony called out, inspecting the cart of alcohol beside the couch, "have the Latino stay while the jocks leave."

"Great idea, Tony!" Marcel called back, enjoying the dirty look she sent to Tony. "Come here, Lorenzo, stand behind your boss."

The two guards looked at Parris, waiting for her instruction. She pointed to the white door; the two men took their leave as Lorenzo stood behind her.

"You didn't say she was so obedient, Tony!" Marcel remarked. "You think she might perform a trick if I asked?"

Tony laughed, pouring himself a generous drink.

"You two trying out a new routine or something?" Parris stood up, hating the way Marcel looked down at her. Marcel retreated from the desk, joining Tony on the couch. Sitting with a heavy sigh, he rested his head on the back of the couch.

"Won't you join us, Parris?" Marcel invited, patting the empty spot between him and Tony.

"If you want to talk to me, then he needs to leave," she pointed at Tony.

"Shut up, bitch!" Tony spat back.

Parris scowled. "If this was a social call, then both of you leave; if this is business, then the puppy leaves."

Tony shot up off the couch, rushing towards the Informant. "Take that jacket off, let's see how those bruises look," Tony snapped back, "I should make new ones that are harder to hide."

She laughed in his face.

"Physical violence comes so easily to the Morettis!" she exclaimed, Tony's face red. "So quick to yip like a dog and then run home with your tail between your legs."

"ENOUGH!" Marcel hollered from his place on the couch. "We're not here to fight, Parris. Tony, have another drink, man."

Tony spat on the white desk before returning to the red couch, downing the rest of his drink and starting to drink from the bottle.

"We're here to give you an opportunity," Marcel continued.

"An opportunity?" she repeated. Lorenzo wiped the desk back into its pristine shape.

"The Wings are going to usurp the Gates," Marcel explained. "The old man is losing it. He lost the Re-Pavement Project. He's asking for another Untouchable. He's losing his grip on the city and it's about time new blood takes it over. We're offering you a chance to keep your protection. As valuable of an asset you are to whoever you choose to side with, you're also dangerous. There will be a bounty on your head once Giovanni is out of the picture."

"Another Moretti in charge?" she made her way to stand in front of the Wings. "What makes you think I want him in charge?"

"Because I know you," Tony spat. "I know who you *really* are, who you went to school with, who you care about. You will fall into place or the Wings will target them."

She smirked at the Head. "You don't know shit."

Tony laughed, "I met a pretty young girl called Angela. Gave her a gun and everything." He paused, waiting for her reaction.

"And?" Parris shrugged, inspecting her nails. Marcel looked at his friend desperately. Tony continued.

"I also met the pending Untouchable—"

"Theo Grayson? I met him, too; Giovanni actually introduced us," Parris cut him off, picking at her nails. "Anything else?"

Marcel shot up out of his seat. *She doesn't care? But Tony said she would care.*

"Hold on, you're not fooling anyone," Marcel tried to reason with her, "These are all kids from STK who happen to know you and you happen to have helped them somehow. Parris, darling, don't think you can fool us. You care about them."

Their grip over the conversation, over the control of information, over the *power* was slipping from their hands and into hers.

Her eyes met Marcel's in a pleased look; he paled at her.

"Don't tell me you came all the way here and made this huge fuss over information you didn't even fact-check?" she asked.

Marcel spun around to look at Tony, who was holding the bottle dumbly. He turned back to the Informant.

"Marcel, darling," she sang sweetly, "don't think you can fool me."

"B-But Janine Johnston, her death was your fault. You pushed her from the roof—" Tony started.

"What did Tony tell you, Marcel?" Parris asked the executive, taking a step closer, all her attention only on Marcel. "Did he tell you that he had dirt on me? That he could control one Untouchable and then have me rat out the old man? That I would guarantee the Wings a smooth rise to the top? Did he promise you that I would bend to your will easily?"

Tony slammed the bottle on the floor, glass flying across the checkered tiles. The smell of alcohol flooded the office.

"YOU'RE NOT GOING TO TRICK US, BITCH! DON'T ACT LIKE YOU DIDN'T BREAK DOWN AT THE MENTION OF JANINE! HE'LL REPLACE YOU LIKE HE REPLACED ME!" Tony shrieked, rushing to her side, his hand going to grab the Informant. Marcel caught the hand before it landed.

"Calm down, man," Marcel whispered. He noticed the way the Informant moved, how her hand went to her waistband.

Bitch was ready to shoot him, Marcel thought as Tony relaxed in his grip.

"Let's have a civil chat, Marcel," Parris invited, opening the white door, the ear-piercing music flooding into the office. She held the door expectantly, as though she knew Marcel would agree.

"No," Tony huffed, but Marcel guided him towards the door.

"We agreed that I would do the talking," Marcel whispered into Tony's ear. "I'll fill you in once I'm done."

Tony looked into his eyes, a swirl of emotion behind the intense blue eyes.

"You better, Marce."

The white door shut, plunging the office into complete silence, soundproof once again. Lorenzo got to work cleaning the alcohol and glass from the floor. Parris took a seat on her red couch, gazing at the executive.

"Isn't this better?" she asked in a relaxed tone, propping her feet up on the coffee table. Marcel stood by the door, thinking of his options, thinking of how he would regain control over the situation.

"You didn't mention the Halos," Parris sang. "I wonder what your boss has in store for them."

"The Halos will operate as normal," Marcel replied quickly. Her smile widened.

"I wonder if Huifen knows about this…"

"Tiffany knows."

"She knows that you're going to go after Giovanni instead of Tony?" Parris pressed back. "You see how he is. He wouldn't be able to control Ciel's underground for a day before he's killed. The only reason he's still alive right now is because he's an Untouchable. Besides, we all know that you would be a better Head."

Marcel clenched his fist, not wanting to show his dissatisfaction with Tony's behaviour.

"You can't play both sides, Marcel."

The sound of glass being swept filled the air.

"How did you know about Tiffany and me?" he asked begrudgingly. Parris tapped away on her phone, already disinterested in the conversation.

"I'm an Informant, how do you think I gather my intel?"

Marcel took a heavy seat on the other end of the couch, slumping forwards, his head in his hands.

"Shit if I know, probably paying a few people on the payroll. Paying the homeless to watch certain people, shit like that," Marcel guessed.

Parris answered without looking at him. "With the rise in the cost of living, you'd be surprised just how easily people can be bought to tell me the little things—who didn't show up to the office, how the mayor needed to be picked up from a mob lounge, lists of new hires in the police force. Homeless people begging where I tell them, too. I'm constantly absorbing information: news articles, online forums, comments on the dark web. It's a full-time job. During my early years, I spent a lot of time at underground clinics; you would be surprised by the things mobsters would tell you while high on morphine."

She continued tapping away on her phone. "Plus, it wasn't hard to figure out. You both were eye-fucking one another at the meetings."

"So what now?" She set her phone down, giving him her full attention. "You came to my club, made a huge show, trusted Tony to a fault, and now here you are, feeling betrayed by your friend, feeling frustrated that he promised *so* much and that he would deliver this time, only to be the one to pick up after him," she delighted in the way Marcel scowled.

"You now know how Giovanni feels about him. So much promise, but no drive to seek it."

"He said you lost your cool when he brought up that high school chick, that it was different this time. He said that he had triggered you with Janine," Marcel tried to counter back, however weak.

Parris shrugged. "He lied to you, Marcel. He's been following me all over the place. It's annoying, really. He made up little schemes that I was brewing when the biggest threat to him was in bed with the Halos this whole time."

Lorenzo resumed his position behind the marble desk. The floor was spotless.

"So, which will it be, Marcel?" she asked, her dark eyes solely focused on the executive. "Who will you betray? Your lover? Or your childhood friend?"

Marcel could not answer. Instead, he marched to the door with his head down-casted, his eyebrows drawn in. His hand hovered over the handle. He looked over his slumped shoulder at Parris, as though he wanted to swear at her, to curse her. He couldn't help but entertain her words—if he was the Head of the Wings, not having to babysit Tony anymore, to get the respect he deserved.

"Oh one last thing, Marcel," Parris sang. "You could have done it without Tony, the Wings. Be the Head of a powerful syndicate; you never needed Tony to begin with."

Stiffly, Marcel nodded. He left without a word, letting the music consume him as he found Tony by the bar, knocking back shots with two girls. Marcel looked up at the opaque glass, knowing that the Informant was behind it, laughing as she looked down at him.

"Are you alright, Lorenzo?" Parris asked as Lorenzo locked the white door. He sighed as he took Marcel's spot on the couch.

"I didn't expect him to remember me or the others, it's been so long."

Parris hummed as she tapped away on her phone. "Tony wouldn't remember, since he doesn't have a direct hand in the trafficking, but Marcel is clever. He would be a threat if he ever took over the Wings."

Lorenzo rubbed his eyes, trying to keep the pain of the years at bay.

"Huifen!" the Informant sang as the Head of the Halos answered. "Where have you been, girlfriend? We need to meet up and catch up!"

"Shut the hell up!" Huifen cursed into the phone.

"You're so mean to me!" pouted Parris.

The predictable "What do you want?!" echoed from the phone. Parris gave Lorenzo a wink as she propped her feet up on the low coffee table.

"Since the Wings were just here harassing me for one reason or another, I just wanted to know if you wanted something from me as well!"

Huifen remained quiet.

"By Wings, I should clarify," Parris continued. "Marcel was here, talking about the Wings usurping the Gates… Not sure if we need to have a conversation about that now."

"Are they still there?" Huifen asked. Parris skipped to the window, looking out to find Marcel dragging Tony and two unfortunate girls towards the exit.

"Lucky you, I have an opening tonight! Come, I'll even show you where I keep my secret knife hidden in my office."

Gleefully, she hung up the phone on the other woman.

I'm checking out a lead, 'Helen.' A few teens have been reported missing, one of them was last seen at a bar called the Loose Screw. – Amir

Parris groaned loudly.

"Another latte?" Lorenzo deciphered the groan.

"Make it a double. My Handsome man is causing trouble tonight," Parris replied, chewing her lip.

"What is he doing?" Lorenzo asked, clutching the door handle.

"Chess pieces do not move on their own. He's going to hit one of mine."

The chimes of bells rang as Amir pushed into the *Loose Screw*. For the early hours of the morning, the bar was filled to the brim. The clients here had a stark difference from *Clueless*'s. The inner city's presence was seen in the way people acted.

The men were older, the drinks were cheaper, and the girls were far too young. He blended in well with his blue flannel and jeans. The nylon floors were sticky with spilled drinks and neglect.

Amir scowled at a man's possessive hold on a girl half his age. The man had a black ring on his pinky finger, which he used to trace patterns around the girl's green eyes. Amir wanted to gag at the sight. He pushed further into the bar, claiming a stool on the wooden countertop.

He had a clear view of the motel across the street. He could see the suite doors facing the bar.

Go home, Amir. There's no gang activity in the Loose Screw. – Helen

What's her deal? I thought the almighty Informant would be more helpful as Helen.

"What's your poison?" a rough voice called out. Amir nodded at the bartender, placing a purple bill on the watermarked countertop.

"One beer, please."

The bartender, who was a few years younger than Amir with a scruffy brown beard, smirked.

"I don't hear 'please' that often."

Did you leave yet? – Helen

"Is that so?" Amir asked with a smile, ignoring Parris. "Us Canadians are known to be polite and friendly."

The bartender gave a short laugh of his own. His sad blue eyes flickered to life briefly.

"Logan," he introduced himself, setting the green bottle down in front of Amir.

"Amir," Amir nodded back.

"You going to be a regular here, Amir?" Logan wiped down the counter. "I could use a friendly regular. Old Benny throws peanuts at me when he wants another drink."

Amir chuckled. Just as he was going to answer, his phone rang. He pulled it out, wide-eyed.

Helen was calling.

"Clingy girlfriend." Amir waved the phone at Logan.

"Godspeed," Logan sympathized.

Parris never called him. It must have been something important.

"Hello, Dear," Amir answered.

"Dear? At least buy a girl a coffee first," Parris bantered back.

"Oh, you!" He laughed loudly. Too loudly. Logan looked over, eyebrow raised. Amir gave him a thumbs-up, a cold sweat travelling down the back of his neck.

"Where are you, Amir?" Parris asked casually.

"At the *Loose Screw*."

"Leave now."

"It's just one drink, Dear," Amir replied slowly. Logan was watching him. "I promise to leave soon. Just… just taking a look around." He wasn't lying. He came to look for any suspicious activity and he'd seen at least ten health and safety violations since entering.

But alarm bells rang after he spoke with the parents of the missing girls. They mentioned that they had caught one of them sneaking off to meet the others here. There were no records of the *Loose Screw* at the CCPD. He had to investigate the bar; he owed it to those girls. His eyes travelled back to the motel across the street.

"Amir, you need to leave that bar. I don't need you there. I need my Queen on his spot," her voice deadly.

"Leave. Now."

"Why?" Amir asked. He could see two people head to the motel. It was the girl he had seen earlier with the gross older man around her. She drunkenly crossed the street, her feet dragged behind her.

"I don't have time for this, a client is coming now. You won't find anything at the *Loose Screw*. The most they do is serve minors," Worry underlined her tone, but Amir didn't notice, he was focused on the girl across the street.

Something's not right.

The instant her head lulled backwards, Amir pushed away from the bar.

"Amir—?"

He hung up the phone. Logan watched him race out the door of the *Loose Screw* and into the night. Amir ran across the street, hand flying to his gun. He banged on the motel room's door. His heart pounded loudly in his ears.

Never again. No more girls going missing. No more Nours!

The second the door opened, Amir rammed his shoulder in, gun raised. The girl was sprawled on the bed, in a state of undress and unconsciousness. Amir roared in anger.

"CCPD, hands in the air!"

Sunrise over Ciel was majestic, the sky painted in pinks and oranges.

This sunrise was sweeter than any other that Amir had the privilege of seeing. Victory filled his heart. His steps were lighter than they'd been in years.

Her parents were so happy to get her back, Amir thought with a sleepy smile. He yawned as he marched up to his apartment. He could deal with the CCPD later, with Captain Chan's glare, with whatever wrench he would try to throw into his investigation, with Officer Sanchez's endless questions.

The kid is safe. That's all that matters.

Unlocking the door, Amir kicked off his shoes. Shedding his clothing, he entered his humble home. The photo of Nour shone under the early sun. He closed the blinds, crawling under his blanket, his tired bones sighing.

He tossed around in his bed. His eyes begged for sleep, but his heart was restless. He pressed call before his mind could catch up with what he was doing in his stupor.

The call rang and rang and rang. The last ring before going to voicemail was when she answered.

"Hello?" Amir said in a quiet voice.

"Yes," came the curt reply from Parris.

"Hi… how are you?" Amir asked, slapping himself in the face.

What am I doing?

"Over the moon."

"Good, that's good," he mumbled, his hand resting on his chest, fidgeting with his cross. "The weather this morning was cold, wasn't it?"

"Did you really just call me to talk about the weather?" Parris asked in a tired voice.

Shit, it is early. Amir lamented as he checked the time.

"I-I don't know, I'm not sure why I called you."

"You're lonely," Parris understood. "Go find a pretty girl to warm your bed, Amir."

"I'm not the type. The first woman I bring to my bed will be my wife."

"And they say chivalry is dead."

She hadn't hung up the phone on him like he had imagined. Yes, they were talking about nothing. But they were still talking.

"What about you? Do you have someone to warm your bed?" Amir rested his hand across the empty pillow beside him, noticing just how cold it was.

"I don't have a bed."

Is she joking? I can't tell.

"I can buy you one."

Laughter rang across the phone. Not the laughter he heard when the Informant was mocking him, not her malicious giggles, but the real laugh he had got a glimpse of in the interrogation room. He smiled into the phone.

"What? I'll buy you one! It won't be the nicest but it'll be something. I'll even toss in a few pillows."

The sweet laughter subsided. He wondered if her eyes crinkled when she genuinely laughed, if she was the type to snort and be embarrassed about it. Parris recomposed herself on the other side.

"I needed that," she admitted.

"Where are you now?" he asked.

The city awakened outside. The construction would soon start. The daily chaos would arrive right on schedule. The symphony would begin playing.

"About to discuss my insurance with the Gates. My policy is almost up."

He sat up. The easy smile was gone, replaced with hard lines of worry on his tanned forehead.

"Parris."

"Amir."

"Are you safe—?"

"Don't call me again."

The call ended.

CHAPTER THIRTEEN

Happy Birthday

Electricity buzzed through STK as the school day came to a close. The volleyball team emerged through the main gates of the gothic school, excited for the weekend.

"Happy early Birthday, Theo!" Nathan called out. An echo of 'happy birthdays' followed as the team clapped a hand on Theo's shoulder. Theo smiled as he waved at his team as he entered the black car.

The Friday afternoon rush hour did not slow the car from weaving through the sea of traffic, rushing towards Old Town. With the weekend finally here, Theo's birthday was the next day. He bounced his knee impatiently, excited to see Giovanni.

He said he had a surprise for my birthday, he remembered as the car stopped in front of the red brick building. Theo made his way to the older man's office; the route became second nature to him.

His second home.

"Hey, boss!" he called out as soon as he walked into the polished office. Giovanni was lounging on the couch, drinking an espresso.

"*Cucciolo*," he warmly greeted back, kissing both cheeks. "Are you excited for your birthday?"

Theo grinned as he took a seat across from the man in one of the armchairs.

"Yes, I am! I got an A on my history assignment and we've been winning our games!" he exclaimed, a childlike smile on his face. "Life is good now!"

Giovanni chuckled at his enthusiasm. "I'm glad you're excited, *Cucciolo*. You deserve nothing but happiness, son."

Theo's ears turned red and he mumbled a thank you.

"I will be picking you up tonight for your birthday surprise," Giovanni instructed as he stood up, abandoning his cup on the table and readjusting his brown suit jacket. "You'll need an overnight bag, so just bring your essentials. I will buy anything you need or forget."

"Where are we going?" Theo asked as he helped himself to some sweets on the table. Giovanni ignored the question, focusing on the view out of his window, looking across his city.

The Stairway Tower watching the conversation unfold.

"There's been a change of plans, *Cucciolo*. The surprise will last longer than a night, so be aware that you will be missing a few days of school."

The comfortable mood in the office shifted. The sweet cookie turned into chalk in Theo's mouth. Theo stared at Giovanni's back, his mouth dry.

"But you said it was only for one night, why are you changing the plan—"

"Like I said," Giovanni spoke over him, "the trip will be running longer than expected." He turned to look at him, his eyes dancing with shadows.

"Not to worry, *Cucciolo*, you'll be back at STK and with your friends before you know it," the older man reassured as he gathered his coat.

An uneasy weight settled in the high schooler's chest. The mafia boss headed towards the door, ruffling Theo's hair on his way. "Now finish your schoolwork. The car will drive you home as usual. Be sure to be ready for eleven tonight."

With the quiet click of the door, Theo was left alone in the office.

He has a good reason for extending the surprise, Theo reasoned. *He always has a good reason.*

The hours went by quickly as Theo poured his focus into his homework, trying not to think of the birthday trip. He wiped the sweat from his forehead, feeling hot in the rather cool office. He felt like he was being watched, despite being alone. A loud knock from the office door startled him as he was told that the car was waiting to take him home. He took the usual path down the elevator and into the back seat of the car. As soon as he blinked, he had been transported from the CCC to his home.

The car dropped him by the curb of his home; nothing was out of the ordinary. Nothing was wrong, except Theo felt different. He felt like this would be the last time he would be dropped off at home. Theo hurried inside, the sun beginning to set. Up the stairs, locking the door once inside his bedroom, his chest tightened painfully once he was finally alone. He crumbled into a ball on the floor, his hands shaking violently.

No, not now, he thought as he tried to regain control of his breathing. *Why am I having a panic attack now? Nothing happened!*

Hot tears sped down his face. *Giovanni has never hurt me, he cares about me! We're probably just going to a cottage.*

A wave of nausea bubbled up his throat and he ran to the bathroom. He vomited into the bowl, gasping for air.

But he would never let you miss school, he argued with himself.

Suddenly the voice of the Informant echoed in his mind, a warning he had heard a lifetime ago when he had asked her if he was in trouble.

"You have no idea."

Theo groaned as he reached for his phone, hitting the call button before thinking his actions through.

"Did you take any pictures of the stash?" Angela asked from the couch, munching on a slice of Hawaiian pizza. Jaya nodded from her spot on the floor. The coffee table was littered with papers, pictures, and pizza.

The girls had been meeting when Raef was out dealing, trying to piece together all the evidence needed to give to Officer Hafiz. The pair had made good progress, Jaya taking pictures of Raef's stash, recording conversations, and keeping records of who he dealt with.

"He said that we'll hit another dealer for more fentanyl soon," Jaya mumbled, her mouth full.

"Then we need to call the police officer soon—"

Angela's phone rang loudly. Jaya saw the way her eyes widened at the screen before rushing to answer it.

"Theo?" she answered, her voice betraying her worry. Jaya motioned for her to put the call on speaker.

"Angie, please," Theo whispered into the phone, "Angie help me." Gooscbumps rose on Angela's arm, her pulse pounding in her ears. He sounded like he was crying.

"Theo, what's wrong?" Angela asked.

"I- He said he'll be taking me away for a while…"

"He?"

"Giovanni!"

"Giovanni said he's taking you away?"

"He said that it's a birthday surprise and that I'll miss school," Theo hiccupped between his words. "He's going to take me. I'm scared. I don't know why, but I'm scared."

"Theo, this is Jaya," Jaya said loudly, and her voice didn't shake like Angela's. "Theo, listen, Giovanni Moretti is the Head of the Gates, do not go with him anywhere!"

"He's coming tonight…"

The girls looked at one another horrified.

Be strong for him, he's calling you because things are serious! Angela reprimanded herself.

"Theo, send us your address, we will come to you!" Angela suggested.

The line was quiet. The girls waited for a response but heard the sound of Theo throwing up instead.

"It's going to be okay," Angela reassured. "Can you send us your address, we will be there soon."

"I need to go," Theo shifted suddenly.

"Send us the address!" Jaya reminded.

"I-I know, sorry… my dad just came home. I'll send it now."

The call ended.

The girls rushed into action, gathering their things and running out of the door. A sole text dinged in the silence.

The only lifeline they had to their friend.

Be there in five minutes, Cucciolo. – G

Theo felt his ribs dig into his lungs. He had his backpack filled with essentials, unsure what to bring. He marched down the stairs as quietly as possible. His dad watched T.V. at a deafening level. Theo turned the front doorknob quietly.

"Where are you going at this hour?" Roger called from the couch, slugging down another beer.

"Getting some air, I'll be back soon," Theo called out, already closing the door behind him. He texted Angela in a panic, waiting at the end of the driveway.

He's almost here. – Theo

Almost there. Stay inside! – Angela

Theo looked wildly around for a taxi, praying that his friends would pick him up first.

But what will Giovanni say when you're not here for him? A voice rang in his mind. Theo tried to reason with the voice. *He will understand that I got scared!*

No, he won't, the voice spat back. *He's been nothing but kind to you, giving you the loan, buying you gifts, watching your games. He's done more than Roger has ever done! Giovanni has never beaten you or embarrassed you in front of his friends! Why betray his trust now?!*

"No, I don't know..." Theo mumbled. He curled into a ball on the driveway, hugging his knees as he crouched down.

"Why are you down there, *Cucciolo*?" Giovanni asked, stepping out of the black car. Theo gasped, landing on his backside, not noticing the black car or the older man at all. Giovanni helped him up, his eyebrows drawn in a worried look.

"Are you alright? You're rather pale, *Cucciolo*."

Theo panted, unable to focus on anything but getting air into his lungs. Giovanni wrapped his arms around him, holding the boy tightly.

"It's alright, I'm here now, son."

The hug did little to comfort him. Theo tried to pull out of the embrace, his eyes blurry. Shades of Giovanni's emerald suit danced across his vision. Giovanni followed him, holding his face in his hands.

Wood and vanilla invaded his nose.

"Breathe, *Cucciolo*. You need to breathe."

The sound of the front door slamming shut refocused Theo's attention.

"Who the fuck is this?" Roger yelled as he stomped down the driveway.

"Dad, please calm down," Theo begged. His father was in a fury, almost within arms reach. His neck and face were red.

"So you've been whoring yourself out?" Roger spat at Theo, grabbing him by his varsity jacket's collar.

"No!" Theo pleaded, "No, Dad, I haven't!"

Spit flew onto Theo's face. "Don't lie, you little shit. This car has been here every fucking night!" Roger yelled.

The smell of beer was prominent.

"So this is how you got that money? Been showing this geezer a good time, eh?"

"No," Theo sobbed. "I did it for you!"

"Get inside the house, NOW!" Roger screamed at his son, raising his other hand, ready to strike.

In an instant, Giovanni grabbed Roger's hand in a death grip. Slowly twisting Roger's arm, he released his hold on Theo. Theo looked between the two of them; Giovanni towered over his father.

"Stop!" Theo yelled. "He'll hurt you!"

"Get inside the car, Theo, dear."

Roger thrashed in Giovanni's hold, trying to pry his arm away. Giovanni was relentless, his arm perfectly still as he looked down at the man with disgust.

"'Theo, dear?' Are you listening to this bullshit?" Roger shrieked at Theo, "GET INSIDE THE HOUSE NOW OR ELSE!"

"S-stop," Theo mumbled. His heart was in his throat as he watched his Dad's face contort in pain.

"Now, *Cucciolo*."

The sound of another car coming down the street caught Theo's attention. An orange and teal taxi appeared under the streetlights.

"YOU USELESS PIECE OF SHIT, YOU'VE ALWAYS BEEN TRASH!" Roger shouted as he lashed about. "NO MATTER HOW MANY BEATINGS YOU STILL TURNED OUT TO BE A WASTE OF SPACE! I'M GOING TO FUCKING KILL YOU—!"

Giovanni punched Roger. His face snapped violently to the side. The sick sound of cartilage breaking rang in Theo's ears. Roger crumbled to the driveway dramatically. Blood covered his face.

"I said *now*."

Giovanni grabbed Theo by his upper arm, pushing Theo into the back seat of the car. The taxi came to a stop behind the black car.

"THEO!" Angela shrieked as she ran out of the taxi. Giovanni slammed the door shut.

The black car was gone.

Angela ran back inside the taxi. "Follow that car!"

"Fuck no!" the taxi driver spat. "Get out! I'm not getting involved." Jaya threw the money at the driver with a curse. The taxi sped off, leaving the girls in front of Theo's home. Angela ran over to Roger, checking if he was still alive.

"What now?" Jaya yelled. "There are no taxis in this area!"

"Shit," Angela mumbled. Roger was knocked out, his nose broken, but he was still breathing. She knew Theo wouldn't forgive himself if Giovanni killed his dad.

"Where the hell is he taking him?" Jaya panicked. "How do we get to him? We don't have a car! FUCK!"

Angela gasped. Her hands flew to her phone wildly, searching for the contact. She hit the call button, her heart pounding loudly.

"Angie?" Logan answered. Noise from a bar echoed behind him. "You've never called before. Is everything—?"

"Logan!" Angela rattled. "Logan I need you to pick me up right now, my friends and I are in trouble. I need to get to *Clueless* right now!"

"*Clueless*?" Logan asked.

"Please, Lo!"

"I'm on my way, Angie."

The black car weaved through the downtown core, purposely driving in circles.

"Breathe." Giovanni rubbed Theo's back. The boy was heaving heavily, panic fully setting in on him.

He stood up to Dad! He even hit him! He hit him hard… is Dad okay?

There was blood! Theo pulled on his hair. Giovanni caught his wrists.

"My dad, you hurt my dad!" Theo couldn't meet Giovanni's eyes. "He was still on the ground and we left him there!" he yelled. His mind raced with images of his dad bloodied and unconscious on the ground.

Giovanni slapped Theo across the face.

Stunned, Theo looked at him with wide eyes. His face stung, but the sound of the slap silenced his thoughts, bringing his focus only on Giovanni.

"Enough. He was about to be violent with you, but I stopped him. Would you have rather he hit you? Beat you like he always does, Theo?"

Theo tried to look out the window, but Giovanni grabbed his face.

"Answer me."

"I-I don't know."

"Answer!"

"I don't know!" Theo cried, his tears never-ending.

Giovanni pushed him into his chest, shushing him. Theo screamed. He was conflicted about his father and wasn't sure whether he should feel relieved, angry, or grateful toward Giovanni. He was sick of the fear but his gut was telling him that he was not out of the woods yet, sick of the dread of eventually going back home to his dad.

Of the consequences.

"Help me... I'm so confused," Theo mumbled into Giovanni's dress shirt, wetting the fabric.

The Head hugged the boy, trapping him in his arms. Kissing the top of his head, he whispered.

"I can make all the pain and confusion go away, *Cucciolo.* Would you like that?"

Theo gripped the man tighter. Smirking, Giovanni called out to the driver.

"Take us to the hotel now."

Angela huffed as they carried Roger back into the home. She wrapped her arms around his torso, the stink of the man adding to her annoyance. Jaya struggled to carry his legs.

"Who the hell is Logan? And why are we going to *Clueless*? We need to be following Giovanni!" Jaya pestered Angela.

"Angie?" Jaya pressed again.

"Logan is a family friend," Angela answered with a grunt, dropping Roger on the couch. Surrounded by the beer bottles, he looked right at home.

"A family friend?" Jaya repeated.

"My sister's high school friend. He said if I ever needed a ride he would take me."

"Wait, the same friend you came to Ciel looking for?" Jaya tried to connect the pieces together.

Angela corrected her, "no, not the same friend. He's a different friend."

"So why are we going to *Clueless*?"

A honk took the girls' attention. Running out of the home, they saw there was a white truck at the end of the driveway. Logan was there, a focused look in his blue eyes.

"Explain on the way," Logan urged.

The girls jumped into the car. Angela explained everything about Theo and Giovanni's relationship to Logan, from the incident with Tony to Giovanni taking Theo tonight. Jaya pitched in when needed. For the most part, Logan was quiet, focused on driving above the speed limit into the downtown core. He was relieved that Angela had called him.

"Why do you need to go to *Clueless*?" Logan finally asked her as he parked near the black building. Jaya held her breath as she waited for the answer.

"Because," Angela explained, "the Informant is going to save Theo."

Angela crossed the street in a hurry. Cars screeched to a stop, honking madly at her.

"Wait!" Logan yelled out, crossing with Jaya in tow.

Angela ran to the side door, pulling it open. A victorious look decorated her face.

I can do it this time. I can see her! Angela thought triumphantly.

The club was alive with people and music. The bouncer was taken aback by seeing a teenager. He tried to grab Angela but she ducked under his reach, pushing past a waitress as she ran up the stairs to the white door.

"Hey!" the waitress yelled. Her tray of drinks sprayed across the marble floor. Jaya and Logan also rushed in. The bouncer successfully grabbed Jaya.

"What is going on?!" the bouncer shouted.

Jaya squirmed in his grip, trying to escape. The bouncer tightened his grip on her arm. Jaya called out in pain. Logan punched him, a deep scowl on his face.

Some clubbers yelled as they backed away from them. Jaya fell to the floor, climbing the stairs on all fours.

Angela slammed the white door open, her eyes landing on the Informant seated behind her desk. Lorenzo hovered just over her shoulders. Jaya and Logan finally entered the office in a pant. Jaya slammed the door shut and locked it.

With a tilt of her head, Parris asked, "To what do I owe this pleasure?"

Pounding came from the door. Lorenzo rushed to open it. The bouncer entered the office, blood pouring from his split lip.

"Ms. Parris, they rushed into the club. I'll take them out now," he huffed. He grabbed Logan by his collar.

"No need," Parris called out cheerily. "Sorry for the trouble!"

The bouncer gave Logan a dirty look as he left.

The office fell into silence. Parris smiled at her guests, her eyes narrowed at Angela.

"Like I said, to what do I owe—"

"Theo Grayson was just taken by Giovanni Moretti," Angela cut Parris off. She stepped in front of the marble desk. "Giovanni said that he would be taking him away for a few days."

Parris's gaze flicked to Logan and then back to Angela. "You just don't learn…"

"Save Theo," Angela demanded. "Bring him back and clear his debt to the Gates."

Both Jaya and Logan stiffened at the tone of Angela's demand. No one ordered the Informant around. Parris sized the girl, her eyes locking onto her determined look.

"Angela, that's not how she works," Jaya whispered from behind. "You don't want to be indebted to her."

"It won't cost me a thing!" Angela spat. Hatred and malice swirled in her mature eyes. "Isn't that right, 'Parris'?"

The Informant leaned back in her chair, amused. Her dark eyes snapped to Logan.

"What do you think, Logan? I assume you're the one who brought Angie here."

"You heard her," mumbled Logan, turned away from the Informant, not able to meet her eyes.

Parris laughed.

"Sorry, but to retrieve the boy from Giovanni would put me in an uncomfortable position," Parris sang. "After all, he's safest with

Giovanni."

"Safe?" Angela shouted. "He's been abducted, you Parrasite!"

"Watch your tone!" Lorenzo yelled back, his neutral expression gone. Jaya jumped at his outburst.

"None of you have the right to barge in here and make such demands of Ms. Parris!" Lorenzo's voice rang in the office, hands clenched into fists.

"Calm down, Lorenzo."

Parris was fixated on Angela. Her voice was levelled, but Lorenzo could tell that the name got to her, the insult that Logan so easily called her, now used by Angela.

"Please. Please save him…" came a quieter sound from Angela.

"Save him for my sister."

––––––––––––––––––––

Theo could not remember the trip from the car to the hotel. He felt lightheaded from crying and the panic attacks. Giovanni had draped his arm across his shoulders and led the way, Theo following silently. They stepped out of the elevator once on the top floor of the hotel. There were two men dressed in suits stationed outside of the hotel room, members of the Gates. They bowed their heads as the pair entered the room.

The room was grand and extravagant. White, black, and gold décor filled the space, transferring them into a palace of sorts. Theo tried to detach from Giovanni but the man crowded his space.

"Come here, *Cucciolo*." He whispered as he led Theo to the lush couch. Theo rubbed his eyes as Giovanni shed his coat and suit jacket, throwing the items across an armchair. The Head went to the impressive bar, pulling glasses and pouring brown liquid into them. Theo looked around; there was only one bed at the far end of the room. Panic hugged his heart as he felt around his pockets, afraid of the messages from his father. He patted his jacket pocket, but nothing was there.

"Where's my phone?"

"You won't need it."

Theo's head was pounding, a severe headache from all the crying and panic finally setting in. Giovanni returned to his side with two glasses. Theo took the one that was being offered to him.

"It will help you relax, *Cucciolo,*" Giovanni promised, raising his glass for a toast.

The chime from a grandfather clock sang. The clock struck midnight.

"Happy Birthday, *Cucciolo,*" Giovanni cheered, clinking the glasses together.

Theo followed his lead. He brought the glass to his lips, drinking the strong liquid. He coughed, lowering the drink, but Giovanni lifted the bottom of his glass, forcing him to drink it all. Theo coughed violently, his throat burning and his eyes stinging.

The Head shushed him as he rubbed circles on his knee. Theo stood up, rushing to the washroom, but Giovanni caught him by the door.

"It's a sin to waste good bourbon," he whispered hotly into Theo's ear, pulling him back to the couch. Theo grumbled as Giovanni took off his blue and white varsity jacket, tossing it away.

"I feel weird, Giovanni…" Theo mumbled, his vision becoming blurry.

Fear flooded Theo's senses, but he couldn't move. His limbs felt heavy. His throat was too dry to cry for help. Theo felt another glass shoved into his face; he grabbed Giovanni's wrist, but he had no strength to stop him. Giovanni pinched his nose, ensuring he drank the whole thing. Some of the bourbon spilled down his chin, but Giovanni pushed it back into the high schooler's mouth with his thumb.

"Be good for me," Giovanni breathed as he pushed his thumb into Theo's mouth, causing the boy to gag. The older man chuckled as he pushed Theo down on the couch, his rough hand wandering over his body. Theo tried to bite down, but he was too weak. He couldn't struggle against him.

He gasped for air when Giovanni let up, but was nauseous when the older man kissed him. The room was spinning. His body and mind worked against one another.

"N-No," Theo groaned.

"Shh, Tony was never good at this, but I'm certain you will be."

Tears sped down Theo's face. His heart sank into a dark pit. He hated the feeling of being weak, the feeling of Giovanni's hands on him.

Loud knocking came from the door. Giovanni cursed, calling for them to come in. One of the guards from outside was holding a phone; he was afraid about knocking at such a time. Theo prayed that the guard would help.

That anyone would help.

"S-Sorry, Boss, but it's the Informant!" the Guard stuttered. "She says that she needs to speak to you now… that it's an emergency!"

The office was dead silent as Parris stood by the opaque window with her phone to her ear. Angela strained to hear but Parris had lowered the volume to where only she could hear the conversation.

After she had asked her to save Theo, the Informant's entire demeanour changed. She wasn't smiling. Her eyes were not dancing with calculations. Her shoulders were tense.

She looked raw.

"Boss!" she sang into the phone. Her tone did not match her expression. "Yes, I know you were busy but an emergency has come up, you see!"

Everyone in the office tensed, waiting to see if she could really save Theo. Logan stared at her back from his seat on the couch. He had his hands clasped together, as though he were praying. Jaya stood by Angela, in disbelief that the Informant had actually listened to her.

Why did she listen to Angela? Jaya wondered. *Who is Angie's sister to Parris?*

Parris saw them in the reflection of the glass.

"There's a missing boy by the name of Theo Grayson. It's a top priority to find him!"

"Is this a joke, *Bella*?" Giovanni growled into the phone. She knew they couldn't hear the conversation, but she measured her words carefully.

"Not a joke, boss. I'm being the most serious I've been in a while."

"I'm hanging up."

"Before you do!" she sang. "I would ask you to leave that boy alone. I can already tell I called at a good time."

Giovanni huffed in annoyance. "'Leave him alone'? Are you telling me what to do?"

"Never, Boss! But I would like to take that boy back and erase his debt to you."

Angela held her breath.

"In exchange for what?" Giovanni demanded.

A sad smile tugged at Parris's lips, "For what you've always wanted."

Giovanni looked at Theo's sleeping form on the couch—the boy he was most excited to take away, to shape and mould, to destroy. But he didn't hold a light compared to *her*.

"You'll take his place tonight, *Bella*. I'll send the address. You will meet me at the Mount Royal Hotel."

The line cut.

Parris turned towards the group, expressionless. She looked at the people in her office. Each one of them hated her for one reason or another. Jaya for forcing her to be her informant, Logan for abandoning him, and Angela…

Janine.

Her trademark smile resumed.

"Go pick him up."

She sent Jaya the address she received from Giovanni. Jaya's eyes widened as she showed Angela the text.

"What did he ask of you?" Logan asked.

Parris ignored him as she returned to her desk, writing on a piece of paper, handing it to Lorenzo with a knowing look. Lorenzo took the list with shaking hands but promptly left the office through a back door.

"You're free to leave and to never come back!" Parris called out cheerfully, tapping away on her phone. Jaya rushed to the door with Angela behind her; the ear-piercing music flooded the office, but Logan was still staring at the Informant.

"What are you exchanging for the kid?" Logan asked again, his eyes focused on her back. He took a step closer to her.

"You're scared—" he started, but Angela's head popped back into the office.

"Logan!" Angela called out, desperate to get Theo back.

The man gave Parris a final look over before he left with the girls, heading to the hotel to pick up Theo.

A piece of himself was left behind in that checkerboard office.

Parris strutted into the Mount Royal Hotel, Ciel's finest. Her heels clacked on the polished marble floor as she entered the elevator. She caught her reflection in the mirror: her hair raised into an elegant bun, a stylish jumpsuit draped over her body, her nails done, and heavy makeup that made her look more 'attractive'.

She didn't look like herself.

Her hand trembled as the elevator did not stop at any other floor. She gripped her purse tighter in an effort to calm her nerves. The door opened with a ding at the top floor. She stepped out, finding two guards standing outside of the hotel room. They silently let her in.

She stepped into the threshold.

Giovanni was seated in a plush armchair, dressed in a wine-coloured bathrobe, drinking a generous glass of whiskey. The room was similar to the hotel he had brought Theo to: marble encasings and gold accents that intimidated the guests, an impressive sitting area with a T.V. mounted to the wall, and a king-sized bed stationed at the ready just beyond the sitting area. Parris stepped into the middle of the room. Giovanni studied her over the rim of the glass.

"A small part of me thought you wouldn't show."

Parris tiredly gestured to herself. "Here I am."

"Here you are," he growled like an animal who finally caught their prey.

Parris refused to make eye contact with the older man. Giovanni's eyes lingered on the deep plunge of the Informant's jumpsuit. It had been nearly nine years since he saw her in anything other than that old leather jacket. His eyes hungrily drank the sights of her well-hidden curves.

"I forget how feminine you really are, *Bella.*"

The Informant scoffed as she strutted to the bar, pouring two drinks. Giovanni's eye twitched in annoyance. He set his glass down on the low coffee table, watching her intently.

Wanting to have control of the conversation, he tried again.

"I didn't know the boy meant so much to you."

Parris returned with two drinks, taking a seat in Giovanni's lap. The older man smirked as his hand wrapped around her hip.

"He doesn't mean anything to me, boss."

His hand travelled to her left hip. She stiffened in his embrace but relaxed when he moved his hand to her leg instead.

"Well, he meant something to me, *Bella*."

He played with the fabric of the playsuit, studying the way she was watching his hand.

"You know what I was going to do with that boy? I was going to mould him into my heir. Into my successor."

Parris rolled her eyes. "The same way you did Tony?"

Giovanni grabbed her face, the drinks in her hands shook.

"Tony was a failure. A disappointment," Giovanni cursed, bringing her face closer to his.

"He was weak, unable to do the simplest tasks… but Theo, Theo could have. I could have made him into a man. He would have fit perfectly in my hand. It was fate that he wandered right to me. If I looked long enough, he almost had the same look in his eyes as you do, *Bella*."

"Your obsession with corrupting the youth is astonishing, Giovanni," she mumbled through squished cheeks.

He chuckled as he released her, his thumb brushing over her bottom lip.

"And you, Parris? You with your silver tongue…"

Goosebumps rose on her arms. Giovanni noticed, delight written on his aging face.

"You've been nothing but cruel, depriving a man of his most basic urge," he continued, his thumb pulling at her lip. "I made you into an Untouchable, but I shouldn't have…"

Parris tried to lean back, but Giovanni followed, whispering hotly into her ear, a possessive growl in his voice.

"I should have kept you all to myself."

Parris shoved the drink into his chest. "I don't want to be sober for this."

Giovanni barked a cold laugh. He took his glass with a raised eyebrow. "You think I'm a fool to drink something you've prepared?" he commented. She shifted in his lap, her dark eyes dancing with deception.

"You drink mine and I'll drink yours!" he suggested; he held the drink out for her.

Parris scowled.

"Come now, *Bella,*" he whispered as he traded their drinks. "Indulge this old man."

His desire for her grew as she drew in her eyebrows, caught in a hard place. Giovanni had always wanted her, from the minute she appeared in front of him to every meeting they had. She was like a shooting star, full of energy but evasive. Making her into an Untouchable meant that even he had to abide by his own rules. She was off-limits to him. That was, until now. Now she was wrapped like a present, ready for undressing. He could see into her complex mind clearly. The gears were smoking from all the turning in her head.

I could still make her mine, he thought as her manicured hand brought the glass to her lips, shaking violently. *I could make her the Head of the Gates. Have her carry me a son. Leave my legacy with her.*

Giovanni watched the Informant finish the entire glass, his heartbeat quickening, waiting for the drink to take its effect.

"Your turn, Giovanni," she whispered, her voice coarse from the burning liquid. He brought the glass to his lips, holding her eyes. He drank deeply, sighing at the taste. Parris pressed herself forward, catching his lips in a rough kiss.

Delighted, he deepened the kiss.

The pair pulled back, panting. Giovanni smirked as he resumed drinking, the brown liquid swishing in his mouth. Quickly, the Informant plunged two of her fingers into his mouth, his hand flying to catch her wrist. She giggled as she played with his tongue.

"Let's have some fun, Giovanni," she whispered seductively as he swallowed the alcohol around her fingers.

She's accepted her fate, he thought as he bit her fingers gently. Excited to see an enthusiastic partner, he threw away the glass. Parris straddled him, diving back in for another kiss.

"You only have yourself to blame," Giovanni warned as he pulled the Informant in.

CHAPTER FOURTEEN

Touchable

Giovanni groaned as the morning sun seared across his eyelids, amplifying his headache. His eyes went in and out of focus as he glanced around the room, finding himself on the king-sized bed, shirtless. The soft lull of the morning warmed him. Locating a clock on the nightstand, his eyes widened. He had never slept in this late before, not in a long time. He must have drunk a lot last night.

Speaking of last night.

"Morning, boss!" Parris called out from the bathroom, already dressed again in her black jumpsuit.

She was styling her hair, pulling at the strands to hide the various dark spots on her neck from the past night. She had bags under her eyes, as though she didn't get any sleep at all. Still, her smile was equipped, albeit a little duller.

Giovanni scanned the hotel room as he sat up, surprised at the mess. Empty bottles scattered around, foil wrappers in the bin, and the strong stench of whiskey suspiciously coming from the couch confirmed it. It had been a wild night. He got up on stumbly legs, feeling like a teenager who was experiencing their first-ever hangover. Giovanni fumbled into the bathroom, sneaking his arms around Parris's waist.

"Those look good on you," he mumbled into her neck.

"They're a pain to cover," she responded as she applied some makeup to the spots.

Giovanni hummed as he pulled her closer, his foggy mind struggling to keep up.

"Last night was electric but... I can't remember much."

Parris looked at the Head of the Gates through the mirror. "Considering you were doing most of the work and drinking 'till you were blacked out, it's a miracle you're alive right now."

Kissing the nape of her neck, Giovanni swayed.

"Why don't you get some more sleep, Giovanni? You look like shit," she recommended.

"Leaving me already?" he whined like a child.

The Informant turned in his embrace, so the pair were face-to-face. "I have a meeting today in Midtown. Besides, haven't you had enough of me?" her eyes were back to their normal intensity, to their normal scheming. Giovanni smiled as he kissed her.

"I'll never get my fill of you, *Bella*."

Eventually, Giovanni took a step back. "Go to work, *Bella*. I'll message you to check-in. I will arrange for our next meeting soon," he whispered gently, his hand resting on her left hip.

"Right," Parris grabbed her bag, leaving the hotel room without a glance back.

Giovanni scanned his own body in the mirror, smirking at the several bites and marks the Informant left.

She'll be the death of me.

Marcel stood under the hot stream, staring at the bathroom wall with a blank stare.

"Marcel, your phone!" Huifen yelled as the sound of the rushing water drowned out her voice.

If we get rid of Giovanni then the whole thing collapses. There would be no order. It'll be open war for Ciel. If I get rid of Tony, then the Wings still have a chance to survive. But then Tony... Tony...

Marcel had been distant since the meeting with the Informant at *Clueless,* leaving the selling of the Wings' products to the other executives, while Tony was off, drowning in his own self-pity with any girl unfortunate enough to get caught in his web.

"Fuck," he groaned as he went back and forth between the two outcomes.

"BABE!" Huifen shouted as she entered the bathroom. "Your phone's been blowing up!"

He pulled back the shower curtain forcefully, more aggressively than he had meant to.

"What?" Marcel called out, closing the water and wrapping himself with a towel. Huifen held his phone out, looking annoyed herself.

"Damn thing keeps blowing up with messages from an unknown number."

"Unknown number?" Marcel asked as he took the device, seeing media files ready for download.

Suddenly, a familiar ding was heard on Huifen's phone in the bedroom, rapid consecutive dings from messages being received. She looked at the Executive skeptically as she checked her phone.

Ten *unread messages – Unknown Number*

"What the fuck is this shit?" Huifen asked as she showed Marcel her screen. Marcel took her phone and placed it next to his on the bed, his eyebrows drawn in.

"I don't think we should open the messages," Marcel cautioned as Huifen hovered over his shoulder.

"Let's just open one—"

DID YOU JUST GET A BUNCH OF PICTURES TOO? – Tony

Marcel's phone beeped again, the pair reading the message hastily.

THE FUCK DOES THIS MEAN?! – Tony

Huifen pushed him to the side, downloading the messages on her phone. Marcel watched in a cold sweat. As the photos loaded on the screen, a wild smile pulled at Huifen's face as she looked at the pictures. She laughed loudly, a cruel sound. Marcel scanned her phone, eyes wide.

There on the screen was the old man and the Informant in some hotel. Several images of the pair making out and undressing the other. The pictures were taken through the hotel window, presumably from across the street. One with the Informant on Giovanni, another with the man unzipping her jumpsuit, one with the Informant kissing the Head in bed. Marcel quickly downloaded the images on his phone, taking a closer look.

There weren't any pictures of the pair in the act, but the implication was there. Marcel answered Tony's call immediately.

"What does this mean?" Tony yelled into the phone, furious.

A final ding was heard as a final message was sent. Tony remained silent as he read it, Marcel and Huifen reading it as well.

It's a free-for-all. – Unknown Number

"It means…" Marcel answered, his mind racing at the new possibilities, possibilities of taking control without killing Giovanni. Not when the old man had dug his own grave by voiding his own agreement.

"Giovanni has touched an Untouchable. I believe we should have our turn, too."

Theo couldn't remember much of his night with Giovanni. All he could remember was being immobilized on the couch after the drink. He remembered how heavy his arms felt, his legs being unresponsive, begging for help.

The next moment he was in Angela's crowded bedroom. She and Jaya watched over him in a tense silence as he came to, his head pounding.

"What—" he started, but a violent cough caught in his throat. Jaya rushed to get water, Angela watched him with a sad look. Once Jaya returned with the water and Theo emptied the cup, he tried asking again.

"What happened?"

The pair looked at one another, as though they had planned who was going to say what. Angela took a deep breath.

"We got you back. You're no longer indebted to the Gates."

"How?!" his voice cracking. He tried to stand up, but Jaya pushed him back down on the bed. "What did you give him? What did you give away?"

"Nothing," Angela responded coldly.

"Don't lie to me, Angie!" Theo cried, "I-I can't handle it anymore. I can't remember last night. Please, I need to know. I have to fix it! I have to fix things with Giovanni. I still owe him the money," he panicked, his eyes pricked. "I need to make sure my dad's alive and then I have to deal with him, too. So tell me what you gave him in exchange!"

Jaya gave Angela a knowing look, as though they had fought about telling him how they got him back from the clutches of the Head. Theo stared at her, the feeling of betrayal too much, his headache worse.

Angela looked at her friends. She knew Jaya wanted to know why the Informant listened to her.

"We went to *Clueless,*" Angela recounted, "I told the Informant to bring you back. To erase your debt. And she did. She owes me."

Jaya watched Theo's face go through a mix of emotions, of confusion, bewilderment, and suspicion.

"Why—?"

"She made a phone call," Angela continued, "and told us to go to the hotel. Once we got there and opened the door, we found you on the couch. You… you were okay. We weren't too late, thank God. It was a little awkward getting you out of the hotel, but Logan did most of the carrying. He brought us all here."

Theo's eyebrows were still scrunched, as though he still didn't believe her.

"It's the truth," Jaya confirmed with a sigh.

"Who the hell is Logan?" Theo asked.

Jaya explained, "but he's a friend of Angie's sister."

Angela waited for the flood of questions that Theo was going to ask but they never came. Theo instead stared at his hands. Jaya waited patiently by his side on the bed, her own mind racing. After what felt like forever, Theo pulled back the cover of the bed, standing up.

"I need to piss," he announced as he left the room. The girls watched him stumble out, noticing how his shoulders slumped down. His tall frame was no longer impressive, instead, he looked like a large target for others to aim at, for Giovanni and Roger to hurt.

The girls remained in silence. Angela refused to meet Jaya's stare, knowing the other girl's patience was running out. Sooner or later Angela would need to tell her a satisfying answer.

"You don't have to tell me… everything," Jaya started. "You don't have to talk about your sister and Parris. You don't have to, Angie. But know that if I had told someone sooner about Raef, I wouldn't be in this situation."

Angela looked up at her and saw her eyes ready to spill over. Jaya's harsh demeanour softened.

"Friends make you strong, Angie."

Angela opened her mouth to reply but nothing came out. She didn't know how to respond.

"Fuck… I-I can't talk about my sister, Jaya. She's nothing like me. She wouldn't find herself in this situation. Nini would have helped Theo ages ago. She would have kept you safe from Raef…."

Angela cursed as tears sped down her face, trying to wipe the pain away. Jaya chuckled as she shed her own tears.

The pair cried in silence, each one grieving for the other and for themselves. It felt silly to cry with another in silence, but Angela was grateful. She wouldn't know what else to say.

The sound of the front door closing grabbed their attention. Angela ran into the living room, calling out, "Theo?"

No answer.

Angela laced her sneakers up without a second thought. Jaya watched from the window, seeing their friend run out the building, towards the subway.

"He left!" Jaya hurried to the living room, rushing to put her shoes on as well.

Jaya's phone rang, stopping her. Raef was calling her. Angela watched her answer with a shaky breath. Angela was torn. She saw the way Jaya flinched at Raef's yelling. She needed to help Jaya escape from him, but she needed to find Theo.

This is what you get for letting people get close to you. The more you care for others, the more you will get hurt when they leave! You never learn this lesson the easy way, a small voice said from the dark part of her mind. *You finally had a chance to speak to Parris directly in her office and you used that chance on Theo! You waste every opportunity.*

"Yes, I understand, I'll head over now," Jaya whispered into the phone, her shoulders stiff.

"Go," Angela instructed, "get the evidence we need for the police officer. I'll go find Theo."

"Angie—"

"We don't have time!" Angela yelled. She left the apartment, running down the stairs, Jaya behind her.

"I won't lose Theo again."

Thank God they got my backpack, Theo thought as he picked it up from Angela's coffee table. He slung it over his shoulders and ran from the apartment. He heard their voices calling after him. But he ran. He already took too much from them. He reached the subway, pausing to think of where he was headed.

He couldn't go home, not yet. With the way Giovanni had hit his dad, he would be asking for a death wish if he went back. He couldn't go back to the Ciel Construction Company, the only other place that he could have called his own. But those days were over now. There was only one place left where he felt safe.

STK it is, he decided as he took the train. *I just need some time alone to gather my thoughts.*

He kept his phone turned off, not ready to deal with the onslaught of messages from everyone.

The school was closed on the weekends; however, being captain had its perks. He punched in the code for the gym, the lock beeping green before he stepped in. Instantly he felt his anxiety settle down as he walked the length of the gym, tossing his bag aside. It was the one place where he was in control of himself with no one's say so.

Theo picked up a ball and spiked it over the net effortlessly, the sound satisfying to hear in the empty gym. He felt his legs protest as his body was still recovering from last night, his mind still foggy. But he needed to do something mindless after the last few weeks.

Angela and Jaya saw right through Giovanni. How was I so easily fooled? He thought as he spiked the ball. *There has to be something wrong with me. Maybe Dad was right, I am worthless. If I was smarter or more clever or something, then this wouldn't have happened.*

He continued to serve the ball across the net, watching it sail through the air at lightning speed, running to the other side to re-serve the scattered balls.

I deserve what happened last night.

"You were always impressive to watch," a voice called from the unlocked gym door.

Theo froze, his blood turning into ice at the voice. He turned around, seeing a familiar suit.

"Come, *Cucciolo*," Giovanni instructed as he held the door open, "let's say our goodbye properly."

Parris skipped down the sidewalk in Midtown, returning from her meeting. Reequipped with her leather jacket, her carefree attitude resumed.

How did you know to check the Loose Screw? *–* Helen

I spoke with the victims' parents. They mentioned the bar a few times, enough for me to warrant a visit. Count my lucky stars that I was there that night. Wait, don't tell me your information network doesn't reach the victims' parents? – Amir

I guess I was too focused on the big picture. – Helen

Her eyes were glued to her phone, having memorized Ciel as though it were the back of her hand. She told Giovanni where she was headed. His messages grew in frequency since she left the hotel.

As though he didn't trust her to come running back to him. She tapped away on her phone quickly as she weaved through the streets. The crowds parted for her, they knew her importance.

A few paces behind her, someone gripped their knife tighter.

Giovanni walked ahead of Theo, his headache still lingering despite the coffee and painkiller. He was delighted at the boy's expression and obedience, still longing for Theo, but he had made a deal.

Besides, the Informant was worth more than a broken boy.

"I did promise you that you could drive my car," Giovanni held the driver's door of his luxurious black car open. There was no driver today. Theo watched as Giovanni held it open for him.

"I was told that my debt to you was erased?" Theo asked, unsure if Angela's words were true.

"Yes, it is. You do not owe the Gates anything."

"Then I don't need to go with you."

The older man looked irritated; Theo watched him push that emotion down.

"I only want to say goodbye, Theo. You have my word."

"Last time I trusted your word I was drugged in a hotel room."

Giovanni barked a cold laugh. Theo hated how he took a step back.

"You've already learned to talk back?" Giovanni boomed in a loud voice, grinning. "Where was this *spark* during our time together?"

The claws of anger pressed into Theo's chest.

"Up to you, but wouldn't you like to thank the person who took your place?" Giovanni suggested. "She didn't want to, but she took it like a pro."

Theo rushed into the car, slamming the door shut. Giovanni chuckled as he sat in the passenger seat.

I'll crash the car with him in it, I swear to God, if he hurt them, if he touched Angie!

"Where?" Theo growled, he gripped the steering wheel tightly. Buckling his seat belt, Giovanni relaxed as he played classical music.

"Around Midtown." He glanced at his phone. "I'll tell you *exactly* where to go."

Theo didn't reply. He drove, going past the speed limit, listening to Giovanni's instructions.

"Left at 14th Avenue."

"Right at Main Street."

For all the weeks Theo had spent alone together with Giovanni: in his office, in the back of his car, in small booths at restaurants. In this moment, Theo's skin itched in his presence, wanting to crawl as far away from the man as possible.

They didn't speak to one another.

Aside from giving directions, Giovanni was content to hum along with the music. Theo felt his breath grow shallower the more he drove, not understanding the Head's endgame.

"Pull aside here."

Theo parked the car along the side of the busy road. His eyes scanned for coily hair or for a small girl with butterfly hairclips, but he couldn't spot Angela or Jaya.

Then who took my place? He thought as he watched the pedestrians.

"You were right, you are a good driver," Giovanni praised as he dialled a number. "You should be able to remember her, it's hard to forget someone so impressive."

The intersection was busy, people emerging from the cracks of the sidewalk. Theo tried harder to scan the crowds of people on the street, not seeing anyone he knew.

Then, he caught a glimpse of a leather jacket.

"*Bella,*" Giovanni purred into the phone, "I see you, won't you cross the road and come and say hi to someone?"

Theo watched the Informant turn around on the sidewalk, her smile widening as she spotted the black car. She waited at the lights.

"Boss! Hearing from you so soon?" Theo heard her through the phone.

She took my place? The Informant from Clueless… *but why?*

"I can't help it, *Bella.* Only a fool wouldn't miss your embrace. Maybe I should put a tracker on you to know where you disappear to," Giovanni suggested, watching her like a hawk.

"So you're the clingy type, I see now—" A loud gasp was heard through the phone. She stopped in the middle of the crosswalk.

A large figure wearing a hood stopped in front of her. The sea of people milled around the pair. Giovanni narrowed his eyes as the figure stepped around her.

"*Bella?*"

Parris fell to the ground, face-down. The figure started running down the sidewalk and down an alley. Someone yelled as they looked down at the Informant. The scream echoed through the phone. Civilians ran to her side, someone called an ambulance, while others turned her onto her back.

Giovanni ran out of the car, his phone clenched in his hand. The sound of the chaos reverberated. Theo rushed out as well, vomit caught in his throat at the sight.

There on Ciel's concrete ground was the Informant. A knife stuck out of her side. A puddle of blood grew in size around her. The Informant stared at the sky with cloudy eyes. A large crowd had gathered around her body, the traffic honking at the mass of people to disperse. The sound of sirens yelled from down the street as the ambulance screamed at cars to get out of the way. The sirens of police followed as someone pointed in the direction the figure ran down.

Theo ran back to the car; grabbed his backpack and tried to calmly walk away. But he looked back to where the paramedics were shouting at one another. The body of the Informant was lifted into the back of the ambulance, police urged the crowd to move along.

The chaos arose instantly, but once the ambulance sped through the concrete graveyard, the anarchy settled down.

Theo saw Giovanni stare at where the ambulance had disappeared. He knew the man well enough to see that he wasn't upset. There was no sadness in the stiffness of his shoulders or in his fists. He wasn't sad that she was stabbed. He was *furious*. Theo watched the Head make a phone call, not moving from the intersection.

"Goodbye, Giovanni," Theo said. Pulling his phone out, he ducked into the subway to vanish.

Ciel was on fire that day.

Angela ran past STK, the sound of sirens shrieking in the nearby distance as she called out for Theo, her voice turning hoarse. She called his phone again with no luck, going straight to voicemail. She had received an update from Jaya that she was out gathering inventory with Raef again. She hoped that she could keep Raef in the dark until they spoke to Officer Hafiz, but Ciel was against her and her friends.

Did you find him yet? – Logan

No, I'm checking the school now. – Angela

Let me know. I can drive by his home. – Logan

The hourglass was running out of sand.

I keep losing focus. Theo and Jaya are consuming my thoughts. I need to be focusing on Parris but they still need my help.

Her phone buzzed to life; Theo's caller ID finally gave her some hope.

"You need to stop ignoring my calls," she huffed into the phone.

"Sorry!" Theo apologized.

"Where were you?" Angela asked as she leaned against the school's black gate.

Theo recounted everything, from the moment he left her apartment to watching the ambulance leave with the Informant. Angela did not say a word the whole time, listening to the events with a certain anger brewing.

"Is she dead?"

"I don't know," Theo answered. "Who is she to you, Angie? Why did she take my place? You do understand what that means, right? What Gio—what *he* was going to do to me? What he did to her?"

"I-I know," Angela stuttered.

Don't think about the details… I asked her to save Theo and she did. What happened after is none of my concern.

"Angie… this isn't like you."

"She owed me a favour. For my sister. And I cashed it in. Parris… I still need to ask her something. She can't die," Angela confessed.

"Parris knows your sister?"

The automated voice of the subway calling out Theo's station caught her attention, thankful for the break in the conversation.

"Are you heading home?" she asked, trying to distract herself from the pain bubbling within her.

"Yeah," Theo answered. "I need to face my dad sooner than later. Plus, being able to see Giovanni and tell him off gave me… confidence? I don't know."

"And you'll be safe?"

"I hope so. Listen, I'll call you once I get there, maybe I can crash at your place again if things turn sideways?"

"Always," Angela affirmed. She sighed as she ended the call, her eyes wandering over her school: the sharp arches, the steeples.

If she's dead, then it's all over. All of this was a waste of time… I wasted my chance by being distracted. But if she's still alive, if Parris somehow crawls back from the gates of hell, then she's mine this time. She can't avoid me anymore. She'll tell me everything.

The roof where her eyes landed.

I'll make her tell me everything.

Theo walked up his street, his dad's car in the driveway. He took in a deep breath before unlocking the front door.

"Dad, I'm home!" he called out.

No response.

"Dad!" he yelled louder again, afraid to close the door in case he had to run for it. "I'm back, can we talk?" He didn't hear movement from upstairs.

Dad's not home? But his car is out front.

"Dad!" Theo yelled again. He jumped when he heard a knock from the front door; he saw an older woman holding a slip of paper. She was their neighbour, ever since he could remember. She was dressed in her nightgown with fuzzy slippers on her feet.

"Mrs. Singh," Theo greeted as he met her by the door.

"Son, I've been watching the window all day waiting for you!" she cried out in a shrill voice.

"What happened?" he asked. He led her to a couch, pushing beer cans away.

"The police came by," she shrieked. "They knocked on your door so loud it woke me up!"

His blood ran cold for the hundredth time that day.

"Why?"

"That Roger Grayson had breached his bail, and he's been arrested again!" she recounted. "They said that I had to tell you since they tried to call you." She handed him the slip of paper.

Theo scanned the page and his heart sank. His dad had breached his bail conditions and was caught with Cloud 9. He would be held in custody until his trial. Mrs. Singh waited for Theo to say something, watching him with old eyes.

"I should be upset," his voice small. "I should be upset that I helped him out the first time and got him his bail money, that I went through so much trouble and hurt so many people to get him out only for him to go and waste it away."

"Son?" Mrs. Singh asked. She could hear the fights over the years, the yelling, and the way Theo cried all throughout his childhood. She held her arms open for him as he cried into her shoulders, his body shaking with a sense of peace he had long forgotten.

A bright light shone into her eyes, disturbing her peaceful slumber.

"Ma'am, are you awake?" a voice spoke from a distance, "Ma'am, we've successfully stitched the wound but you need to rest until the doctor sees you. You're currently at St. Katherine's Hospital."

Parris groaned as she turned her head towards the voice.

"Ma'am, what is your first and last name? We did not find any wallet or personal identification on your person when the ambulance brought you in," a nurse spoke to her right, the sound bounced around in her mind.

"Vitals?" she asked with a dry mouth, fighting to open her eyes.

"The doctor will tell you everything—"

"Vitals hit?" Parris yelled. The hospital room finally came into focus. She felt an intense pain in her left side, tightness from the stitches.

"No…" the nurse responded hesitantly. "But the doctor will go over your procedure—Ma'am, you can't take out your IV!"

The Informant pulled at the instruments connected to her arm with a grimace. The nurse yelled at her to stop, but she ignored them.

"I need your phone," Parris demanded as she sat up; her head rushed and her side protested the movement.

"Ma'am, I insist that you lie back down immediately; you were stabbed and lost an incredible amount of blood!" the nurse yelled in disbelief.

Parris glared at the nurse, struggling to get out of bed.

"I won't say it again," she warned, grabbing a hold of the nurse's collar, an urgency in her voice.

"Give me your phone before I have the Halos shoot your hands."

The nurse instantly handed over their phone. Parris struggled to focus her eyes on the screen.

Shouting was heard down the hall. The nurse rushed outside to see what the commotion was about. Parris leaned on the wall as she strained to stand. Her stab wound was on fire. She ignored the pain as she dialled a number.

"Lorenzo, what happened?" she whispered.

"Wings are in the hospital. Giovanni has sent his men to St. Michael's hospital instead. No one knew where you went!" Lorenzo answered, his voice desperate. "Images of you in bed with Giovanni have been circulated to the executives and Heads of the Halos and Wings! You're no longer Untouchable!"

The sounds from the hallway grew louder.

"Last thing I remembered was being stabbed." She stepped out into the hallway, leaning against the wall. "I need to escape."

"Where is Parris!" a voice yelled at the nurses' station.

A group of men wearing black rings on their pinkies harassed the nurses. A security guard approached the group but was quickly punched in the head. Patients yelled as the nurses called for help; the man who yelled produced a gun, pointing it at a nurse.

Parris cursed as she ducked into another hallway, nurses and security guards rushing towards the nurses' station.

"Where are you?" Parris asked as she found an elevator.

"The Wings will recognize me if I bring the car close to the hospital," Lorenzo panicked. "What should I do?!"

Parris groaned as she held her side, warm liquid soaking the hospital gown.

"So the Wings are after me? They must be hoping to finish the job, then… Lorenzo, take the staff and go into hiding until I say so. Tell Owl I'll be there soon," Parris instructed as she pushed past the police, who rushed into the elevator on the ground floor.

The hospital alarm rang. Those in the lobby looked around confused, while those coming out of the elevator screamed at them to run.

"I'll contact you when things are ready."

"But, Ms. Parris!" Lorenzo protested, but stopped himself. He could hear her laboured breaths through the phone and the shouting over the hospital speakers.

"Code Silver on level five, all security please report to level five!" a voice announced on the hospital speakers.

"I'll do as you said, boss!"

Parris followed the crowds outside of the hospital. She made her way towards the dumpsters outside. Looking down at her side, she saw the red blotch increase on the hospital gown. Dialling another number, her vision started to blur.

"This is Logan O'Brien."

"Pick me up from the south entrance of Saint Katherine's Hospital near the garbage," Parris whispered. She slid down behind the dumpster, her legs no longer solid.

"No."

She yelled in pain when her side pinched the stitches. "I know you will!" she cried, almost desperately.

"I know you will, Logan—"

Logan hung up the phone.

Parris stayed still behind the dumpster on the floor. She heard sirens race by. She heard the officers enter the hospital. She heard everything. From her spot with the garbage, she was hidden from the world. Applying pressure to her stitches was all she could do while she waited and listened. She fought sleep, she fought the pain, she fought to survive.

But she couldn't fight forever.

Just as the blackness in the corner of her vision was about to take over, she heard him.

"A Parrasite among filth," Logan spat at her. She couldn't open her eyes anymore but she smiled in his direction.

"Be a dear and take me away from here?"

"I heard a lady got stabbed in Midtown today," he said as he removed his sunglasses, looking down at her. "Guessing it was you?"

"Bingo!" Parris sang with a grimace.

"Does it hurt?" he asked as he wrapped her arm across his shoulder. He yanked her up suddenly, pulling at her wound.

"YES!" Parris yelled as her eyes shot open. She shook from the pain, the blood stain growing larger.

"Good."

Logan dragged her to his car. He glanced up as the police escorted the arrested Wings into their cruisers.

"You probably caused all this, didn't you, Parrasite?" he asked as he slammed her door shut. Parris leaned the seat all the way back, in an effort to hide herself. Logan sat behind the wheel, refusing to look at her. But the sound of her laboured breathing pulled at his conscious.

"Where to?"

When she didn't answer, he looked over to find the blood stain on the hospital gown alarmingly large.

"Hey!" he yelled, slapping her face. "Wake up! Where the fuck am I taking you?" He placed a hand on her face, feeling it heat up.

"Shit," he mumbled, "a fever."

"Corner of Carin and 9th," Parris muttered weakly. "Safe space."

Logan drove in silence, only the sound of the Informant's laboured breathing filling the space. Every time he would glance over, she was doing worse. He focused on driving instead, watching the city turn into the sketchy side of town.

"We're here," Logan announced, searching for a sign for a clinic.

"Number nineteen, park in the back. Then knock on the door three times," Parris instructed. Her eyes closed, her voice weaker.

Logan did as he was told and waited by the door, knocking three times. A woman in a white doctor's coat instantly answered. She had sharp cheekbones and sharper eyes. Her graying hair was pulled into a tight bun. The doctor's sharp features morphed into a sad expression.

"Quickly now," the doctor rushed to the truck, "she might have bled out already."

The doctor opened the door and gasped when she saw the Informant. She called for Logan to carry her inside while she prepared. Logan huffed as he went to lift her down the stairs, deciding to carry her bridal style for the sake of her wound. Once at the bottom, the doctor had prepared a cot for her. Parris whimpered as she was placed down, and the doctor rushed over with bandages.

Logan stood there, unsure of what to do. He was still unsure of why he actually saved the Parrasite when she called.

"Well, don't be useless!" the doctor yelled at him. "Boil some water!"

"Owl," Parris groaned from the cot, "don't be mean to him. He's sensitive."

"Oh, great," Owl sighed. "Now she's delirious!"

Still unsure of himself, Logan rushed to boil some water. *Just keep your hands busy,* he told himself as he watched the doctor hook an IV into the Informant.

You can ask Dr. Brown why you helped her later. He brought the hot water to Owl. He watched the Informant disappear under the drugs, her pained face soothed over. A stray tear escaped from the corner of her eye.

Just because you helped her doesn't mean it changes anything. It doesn't make up for Janine, for abandoning me.

He listened to the doctor's instructions as she pulled the curtain to undress her patient. He gathered the items asked of him. He brought them to Owl, watching her expose the Informant's left side.

She's still a Parrasite.

He grimaced as he saw the state of her side. Burn marks, a variety of scars, and bite marks, some old and others recent. His eyes lingered on the 'G' branded on her side. They were deliberate. The stab wound and the fresh ruined stitches were the priority for now.

She's still at fault.

Listening intently as he helped Owl, cut the string where he was asked. Watching the doctor work to save her.

I'll never forgive her.

One Day Ago.

"You only have yourself to blame," Giovanni spoke as he kissed the Informant, his hands travelling all over her. Parris tried to meet his intensity but could feel the bile rise in her throat.

The groping and grabbing were aggressive. The hunter's claws stuck in their prey's side. Just as his hand slid the zipper of her jumpsuit down, his head slammed back against the armchair heavily.

"Ugh, finally," she stood from his lap. She slapped Giovanni's face for good measure, the sound ringing in the hotel room.

No reaction.

She smirked at her nails. She never spiked the drinks, like she knew Giovanni would have thought. He was so simple-minded, after all.

Who knew benzodiazepine sealed under an orally disintegrating film below my nails was an effective way to knock someone out? She thought gleefully to herself.

Parris quickly sent a message to Lorenzo, letting him know her plan worked. Pulling the curtains closed, she looked around the room.

She got to work.

She picked up the television remote, playing an adult video, making sure the volume was loud enough for the two guards outside to hear. The obnoxious moans of the woman were convincing enough.

Parris hummed as she removed her heels, grabbing onto Giovanni in a pack-strap carry towards the king bed. She positioned him on his back, removing the robe. The older man was out like a light.

Karma for too much shit to list, she thought as she continued about her plan.

Scattering the Head's clothing around the room haphazardly, she picked up the bottles of alcohol and proceeded to spray some around the room, the couch, and down the drain. She had to make their night of passion believable. Retrieving a facial suction cup from her bag, she began to spread hickeys across Giovanni's torso and neck, biting him for extra measure. Leaning him forward, she scratched his back until there were angry red lines.

It felt therapeutic hurting the older man.

Opening two condoms and filling them with body wash, she tied them off and tossed them towards the bin, purposely missing.

I need some of you undressed as well. – Lorenzo

Parris grumbled as she pulled the curtains back again, removing her jumpsuit to mount the older man, kissing his unconscious lips as she posed in her underwear, waiting impatiently to receive Lorenzo's text.

Done! – Lorenzo

Prepare yourself for tomorrow. You better not miss! – Parris

Pulling the curtains closed again, Parris finished her scheme by making hickeys on her neck in the washroom mirror. Once satisfied with her work, she pulled at her hair, making it frizzy.

Looking at herself and around the room, it did look like a night of wild passion. She dressed in her jumpsuit, rubbing her bare arms. Lying on the couch, she watched the clock tick slowly.

He'll wake in six hours.

She could knock down the King here and now. Snuff him out before the first light of dawn. But it wouldn't be game over. She needed to break the entire chessboard, so the game could never be played again.

Parris stared at Giovanni, her eyes refused to blink, refusing to lower her guard in his presence, even with him like this.

After all, the devil is still the devil.

279

CHAPTER FIFTEEN

Ghosts and Pitchforks

Tony took a long drag of his cigarette, exhaling the smoke with a sigh. Gathered around a circular table were the Wings and Halos in the Wings' boardroom in the old office building. The room was filled with twenty-odd people. The two organizations had never had a meeting where all the Executives and Heads were present, where the Gates were not invited. Most of the executives were dressed in suits, this meeting deciding their future and funerals. These were unprecedented times.

Leaning on the table over a map of Ciel were Marcel and Huifen, each equipped with a marker, dividing up the city.

Claiming parts of the Gates' turf.

"We will take the brothels," Marcel decided. "It'll be a good place to sell our products."

"Then we take the underground casinos and Financial District." Huifen circled in green.

The Head and Executive were working in unison, while Tony watched from the side. He had disappeared the past few weeks, drowning in alcohol, drugs, and women. His last visit to *Clueless* affected him harder than he imagined. He was content to live the rest of his days in his dark room while Marcel ran the organization but the pictures reignited something within him, his hatred of his father coming back full-force after almost ten years.

With the disappearance of the Informant, tensions rose. If she was confirmed dead, then all hell would break loose from the Gates. The Halos and Wings worked on the battle plan, buying weapons and recruiting the smaller gangs into their fold.

Clueless had been on lockdown, not opening its doors to anyone. The

Gates were searching the city for the Informant, too preoccupied to realize the conspiracy against their Head.

"And the protection brackets in Old Town and the East?" Tony asked as he tapped on the map.

Huifen narrowed her eyes at Tony. "The Halos get Old Town, as we are the oldest of the organizations."

Tony snubbed the butt into the map, burning an ugly hole. "Then the Wings get Midtown and that damned school. I'll take fucking pleasure in burning it to the ground."

The pair glared at one another; tension rose in the room.

"We don't get shit if we start fighting," Marcel announced loudly. "We need to cooperate in order to push the Gates out. Don't forget, the old man still has more assets than both the Halos and Wings combined. But he's distracted now, and this is the time to strike."

"The Wings couldn't even kill the Informant in the hospital," Huifen yelled. "How do you lose someone who's half-dead?!"

"We lost some of our men because the Halos didn't have the balls to go in themselves! The CCPD has to keep them in custody until the news calms down. She's useful but she knows too much, and we can't risk leaving her alive. As much as she knows about the Gates, she also knows a shit-ton about us!" Tony screamed back.

The executives were shuffling amongst themselves, not sure if a shoot-out was going to happen as they watched the Heads.

"ENOUGH!" Marcel shouted, resting a hand over Huifen's. Tony glanced down rapidly at the two. Just as quickly, Marcel retracted his hand, as though nothing had happened.

"The other Untouchables will remain Untouchable. Giovanni is turning the city upside-down looking for the Informant. If we fuck with the school, then it would bring the Gates down on our asses. We cannot cause a full-out open war, we need to choose our targets wisely. That includes you, too, Tony. The Informant got away, no sense in burning the whole thing down…"

Huifen took a deep breath as she calmed down, her shoulders not as stiff. Tony watched her like a hawk, suddenly coming to a realization.

Tony lit another cigarette.

"I heard a thief was spotted at STK…" Huifen stared at the school on the map. "Someone who stole from me personally."

"Tiffany—" Marcel warned.

"I don't care about territory if there's no loyalty," Huifen spoke over him. "But to steal from me personally and live in my city?"

The executives took a step back from the Head of the Halos, often forgetting there was so much more to the chemical engineer. As cute as she dressed, Huifen mostly saw red, making a point to shoot the hands of those who stole from her in front of her organization, to then shoot them between the eyes and dump them in the harbour.

"I heard dear old Raef is back to his old ways."

"This feels silly," Angela complained as she scooped the guts from her pumpkin. "It feels silly to come to school when there are gangs and mobsters involved in our lives outside of these walls."

"And we're here carving pumpkins," Theo finished her thought as he mapped out the face on their pumpkin. Angela scoffed as their homeroom teacher handed them their carving set.

Lucy happily switched seats back with Theo, mentioning that Angela seemed more at ease with him than her. Theo was doing better after sleeping in an empty house, sleeping off the drug from the hotel. He had told Angela about his dad and she was glad to see him at peace after so long.

"I feel like we're cosplaying high school students," Angela continued, stabbing the eye out. Theo laughed, and the pleasant sound tugged Angela's lips into a smile.

"And Jaya's okay telling that officer everything?" he asked.

Angela hummed. "Yeah, we have a lot of evidence against her ex, but she can't shake him off. Plus, she's worried about her family, since he knows where she lives. We just need enough to lock him up for a long time."

"He doesn't have any connections?" He looked up at her. "No one to go after Jaya once she goes to the Blues?"

Their pumpkin was basic, the pair not having enough energy to be creative after such an exhausting weekend and midterm season starting.

"She said he's all alone, that's why he came back to her."

The pumpkins were for the Halloween party. Angela wasn't planning on attending, with the way her year had been, but Theo had been convincing her otherwise. It felt good to have him back. She missed him.

"You still haven't told me why the Informant took my place," Theo stated nervously. "I won't let it go, you know." She didn't respond, focused on carving the mouth. Angela had kept silent since the night they retrieved Theo about the Informant. Both he and Jaya pestered her, but she refused to answer any questions, especially after the incident at the hospital hit the news.

Angela had tried. She really had, but the words wouldn't come out. No one ever asked her about Nini anymore, not her parents, not her aunt.

"Who is she to you?" Theo asked in a tired voice.

Angela sighed deeply. First period was ages away from over. Theo would just ask again and again and again.

"Parris was my sister's best friend," Angela shared. Theo's eyes widened in surprise. "My perfect sister who had everything she could have ever wanted. Family. Friends. Grades. Nini really did have everything. You know, she had a full scholarship to U of C's biomedical program," Angela recounted with a small smile.

The floodgates were open. She got to talk about Nini to Theo!

"She was stupid smart! Smarter than you for sure, Theo." Angela looked up at him, a fond look on her young face. Theo memorized the way she looked at that moment. Happiness finally peeked beneath the mask she always wore.

"She was worse than my parents when it came to scolding me on my homework. God forbid I get a C+ on my science fair project!"

Angela smiled at their pumpkin, reliving the warmth of her childhood memories with her sister.

"But she did always take me out for ice cream after my spelling bees and tests, always took me to the park when I would ask… God, I love Nini so much."

Their pumpkin was complete. A wide smile and sharp dead eyes peered back at her. Theo remained quiet; he often forgot that Angela had a sister.

The smile on her lips turned into a scowl.

"Parris is a Parrasite," Angela spat, stabbing the carving tool into the pumpkin. "She didn't value her friendship with Nini. The precious hours she got to spend with her. Ever since I came to Ciel, she's been avoiding me. I need to confront her. I need to confront her about why she didn't love Nini, why she abandoned her when she needed her the most."

She looked back at Theo. Her mask was back in its place.

"That's why Parris owes me."

The past few days at Owl's clinic had been strange for Logan. Often Owl would tell him that he could leave whenever he wanted to, but he couldn't move from his spot on the dusty couch. He would go to work at the *Loose Screw* during the night then come back in the early hours of the morning.

Somehow a cup of coffee would materialize on the coffee table for him once he woke up. He stayed there for days, watching a variety of people enter the clinic with different wounds, the way Owl intimidated even the most dangerous gangsters.

One of the days, a teenager dropped off a package for him, a plain shoebox with a single cellphone inside and clothing. Inside was a note that only had the letter 'P' on it. It was the Informant's phone. He had turned it on but the password prevented him from snooping any further. He had placed it by her bedside, and left immediately after to return to his spot on the couch.

Feeling more anxious as the days ran by, he walked by the Parrasite's bed, pulling the curtain back. He inspected her face, seeing the hollows of her cheeks prominent on her face. She had lost an insane amount of blood, and factoring that with exhaustion from the lack of sleep for years, Owl's guess, her recovery would take a long time. He laid a hand on her forehead, the fever resurfacing every so often. Owl had told him that the chances of infection were high. He dipped a towel into the ice water by her bed, wringing it out before placing it on her.

Don't be so gentle with her. She doesn't deserve it.

When he asked Owl about Parris's left side, about the scars and burn marks, the doctor looked away, pursing her lips in response. Logan's phone rang quietly in the room. He stepped outside of the clinic under the autumn sun as he answered.

"Doc."

"Logan!" Doctor Brown replied. "I was worried when you requested an urgent phone session, is everything alright?"

"I—"

"Logan?"

"I don't know how to feel."

He told the good doctor about taking the girls to the Informant, to watching the way she shook while on the phone with someone. He confessed that he didn't want to save her but his body moved on its own before his mind could catch up.

"And now?" Doctor Brown pressed. He leaned against the clinic wall, unsure of what to say.

"Maybe," she suggested lightly, "since you still care about Janine after so long, maybe you do still care about Parris, too, even after all this time."

"No," he replied weakly, not believing his own words.

"Then why haven't you left her side?"

He knew the reason; somewhere deep down, he knew. It was the same reason he rushed to her office after Tony left, the same reason he needed to know what she had exchanged for Theo. But he couldn't bring himself to forget the years of pain and betrayal and loneliness she made him feel, the way she abandoned him. His heart refused to forgive her.

"I need to go now, Doc."

"Open yourself to the possibility that she still cares about you, Logan, that she still cares about you and trusts you enough to save her!" she said quickly before Logan cut the line. He stood in the cool breeze, fidgeting with his phone.

When he had his fill of the world, he ventured back down into the clinic.

Jaya laughed loudly as Theo left Angela's room, dressed in his costume. Angela rushed from the bathroom to see. In the middle of the living room was Theo dressed in a nightgown, gray wig, and reading glasses on his head.

"This belongs to my neighbour," he did a little spin.

Jaya wiped the tears from her eyes. She howled at his silliness.

"Mine is funny while yours is clever!" Theo exclaimed. He poked one of the cereal boxes stapled to Jaya's shirt. She had covered herself in cereal boxes and blood.

"A serial killer of sorts," Jaya replied in shaky breaths as she calmed herself down.

"You two are a riot!" Angela called out, rushing back into the bathroom to finish getting ready.

The pair followed her. Theo snapped a picture of the three in the mirror. Angela scolded him, saying she wasn't ready yet. Her costume was not as creative as the others, as she had settled for cat ears and an all-black outfit.

Nini used to make me the best costumes, Angela thought with a smile.

Deciding last-minute to attend the Halloween party, she offered her place for them to get ready. Theo's house was too far from the school, and Jaya's place would be too chaotic with her younger siblings.

The trio made funny faces in the mirror as Theo snapped too many pictures. Once satisfied, they made their way down to the street where Theo's dad's car was parked. Angela sent a picture of them to her parents.

Heading to the Halloween Party now! – Angela

Mom loves Jaya's and Theo's costumes. You look beautiful, Angel. Have fun and be safe. – Dad

It was an upgrade to drive around the city. Jaya sat up front, blasting her music through the speakers as Theo sped through the streets. The lights bled into streaks as the pair screamed at the top of their lungs along with the loud music. The feeling was electric as Angela watched them sing off-tune, Theo's wig bobbing about his head. They acted as though they didn't have a care in the world, as though they were never involved with the gangs, their families were safe, and their biggest concern was finding a good university to attend.

Is this what normal feels like? To have people love you and excited to live life with you? Angela thought. *Did Nini feel like this with Parris and Logan?*

Honking the horn at some seniors walking towards STK, Theo pulled into a free spot on the street. Jaya hopped out, looping her arm with Angela as they skipped to the front door. Theo donned the glasses and sprinted behind the girls.

Halloween in Ciel City was exciting, as civilians were dressed in costumes of their own, flooding the street, each one having their own plans for the evening. The high schoolers marched up the steps of their school, handing their student IDs to their teachers, who manned the door.

"I trust you two to behave tonight," Principal Patel instructed with a stern look as he returned Theo and Angela's IDs.

"Yes, Sir!" Theo saluted him. Some students snickered as his wig finally fell off.

Jaya was right, it totally looks like Hogwarts! Angela thought as she looked around in awe. The school had transformed for the party. The jack-o-lanterns they had carved lit a path towards the gym.

"Over here!" yelled a member of the photography club. Angela slung her arms across Theo and Jaya's shoulders, standing in the middle. Jaya balanced on her tippy toes, complaining about their heights. Theo wrapped his arm around Angela's waist, beaming at her.

The three of them smiled for the camera.

Bats, cobwebs, and streamers decorated the gym. Lights flashed with different colours, a smoke machine was working overtime, and a DJ played on a built stage. It felt more like a nightclub than her school's gym.

Bodies of the students moving to the music in different rhythms made Angela feel a little self-conscious. She had never been to a school dance before. Floods of neon orange pylons that were stolen from the Re-Pavement Project were adorned by a rowdy basketball team. Theo called out as he spotted the volleyball team. Grabbing Angela by the hand, he brought her and Jaya to their circle in the middle of the dancefloor. She greeted the players she knew, laughing as someone made fun of Theo's costume.

"I like your ears!" Nathan, who was dressed as a mad scientist, yelled in her ear.

"Thanks!" she yelled back, pressing into Theo's side as she tried to jump along with the group.

The next moments were a blur of dancing, music, and lights. Angela's cheeks hurt from smiling and laughing. She followed Jaya towards the punch table, sipping from a purple cup. She waved at her history teacher, who took a sip of the bowl, making sure it was alcohol-free. She brought a cup for Theo, who was the life of the party. She cheered him on as he and Nathan began to dance in unison.

The DJ called into the microphone, "Let me hear you make some noise, STK!"

The gym erupted with cheers and screams from the students. It felt good to let loose, seeing the teachers tap their feet to the beat as the students flailed their arms wildly. Jaya spun her around, her cereal boxes losing integrity as Jaya jumped up and down. Theo held his arm out for Angela to take. She grabbed on and he spun her around while singing the song. Angela shouted as she spun him in return, his wig bouncing everywhere. They held one another close as they danced and sang, Theo's ears pink.

A shrill yell was heard in the distance, but the students continued partying. The sound of the gym door slamming shut caused some students to look over, but the party endured. It wasn't until the music stopped and silence filled the gym that everyone's attention was caught.

Everyone looked around, trying to understand the sudden silence. Angela looked towards the DJ booth, confused about why the music stopped. Then she saw someone on stage, someone familiar, with their ugly smile and chain hanging from his pocket. Only when she saw the look of horror on Jaya's face did she remember.

She had met him in an alley in Chinatown.

"Hello, STK!" Billy yelled into the mic. The students looked around confused, and the DJ held his arms up, frightened.

"What a fun party!" he continued. "I remember my high school Halloween party, although we had spiked the punch bowl by now!"

"Excuse me!" Principal Patel yelled as he ran towards the stage. The sea of students watched him sprint in his perfect suit. "Who do you think you are? This school is protected!"

"Hm, is it, though?" Billy asked as he leaned against the turn tables. Angela looked around, noticing more Halos filling the gym, blocking the doors. There were between twenty to thirty Halos, judging by the chains hanging from their pockets.

"Leave now!" Patel jumped onto the stage, his fist shaking. "This school is protected from scum like you!"

"We'll leave when we get what we want!" Billy yelled, causing the speakers to echo loudly. The students covered their ears. "The Halos are looking for a rat. He's been spotted around STK as of late."

"Jaya," Angela whispered, the smaller girl shook. "Jaya, let's run!"

"Where is Rafael Gomez?" Billy asked the silent crowd.

Some eyes wandered to Jaya.

"How dare you treat an Untouchable this way? Do you think that the Gates will allow for this?" Patel bellowed furiously as he stepped closer to the man.

"Nah, shut up!" Billy shot Patel in the leg.

Chaos erupted as the students ran for the doors screaming. Billy continued yelling into the microphone, "Anyone who knows where the rat is and doesn't speak will get their hands shot!"

Angela grabbed the frozen Jaya and pushed along with the students towards the door. The sound of gunshots echoing in the gym only motivated them more to escape.

It was a stampede of students.

"JAYA!" a Halo called out as he pointed a knife towards the girls.

"NO!" Angela screamed, covering Jaya with her body. The Halo was tackled from the side. Theo struggled to pin him down as the students filed through the unmanned door. Angela kicked his face, feeling the bones in his nose break beneath her shoe.

The knife scattered across the floor, gone under the mass of people.

"MOVE!" Theo screamed as he grabbed Jaya, leading them further into the school. Angela pulled the fire alarm down, the ringing adding to the commotion of people escaping from the gym. More gunshots were heard behind them.

The students tried fleeing through the front door but more armed Halos met them. Theo grabbed a clown mask from the ground, leading them down the science hallway. Angela ran ahead of the pair, checking for an unlocked classroom. She began to panic as all the doors were locked. Theo glanced over his shoulders, the students running in different directions, trying to find a way out of the school.

"Here!" Angela whispered as she found an unlocked door. She locked it behind them as other students ran down the hallway with a scream. Theo placed the mask over Jaya's face.

The trio hid behind a lab bench, the sound of their panting filled the room along with the fire alarm. The rush of people outside and more gunshots were heard. Not before long, the sound of police sirens joined the turmoil. Angela glanced over at Jaya, who sat on the other side of Theo, seeing her chest heave. Theo rubbed her shoulders, trying to comfort her.

Angela opened her phone, turning down the brightness. She received a message from Lucy asking if she had made it out alive. She looked at Theo's screen, seeing a plethora of messages on his. Jaya was messaging someone, too.

The contact was saved under the letter 'P'.

Some students were also hiding, while some had found an unlocked window and climbed down from the second floor. Others were in the gym still, trying to tell the Halos they had nothing to do with Raef.

The fire alarm stopped, leaving the three in silence. Only the sound of their panting was heard in the dark science lab.

A loud bang came from the door. The trio jumped. Angela made a noise of surprise, and Theo slapped his hand across her mouth.

"Police, open up!" a voice called from the other side. Theo shook his head as Jaya turned towards the pair. Angela looked around, noticing a few glass beakers within arm's reach. She grabbed a few, handing them to her friends, who understood.

The sound of the door unlocking caused them to be still, ready to fight. A man entered the room, flashlight and gun in hand.

"CCPD, is there anyone in here?"

Jaya shrieked as she threw the beaker at the officer. Angela and Theo grabbed at her to stop. She missed, and the beaker crashed into the wall next to the officer. He flicked the lights on, lowering his gun as he approached the students.

"You're safe now," Officer Amir Hafiz spoke gently, pocketing his flashlight. "We've apprehended the intruders. The CCPD is currently looking for missing students."

Theo slumped on the bench, the adrenaline exiting his system. Amir studied the group closely, his eyes stopping on Angela.

"I've seen you before," Amir remembered as he stepped closer to the trio. "You were attacked by Tony Moretti," Amir successfully recounted. His walkie peeped as someone spoke to him from the other side, Amir responded.

"Is this him?" Jaya asked from behind the clown mask, forgetting to take it off. Angela took a step forward towards the man, feeling that this was more than a coincidence for the officer to find her and her friends.

As though fate had brought him to her.

This was her moment to help Jaya, to save her, just as she had helped Theo.

"Officer Hafiz, we need your help."

Amir nodded at the girl, as though he knew she would say that.

"Let's get you three down to the station."

Owl flew between the different patients at her clinic, most of them left after she patched them up and gave them a talking-to. But Parris remained in and out of consciousness. Owl tore the curtain back as she entered the small room, finding Logan knocked out by her bedside, reading a medical book from her collection. She slammed down her tray, awakening the man, the book falling from his grip.

"Not going trick-or-treating?"

Logan rubbed his eyes as he leaned down to get the book. "They don't teach you bedside manners in medical school?"

"I wouldn't know, I never went." Owl was busy checking Parris's vitals. Logan glared at her, as though the sleepless nights at the clinic were for nought.

"Relax." He did not. "I watched my mother growing up. I know my stuff. Even taught Parris a little back in the day."

"She really does know her stuff," came the hoarse voice of Parris from the bed, awoken from the multiple thuds of falling objects.

"You've been in and out, kid. How are you feeling?" Owl asked, worry entrenched in her frown lines. Parris didn't answer, instead looking around the room, craning her neck.

"Phone."

Logan moved quickly, giving the Informant the phone from her side table. She took it with weak hands, struggling to bring the device to eye level.

They remained silent as they watched the Informant read through her messages.

"The Halos invaded STK," she announced to the quiet room. Owl's eyes got impossibly wide. "Multiple shootings, no one confirmed dead, suspects apprehended."

"They're attacking the Untouchables," the doctor said. "Do they think the Gates would allow for this?"

Parris scanned through her phone, seeing multiple messages and missed calls from Giovanni.

The Informant had a pained look on her face as she continued reading through the endless messages. She tried sitting up but gasped when it pulled on her stitches. Owl stopped her with a hand on her shoulder.

"And just where do you think you're going, Parris?"

"This has to end."

"End with you dead from an infection, brat!" Owl warned as the Informant pushed back. "Logan, talk some sense into her."

He looked down at the Parrasite, seeing her struggle against the doctor's hand. Her phone lit up with new messages as though she were responding to a sinking ship.

Is she the reason the Big Three got along? Could she put an end to the incoming gang war?

"Take me to Port Front Central," Parris looked directly at Logan.

Owl increased the frequency of the drip in the IV with one hand, while holding down the Informant with the other.

"Absolutely not! Stop being suicidal, Parris!" Owl yelled at her.

"NOW!" the Informant shouted urgently. "No one else can get those idiots to agree. There's a bloodbath coming, and you and Angie will get swept up in it. You said that you didn't care for me, Logan. So bring me there. *Now!*"

Logan caught the doctor's wrist, moving without thinking. Owl's piercing eyes bore into his soul, making him shudder. He was doing it again, helping the Parrasite without thinking, as though her wishes were his commands.

"Owl," Parris whispered uncharacteristically gentle. "Thank you for your help, but it's time I go."

The doctor released her grip on her, looking away, redness in her sharp eyes. Owl helped her to a seating position, shooing Logan outside so she could dress the Informant. He waited in the waiting room of the underground clinic, his mind running in circles.

Leave her. LEAVE NOW!

"Let's go," Parris called out. She was dressed in her usual attire, minus her leather jacket. She held her side as she took a laboured step up the staircase. Logan jumped when Owl placed her hand on his shoulder.

"You take good care of that one. We can't lose her. At least, not yet. The game is still in play." The doctor's eyes were glazed over, as though she were in mourning.

"I'll try," Logan mumbled, not sure why he said so. Parris panted from the top of the staircase, pushing open the metal door.

The night welcomed her back into its embrace.

"Where to?" Logan asked bitterly as he started the car, the Informant sitting with a grimace.

"Port Central Front, Warehouse Number Forty-Six." She was already busy on her phone. Logan huffed as he started down the road, promising himself that he would drop her off and never look back.

The ride to the warehouse was silent. Parris tapped urgently on her phone, responding to an onslaught of messages. Logan would glance over every now and then, but he never caught her eye.

He cursed at himself as he watched the Informant disappear into the abandoned warehouse. Parris left without a word or a glance back.

Leave already, you said you would leave!

"Shit," he mumbled. He parked his truck down another alley.

Hopping out, he searched for another entrance into Warehouse Number Forty-Six. Logan found a rusty fire escape that groaned as he placed his body weight on the first step. Stepping as carefully as he could, he tiptoed up the fire escape, nudging the old door open. Finding himself on the second floor, overlooking the body of the warehouse, Logan lay on his stomach on the metal grate floor. He watched the Informant sway in the middle of the gutted floor that was covered with graffiti. Exposed support pillars and harsh lighting made the place all the more unwelcoming. Parris was dressed in her leather jacket.

Her jacket? Lorenzo must be close by, he thought to himself.

The metal creaked under his weight; Logan winced, praying that she wouldn't notice. The slightest turn of Parris's head towards his direction was the only indication that she heard. Parris turned her attention to the sound of three cars entering through the garage door.

Three black cars pulled into the warehouse, stopping in a semi-circle around the Informant. Four individuals exited the vehicles. Logan's eyes widened as he understood. She was calling for a meeting of the Heads of the Gates, Wings, and Halos.

"*Bella*!" Giovanni called out as he rushed to her. Logan watched the older man stroke her face, and his blood boiled. He could tell she was uncomfortable; it wasn't hard to see. Her shoulders were as stiff as marble.

"Not now," she muttered as she took a step back, holding her side. "We're here to discuss a cease-fire."

"You're a hard bitch to kill."

Parris glared at Tony. Giovanni turned around slowly, staring at his son with red eyes.

"You admit to stabbing her?"

Marcel stepped between the pair.

"The Wings didn't stab her, but we did send our men after her in the hospital," Marcel admitted.

In an instant, Giovanni was in Tony's face.

"A lowlife decided to stab her and suddenly the order is gone? She's an Untouchable. My Untouchable. How dare you break the simplest terms of our agreement! Why is it so hard for you to *listen*? Didn't you learn your lesson, boy?"

Marcel tried to approach the duo, but Giovanni pulled a gun, aiming at Marcel.

"I always knew you were smart, Marcel. I know you've been pulling the strings behind the Wings. That you're the *real* Head. You haven't usurped this piece of trash and taken over yet, and I respect you for respecting my agreement. He is an Untouchable, unfortunately," Giovanni spoke, barely looking at Marcel.

"But," Giovanni continued, "I'll grant you permission to kill him. Because if you don't, then I will. And you know that I won't be gentle."

"BASTARD," Tony roared, pushing his father square in the chest.

The sound of a slap echoed in the empty warehouse. Giovanni backhanded Tony across the face.

Huifen watched from the back, not wanting the attention of the Head of the Gates. But she found his chestnut eyes, the gun still pointed at Marcel.

"Tiffany."

A shiver went down her spine.

"Tiffany," Giovanni growled, "sending the Halos into my school?"

She croaked; she opened her mouth but nothing came out. She could feel the anger roll off of Giovanni in waves. She prided herself on being fearless, but in that moment, she felt like a little kid again, hand caught in the cookie jar.

"Huifen!"

She jumped.

"That school was not to be touched. It was not to be raided. It was to remain pure, but you've tainted it."

Huifen tried to approach the older man, but he shot the ground next to Marcel's foot.

"HOW IS IT OUR FAULT YOU'RE LOSING YOUR EDGE?" Tony yelled, recovered from the shock of the slap. Being hit by his father for the first time in ten years stunned him. Being touched by his father again…

Giovanni peered down at his son with disgust.

"You were the one who lost the Re-Pavement Project! We follow your rules if you provide us opportunities," Tony continued yelling. "You! Not the Wings, or the fucking Halos, but YOU! You were the one who touched her! You tainted an Untouchable first! Why are you blaming us for FOLLOWING YOUR FUCKING LEAD?"

Once he had poured out his frustration, Tony panted heavily. His piercing blue eyes caught his father's chestnut ones.

"Last I checked," Giovanni calmly announced. Hunger filled his chestnut eyes as he stalked up to Tony, his lips tugged into an ugly snarl. "You were the one who started this all. You decided to fuck with an Untouchable all those years ago. Sleeping with that STK student."

The calmness in his voice made him all the more off-putting. Tony knew what the look meant, what the hungry stare could only mean for him. Giovanni's polished shoes crept along the dingy floor. Without meaning to, Tony took a step back as Giovanni continued his advance towards him slowly.

"You were the one. Not the Gates, or the Halos, or the Wings. But you. Then, you decided to hurt my Informant and my boy. Imagine my surprise when Theo Grayson said he was assaulted right outside of that school. That *you* dared to touch him. Another STK student."

"Stay back…" Tony whispered.

"The loss of the Project impacts your business. Impacts the Halos' business. Not mine." Giovanni continued his stalking. Tony's back hit against one of the cars. His eyes frantically looked around for an escape route, but there was none. Marcel and Huifen were frozen in place. Giovanni was within arm's reach. The Informant watched from a distance.

Tony was a cornered animal.

"You needed that Project. Not me. The Untouchables are meant to be respected for the sake of our shared business. Respect for the Untouchables meant respect for me."

Tony cowered away from his father, never inheriting his height and stature. He was little. He was weak. Giovanni's physical presence was all-encompassing. There was only *him*.

"Stop…"

"But you still haven't learned that lesson."

Giovanni brought the gun next to Tony's ear, firing another bullet. Tony gave a yell as he covered his ears, a violent ringing in his head.

Once Tony was disoriented, Giovanni brought the handle of the gun across Tony's face. Blood spurted out from his broken nose. Giovanni grabbed Tony's face, slamming his head back into the car. Tony tried to grab the offending hand, but his mind was beginning to fog from the onslaught.

Marcel continued facing forward, the sound of the Moretti family behind him bringing him back to the hours he would wait for Tony outside of the Head's office in the CCC building, and how he had to be the one to pick up the pieces Giovanni constantly broke.

Huifen stared at the way the older man behaved, seeing the animalistic rage in the way Giovanni effortlessly hurt Tony, the smile on the older man's face all teeth. She was used to violence, they all were, but watching Giovanni was like watching a wild animal destroy for sport, not for food.

"After all that time and effort I spent on you. You failed to apply any of the skills I ingrained into you," Giovanni snarled.

The sound of Tony's skull meeting the metal of the car echoed in the warehouse. Giovanni continued bashing Tony's head into the car.

Marcel squeezed his eyes shut at Tony's cries. Giovanni kicked Tony's shins, his body crashing onto the dirty floor in a heap. Giovanni dug his heel into Tony's groin.

Tony wailed in pain and humiliation. His hands tried to pry his father off.

"I taught you well. Even how to use this prick. Maybe too well. Tell me. Was it worth it? Was she a good lay for you?"

Tony choked on his cry. Huifen's eyes widened in realization and disgust. Giovanni grinned. He wanted to see blood. He *needed* to see tears.

"Was she better than me, boy?"

"Please, s-stop!" Tony begged. His face was red. Tears collected in his eyes. Giovanni kicked him in the head. Tony cried out, his body going limp on the ground. Tears finally broke through.

"*Answer me.*"

Returning the gun to its place, Giovanni held Tony's left wrist. One by one, he broke each finger with a clean snap.

"Don't tell me you've missed this?" Giovanni growled, his ears hungry for more sounds of pain. He was in his element.

Snap!

"Ahh! Please, enough!" Tony screamed, his chest heaving.

Snap!

Tony continued to scream. The sounds of the bones snapping into unnatural positions were pleasant to Giovanni's ears.

Snap!

"I've never treated *her* like this," Giovanni whispered.

Snap!

"I wasn't going to treat Theo like this either."

SNAP!

"NO MORE!" Tony cried. His entire left hand was misshapen. The fingers, once pale, were now red and blue and stuck out at odd angles.

"Only you. Only *you* were this special."

Giovanni's eyes gleamed at the way Tony tried to curl away.

"On your feet! I tried to raise a man after all." Giovanni grabbed Tony by the neck, putting him back on his feet.

"Mercy…" Tony mumbled. His head lulled around, concussed from the assault.

Giovanni laughed loudly.

"You were the one asking for my attention!" He grabbed Tony by the chin. "I'm just giving you what you've been asking for, b*egging* me for."

"Marce—!"

Giovanni's fist rained down on Tony's left side. The cruel crack of his ribs filled the warehouse. Marcel winced. Huifen shook, glad she wasn't on the receiving end of Giovanni's attention.

"None of that now. He won't help you. He's never helped you before, has he?" Giovanni mocked, his canines prominent.

"This has always been an *intimate* family moment."

They all killed for business routinely, but this was different. Marcel and Huifen relied on guns and grunts to get their message across. But Giovanni just needed himself. Marcel knew what happened behind the office doors at the CCC, the reason why Tony walked with a limp, what Giovanni enjoyed more than anything.

Breaking his prey down.

Another gunshot echoed in the empty warehouse, and Tony cried as the bullet sailed through his left palm. His left hand was useless now. The sound of his body crumpling to the ground brought everyone back to reality.

"Such a shame to the Moretti name. I should have castrated you before kicking you out," Giovanni spat at him, returning the gun.

"Let this serve as a reminder," Giovanni declared, out of breath. His shoulders rose as he panted deeply. Tony trembled on the ground, cradling whatever of himself he could hold. Blood pooled around him. Giovanni turned his back on the battered form of his son on the floor.

"Does this mean we have a cease-fire?" Parris asked, breaking the intense tension in the warehouse.

"The status quo still stands," Giovanni returned to her side.

"Any objections?" he asked, turning to face the co-conspirators.

Nobody spoke; they couldn't disagree with the older man, not able to meet his eyes. His influence aside, his physical brutality left their mouths dry.

"Then I will take my leave." He kissed the Informant's hand. "And we shall meet soon, *Bella*. I am relieved to see you walking about."

Parris forced a smile.

Once Giovanni's car drove out of the warehouse, Marcel rushed to Tony's side. Huifen promptly left, no comment this time. Parris swayed out of the warehouse without a second glance at the Wings; her balance was off as she was busy making a phone call.

Logan finally let out the breath he had been holding. He could feel the goosebumps on his arm slowly settle as he watched the battered man be lifted into the back of the last car before it too left the warehouse in a hurry.

It felt silly to be dressed in their costumes, sitting in the police station on Halloween, but there they were. Angela bounced her leg anxiously as she sat in an uncomfortable chair in Officer Hafiz's office. The vomit-coloured walls did little to comfort the teenagers.

Jaya sat next to her, still wearing the clown mask. Officer Hafiz had instructed her to keep it on, to maintain her privacy. But safe in the office, she was too lost in her thoughts to remember to take it off. Theo stood behind the girls, leaning against the wall, pinching the bridge of his nose.

I saw the news! What happened? Are you okay? Were you hurt? Where are you now? Why won't you answer your phone? – Dad

I'm safe! We left the party early, so we weren't there when that happened. I'm with Jaya and Theo. We're at Aunty Kim's place. I'll call you later. – Angela

The sound of the door opening caught their attention. Officer Hafiz entered with a tray of three steaming cups of hot chocolate. He placed the tray on his desk as he sat on the opposing side, removing his hat with a sigh.

"A cat, a cereal killer, and a granny," he mumbled to himself, slightly amused. "Help yourselves," he invited as the trio remained in their spots.

Theo took a cup first, muttering about needing something for his headache. Angela took one of the steaming cups. She recognized the smell, the same brand of instant mix she bought for her aunt's place. That gave her some comfort as she took a sip, careful to not burn herself.

"So, are you three here to tell me exactly why the Halos were at your Halloween Party tonight?"

Angela felt Jaya's and Theo's eyes land on her.

"Before we say anything, we need assurance that we will get immunity, that those of us involved will not be charged with any crimes, that we will be safe," Angela demanded.

Amir watched the kids sadly. "I will ensure that you all are safe. I'll draft the immunity agreements myself," Amir pledged.

Shakily, Jaya removed the clown mask. With a deep breath, she told the story of her and Raef meeting one another in STK, how Raef got caught up using and selling drugs, which led to his expulsion last year. When he was caught stealing from the Halos, she was spared when he disappeared. Then, when he resurfaced, indebted to the Gates and with the Halos still after him, the pair would gather supplies before the Halos would cut off other dealers. He would do this in order to resell and pay off his debt to the Gates. Jaya recounted the painful story with tears speeding down her face, her hot chocolate turned cold by the end of her tale.

"You were there at *Fresh to Go?*" Amir asked as he continued taking notes.

"Sorry," Jaya whispered meekly, "I didn't have a choice."

Amir smiled. "You gave one of my officers a run for her money. Are you on the track team?"

"No! I hate sports." Jaya laughed genuinely.

The air in the office was lighter the longer they spoke. Amir was easy to talk to, his warm concern refreshing to the group. The high schoolers were glad he was the one to find them.

"And tonight?" Amir prompted.

"They came in looking for Raef or for someone who knew Raef," Jaya recounted. "The fact that they attacked an Untouchable makes no sense. I thought the school was protected, but then they shot Principal Patel…"

"Your principal is okay, they took him to the hospital. He should make a speedy recovery. What are you proposing, Jaya? You said you had incriminating evidence that you've been gathering."

"I want him out of my life. I want to graduate and go to university and be done with him!" Jaya exclaimed. Angela handed her another tissue, a pile building on the small girl's lap.

"I want to be free of him, please, Officer Hafiz."

"And is there anything that you forgot to tell me?" Amir asked, watching Jaya carefully.

Jaya hesitated, not sure if she should speak about the Informant and how she had been coerced into gathering intel for her.

"No, nothing, Sir."

He nodded as he continued writing, Angela attempting to read the notes upside down.

"This is what I can tell you three," Amir finally looked up. "Give me the evidence and I will take care of the rest. Jaya, I will see that you are free from this jerk's influence."

Jaya blew her nose loudly in response.

"Thank you, Sir," Theo chipped in, "but we have to make sure Jaya is still safe even after Raef is arrested."

"Change is coming to Ciel City, Theo," Amir stated confidently. "A new Ciel where gangs won't dictate your lives. That I can promise you kids."

"Are you going to tell our parents now?" Jaya asked in a quiet voice.

Shit! Angela thought. *He can't report this to Mom and Dad. I can't have them pull me out now.*

Amir glanced at his phone. Angela tried to peek at the screen. He was reading a message from 'Helen'.

"There's a new city by-law," Amir read the text. He wasn't happy with what he was reading, but he swallowed around his discomfort.

"Since all three of you are seventeen, you may choose to disclose the events of tonight to your parents. I would suggest you don't… just until we've dealt with Rafael. The fewer people who know, the easier it will be."

Donning his jacket, Amir watched the high schoolers stand up. "Now come on." He held the door to his office open, the trio filed through, and Jaya re-equipped her mask.

"I think I should have some candy in my police cruiser; it is Halloween, after all."

The STK students followed Amir into the car. Jaya had calmed down remarkably as she conversed with the officer. Theo was excited that Amir also played volleyball, exchanging ideas of having a CCPD vs STK game.

Amir had been kind to them, gentle, even. He made Angela feel safe and cared for, like an older sibling, like how Nini used to take her to the park and fuss over her scraped knee, or when she told their parents that she broke the ugly vase from Aunty Kim when Angela had been throwing her ball around their home.

Why didn't we go to him sooner? Why are good people so hard to find? Angela thought as she sat in the car with Theo and Amir, waiting for Jaya to return with the physical evidence from her home.

"When you said change is coming… did you really mean that,

Officer?" Theo mumbled in a quiet voice.

Amir looked between him and Angela in the rearview mirror. His green eyes radiated warmth.

"I meant every word."

CHAPTER SIXTEEN

Silver Plate

The next day was a cause for celebration for Jaya. Today was the day Raef would be arrested.

Today the nightmare would end.

I'll be able to finally focus on graduating. On university applications. On my future without this looming black cloud. This is going to work out!

She rushed around her home, getting ready to stake out Raef's apartment. Officer Hafiz had told her that he would send an officer to pick her up and confirm Raef's location and identity in order for them to make the arrest.

When she had given him the evidence she had collected, hope filled her chest. Officer Hafiz had been alarmed at the sheer volume of evidence: photos of illicit drugs, a USB full of recorded conversations, and a list of other dealers and suppliers. But it was him pushing all the evidence aside, focused only on Jaya asking in a calm and controlled voice if she was okay, that had cemented his image in her mind.

He was a good person.

"This is more than just probable cause," he remarked as he flipped through the photographs. Jaya hugged Angela tightly, excited that the laborious work had paid off.

"You kids have a knack for criminal investigation," Amir praised them.

The students had the day off from school as the police conducted an investigation of STK. Jaya's parents had been disturbed when they heard the news and Jaya's filtered version, but she assured them that nothing had happened to her.

Another easy lie she sold them.

"Appa!" Jaya yelled. "I'm heading out now, I won't be home until late. I'm studying with Angela for our midterms!"

"Stay away from Midtown! Crazy people entering the school," her dad shouted from somewhere in the house. A crash of toys and crying followed.

It was a dark and cloudy day, and Jaya pulled her rain jacket around herself tighter as she walked up the street. She found a police cruiser parked up the street. She knocked on the window politely.

"Hi, Officer Hafiz said I would find a car here for me?"

A woman officer smiled kindly at her.

"Jaya Sharma! Come on in, my name is Officer Sanchez, Officer Hafiz told me the situation."

"How much did he tell you?" Jaya buckled up.

"He told me enough; he said that this was highly confidential," Sanchez answered cheerily.

Officer Sanchez began driving towards the address of Raef's apartment. Jaya took in a deep breath, ready to do the impossible. Officer Sanchez did not make conversation, focused on driving and humming along to the radio. Jaya was thankful for that. After last night, she just wanted to mindlessly stare out of the window at the passing buildings.

"Oh, you missed the exit."

The radio grew louder as Officer Sanchez turned the dial-up.

"Officer Sanchez, Raef's apartment was back there," Jaya explained.

"I know," she replied cheerfully. "But we're not going there."

A cold sweat dripped down the back of Jaya's neck.

"But Officer Hafiz said that we would confirm his location and appearance together. Then I would be returned home so you can make the arrest."

"Plans have changed, Jaya."

The car sped on the highway, the traffic lessening as they drove away from the city center, towards the west end. Jaya frantically pulled out her phone.

"Put that away," Sanchez tapped the gun in her holster. "Don't be so worried. Just sit back and relax, Jaya."

Jaya stared at the gun. She clasped her hands together as they pulled into a pier, seagulls flew overhead. There were a few cars parked at the pier and a group of individuals gathered together. Jaya gasped; she recognized the high pigtails from afar.

"Come on, you shouldn't leave the Head of the Halos waiting," Sanchez instructed.

Huifen's eyes lit up when she saw Jaya. A cruel smile and a gesture to approach were the only orders Jaya needed to follow Sanchez towards the crowd. Huifen stood in the center with her executives around a body on the floor.

"Jaya Sharma in the flesh!" Huifen welcomed in a loud voice. "Twice in one year? Someone has a death wish!" The group of executives and grunts snickered as Jaya stiffened at the sight of the body on the floor. Sanchez grabbed her neck from behind, forcing her to watch.

On the pier was Raef, bloodied and bruised. He was gasping for breaths, his nose bones shattered. Huifen grabbed Jaya's face, her nails digging into the flesh of Jaya's cheeks.

"I really should be thanking you for delivering this piece of shit to me. I got heat for sending my men to STK, but sometimes you need to smoke out the pests in order to terminate them."

Jaya's chest heaved; the words being spoken did not register as she looked at Raef. His eyes were swollen and black. She wanted to gag, but warm liquid travelling down her cheek brought her attention back to Huifen.

"Please…"

"Please what?" Huifen spat.

"Please leave me out of this."

The Head stepped away from Jaya, circling the damaged body on the floor. Huifen sighed dramatically before stomping on Raef's hand. His wail echoed across the pier.

"I did leave you out of this, Jaya. When I decided to take the Informant's offer in your place. I let you leave the mess this thing made."

"JAYA!" Raef yelled, spit flew from his mouth. "HELP!"

"But she did help!" Huifen continued, stepping off the boy. "She ran to the CCPD! Truly, thank you for giving us everything. Finding this piece of filth had been difficult."

"I didn't!" Jaya croaked, her voice distant to her own ears. "I never meant for any of this! I just wanted to live a normal life. I wanted to be free! Officer Hafiz promised me that!"

The Head rolled her eyes. "Is that the delusional greenie, Sanchez?"

The hand on Jaya's neck tightened. "Yes, the same one who found Cloud 9 at *Fresh To Go,*" Sanchez answered.

"Fuck him!" Huifen groaned. "I paired you with him specifically to make sure he wouldn't find jack shit, Sanchez! *Fresh To Go* was a vital stash for us."

Jaya felt the way the officer stiffened behind her, afraid of the Head's wrath.

Officer Hafiz didn't betray me?

"Stealing from me was bold, but living in my city afterward was idiotic. It was only a matter of time. Come on, thank Jaya for telling us how to find you," Huifen mocked as she kicked Raef's arm out.

Raef looked up at Jaya, his eyes clouded. She looked into them, the eyes that brought her so much joy and then pain. She couldn't bring herself to think this was justified, that he deserved this. Not like this.

"Jaya…"

Huifen shot his hand. Jaya jumped, the sound echoing on the pier. The seagulls fluttered overhead. Raef remained silent; he had nothing left to scream with. Blood gushed from the wound, Jaya could see the veins and the exposed nerves. Huifen stood back, waiting for an executive to turn him around to expose his other hand.

"Can't forget about this one, too."

The blood under Raef grew and he stopped moving. Jaya clenched her eyes shut as Huifen shot his other hand. Again, no sound from Raef.

A third shot rang across the pier.

When Jaya finally opened her eyes, Huifen was in front of her.

"I should shoot your hands as well, Jaya."

Jaya openly wept, not able to handle anymore. She saw where the third bullet hit its mark: between Raef's eyes. He was gone. The boy she once loved and then feared; she had witnessed his murder.

She had killed him.

"But you did give him up to me, so I will count that as even."

Sanchez released her. Without that hold, Jaya fell to the ground sobbing. She couldn't see or hear anything, her crying shaking her violently. The world was cold. It was the colder press of metal to her head that brought her back to reality.

"If I see you again, Jaya, I will kill you."

The young girl hugged herself as the members of the Halos left after pushing Raef's body into the water. Even Officer Sanchez walked away silently, not bothered by the murder she had abetted. Jaya felt a drop of rain on her head as she stayed on the pier sobbing.

The sudden downpour was surprising as the weather changed drastically. Amir ran to the car, entering the backseat in a huff as he pushed his wet hair back from his forehead.

"They didn't mention rain today," Lorenzo commented from behind the wheel.

Amir looked to the Informant in the back with him. He had heard about the stabbing in Midtown, the same day after they had their meeting. When he had lost contact with her for a while he had assumed the worst. He would never admit it to her, but he was relieved she was alive.

'Alive' was subjective. He could see the way her hand clenched her side, the tightness in her eyebrows from exhaustion.

Ever since that night at *Clueless* a few weeks ago, they had been meeting in secret like this, while still communicating through messages as Helen whenever she needed something from him. It was good to spend time with her.

Even if she was a powerful mafia informant.

"It'll clear up soon," Parris sang. "Sometimes sudden downpours need to happen to clear the air."

Lorenzo drove around Ciel, the usual route taking significantly longer. Cars insistently honked at one another as more lanes in the downtown core were being closed. Construction workers placed ugly orange pylons, closing some streets and restricting the movement of the flow of traffic.

"The Re-Pavement Project is underway," Amir commented as he watched from the window. Parris had told him about her plans that night, and she had explained what was to come. Amir had been shocked but promised not to tell a soul. When he had told those kids change was coming, he had meant it.

Those kids, Amir thought. It was a meeting some time ago when the Informant had mentioned that some STK kids were caught up with the gangs. When he had pushed for more information, she kept quiet.

Those kids… Angela, Jaya, and Theo were the ones she had meant.

"Your meeting with the Heads worked out," he continued. "The Halos haven't been resisting the investigation and small gang violence has decreased."

Parris hummed as she stared out the window. "And those kids you picked up last night?"

Amir smiled. *She does care about them.* Her first message to him since she disappeared was to have him check the science labs of STK on Halloween. She had sent him to save those kids.

"Don't worry about them," Amir said as he checked the time. "I told Officer Sanchez to pick up the girl, Jaya, to scout the apartment."

It was the slow turn of her head that told Amir he had messed up. Parris looked at him as though he had said the stupidest thing in existence. Just then, her phone rang.

"Yes?"

"I'm done!" came the frantic shrill of Jaya. Amir checked the time again; he told Sanchez not to make the arrest without him. It was still too early in the day; he instructed her to only stake out the apartment.

What happened?

"I am done with your shit!" Jaya screamed. "They killed him! They shot him in front of me!"

"Who was it?" Parris asked, her eyes never leaving Amir.

"Tiffany shot Raef! That officer who picked me up brought me to his fucking execution! She's a part of the fucking Halos!"

Realization plunged into Amir's stomach like a ton of lead. Slowly the warning of the Informant all those weeks ago rang in his ear.

"I wouldn't trust a soul in that division, Officer Amir Hafiz."

"I want out! I'm not working for you anymore," Jaya sobbed. Amir could hear the panic and pain in her voice. He had done this to her.

"Jaya, where are you now?" Parris asked, her frown deeper than ever.

"There's nothing left to protect me from! Not from Raef or the shitty Halos! It's over, go fuck yourself!" the high schooler yelled before ending the call.

The car was quiet as they digested the news. Amir rushed to call Officer Sanchez, to confront her. Parris slapped the phone out of his hand in a sudden outrage.

"I warned you."

He looked up to see a storm brewing in her eyes.

"You're a *fucking* idiot, Amir."

Amir's voice caught in his throat. He didn't know how to respond, how to make up for the harm he had done. He had believed that Kristina Sanchez was on his side. She had made that speech to him when he had first transferred. She admitted to the squad that she helped him investigate Cloud 9. She gave him looks of adoration as he walked past.

Those looks of admiration turned into an ugly look of manipulation as he remembered her insistent prodding. He remembered the way she would ask for his source of information: how he had known about *Fresh To Go, h*ow he even got the warrant in the first place, the countless times she would knock on his office door, asking what he was working on, the way she would so readily offer her help. He should have listened to Parris. Amir wanted the Informant to be wrong about Sanchez, he wanted to believe that she was capable of making errors like the rest of them. But he should have known that she knew better.

The sting of betrayal and the feeling of humiliation made him stare at his hands.

The rain had finally stopped, the clouds slowly making space for the sun to peek through, to have a look at Ciel.

"This is the last time we'll meet in person," Parris declared as the car came to a stop where it had picked the officer up. "Be sure to play your part well, you won't get a second chance."

"I'm sorry, Parris."

She didn't play with her phone, as he was accustomed to when she would wait for him to leave. She sat still, staring at the headrest of the driver's seat. Amir didn't want to leave yet. He didn't want this to be the last time.

"I'm sorry that you have to live like this. All I could do was only save one person. Clearly, I'm not cut out for this job," he continued when she didn't respond. Lorenzo looked at him through the rear mirror.

"I'm sorry you lost your STK informant and that I ruined some of your plans."

"Enough."

But he couldn't stop. He was never good at saying goodbye.

"As trivial as it was, getting messages from Helen made me feel not alone. It felt nice to have a friend in this city."

She is my friend.

Parris turned towards him; he could see the bags under her eyes. Her cocky smile wasn't there anymore.

"I pray you find peace, Parris," he gripped the handle of the door. "When this blows over, maybe we can have a drink together again. I'll get you a Ciel latte!"

"You remembered my order from *Jim's?*" she chuckled, a light flickered in her drained eyes.

Amir smiled, dread sunk into his heart. Those dark eyes weren't as shadowy as he had thought, not when the sun shone into them.

They were warm.

"How could I forget?"

The sound of the news channel echoed in the apartment. Angela needed background noise to think.

"The Re-Pavement Project is underway in the Downtown Core. Expect lane closures, increase in travel time, and detours. Mayor Robert encourages people to avoid the Downtown Core this weekend," the T.V. announced.

Angela sat on her bed, the shoebox in front of her. She had pulled all the curtains of the apartment closed, in case someone was watching her.

I've helped Theo and now I've helped Jaya. I got them back. They're safe now, finally. My grades aren't enough for a scholarship but I can work on them once I've done it. Parris is still out there. She's alive. I know she is.

"Hi, Dad," Angela answered her phone.

"Hi, Angel," he greeted back. His tone was tense. Angela knew what was coming next.

"Angel, your mother had another… episode. She's been having a rough time since last night's news broadcast on the attack on STK. The counsellor thinks it retriggered her."

Of course it did, Angela thought bitterly.

"You didn't come home for Thanksgiving, but maybe you can come home this weekend? Stay with her a bit?" her dad asked. She knew he must be at the end of his rope. Taking care of his wife, raising a child, and working full-time was beginning to take a toll on him. Especially after ten long, painful years.

"Dad, it's midterm season."

"I know… I know. She keeps mentioning her."

Angela pressed her trembling lips into a line. She tried not to resent her mother. Angela had tried to throughout her entire childhood, not when her mother would cry throughout the night, praying for Nini, not when her father took on the endless weight of trying to give them a semblance of a normal life, not when Angela was alone, crying herself to sleep hugging Nini's pillow.

"I'm not Nini, Dad."

I'm sorry, Dad. I know that this hurts you.

"I understand. Please focus on your studies, ignore everything I just said," her father hide the hurt in his voice.

"Tell Mom that I love her and I'll see her once I finish my midterms."

"I will. Work hard, Angel."

The line cut.

Rubbing her eyes angrily, Angela refused to cry. She returned her attention to the shoebox, pulling the gun out. She hadn't touched it since the night Tony gave it to her.

That night was a lifetime ago.

She was different then. Ciel City was easy to navigate. It had been easy to find the Informant. But the gangs got in her way. Her friends got in her way.

Every time she wanted to talk to the Informant, Parris was whisked away.

She received a phone call from Jaya, but she ignored it. She figured that they would have arrested Raef by now.

Good for her, she thought as she typed two separate messages on her phone, hitting the send button with more pressure than she had meant.

One to Parris and one to Logan.

Lastly, she called Theo, asking him to give her a ride. He quickly agreed.

I'll finally ask her. This time we will have a private moment to talk. No worming your way out of it, Parris.

Angela checked the gun, to make sure it was actually loaded. Once everything was ready, she waited by the door. She looked around her aunt's apartment, her home for the past few months.

The 'A' and 'J' letter magnets on the cream-coloured fridge. The bulky television console. The flower lampshade in the bedroom.

Guilt weighed heavily on her heart for how she treated her parents, but she pushed it aside. She would be a better help to her dad after tonight. She would comfort her mother after tonight. She would get her grades up once she spoke to her.

When she received a message from Theo, she left the empty home.

Theo's car slowed down as it approached its destination: a low abandoned building, with a fire escape attached to the side. It was a laundromat back in the day. The faded sign read:

Johnston's Family Wash.

Angela had sat in silence the whole ride over, a hard look on her face. Theo had asked her a million questions but Angela ignored him. He tried making conversation about Jaya and the Officer instead, but that fell through when he realized that he hadn't heard an update from Jaya.

"You can park on the side; I'm heading up to the roof," Angela uttered. Theo did as instructed, parking the car near the fire escape.

"Wait for me here; it shouldn't take too long, Theo."

"Why can't I come up with you? What are you even going to do on the roof, Angie?" Theo asked, his hands gripped the steering wheel harder.

Checking that the contents of the bag were still there and had not magically disappeared, Angela opened the door.

"This is something I have to do on my own. I've been waiting ten years to do this, so just wait for me here, please."

Worry entrenched further on his features. "You would tell me if you were in trouble, right, Angie?"

"I'll be back soon."

The door closed behind her.

Angela climbed the fire escape, the stairs groaning at each step. The sound of her footsteps on the roof's gravel made her stomach turn, but bile rose when she saw the figure seated on the edge of the roof.

The familiar leather jacket was equipped like a shield.

"About time you showed up," Parris called out over the sound of local traffic and the soft wind.

"I thought you would get cold feet." Her voice lacked the usual upbeat smile. She looked out at the distance, her back to Angela.

Watching over Ciel.

The city's skyline started to twinkle as the sun set in the distance. The sky acted as if it hadn't cried its heart out just earlier that same day. The Stairway Tower still stood proudly among the rest against the purple sky. Watching the roof.

Angela reached into her bag, pulling out Tony's gun. She threw the bag across the rooftop, pointing the weapon at Parris's back. Angela's heartbeat pounded loudly in her ears. With a shaky deep breath, she called out.

"Look at me."

Parris stood up slowly from the ledge, turning around to look at the girl. Her dark eyes peered into Angela's soul.

"I didn't think you would come, either," Angela responded. "You've been avoiding me since I've returned to Ciel City."

"Can you blame me? You're pointing a gun at me." Parris chuckled at the gun. "Come to kill me?" Parris asked amused.

"The gun is to make sure you don't worm your way out of this," Angela exclaimed, gripping the gun with both hands tighter.

Parris barked out a cold laugh.

"Is it, now?" she mocked. She swayed closer to the high schooler, until she was within arm's reach, a hand on her stab wound.

"Well, then, go ahead, your chances of actually hitting me should be better now."

Angela's arms shook from the weight of the foreign weapon, and from the years she had spent dreaming of this moment, of confronting Parris, of finally knowing what happened.

Parris heard the battle in her head and took another step forward until the barrel of the gun was pressed against her forehead.

"Go ahead, Angie."

Angela faltered for a moment. Peering into Parris's eyes, she did not see the usual glee and sharpness there, just a dull colour staring back.

"Why didn't you save her?"

"You're going to have to be more specific—-"

"Why didn't you stop Janine from jumping off STK's roof ten years ago?" Angela exploded.

The gun shook violently in Angela's hands. Tears pooled in her eyes, refusing to break through. Parris watched her coldly.

Anger roared in Angela at her silence.

"I saw you! Mom and I went to drop off Janine's lunch that day and we were early. I saw Janine on the ledge from the car window and then I saw you! You just stood there, you didn't try to save her. YOU LET HER FALL!"

Parris remained quiet as her cold eyes were analyzing the new information. Angela could not hold herself back; she screamed in the Informant's face.

"ANSWER ME! WHY DIDN'T YOU STOP MY SISTER?"

The gun was now a rattling mess. Angela's eyes were red. Tears fell down her face in waves.

"Do you want to kill me, Angie?" Parris finally asked, completely avoiding Angela's question. Angela dug the gun into Parris's forehead.

"Answer the *fucking* question!"

Parris took a step back, the gun shaking flimsily in the air without her.

"No. No, I don't think you're a killer, Angie. You won't even shoot me. I think you just want someone to blame. Someone who isn't Janine," Parris understood.

"Of course I blame you! You're the reason my sister is gone!" Angela howled.

The sky was darkening quickly now. The sun ran from the confrontation.

"You could have saved her! You could have pulled her back from that ledge. Instead, you left her up there to jump!" She hated the way the Informant was reacting. That cool and collected face made her blood burn.

"And what makes you think she had wanted saving?" Parris replied steadily.

Angela scrunched her face in both disgust and confusion, *What the hell kind of question is that?* When she did not reply, Parris continued.

"Your sister had made her choice. Nothing I could have said or done would have changed her decision."

"LIAR!" Angela exploded. "You always make up stories and lies to suit you! For fuck's sake, your name isn't even Parris. You *always* lie!"

"Not this time, Angie."

"Why did she jump, then?" Angela finally asked.

The one question that had plagued her family for the last ten years. The question that haunted her thoughts. Her daily life. Nini was so happy, there was no reason for her to kill herself—not before her high school graduation, not right after her Homecoming party, not when she had promised Angela to take her to the park that day.

"Janine decided that killing herself was the right thing to do," Parris answered sadly.

Angela's hands shook violently, the gun heavier now. Her resolution faltered. That answer wasn't adequate. It didn't fill the gaps.

"I don't believe you!"

"Janine had her reasons for killing herself that day," Parris continued.

Is Parris even telling the truth?

"She had dug a hole and decided that staying in that hole was better than climbing out of it. She couldn't look past the present moment. No thoughts of graduation or university convinced her to step down."

"Fuck!" Angela cried. This couldn't be the answer. This couldn't be the answer she had been waiting ten years for.

"This is what you wanted, Angie. You wanted to know. No one could have convinced her otherwise, not me and not you. You couldn't have saved Nini."

"DON'T YOU DARE SAY THAT!" Angela roared.

Parris stopped. She watched Angela's face, full of tears and pain. Parris was more tired than she had been in years, the stabbing paling in comparison.

"Don't you dare say I couldn't have saved her."

Theo anxiously tapped his fingers against the wheel, itching to run up the stairs to check on Angela.

Bright headlights approaching caught his attention. Another car pulled into the alleyway beside the fire escape. A man with a short scruffy beard stepped out of his white truck, looking up to the same rooftop that Angela was on. Theo exited his car, calling out.

"Who are you?"

The man looked at Theo with narrowed eyes before he realized. "You're Theo, right?"

When he saw the puzzled look on his face, the man continued. "I carried you out of that hotel. Angie asked me to help her. My name is Logan."

"Nice to meet you," Theo approached Logan.

"What are you doing here, kid?" Logan asked.

"Angela asked me to drop her off and wait for her. She's supposed to do something on the roof... you?"

Logan looked confused. "She asked me to come here because she had something important to show me. Something about confirming a story. But why atop the old family business?"

"Old family business?"

The voice of Angela crying, "DON'T YOU DARE SAY THAT!" carried down from the rooftop to the alley.

Immediately, both of them began running up the fire escape.

Angela kept the shaky gun pointed at Parris, her eyes starting to blur from the constant tears.

"That's a lie! I could have convinced her! I COULD HAVE SAVED HER!" she shouted.

"You were a child, Angie," Parris spoke gently. "You were too young to understand that it wasn't your fault. You still are. You were enough for Janine. Your parents were enough. Janine loved you all so much."

"If I was enough, then why did she jump? She wasn't depressed nor did she have suicidal tendencies. She didn't even leave a note! There's no way she had planned on killing herself that day. So, what did you tell her?!"

"I told her to step down. To think of you, Angie... You look just like her."

Angela screwed her eyes shut; her heart ached beyond measure. She'd been told that her whole life. Janine's younger twin. Nini's younger half.

Parris smiled painfully, her hand holding her left side. Angela was at least happy that she was in pain. She wanted her to hurt. She wanted her to feel pain when all Angela had felt the last ten years were pain, loneliness and abandonment.

"Why didn't you at least pull her back from the ledge?" Angela shouted.

"I didn't physically try to stop her from jumping, I admit that," Parris answered. Her dark eyes flickered with grief. "I plead guilty, judge. Go ahead, executioner."

Angela roared in anger.

"A time like this, and you're still playing your stupid games?! I hate you! You just want the easy way out! You're a sad person that no one can love. You're barely even human! You don't deserve to live; you should have been the one to jump, not Janine! YOU DAMN PARRASITE!"

"If hating me makes it easier, Angie, then hate me. Go ahead. Shoot me. It'll make you feel better. At least, for the moment."

"You want me to shoot you?!" Angela asked, mortified.

"Come on, don't lose your edge now," Parris commented. Her eyes were darker.

Why does she want me to shoot her? What is she trying to do?!

"I'm not playing your games, Parris!"

"No games this time, Angela," Parris sang. "Don't you blame me for Nini's death? Prove it. Shoot me right *here*." She tapped the middle of her forehead.

"I'm not a killer—"

"If you really loved Janine, you would shoot me."

Anger roared in Angela, blinding her in a fury of red. She held the gun up against Parris's forehead.

"Sing, oh goddess, sing of the wrath of Angela Johnston," Parris closed her eyes, pushing her forehead into the barrel.

Accepting her fate.

Gulping for air, Angela pulled the trigger.

Click!

"Safety's on," Parris instructed.

Angela threw the gun away with a cry. Before Angela could pull her thoughts together, she was tackled to the ground.

"No! NO!" she yelled, fighting to throw the figure off her. Parris would escape again!

"DON'T LET HER GET AWAY!" Angela begged.

Theo pinned her arms down to the roof. Logan grabbed onto Parris's wrist, even though she did not make an attempt to escape.

"Of course, this is because of you," Logan spat, his grip tightening. "What happened here?"

"Theo," Angela bellowed. "Theo, get off me right now!" The boy ignored her, not able to look at her. "Don't let that monster escape!" she screamed, her face turning into an ugly shape.

"She's not a monster!" Theo yelled back, his eyes screwed shut. Angela continued to fight against him. He was baffled as to why his friend was acting like this.

And why she had a gun!

"She saved me from that disgusting creep, she helped me escape my debt! I owe her my life!" he tried to reason with Angela. But his friend shook her head frantically, as though he had been infected.

"Angie, she's a victim of all this, too!" Theo pleaded. "Please see that!"

Parris is a victim?!

"She doesn't save people, she plays with their lives!' Angela spat. "She could have saved my sister's life but chose to sit back and watch!"

"What is she talking about?" Logan asked Parris. She looked at the ground, refusing to meet his eyes.

"Answer!" Logan yelled. The days in Owl's clinic meant nothing to him at that moment. Nothing mattered except for Angela's words and his own pain.

Angela shrieked into the night as she thrashed in Theo's hold.

"She killed Janine Johnston! She was up there on the roof with her, Logan! She didn't save her. She let her jump to her death, she admitted it herself. My sister! Your friend!"

Logan stopped dead.

All the years he had spent in that elegant office beating himself up for not doing anything. All the years he had blamed himself for not being there for Janine.

"Is that true?" he asked Parris in a scarily calm voice.

The Informant avoided everyone's eyes, futilely attempting to tug her arm out of Logan's death grip. Logan grabbed her face, spit flying.

"IS THAT TRUE?"

After a pause, Parris finally answered, meeting Logan's eyes.

"I didn't stop her, Lo—"

Logan punched Parris square in the face.

The next moments were a blur as Logan continued his assault on Parris, Theo rushed to stop him, and Angela scrambled for the gun. Theo managed to grab Logan's arm, pulling him off of the Informant. Parris doubled over in pain, clamping her stomach. Angela grabbed the gun, pointing it at the Informant with a crazed look.

She can't escape!

The click of the metal snapped everyone back to reality.

"Angela, stop!" Theo pleaded, struggling to hold Logan back. "You're angry but this won't bring back your sister!"

"Nobody move!" Angela shrieked, her voice turned hoarse, only focused on Parris. She was losing herself again to the anger, to the pain of loss, the bottomless pit of agony she had to harbour ever since Janine jumped.

"Tell us what happened!"

The sound of panting filled the chilled evening air. All eyes fell on Parris. Her shirt had a dark spot, blood quickly gathering on the fabric. She took in a deep shaky breath before she spoke.

"I had noticed Janine became more distant."

Angela trembled. Fresh tears raced down her face. Even Logan stopped his struggle against Theo, holding his breath.

She's going to tell us the story.

"I would try to find her after school, but she would always disappear. One day, I finally found her before lunch. She had climbed to the rooftop. I followed her. Watching her, I saw the way she threw her bag across the roof. She stood on the ledge, peering over. I had asked her to step down, not really knowing what she was up to. I joked with her, saying that she would be the news of the school if she tripped. When I realized that she was up there for a purpose, I asked her to step down. She had told me that she had no choice, that she had to jump."

Parris's retelling drew them into her memory.

"I asked her why she had no choice. Janine said that she had messed up. Messed up and got herself involved with the mafia. That's why she always skipped our after-school meet-ups. She said that she was fucking a high-level executive of the mafia."

Goosebumps rose on Theo's arm despite his warm varsity jacket. His grip on Logan slackened. Parris looked over to Logan.

"That's why she was always bailing on us. She kept digging that hole, making it bigger. That idiot, if she had just told us earlier!" Parris yelled. Her dark eyes were livid with anger and frustration.

It was the first time Angela had seen a genuine emotion on the Informant's face.

"She said that they were going to move into the school, into her personal life, and involve her friends with their activities. She wanted to protect them—us. She thought that by jumping off the roof, the mafia would leave her loved ones alone."

She's lying, she's lying, she's lying!

Angela took in a breath to protest, but Logan beat her to it. "What do you mean 'involve'?"

"They would take us away, play with us, have us distribute their drugs, or sell us."

"DON'T LIE!" Angela yelled, the gun still pointed at her sister's best friend.

Nini wouldn't have gotten herself involved with the gangs. She was too smart to get caught in their web!

"She's not lying," Logan replied. His blue eyes filled with grief, realization, and pain. "She's not lying."

Parris continued, "I tried to calm her down. I tried to tell her that we could go to the police, that help was available."

The soft wind blew between the four of them. Parris contemplated her next words.

"I then asked her to step down, for me, to remember that I was her friend, her sister, that I would stand by her through thick and thin… she just smiled at me."

"Enough," Angela whispered.

"She had warned me to stay away from the Syndicates, to never go outside alone, to watch out for myself."

I've heard enough.

"I rushed off to find someone who could help… that's when I passed Logan in the hall. By the time I had reached a teacher, I heard yelling from the courtyard—"

Parris collapsed, her legs giving out under her. The colour drained from her face.

"I'm sorry, Angie," Parris whispered before her eyes closed. Theo rushed to her side, applying pressure to her stab wound, unsure of how to help.

Angela dropped to her knees on the roof, the gun cast aside.

"Nini…" Angela sobbed.

Nini was involved with a gang member… she had willingly decided to jump. Janine decided to jump.

"Angie?" Logan whispered as he sank in front of her.

"Nini's gone, Lo," Angela cried. Her chest shuddered as it fought against the realization.

Janine decided to leave me!

Logan held her close as she cried.

"It's not fair," Angela wailed into his chest. Logan held her tightly, a pained look on his face. He refused to cry, not in front of the kids.

"Angie, it's okay. I'm here for you," Logan shushed her. "I should have reached out sooner, checked in on you. I should have been here for you."

Slowly, Angela began to calm down. He called for Theo to take her home. Theo obediently nodded, holding Angela tightly as he walked her to the car. Theo spared one last look at Parris before descending the stairs with Angela.

Logan looked at the unconscious form of Parris on the roof. He carried her down the fire escape carefully, setting her battered form down in his car for the second time. He contemplated between going back to Owl's or *Clueless*. In the end, he decided to make her Lorenzo's problem.

The car trudged along, and Logan finally allowed himself to shed tears for his old friends.

CHAPTER SEVENTEEN

Catharsis

It was difficult carrying an unconscious woman around downtown without a few weird glances from people. It didn't help that Logan hid the gun Angela had used in his waistband. Logan grimaced as he carried Parris to the side entrance of her club, kicking at the door until someone opened it. He thanked God that it was Lorenzo who opened it and not the security guard he had punched.

Lorenzo took one look at his boss before he led the way to the white door silently. The deafening noise of the club pierced Logan's ears painfully. The clubbers were too intoxicated to notice the odd sight. Logan carried her up the stairs quickly and into the quiet checkerboard office. He placed her on the low red sofa, ready to let her staff deal with her mess. He was out of his depth.

She was there when Janine jumped.

He collapsed against the opaque glass, crumpling to the tiled floor, wishing the chessboard floor had opened up and swallowed him right there and then. The events of the night came crashing into his mind all at once: Angie's face, the story from the Informant, and the way she apologized to the kid!

She had the chance to speak to Janine before she jumped! She tried to talk her down. I didn't know...

"Logan!" came the distant voice of someone calling his name. "Logan, focus on my voice!"

But Logan didn't want to focus on anything— not when his heart sunk into his chest, not when he blamed himself for failing Janine alone for the past ten years, not when *she* had the chance to talk with Janine before she jumped! His chest was shaking violently, his lungs refusing to fill with air.

"Logan O'Brien!"

The slap to his face grounded him. He looked around in a daze; Lorenzo crouched down to eye level with him.

"I can't help the both of you!"

He saw the scared expression of Lorenzo, often forgetting how young he was. He should have been in college, stressing about midterms, not in this life that demanded more than anyone could give.

"Sorry," Logan mumbled as he rubbed his eyes. "Sorry, go fix her."

Lorenzo stood in a huff, glancing at his boss. "Her wound was agitated, and given her slow recovery, whatever happened was just enough to put her to sleep. Nothing too serious. I would rather not bother Owl."

Logan watched the slow rise of her chest as she slept on the red couch. Lorenzo glared at him with narrow eyes.

"So, what happened to her?" Lorenzo asked, accusingly. When he was met with silence, he sighed as he headed to the white door.

"When she awakens, call line two on the desk phone. I'll come up with a few things. If you need anything, there's a first aid kit in the door behind her desk."

The white door shut gently, leaving Logan with Parris.

Time passed differently in the office as Logan watched Parris. He had felt her forehead, feeling the fever resurface again. He pushed open the only other door in the lush office, finding a humble backroom with a bathroom and staircase leading up somewhere.

Probably to the roof, he thought as he removed her leather jacket, seeing the wet stain of her shirt. He placed a towel between her stomach and the shirt, not having the heart to undress her.

He sat on the coffee table, wringing a wet cloth, applying the cold compression to her forehead, just as he had in Owl's clinic not too long ago. He had to do a mindless activity as his brain processed the new information.

I punched her hard, he thought as he saw the bruise bloom on her cheekbone. But he hadn't meant to hurt her; his body acted before he could realize he was punching her all over.

"Way to give a girl mixed signals," came the sarcastic voice of the Informant. "One minute you're punching the ever-living daylight out of her, the next you're as gentle as a flower."

The atmosphere in the office changed from dread to tension.

"You're burning up," came the dumb reply of Logan.

Parris rolled her eyes. "And whose fault is that?" she snapped back, her voice and face betraying just how weak she was. He looked away, ashamed of his actions.

Parris sighed and the hard look in her dark eyes softened. Logan watched her stare at the office wall, the way her body melted into the couch, beyond exhaustion.

"I'm sorry for hitting you," Logan whispered. Parris closed her eyes, but Logan saw the flash of hurt in them.

She was so easy to read. But her expressions and words never aligned. He couldn't understand why she acted the way she did—distant, cold, and cruel. But that's not how she was with him, once upon a time, and certainly not how she was around Janine, either.

They sat in silence. He wrung out the cloth several times, forgetting to call Lorenzo. He watched her face, wanting to know what she was thinking now.

Was she thinking of Angela and how she had hurt her? Or was she thinking of all the ways she had failed Janine? Like I am.

"I think about you sometimes. About the look you get when you realize it's me," Parris admitted quietly. "You always look at me with such anger."

He stopped midway through wringing the cloth.

"And yet, I understand why. You deserve to be angry at me for Janine."

"You think I'm still angry about Janine?" Logan asked dumbfounded.

"What else?" she mumbled. "Janine was your everything."

"Janine is gone," Logan said firmly. "It still hurts but that's not what this is about. I'm angry that you left me! That you abandoned me. That we didn't matter to you. That you act like *I* didn't matter to you!"

Parris screwed her eyes shut.

"Janine wasn't my everything," Logan admitted. He placed the cloth back on her forehead, his lips trembled.

I can't say it.

A flickering light caught their attention as Parris pushed away his hand, sitting up hastily. She looked at the white door with wide eyes.

"Go hide in the backroom, and don't come out no matter what!" Parris instructed a confused Logan, panic in her usually controlled voice.

"What's hap—?"

"Move now!"

Logan rushed behind the backroom door just as the office door opened and a lone man entered. Logan watched from the small window in the door, watching an older man in a smart black suit close the white door gently behind him.

It was the same man from the Head meeting, the same one who bruised and bloodied the Head of the Wings without so much as breaking a sweat, the same one who touched her so easily.

"*Bella,*" he greeted as he strolled in front of the Informant.

Parris's signature smile instantly resumed on her face, but the pain from her wound and fever showed.

"Giovanni!" she exclaimed as she studied his demeanour. "Another unexpected house call so soon? I really am the luckiest gal!"

Giovanni chuckled, throwing down a file on the coffee table. His eyes watched the Informant as she reached for the document, seeing her wince as she leaned forward. Her eyes quickly scanned through the pages of the medical report.

"You know, *Bella*," Giovanni began as he stalked his way around the coffee table to stand in front of her. "As splendid as I am sure our night together was, I couldn't remember a damned thing about it."

Logan held his breath from behind the door.

The Informant looked up at Giovanni briefly, before diving back into the medical report in her hand. Giovanni watched a lone streak of sweat bead down the side of her face.

"So, I took a blood test the next morning, and to my surprise, they found traces of what are commonly known as 'date rape' drugs."

Giovanni slammed his foot down on her stab wound. Parris hollered in pain, her hands flying to pull the foot off. But she was too weak to move it. Tears swelled in her eyes as she glared at the older man.

"You drugged me, *Bella*? Even after everything I've done for you?" he pressed into the stitches, his chestnut eyes on fire. "How dare you think that you could take advantage of my kindness?" he yelled loudly. Parris gripped his foot harder, trying to pry it off.

Logan's anger swelled at the other man, pushing the door a sliver open before Parris yelled.

"Don't move!"

Logan stopped immediately; he knew that was directed at him. Giovanni gave her a confused look at her strange behaviour before removing his foot.

Parris gasped in relief, but Giovanni dove in for a kiss. She struggled against him, snapping her face away.

"You owe me a debt now, Parris! And I plan on collecting interest," he clawed into her side, rooting her to the couch as the other hand clasped her chin.

"Get off me, Giovanni!"

"Did you think you were special, Parris? That you really were untouchable?" The older man laughed cruelly at her. Parris continued to struggle against him but ceased when he clawed at her side, pulling at the stitches.

Still and silent, she looked at the thug in front of her with raging eyes. Giovanni's eyes darken.

"I own you, *Bella*."

"You don't own me. I am not a possession."

"I created you! You wouldn't have gotten this far if not for me. You've always been mine, Parris. You're my perfect creation. My *favourite* child."

The backroom door slammed open.

"Get off her!" Logan yelled, entering the office with Angela's gun in hand, shaking as he pointed it at Giovanni.

Giovanni gave him a bored look before sitting on the red couch and hoisting Parris into his lap. She cried out as he began to paw at her side.

"I said get off!" Logan yelled again, his words not carrying any weight to the Head of the Gates. Parris was breathing heavily, lightheaded.

Giovanni pulled her head back by her hair, asking, "And who might this be, *Bella*?"

She kept silent, crying out when he pulled the skin off her wound.

"A nobody!" she answered desperately.

"Hm, even a nobody has a name," he mocked. He watched the way Logan's resolve began to falter at his indifferent attitude. The feeling of the Informant's struggle against him fueled his desire to consume her.

"Someone I went to school with, no one important!" Parris rattled, the pain overwhelming. She refused to meet anyone's eyes, wincing her dark ones shut.

The clashing of realities was too much.

Logan just stood there, gun pointed, hands shaking. Giovanni tightened his grip on her.

"He looks familiar," Giovanni thought out loud. "Is he your lover?" he asked, his eyes sizing up Logan, a hint of envy in his deep voice.

When she didn't answer him, he grabbed her stomach again, pulling at it.

"No!" she choked. Logan took another step closer to the couch, the gun still readied.

"I said get off her now or I'll shoot!"

"Don't shoot him!" Parris cried back at him, a wild look on her usually composed features. Logan looked at her in distraught. Giovanni barked out a cold laugh.

"Don't shoot him," she repeated as she tried to control her emotions.

"Parris…" Logan slowly lowering the gun in disbelief.

"Either you leave or you watch quietly, kid. Your choice," Giovanni growled victoriously.

With that Parris began thrashing against Giovanni's hold on her. He lowered her to the couch, boxing her in, kissing her neck.

"GIOVANNI, YOU SON OF A BITCH!" She screamed as he held her down, beginning to unbutton her pants.

A gunshot rang in the room.

Giovanni and Parris both looked at each other surprised. Giovanni sat up; the red couch behind him now sporting a bullet hole, inches above where the Head had just been.

"I said get off her," Logan demanded, his hands no longer shaking.

They were steady. Parris looked between the two men, for the first time unsure of what would happen next.

Slowly, Giovanni smirked at Logan, a hint of amusement in his eyes.

"Well my boy, to shoot at the Head of the Gates is asking for a death wish." He looked down at Parris. "But you knew that, didn't you."

Parris scowled at the older man. He sighed, bending down to plant a kiss on the crown of her head.

"I will be expecting payment soon, *Bella*."

Standing up, the STK alumni watched as he straightened his suit. Giovanni clapped his hand on Logan's shoulder.

"You would leave Ciel within the next twenty-four hours if you were a smart boy." With that, the Head left the office in a calm walk.

The white door closed with a click.

Trying to get air into her lungs, Parris breathed deeply through her nose and out through her mouth. After a few moments, she hesitantly looked at Logan. She found him smiling and whispering to himself, his eyes gaping at the ground.

"I did something. I *finally* did something! Did you see that, Janine? I saved her! I did something!"

A pained expression decorated Parris's tanned face before she threw up on the floor.

Theo would be lying if he said he wasn't tired. He rubbed his eyes as he watched Angela hiccup in her sleep. The autumn sun was already up and hiding from them behind dark clouds.

Angela had not stopped crying well into the night, mumbling for Janine. Theo was not able to get her to focus on anything else. She refused to enter the apartment, which prompted him to drive around the suburbs to tire her out. When the early light of dawn had started to peek, she had collapsed into her bed.

Groaning, he made his way to the kitchen, searching for coffee. He hated the stuff but he remembered the way Giovanni drank it for energy, often consuming several cups a day. He had liked that latte Giovanni had ordered him when…

He shook his head, trying to shake the older man out of his thoughts.

He opened the cream fridge, looking for milk. Pausing, he looked intently at the magnets. He had never paid any mind to the magnets before.

The letters 'A' and 'J'.

J for Janine.

Angela had said her sister had died, that she had killed herself. He still did not fully understand, since he was more focused on stopping his friend from hurting herself or the Informant on that rooftop. He felt embarrassed for never asking Angela more about her sister.

The perfect STK student.

When he thought more about it, he felt stupid not having asked her any simple questions, like why she seemed to have a distaste for the city before even exploring it, or why she was obsessed with the Informant. He should have known Angela's sister was gone. The signs were there.

"Hey, Jaya," he answered his phone, thankful for the distraction. "Yeah, no, Angela's had a hard night, that's probably why she didn't answer your call… did you know about her sister?"

"Her sister? I know that Angela has a sister, but she never talks about her," Jaya answered.

"Yeah, her name was Janine Johnston." He poured the milk into the coffee, turning it into an inviting colour.

"Did something happen?"

Theo told Jaya over the phone, about the night and the gun, about the Informant and Logan, about Angela's rage and tears.

"I'm on my way, Theo," Jaya said, hanging up the call.

Theo checked back on Angela, glad she was still asleep. He sat on the couch, thinking of the situation. He sighed as he shook his head, not wanting to speculate until Angela awoke. He searched for the remote, looking through the television console. He opened a cabinet door, finding old photo albums. He glanced over his shoulder, hearing light breathing from Angela in the bedroom; he opened the album.

Old news clippings were shoved into the plastic protectors. Titles that read, *Suicide at St. Kathrine's School!*, *Gifted Student Commits Suicide, STK Student Kills Herself without a Note*!

The pictures were of a young girl, strikingly similar to Angela. The same round hairstyle, big eyes, and full lips. Theo's blood ran cold as he read the descriptions.

Young Janine Johnston, daughter of Philip Johnston and Heaven Williams, owners of the Johnston's Family Wash*, and older sibling to a younger sister, jumped from the famed STK rooftop. Janine was reported to be a bright student, top of her class in Physics and Chemistry, having accepted an early invitation to the University of Ciel's prestigious Biomedical Program. Police and family were unable to find a note explaining why this child took her own life.*

Theo had known about a suicide at his school. Gossip and rumours of finding the lost suicide note would resurface every so often. Finding the note was a folktale of sorts to the students.

He continued to flip through the photo album, finding pictures of a young Janine next to her parents and another woman who looked like her father.

Maybe her aunt?

Photos of Janine and a young Angela. The smiling faces of Janine with a girl and boy at a school event. He felt sick for looking through someone's memories, for being so close to Angela without knowing who she was.

That's why she was so nervous on the first day. She was visiting the last site of her sister. Living with that knowledge, she had to fill in the gaps as to why she jumped, why Parris gave up on her friend.

He hurried to open the door, not wanting to wake Angela. He let Jaya in, noticing the puffiness of her eyes. She wasn't wearing her iconic butterfly clips today.

"How did everything with Raef go?" he asked in a hushed voice.

"It's over now," Jaya replied coldly.

Theo showed Jaya the news clippings, along with the family photos.

"No wonder she blamed Parris; she thought she was at fault for her sister's death. She wanted revenge for her sister," Jaya understood, going through the pictures, pausing at the picture of the trio.

"It was always in front of us, but we were too caught up in our own shit to realize," Theo conceded, his eyes drawn to the smile on Angela's face. Her smile was wide as she rode Janine's shoulder in a park.

"That's not true," Angela corrected by the doorway, startling the pair. Jaya jumped up, running to hug her. She held her tightly.

"It wasn't a secret for anyone to discover," Angela confessed in a low voice. Jaya pulled back, looking at her with sad eyes.

"I just thought that if I could confront Parris, I could finally hear the full story. What she said to my sister on that rooftop… it's been haunting me for the last ten years. She wasn't Janine's friend. Parris didn't try to save my sister. She never tried to pull her back from that ledge. She just let my sister jump… that's not what a friend would do."

"You wanted someone to blame," Theo recognized immediately.

"Hurting others doesn't make you hurt less, Angie," Jaya stated wisely, pulling back from her friend.

"You planned on spending your entire senior year looking for her?" Theo asked from his spot on the floor. "What if you had never met?"

Realization hit Jaya. "That's why you wanted to go into Chinatown. You wanted to explore the different turfs!"

"I knew she was still in Ciel City," Angela recounted. "I noticed she had removed herself from the yearbook when it came in the mail after we moved away from the city. I assumed she was trying to cover her tracks, to lie low. I thought that she may have joined a gang, I just didn't know which one, so I had to check them all. My luck that she appeared to me in front of the Halos, learning about Untouchables in Ciel… I remember when I first saw her after ten years in that alleyway, it was like seeing the monster from your nightmares."

The three of them remained silent, Theo and Jaya looking at Angela with concern.

"But she said she tried to talk Janine down!" Theo blurted. "She had tried to convince Janine to go ask for help!"

"And you believe that?!" Angela yelled at him, causing him to flinch. "Just because she took your place doesn't mean you should put her on a pedestal! Not every kind action from an adult is meant to be treasured!"

That shut Theo up.

"Hey!" Jaya reprimanded her. "You don't mean what you're saying. You're just hurt and it's easier to deflect the pain than to face it."

"I've faced this pain for a decade!" Angela cried fresh tears in her puffy brown eyes. "I've missed my stupid sister every single day of my life since she jumped! Her stupid friends who couldn't pull her back from a fucking ledge! She jumped and she left my family! She left *me*! How could she leave me? Leave my family in pieces?"

Angela sank to the floor.

"Angela…" Jaya sat on the floor next to her. Even Theo appeared on her other side in an instant, already forgiving her harsh words.

"Was I not enough?" Angela sobbed as Jaya pulled her into her arms. "Am I not enough? Even the two of you left me… I'm never enough for anyone. Even Aunty Kim couldn't wait for me to arrive in Ciel. If it was Janine she would have cancelled her work trip in an instant. I'm fucking worthless to everyone."

"You're not worthless, Angie," Theo reassured.

"I just want to be with Janine again!" Angela sobbed as Theo held her.

Angela said all the words that plagued her for the past ten years, all of her insecurities, all of her hatred for Janine for leaving her alone. Jaya rubbed her back, shushing her, whispering comforting words.

"I don't know how we can exactly help you, Angie," Jaya comforted. "But know that Theo and I are here. We won't ever leave you again."

Jaya and Theo shared a look. They meant it. They would never leave Angie again. Jaya continued.

"You've helped us both *so* much in the short amount of time you've known us… You work hard to keep your friends safe, something we need to work on. You're our friend. Family, really. We care about you."

"You're constantly pulling us back from our own ledges," Theo confessed. "Without you, I would have experienced a fate worse than death."

"You grabbed onto us and refused to let go. That's what makes you a great friend, Angie. I don't know your sister, but I know she would have been proud of you. She would be proud of how you love others," Jaya confirmed.

Nothing else mattered in the world at that moment. Not the Big Three, the CCPD, or even school. Only the thought of being able to rely on one another fueled them.

The group of damaged children stayed there on the living room floor, comforting one another from the horrors that were thrust upon them.

CHAPTER EIGHTEEN

Janine Johnston

The halls of STK were welcoming as Janine left her biology class, merging into the flurry of blue, white, and gray. The sounds of the students milling through the open door were like the trumpets of freedom, the school day coming to a close. The noise pollution from the hallway was electric as the students excitedly made their way home to prepare for that evening: STK's Senior Homecoming.

Janine waved at a few passing classmates as she opened her locker, placing the heavy textbook within. She slid her phone open, checking the message she had received with a wide smile.

Pick you up down the block, Princess. – T

Excited, she closed the locker with a blush.

"Whatchya smiling at?" asked a girl who leaned against the lockers. Janine gave a little jump as she shoved her friend playfully. Her soft curls framed her dark eyes as they shimmered back at Janine.

"Don't scare me like that!"

"Don't be so easy to scare then!" the girl replied with a cheeky smile. Janine rolled her eyes as she hugged her friend.

"You always cause so much trouble, Achilles," Janine said, walking down the hallway with the girl in tow.

"*Au contraire*, Patroclus! I cause enough trouble to keep things interesting!"

The girls giggled together, the noise of the hallway fading away, the pair only hearing one another.

Janine looked at her friend warmly. "Our history skit was iconic. Mrs. Foto was laughing the whole time!"

Her friend shook with more laughter. "I like our modern re-telling of Amy and Patty! Maybe I should change my name to Achilles for the rest of the year? A Homer-age to our greatest performance!"

Janine shoved Achilles again for the bad pun.

"Achilles? Well, it's not far off from Al—"

"Make way!" yelled a rowdy student as the basketball team ran through the crowded hall. Janine smiled at their silliness. Achilles rolled her eyes with a grin.

Achilles held Janine's hand. "I'll see you later tonight?" she asked, her mood turning suspicious.

"Of course!" Janine replied. "I promised you and Logan that we would go together, our last hurrah of senior year! We need to party tonight before tomorrow's exam review."

The other girl smiled. "Just like you promised the movies last week? You stood Logan and me up! Are you trying to set us up?"

Before Janine could answer, she heard her name being called. "Ms. Johnston!" yelled Principal Patel from across the hall.

Achilles gave Janine a wink as she ducked away. She disappeared into the sea of students instantly, Janine not even catching the back of her head.

How does she do that?

"Yes, Principal Patel?" she answered politely as the man approached her.

He straightened his already perfect suit. "Ms. Johnston, I just wanted to congratulate you on winning the physics award last semester. Now I am being told that you will win the chemistry award as well! I know that you are a very serious student and STK could not be prouder of your performance. You may come to be our top student ever!"

The bright student blushed as she thanked her principal. "I just enjoy science, that's all!"

"And an early offer to U of C's prestigious biomedical program I hear?"

Janine nodded. "I'm planning on attending this fall! Just have to make sure to get the top score on the chemistry exam next week for my full scholarship!"

"I look forward to your continued successes, Ms. Johnston! After all, you're one of STK's brightest stars. I expect the same of your sister when the time comes."

"Angie's still in elementary now, but soon enough she'll be walking down these halls," Janine said, a fondness in her voice. "She's even brighter than me!"

Patel patted her shoulder gently as he beamed at her. "Continue the hard work!"

Janine waved at him as she made her way through the iconic gothic archways, leaving her school and classmates behind as she walked on the busy Midtown sidewalk until she spotted the red sports car. Giddy, she sat in the passenger seat, tossing her bag into the back somewhere.

"Hey, Princess," purred Tony as he kissed the younger girl. Janine mumbled a small 'hi' back at the man as the car zoomed through the streets of Ciel. One hand was on the wheel while the other rested on her thigh.

"What do you have planned for our date today?" she asked excitedly.

The hand travelled higher up her thigh. "The hotel," came the short reply. She started to play with the end of her skirt, pulling it down.

"Right, but I have my homecoming tonight- so I don't think the hotel right now is a good idea, Tony."

Tony looked at her briefly at the red light. "You never complained about the hotel before, Princess."

"I-I just don't like how rough you are—"

Tony shushed her before he answered his phone. "Yes, Dad?"

She couldn't hear what was being said, but by Tony's reaction, it wasn't anything urgent.

"Okay, I'll see you at the meeting tomorrow. Bye." He pulled off to the side of the road, finally giving the high schooler his full attention.

"What do you want, Princess?"

"I want a cute and romantic date with my boyfriend!" Janine pouted, she crossed her arms across her chest. Tony chuckled as he caught her chin.

"So you're saying that I haven't been cute or romantic?" he asked, leaning closer.

"Like you read my mind," she whispered into his kiss.

"Would buying a fancy dress for my girlfriend count as cute and romantic?"

"It would be a start!"

"Do I seriously have to call you Achilles now?" Logan groaned as he played with his black bowtie by the gates of STK. The damn thing was close to choking him. Achilles was spinning in her short sparkly black dress, not a care in the world.

"This is crucial, Logan! You can't ruin my final moments of high school by *not* calling me Achilles."

He sighed at her antics, having gotten used to them for the past four years. It was better and more amusing to play along. He smiled shyly as he watched her spin, the streetlight bouncing off her dress.

Like a shooting star, Logan thought.

"Hot dog!" Achilles whistled as Janine appeared. She was wearing a high-low silver dress that screamed elegance.

"You look great, Janine!" Logan complimented as he hugged her.

"Thanks, Lo!" she beamed, her hair sporting sparkly hair clips that made her shimmer. "Did you tell Achilles how beautiful she looks?"

Logan blushed. Janine giggled and winked at her friend. Achilles was too busy enjoying the twirl of her dress to listen, but she did try to hide a smile of her own.

The trio entered the gothic church together. Balloon arches and lights converted their high school into their *Under the Stars* Homecoming.

"Over here!" yelled a member of the photography club as the trio walked through the school's foyer. Achilles got on her tiptoes to sling her arms across their shoulders, thankful they bent a little for their shorter friend.

The three of them smiled for the camera.

"Let's go!" Achilles cheered as they entered the gymnasium, music blasting on the speakers. Janine squealed as she grabbed her best friend's arms and dragged them to the middle of the dance floor. Logan laughed as Achilles spun him, the pair of them fooling around. Janine took a picture on her slide phone.

The party continued as the trio screamed the lyrics to the songs, dancing with one another for what seemed like hours. The basketball team tried to get their coach to join the limbo competition. Even Mrs. Foto pulled out her dance moves from the eighties.

Their homecoming vibrated with life.

Janine watched her friends, the way they didn't have a care in the world at that moment. No stress of exams or deciding which university to attend; the only thing that mattered was singing and dancing together.

I'm here, time to leave. – T

Janine pouted as she read over the message. She didn't want to leave yet. It was her senior homecoming! Not to mention Logan and Achilles would be upset if she left early again.

Ever since Tony first approached her at the mall while waiting for her mom to finish getting Angela new clothes a few weeks back, he had consumed all of her free time. She had enjoyed the attention of a man in his twenties, his charming words, and dazzling smile. He was her secret to keep. It wasn't that she needed attention. She had the love and care of her friends and family. But the way Tony desired her was all-consuming. Tony worshiped her, as though Janine was the most beautiful girl in the whole world. He would constantly say that to her. Along with the impressive gifts he always bought her, how could Janine not be interested? Her first boyfriend was such a sweetheart, after all!

Sparing one last look at her friends, she yelled something about the washroom before heading out through the gymnasium doors. Her heels clacked in the empty halls as everyone was inside having a ball. She spotted the red sports car parked on the street.

Tony lowered the window, whistling as she strutted towards him. Janine giggled as she sat next to him, his lips immediately attacking hers.

"Now we go to the hotel," whispered Tony.

Principal Patel watched the car speed away from his school. He stood under the gothic archway, his eyes narrowing at the driver of the car.

"That doesn't look right," Achilles sang from behind Patel, causing the man to jump with a yip.

"If I said it once, I've said it a million times!" Patel roared at her as she rushed back towards the gymnasium.

"STOP SNEAKING UP ON PEOPLE!"

The soft hum of a vacuum from the hotel's hallway made its way into the room, clearing the soft morning lull Tony was enjoying.

Tony took a deep drag of the cigarette as he looked through Janine's phone, seeing the message to her parents about spending the night at an Alexandra's house. He scrolled through the camera roll, finding another young girl equally delightful in a black dress. A soft groan brought his attention to the girl in his bed.

"Morning, Princess." He kissed her temple as her eyelashes fluttered open.

"I'm not late for the exam review, right?" Janine mumbled.

"No, I'll drop you off."

She curled into a ball, fighting off sleep. Tony sat on her side of the bed, still interested in the girl in the picture.

"Is she a friend of yours?" he asked. Janine opened one eye, looking at the picture.

"Hm, she's my bestie."

"She looks like a wild time."

That woke Janine up. The pleasant morning lull vanished in a second. She sat up, looking at Tony with sharp eyes.

"What does that mean?"

"Just saying. She's got a cute face and a nice rack at such a young age, she must be making her way through that school like a wildfire." Tony snickered as he zoomed in on Achilles's face and body. Janine got up abruptly, digging through her overnight bag for her uniform.

"I don't appreciate you speaking about my best friend like that, Tony."

Tony slapped her behind. "Is someone jealous? I thought you were besties?"

"Stop talking like that."

"Maybe she would be open to joining in on our fun? She looks like the freaky type—"

Janine turned around, her palm ready to strike his face, but he caught her hand with ease.

"Ready for another round, Princess?" Tony suggested with a smirk.

A rough knock on the door stole their attention.

"Hide," he whispered to Janine. She crawled under the bed. Tony threw her dress and bag into the closet, rushing to open the hotel door. Janine lifted the bed linen to catch a glimpse of a large man in a smart suit entering the hotel room.

"Dad!" Tony exclaimed as he greeted Giovanni with a kiss on each cheek. "The meeting isn't until later today—"

Giovanni punched Tony across the face, his body thrown to the ground like a ragdoll. Janine clapped her hands over her mouth. The Head reached down, pulling Tony up by his hair.

"Imagine my surprise when STK's principal called me late last night saying one of their most gifted students entered your car."

"Dad I—!"

The older man pushed his son into the side table, the lamp smashing on the ground.

"An Untouchable means that that school is not to be interfered with by the Gates, and my son is trying to get into the pants of a *high schooler*?"

Another crash. Tony cried as he was pinned to the wall by his throat.

"The Gates promised the security of that school. The mayor entrusted this to my organization, to keep the crime controlled around that school and its students. Ciel City needs this school to boost its image and draw in more youth. The Halos have agreed to my terms and have kept their drugs out of that building, and my son is trying to get his dick wet!"

Janine watched in horror as the man relentlessly punched Tony.

The Gates? As in the mafia? Tony is a part of the mafia? Janine's thoughts screamed in her head.

A rapid series of knocks came. A hotel maid unlocked the door, entering in a rush.

"I heard something crash, is everyone alright?!"

The maid caught sight of the gun peeking out of Giovanni's waist.

"HELP!" the maid yelled.

The sharp sound of a bullet finding its home between her eyes caused Janine to bite her tongue. The maid dropped to the ground with a loud thud, blood beginning to pool around her lifeless body. Her dead eyes peered into the ceiling.

Giovanni held his gun steady, barely looking at the maid. Tony panted as he tried to catch his breath. Janine shook under the bed, tears in her eyes as she watched the dead body. Voices were heard through the open door, the sound of the gun causing a commotion.

"If anything happens to that school, to that girl, Janine Johnston. If a single hair on her head is hurt during her time at that school," Giovanni spoke as he returned his gun, straightening his suit.

"You'll be dead, *Cucciolo*."

The door slammed shut behind him.

Janine bolted out from under the bed, retrieving her bag from the closet in a hurry.

"Janine!" Tony croaked from the floor, but she had already left the hotel room, running at full speed towards the subway and away from the mess she had wandered into.

What the fuck was I thinking!

She stared at the floor of the subway, unwilling to believe that she had been seeing the son of the Head of the Gates. The son of a murderer! She never questioned Tony when he said he owned a few businesses, but his endless supply of money now made sense. He was a criminal. He came from a family of criminals and today proved it.

The sheer violence that she had never experienced before. The way his dad killed the maid without a second glance.

He said that STK was an Untouchable... What if I get in trouble for sleeping with him?

"Nomos, Nomos Station."

Janine ran through the subway barriers and up to the concrete street. She continued through the soul-sucking green doors of the CCPD 97th

Division. Once inside the lobby, she looked around wildly.

An officer! Any officer will do! She spotted a middle-aged male officer speaking with the receptionist. He pulled out a handkerchief, wiping his sweat-soaked face.

"Excuse me!" Janine called out. She panted heavily as she tried to catch her breath. She read his badge.

Officer J. Chan.

He can protect me.

"Yes, dear?" Officer Chan asked calmly. "What's the matter?"

"I've just witnessed a crime!" Janine panted, her eyes pricking. "I just saw someone shoot a maid down at the Mount Royal Hotel! I left Tony behind because his dad said he would kill him for messing with me!"

"Woah, woah, wait a minute," Officer Chan said, hands out. His eyes darted down to her uniform before his eyebrows shot up. "Tony? As in Tony Moretti?"

He can do something! Janine allowed hope to fill her chest.

"Yes, him! His dad shot the maid—"

"Get lost, kid."

Her chest caved in on itself.

"What?"

"Go to school and act like this conversation never happened." Chan turned his back on her.

"But someone is dead!" Janine yelled. A few other officers turned to look.

"Stop lying!" Chan shouted from over his shoulder. He said the next words in a whisper. "The Gates make sure no one messes with Tony Moretti or your school. You're an STK student, so you're also off-limits. If Tony Moretti touches you that's none of our business. Now leave before I put you in the back of a police cruiser and take you to school myself."

Stunned. Janine was beyond stunned. No words could explain the frustration she felt in that moment, the defeat that filled her lungs with concrete. She left the CCPD, not remembering the ride to school, not remembering when her feet had obediently listened to the officer. Her thoughts consumed her entirely.

The black gates of STK appeared before her.

"Princess!" a voice called out from behind. Tony left his car in a rush.

"Leave me alone!" Janine yelled.

Tony caught her upper arm in a vice grip. "Why did you leave?!" he yelled back at her.

His once-handsome face looked ugly now to Janine. She thought that he was mature, that a man in his twenties taking an interest in her meant that she was also mature. And mature meant wise. But in that moment all she could feel was stupid.

"I didn't give you fucking permission to leave!"

"I don't need a criminal's permission!"

Tony's face turned red with fury. "You think you can leave me? I know where you live, Janine. I know all about your family. You think you could walk out on me?"

"Did you miss the part where Daddy beat the living shit out of you for talking with me?" Janine screamed back at him.

"You're mine, Princess," Tony spat back at her. "Today's your last day at this school. From now on, you're going to stay with me. We'll fuck, have a grand old time, and the old man can't give me shit since you're not part of STK anymore."

"Like hell, you freak!"

"Or maybe I should find your friend and pick her up. I'm sure she would be fun to play with. Hell, I might even invite a few of my guys to mess her up."

That silenced Janine instantly.

"Don't you dare touch her, Tony."

"I'll tell you what." He leaned in. "If you don't come with me after school today, I swear I'll hunt down that girl and have the Gates cut her up into pieces. But not until we've had our fill of her. You already know, Princess, how I like it; do you think she'll like it, too?"

The whimpering pup from earlier was gone and replaced with a wolf.

"Of course, how could I forget about your sister— Angelica, was it? I know a few pervs that enjoy a younger girl from time to time. So, you'll wrap up your affairs today, say your goodbyes, and I'll be here to pick you up, Princess."

Ice pressed against her insides as Tony threatened her best friend and sister.

Angie...

"PERVERT! FIRE! GEEZER! HEEEEELP!" came the roaring voice of Achilles as she yelled at Tony. Pedestrians looked over at the group, eyebrows raised as Tony released Janine immediately.

"Pervert! Fire! Geezer!" Achilles continued yelling at Tony, fury in her dark eyes. "HELP!"

"Fucking bitch!" Tony spat at her. He stepped back from Janine.

"You're the perverted bitch!" Achilles spat back quickly. "You know it's a crime to touch underaged girls, don't you?"

Spitting at the man, Achilles pulled Janine away, leading her to the entrance of STK. Her dark eyes still glued to Tony. She gave him her middle finger.

"The fuck were you thinking, Janine?" Achilles whispered. They entered STK, Tony still watched from the sidewalk.

"Janine?" Achilles asked again, her friend completely zoned out.

He said he would take them away...

Achilles sighed as she walked her best friend to her chemistry review, making sure she sat down before leaving the shocked girl.

Debating on whether she should tell Patel what had happened, Achilles knew that he couldn't do much. He didn't do anything when he saw Janine leave with him last night. She headed to her own review session fuming.

Janine pulled out her notebook robotically; her body was seated at her desk but her mind was in outer space.

They're not safe. Mom and Dad...he's dropped me off at home before! Even at Aunty Kim's! Does he know about Logan? He was in that picture, too. Fuck!

She dug her pen deeper into her paper, redrawing the same line over and over again. Janine's mind came up with every worst-case scenario. All of them involved her friends and family being subjected to Tony's words or his father's violence.

He saw her in person, too!

The period passed by quickly, Janine not having retained any information about the upcoming exam. Her phone buzzed with messages from her mom and friends, but they went by ignored.

The voice of Officer Chan dismissing her replayed in her ears. If the police couldn't stop Tony, then Janine had to leave with him.

But his dad said that if anything happened to me, he would kill Tony. He really would. God, he killed that poor maid! He shot her down without even batting an eye... a ruthless monster. Has Tony killed someone before? What if he brings a gun with him today after school?

Janine gazed out of the window, her mind slowly coming to a conclusion.

Something has to happen to me today. I need to hurt myself.

The shrill of the bell dismissed her. She couldn't hear the greetings from her fellow classmates and friends. She wandered through the school, not bothering to attend her English review session with Achilles and Logan.

I need to do something today. Something big enough that will stop Tony.

Her subconscious already knew. Her feet dragged her to the stairwell, the vaulted hallways deserted after the flurry of students. Janine began to shake uncontrollably as she marched up the staircase, one foot in front of the other.

If I jump, then it will make the news. The Gates would know about it. If I break my leg or arm then maybe that'll be enough. His dad knows my name. He told Tony that nothing could happen to me.

With every step her conviction grew.

The Gates will stop Tony. His dad will kill him. He was beating him to a pulp just for being with me... he'll shoot him dead this time.

Her phone buzzed insistently. Her mother sent a message about lunch, Logan asked where she was.

I need to protect them.

Her feet brought her to her destination. Her chest quivered as she pushed against the heavy metal door.

The rooftop was unwelcoming.

The sound of the door against the concrete floor was like nails on a chalkboard, but Janine couldn't hear anything anymore. She couldn't hear the sound of the street or the whistle of the wind. She could only hear her quickened heartbeat.

Janine stepped onto the rooftop. Her black uniform shoes continued relentlessly across the span of the floor. She threw her bag away, no longer needing her extensive notes.

The sun neared its zenith for the day, glaring at her, as to warn her, to stop her. But Janine did not stop. She marched to her destination, to the edge of her beloved school. She peered over, her knees shaking from the height. Six storeys up, the courtyard below appeared further than the staircase suggested.

I'll hurt myself somewhere where everyone will see. It'll make news and Tony will leave them alone. He'll leave me alone. The CCPD won't help. Patel didn't help. I have to do this.

"Careful, you might trip."

Janine tensed as she turned around to her best friend. She stood by the door, taking in the scene before her. Janine had wanted to do this quickly and alone, so she couldn't back out. Her being here made it harder.

"If you trip then you might make it on the STK news channel—"

"You need to leave."

"You need to get down."

The girls looked at one another, so much shared history between them. Janine saw the endless thoughts and ideas that projected through her dark eyes, the gears turning.

It was captivating and intimidating.

"I need to do this."

"Do what, kill yourself?"

"No, not kill myself… just hurt myself in a public place."

The other girl held her hands up as she approached the ledge, standing close to Janine, close enough to grab her.

"What does that mean, Janine?"

Janine told her. She told her everything. From her initial meeting with Tony to his threats earlier that day. The CCPD's officer's dismissive attitude. She told her about Tony's threats to her and Angela. Janine poured out her soul to her best friend.

They stood on the roof for a while, but time didn't matter anymore. Another bell rang. Janine finished her story, waiting for the flurry of insults and reprimands from her friend. But it never came. She stayed silent the entire time, absorbing all of the information. Processing it.

"And you think by jumping, all of this will end?"

Janine nodded, a few stray tears escaping as she looked back over the ledge at the courtyard.

"It will end."

"And what if you *do* end up killing yourself? Huh? What happens then? What about your parents? Angie is still so young. Won't this destroy your family?"

Dark eyes began to prick as she watched her friend stare at the courtyard silently.

"What about Logan? And university? And our grad trip?! We can't go to Banff if you're dead!" she cried, grasping at strings now.

"We were looking forward to that trip, weren't we?" Janine laughed softly, a pained expression on her face.

"Janine please think!" she pleaded. "This plan doesn't make any sense. There is no guarantee that Tony will leave you alone or that his dad will kill him. You're frightened and you feel like you're the only one who can fix this. Come down, let's think of a plan together. You know I always think of the best plans!"

Tears sped down Janine's face as she refused to turn back to look at her. She had to do this. She needed to hurt herself. She needed to put her life on pause, long enough for Tony to be dealt with. Long enough that she'd be safe. Her family and friends to be safe. University and their graduation trip would have to wait.

"What about me?!" cried the girl. "What about me?"

Janine wiped her eyes, turning back to look at her friend. Her sister. She said her name gently. Not one of her made-up names, not Achilles, but her real name.

The wind picked up the soft sound.

"I'm sorry for being a shitty friend. But… in case you're right and I do die… you are my note to this world. You need to stay safe. Never interact with the gangs or go looking for trouble! Promise me that. Promise me that you'll look after Logan too. You mean a lot to him."

"Janine—"

"You knew that I was messing around with an older guy and yet you tried to help me! You always help others and it's a shame when you don't care about yourself… When you visit me in the hospital, make sure you bring donuts from *Jim's*."

"Stop."

"I love you," Janine whispered.

"I love you, too."

Janine turned back around, not able to look at her any longer. A moment longer and she would have stepped down to the rooftop. A moment longer and she would put everyone's lives in danger.

I have to protect Angie.

The other girl ran through the door, calling over her shoulder, "I'll get help, just wait, Janine!"

Maybe I should pray, Janine thought as she looked up at Ciel's blue sky.

The other girl rushed to Principal Patel's office. She ignored Logan as she crossed him in the hall. He looked at the stairwell and decided that he should look there for Janine.

The sense of urgency from his other friend worried him as he climbed the steps two at a time. He slammed the door open, his eyes landing on Janine standing on the ledge.

"Janine!"

She sighed, not having the heart to tell her tale again.

"I'll grab you, hold still!" he shouted but she yelled at him.

"Stay back or it'll look like you pushed me!"

Logan froze by the door.

"What are you doing?!" he asked desperately. She kept her back turned towards Logan. Knowing that if she saw him, she might not be able to jump. He saw the discarded bag and gasped.

"Janine, wait!"

"Logan."

He clamped his mouth shut hearing his name, not knowing how to help her and not wanting to aggravate her.

"Logan," Janine repeated gently. "This… this is not because of you. You've been a dear friend and I'll always cherish our time together. This is because of something else."

Silence followed. Even the wind decided to quiet down and watch.

Now or never. For their safety. For Angie.

Janine took in a deep breath as she took a step off the edge of the roof.

"PATEL!" shrieked the other girl in the hall, running at full speed to his office.

"Help!" she yelled.

A bloodcurdling shriek erupted from the courtyard. She ran wildly towards the scream. She caught herself by the grand doorway of STK.

There on the ground of the courtyard was the body of Janine Johnston. A few students screamed at the sight, drawing the attention of some pedestrians. Janine was lying face-first on the ground, a splash of red entrails surrounding her. Her limbs and bones stuck out at odd angles.

The image seared into her mind.

"What's happened?!" yelled Patel as he pushed past the girl, stopping as soon as he caught sight of Janine.

"Oh, dear God!" he cried as he rushed to Janine.

A few faculty followed him out, trying to cover the mangled body.

Someone called for the police while others yelled at the students to get inside.

The girl disappeared.

Marcel rolled to a stop in Old Town. He parked in front of the Ciel Construction Company. He was excited to finally attend an executive meeting of the Gates. Going over the numbers of the human trafficking department, he itched to start his own syndicate one day.

He greeted Tony with a pat on the back as they rode the elevator up together. He saw the new bruises on his neck and knew that Giovanni was the culprit again.

"I need a safehouse for tonight, Marce."

"Another unfortunate soul?"

"I'm about to have a long-term houseguest."

Marcel sighed as he checked over his folders. "Still that high school girl you've been on about?"

They entered the office of the Head of the Gates. Tony's grin instantly dropped as he saw the furious look on his father's face. He knew that that anger was directed at him.

Other executives in suits stood against the office walls, giving the man as much space as possible. Marcel stood against the door, unsure of what was happening. This wasn't like the times he would wait for Tony's 'insurance' with Giovanni.

Something was different about this time.

"One of STK's brightest students just jumped from the school's rooftop with no note," Giovanni recounted as he stood up slowly. Marcel saw the way Tony's knees violently shook.

"Patel confirmed, it was the same girl who got in your car last night. Officer Chan also just called. Apparently, she tried reporting you and me to the CCPD this morning. Her name was Janine Johnston."

Giovanni calmly slid a knuckle brass on his right hand. Tony knew he wouldn't be leaving with only a few bruises this time.

"Let this serve as a message to anyone, including my own son, of what happens when you touch an Untouchable."

Present Day.

Angela couldn't escape Theo or Jaya. The pair took shifts spending the day with her to make sure she didn't try to hunt down Parris again.

It was like being on suicide watch.

It was only when the sun began to set when she made a huge show of yawning and getting ready for bed, did they trust that she would be alright on her own. And Angela was. She had messaged Logan, assuring him she was alright. She had even called her parents, however brief the call was.

She was fine until the moment she received a message telling her to meet her on the rooftop of STK.

It was the first and only time the Informant had invited Angela to meet, just the two of them. Angela pushed open the heavy metal door stepping onto the same roof Janine had chosen to end her life on. She looked around, noticing the high fence surrounding the ledge.

The school's attempt at suicide prevention.

Angela somberly walked up to the Informant, who was watching the dark clouds pass by. Parris was drained. Her body was still not healed from the initial stabbing, the never-ending fever, or Logan and Giovanni's fury. Angela leaned beside her against the fence, looking up at the sky.

"I still hate you."

"I don't think you'll ever stop."

Angela finally looked at the woman. Parris smiled as she watched the cars pass by.

"It's okay, I'm used to it."

Angela stopped the tug of empathy on her heartstrings before her fire of hatred could flicker out.

"So you spent the last ten years trying to find me? I must say, I'm honoured," Parris sang, her sarcastic bite lacking its usual theatrics.

"Don't flatter yourself," Angela replied. "You're the reason my sister is dead. Nothing you can say will change that."

"You still don't believe me? Or is it easier to blame me and not Janine?"

Angela sighed tiredly.

"It's not fair that I lost my sister and you're acting like nothing happened. At least Logan has the decency to care about everything. You kept hiding and avoiding me."

Parris hummed.

"Logan… I remember you having a little crush on him when you were younger," Parris reminisced.

Clenching her jaw in response, Angela glared at the fence. But Parris noticed the tint of red on her cheeks.

"Besides, you wouldn't have accepted my help. You needed someone to blame. You could not accept that Janine wasn't perfect. The image of your sister you had made was too strong in your mind. Your mind decided that I was the reason she jumped, that I had tricked her somehow. That's the only way you could maintain her perfect image. I think that no matter what I do, you would still find a way to pin it on me."

Angela watched Parris speak. Her words resonated with her, despite trying to tell herself that she was wrong.

My perfect sister…

"Why did you want me to shoot you?" Angela asked, shifting the focus off her.

Parris hummed to herself.

"I wanted to test your resolve. I knew the safety was on."

Even with a gun in her face, she was still playing her mind games.

They watched a kid walk with a balloon on the concrete sidewalk. Her parents laughed at her delight, taking a picture of her holding the ribbon tightly.

"Do you know which executive she was seeing?" Angela pushed.

Parris pinched the bridge of her nose; the gears behind her eyes would start smoking soon. She didn't answer right away.

"If I tell you, you'll just be reckless with the information. I don't want you in trouble or dead, believe it or not, Angie."

Angela nodded, not really sure if she could force the Informant to tell her anymore.

The pair stood there—the girl who lost her sister and the girl who lost her best friend. The wind sang a song for them, blowing between the leather jacket and denim jacket.

"Do you want vengeance for Janine, Angie?"

Dark eyes met angry ones. Angela fidgeted from the intensity.

"More than anything."

"Then I'll give you your chance at vengeance."

Logan paced the span of his living room, his mind reeling with the threat from the Head of the Gates.

Do I leave Ciel? Shit, what if the day is already over? Should I have gone to the police?

After returning from *Clueless*, he should have packed the car and left. But exhaustion won and he slept like a dead man.

Well, either way, he was a dead man.

A sharp knock plunged his heart into his stomach. He slowly pulled the gun from his waistband, the same one he had used to shoot at the

Head. Taking cover by the wall, he waited.

"Open up, the food will get cold!"

He opened the door quickly, his eyes wide as the Informant stood before him with a paper bag with a grease stain.

"About time!"

Parris entered the humble apartment as though she owned it. Logan locked the door behind her. She plopped the bag of food on the coffee table; Logan watched in disbelief as she lowered herself down on the couch.

"Grab some plates, don't be a rude host, now!"

He pulled out a small dinner plate and a popcorn bowl, only having one of everything. He had never had a guest over before. His own family refused to visit him in Ciel. The raised eyebrow was all the Informant commented before she placed a large pecan butter tart on each serving plate. Logan sat on the other end of the couch.

"*Jim's?*" he asked, taking a big bite.

"Naturally, they make the best in the city."

The still-warm gooey goodness was nostalgic for Logan, bringing him back to the days of his youth, of wandering around downtown with his friends, stumbling upon *Jim's* and their mastery of the baked goods. The sticky sugar somehow calmed his fried nerves. He smiled as he took another greedy bite, not having put anything in his stomach for more than twenty-four hours.

"I knew you didn't eat." She placed another one on his plate, which he gladly chomped down on. "We haven't shared a meal together in a long time."

Suddenly, the treat was too sweet. He looked at her, his mind caught up. She had to be here for a purpose. For a *damned* good reason.

"I need that gun back," Parris started.

Logan retrieved it wordlessly, placing it on the empty seat between them. She picked it up with a sour look before placing it in her waistband. She then pulled out an envelope from her leather jacket, set it down on the coffee table.

Logan pulled the contents of the envelope out with sticky fingers. He gasped as he saw the plane ticket. A one-way trip to Banff, Alberta. The envelope jingled as he pulled out a set of keys, a slip of paper with an address, and a wad of cash.

"The fuck is this?"

"It's a plane ticket; you see, a plane is this great big machine that—"

"DON'T FUCK WITH ME!"

Parris stood up, only having taken a bite from her treat. She headed towards the door, stopping to speak over her shoulder.

"Leave before the Gates find the time to kill you."

Logan grabbed her arm gently. "Come with me," he begged. "Come with me and we can leave this all behind!"

She couldn't look over her shoulder. She couldn't look at her old friend.

"PLEASE!" he pleaded, his heart not able to take anymore. Her indifferent attitude unsettled him.

This wasn't the same person he would follow blindly. This wasn't his friend he had lunch with on the school's stage when they weren't supposed to. This wasn't the same girl he had danced with at homecoming.

She wasn't her.

"I-I don't understand! Why did you leave me after she jumped? Why do you act the way you do? *Why*?!"

The sweet turned cold. Logan held his breath, praying that she would answer him this time, that she would finally give him a reason.

"Why did I have to lose you both that day? Was I not enough?"

Dark eyes stared back at him through a mess of hair. He knew her better than anyone else. He could see her emotions so plainly that it was shocking when others found her hard to read. She wore her heart on her sleeves. Even now Logan could see her.

Not Parris or Achilles but *her*.

She didn't want to stay in Ciel. The city wasn't good to her; it wasn't good to him, either. She was scared of something. Logan's lip trembled as he waited for her.

"Logan, I—" she said softly. "She's not coming back. Not Janine or the person I used to be. You need to move on. Heal with time… I have to go now."

His hand fell to his side, defeated. He watched her leave. He stood there, listening to the sound of her footsteps until they disappeared. He stood there, a man with nothing left.

Parris slid into the back of the car; Lorenzo started down the road.

"I'm calling for a meeting at *Clueless*," she announced.

Lorenzo glanced at his boss through the rearview mirror, unsure of the storm brewing in her eyes.

CHAPTER NINETEEN

Siege of Troy

There were too many construction workers for an overnight shift. Giovanni's eyes scanned over the workers who materialized from the cracks in Ciel's concrete from the comfort of his car. His own company could never supply this much labour, even with the Wings' products. His chestnut eyes narrowed at the workers who wore bulky construction jackets.

The night's temperature was cool but not *that* cold.

Something is happening, he thought. A worker who held a stop sign approached his black car. She spoke to his driver in a commanding voice.

Giovanni waited impatiently. He had places to be. Namely, he had to be at *Clueless* for a meeting called by the Informant. His creation was welcoming him into her space.

He would not be late for that.

"Sorry, Sir," the driver informed once the divider slid down soundlessly. "But the roads are closed for the Re-Pavement Project. They are only permitting foot traffic into the core of Downtown."

Checking his watch, Giovanni sighed as he opened the door.

"Tell my men to walk down from Elderson Street. I will meet them there."

Ducking out of the car, he walked down his city's streets. The sea of neon orange and yellow stuck out like a sore thumb against the grays and shadows of Ciel's nighttime.

He checked his watch. It was almost four a.m. Almost time.

Giovanni observed the few Halos and the group of Wings conveying on the black building also on foot. Their chains and black rings made them obvious to spot. But there were no pedestrians, or CCPD officers, for that matter.

Giovanni messaged his executives as he approached *Clueless*, his eyes darting across the eerie street.

Have all level Gates close to the Downtown Core, converge on Clueless. Stay armed and ready. – G

Ciel City was too empty. It was too quiet.

Too still.

Giovanni approached his executives in front of the club. His men asked why the streets were closed, others asking where everyone was. Giovanni narrowed his eyes at the front door of *Clueless*.

A storm is coming.

Waiting for a storm was worse than actually enduring the storm. At least, that's what Angela thought as she sat on the floor of her aunt's apartment fully dressed, lying in wait. Jaya and Theo sat across from her on the couch, unsure of why she asked them to come over so late, but they came nevertheless.

They sat in silence. Angela was not able to say why they were there, not until she was told herself. She checked the clock on the wall.

It was almost time.

"If you both were offered a chance at justice, a chance to get revenge on those who've hurt you, would you take it?" Angela asked, fixated on the coffee table.

Jaya and Theo shared a look.

"Justice and revenge are not the same thing," Theo answered. "You don't heal from getting revenge."

Jaya nodded along, trying to see behind the well-crafted mask Angela was wearing now. She was beginning to be able to look past it.

"But would you? If Parris had a way to give you revenge, you would take it, right?" Angela pressed, her tired eyes pleading at them, at her only two friends.

She needed to know if they were with her, if they would really help her get revenge for Janine, or if all their promises were empty nothings.

It was almost time.

"Jaya, don't you want justice for what the Halos put you through? For attacking you and making you fear every step you took outside of your home?" Angela asked, strangely calm.

Jaya's eyes watered, tears threatening to fall. The image of Raef dead was still at the forefront of her mind.

"Theo." Angela changed tactics. "Wouldn't you want justice for everything that creep did to you?"

"What is this about, Angie? I'm not going to help you kill the woman who saved me," Theo stated. He clenched his jaw, not wanting to think about the older man.

The clock struck four. Angela received a message.

Vengeance is at Pier 3. – Parris

Angela gasped; a small part of her surprised the Informant had actually messaged. That she was honest about giving her a chance at vengeance. Her resolve hardened. Angela sent a message to Logan, letting him know the plan.

"I am offering you both the only chance at getting back at those sons of bitches for all the horrors they've done to you. Parris is going to give us *all* a chance to get back at them!" Angela exclaimed.

"Parris?" Jaya asked.

Angela jumped up from her spot, rushing through the front door.

"Wait, Angela!" Jaya called out, following her out the door. Angela was already running down the stairs, her heart leading her. Theo easily caught up, behind her by a few paces.

"Where are you going?" he asked, noticing just how fast Angela was.

"Vengeance is at Pier 3! Parris is meeting us there. Come on!"

Angela ran onto the street, her friends behind her. Jaya ran stride by stride with Theo; Angela glanced back and ran faster than she'd ever run in her life.

All of her runs through Ciel City paid off. She ran through the quiet streets, the wind whipping at her face. No cars tonight. They would have to run into the Downtown Core. The Re-Pavement Project started tonight. Angela had to get to Pier 3 first. She had to get there before it was too late to avenge Janine.

Before her chance escaped her again.

It was loud in the CCPD's 97th Division's Lobby. The blue-clad officers gathered together in a herd, their shoulders touching one another, as though they were packed like a can of blue sardines.

"I thought you were patrolling the Port Front?" an officer asked her blue-clad coworker beside her.

"No, my shift changed. I thought you had the Core route?" he replied.

Confusion filled the lobby.

Officers asked one another why they were gathered at headquarters, asking who was out on the streets.

"What do you mean Captain changed your schedule?!"

"What about you, Sanchez?"

Officer Sanchez looked around the lobby, her suspicion continuing to grow. Her schedule had suddenly changed a few days prior. Then, according to a few of her peers, theirs changed just a few hours ago. Now every member of the CCPD was called to the 97th Division for a meeting called by their captain.

"Something's not right," she whispered.

Her eyes searched for Captain Chan, the only person who could clarify this mess. She saw a figure climb on the welcome desk, standing righteously in front of them.

Hafiz, she thought with a scowl.

"Attention, Ciel City Police Department!" Amir shouted from atop the desk.

The talking dipped into silence as his co-workers stared at him.

"My name is Officer Amir Hafiz, head of the Anti-Gang Task Force. I was the one to call this meeting tonight."

"Where's Captain Chan?" asked an officer behind Sanchez.

"Under arrest."

The CCPD officers froze in shocked silence, murder in their eyes. Sanchez pushed through her friends, reaching the desk.

"Who arrested him?" she called out in a loud voice.

"I arrested him." Amir looked down at her, disgust on his face. "I arrested him just five minutes before coming down for this meeting."

Fire burned in her eyes as she gave an ugly scowl at him. "You hurt one of our own, greenie?"

"Not just him," Amir called out, no longer looking at Sanchez. He spoke in a loud, unshakable voice. "Everyone in this building is being put under arrest for suspected connection with the three syndicates of Ciel."

A few officers laughed, while others itched forward towards him.

"And how do you intend to arrest us *all*, Amir?" Sanchez gloated, strengthened by the sheer number of her comrades in the lobby also glaring daggers at the greenie.

"No, I won't be arresting any more CCPD officers tonight. But the federal guards will. It took a lot of time, patience, and planning, but the federal guards were able to infiltrate the CCPD."

Just then the green glass doors of the CCPD slammed open. A flood of neon orange and yellow jackets filled the lobby. The federal guards posing as construction workers pointed their assault rifles at the CCPD. A few federal guards dressed in balaclavas descended the spiral stairs from Captain Chan's office, the captain in cuffs.

"Captain!"

Captain Chan was enraged, his eyes threatening to pop out of their sockets as he scanned the lobby of his division. The officers looked around, trying to understand the ambush.

Surely someone knew this would happen. Someone had to have seen Amir's request for the federal guards. He couldn't have orchestrated this trap himself—he was too naïve to.

Sanchez bolted for her phone, sending Tiffany a message about their situation.

The message wouldn't send.

"All communications have been successfully cut, Officer Hafiz!" a woman in a construction jacket called out from the entrance.

"Officer Hafiz!" Captain Chan barked out. "What is this?!"

Sanchez glared at Amir as he made his way to the green soul-crushing doors. The CCPD parted for him.

"This is change, Captain Chan."

The sea of neon outnumbered the blue. Amir read a message on his phone.

Pier 3. – Helen

Amir looked over his shoulder at his enemies—past Sanchez's glare, past the look of murder in the eyes of the tainted officers of the law, at the pest in his new house.

"Or, as my friend would say, checkmate."

———————————————————

The atmosphere was tense inside the club. Tony cussed as he was patted down for weapons. It was enough that they had to walk all the way to the club with the road closures, but now the Informant had made it a weapons-free meeting. Marcel sighed as the security took another gun from Tony's waistband.

"You can pick this up from coat check on your way out," the security informed as he went to search another Wing executive.

The club was full of members from all three syndicates, the biggest meeting Ciel City had seen in the last five years. Marcel spotted Giovanni by the foot of the stairs staring at the opaque glass of the office. Huifen was not far behind as she scanned the club. Marcel followed her eyes as they landed on the bar.

The usual spotless marble bar was closed, with a metal grate covering it.

Something is happening, Marcel thought, grateful that he instructed the Wings to stay close to the club in case of a shootout.

A Gates executive bumped into him, a Halo executive right behind him, muttering about the filth in the club.

Marcel felt trapped. It was uncomfortable being this close to their enemies from rival syndicates. Tensions have been higher than ever since Halloween.

Since Giovanni asserted dominance over Ciel.

Tony held his ribs as he swayed in, his left hand wrapped in heavy bandages. His latest beating from Giovanni still felt fresh. He, too, took a glance around, scowling at the sheer number of members from rival gangs.

"Where's the fucking Informant?!" Tony yelled in a loud voice over the chatter. "She's the one who called this shitshow, so where is she?"

The glass turned transparent.

Drawing all eyes to the Informant who stood tall in front of them. She wasn't wearing her signature leather jacket, but her smile was there. The woman before them was neither the Informant nor Parris. It was someone they hadn't seen before. Her dark eyes scanned over the executives and Heads, a delighted look on her face as they waited quietly for her. She held a microphone to her mouth.

"Thank you all for coming on such short notice," she sang. "Truly, it means so much to little old me that I could gather all of Ciel's gangsters in one club. This iconic meeting of the Gates, the Wings, and the Halos will not be forgotten."

Her voice echoed in the club.

Everyone held on to each and every word she spoke. Marcel grabbed Tony, bringing him closer to the stairs, noticing Huifen just behind Giovanni.

"The reason for tonight's meeting is a special one—a reason I've been contemplating for the past ten years."

The televisions in the club came to life as a picture of Janine Johnston flashed before their eyes.

"I hope a few of you remember why Tony Moretti had to leave the Gates ten years ago. It was all because of this girl, Janine Johnston. My best friend."

Tony gulped.

"She was a student with me at St. Katherine's High School, where Tony Moretti, the first Untouchable, would pick her up after school. STK's top student, messing with the second Untouchable, an Untouchable Giovanni Moretti made."

"What is the meaning of this?!" a Wing executive yelled out. Parris held her finger up to her mouth, demanding silence.

"Janine has everything to do with tonight," Parris spoke in a low voice. "It was when Janine killed herself to escape from Tony Moretti that Giovanni Moretti ostracized him from the Gates. Giovanni couldn't kill Tony; he would have voided his own agreement if he did. So Tony was allowed to live another day, despite breaking his father's agreement. But it must have hurt dear old Giovanni to kick his only child out of the Gates, a syndicate he'd dedicated more than thirty years of his life towards. His legacy."

Her eyes met Giovanni, her mocking tone setting his blood aflame. She smiled maliciously at him.

"But Giovanni was used to hurting children."

The Head of the Gates marched up the stairs, banging on the white door, but it wouldn't open. Parris continued her tale, the club still quiet. Giovanni's anger faded into a dull banging in the background.

"Not long after, Huifen Ping took over the Halos by killing her own mother and consolidating the Halos as Ciel's drug dealer. Congratulations, Huifen. You've been ruthlessly successful since."

Huifen glared daggers at the Informant, not taking the bait of her taunting. Parris turned her attention to Marcel.

"After Janine's death, Marcel Gagnon form the Wings, with Tony Moretti as the figurehead. Grooming young girls online to be sold, trafficking foreigners and holding them hostage for labour—perhaps the Wings are the most cruel of the Syndicates. I would buy from them, to release their 'catches', but I couldn't buy them all."

Is this her plan? To make us angry with her? Marcel thought, meeting her eyes. *What does she get out of this?*

"Of course, none of tonight would be possible without the Gates losing the Ciel Re-Pavement Project!" she exclaimed excitedly. "Truly, a big round of applause to the Ciel Construction Company for losing the bid. It was hard to get the deal, but City Counselors are finicky beings, right Giovanni?"

She won the bid for the Re-Pavement Project? Marcel thought, surprised. *But what does she gain from the construction deal?*

"Now for the best part!" she squealed. "Thanks to communication jammers, you've all been unaware of the raids on all of your safehouses, your weapons, your drugs, your storage facilities, and your headquarters!"

"WHAT?!" a Wings executive shouted.

"Someone call the lookouts!" a Gates executive commanded.

"She must be joking!" a Halo gasped.

Giovanni continued to ram his shoulder into the white door, only seeing red. Huifen shrieked at her executives to check on her stashes.

It was madness.

The screens of the club flashed with different bank accounts, all belonging to the Big Three. Names of businesses they owned and shell corporations were broadcasted.

"But wait!" Parris laughed as she watched the chaos. "There's more!"

Marcel held his breath as he watched the Informant, never appreciating just how cruel and cunning she really was. Parris vibrated as though she was about to spoil the ending to the most anticipated movie.

"There was no Re-Pavement Project to begin with! I had the mayor create the entire project to increase inter-gang tensions, and boy, oh boy, did it work! At the first instance of the Gates losing power, you all scrambled like rats for a piece. It pays to have the mayor in your back pocket, right Giovanni?!"

Parris howled with laughter as lumps of coal formed in everyone's throat. She glowed at their stunned faces.

The years of planning were worth every moment.

"Every single construction worker you've seen for the past few weeks are the good federal agents of our great nation, equipped with valid warrants to search and seize every safehouse and gang hideout I know of. And I know *all* of them."

"Bitch!" Huifen cried as she joined Giovanni, trying to pry the white door open. Tony stood there too shocked to be angry yet. His entire world unravelled right before his eyes.

She wasn't just an Untouchable, she was unstoppable.

"Ciel City will be cleansed of its filth. At dawn, the Gates, the Wings, and the Halos will cease to be. That is my promise. My promise to Janine Johnston."

Marcel rushed to the top of the stairs, pushing against the door. His life's work was down the drain. His every ambition and sacrifice was lost to the likes of *her*.

"Every member of my staff were people I bought from the Wings. Not 'products' but actual people. They will get their revenge on you, the scum who tore them away from their families and friends, who stole their lives away."

The staff of *Clueless* materialized behind the metal grates of the black bar.

Guns aimed at the executives.

"You can open fire now, I'm finished monologuing."

An execution was ordered.

The staff opened fire in a blaze of lights; executives of every kind ran for cover or to find an escape, but the club was locked down. There was no way to escape. The sound of guns and killing were horrific. Blood sprayed the body of the club with no artistic intention.

Only the desire for revenge.

Tony finally limped up the stairs, pushing against the white door with everything he had. Huifen screamed curses at the Informant. Marcel raged in silence. Giovanni rammed his shoulder against the door, fury painted across his face.

It opened.

The gangsters collapsed into the checkerboard office, the chess pieces knocked over.

The game was won.

Tony slammed the door shut, the sound of the death sentence cut off into a startling silence. Parris was already gone from the office, the back door swinging open after her.

"Under the table!" Huifen screamed at Marcel. He dove for the table; his hand found a knife handle.

The only weapon they had.

Marcel looked at the knife dumbly, unsure of what to do with it.

"Kill him!" Huifen screamed, her face a ruby red as she pointed to Tony. "Then we'll kill the old man!"

Giovanni had already disappeared through the door after the Informant. Tony looked over his shoulder, at the blade in his friend's hand.

"Marce—?"

"NOW!" Huifen bellowed in a crazed voice.

Marcel yelled as he plunged the knife deep into Huifen's throat. She stared at him with wide eyes, the blood caught in her lungs gurgling as she tried to speak.

"Go!" Marcel cried out, distraught as he watched her body slide down the glass, leaving a bloody trail behind. Tony continued after his father and Parris.

Not sparing a glance back at Marcel.

A gunshot rang in the room, a bullet finding its home in Marcel's knee. He howled in pain as he fell near Huifen.

Behind the red couch stood Lorenzo, gun-cocked at the executive.

"You—!"

"For all the lives you've *ruined*."

Lorenzo shot another bullet in between Marcel's eyes, his dead body launched near Huifen's.

Lorenzo took a shuddering deep breath as he looked down at the club, at the countless bodies that littered every surface. The staff waited on his order to make a run for it. He looked to where the Informant had run to.

"Please, God, let her win."

Parris slammed the door to the roof open, jumping onto the fire escape, climbing down as fast as she could. She heard the gunshot, knowing that Lorenzo was successful.

Two less things to worry about.

"BELLA!"

Giovanni bellowed as he climbed down the fire escape after her, keeping an impressive pace. She risked a glance over her shoulder, the Head unsurprisingly in great shape as he closed in. Tony was just then making his way onto the fire escape.

Parris landed on the asphalt, running down the street towards the Pier.

Little bitch was acting up her injuries, thought Giovanni as he landed heavily on the asphalt. *She's running like prey in the wild.* He took off after her.

A sudden explosion of fire did not distract him from the Informant. Giovanni's intuition had been correct, and his men gathered around *Clueless* battling members of the Wings and Halos once communications were cut.

Low-level Wings had set a car on fire. The different gang members were fighting one another, their truce no longer in effect.

The flames drew the criminals to *Clueless*, like moths to a flame. Construction workers armed with guns sought to arrest the gang members.

Parris ran through Ciel City. She ran past the brawls, the Halos stabbing the Gates, the federal guards calling out for order, the Wings who fired at the Halos, and the construction workers who were arresting the gang members.

Blood filled the streets of Ciel City.

Parris ran as hard as possible towards the Pier, Giovanni not letting up behind her. Her side burned from the physical exhaustion. The wind whistled in her ear as she dodged the flames of another burning car. This one was a police cruiser.

The flames grew, engulfing parts of the city. Sirens were blazing in the air.

Her heart hurt, but she continued. Her declaration of war fueled the rage in Giovanni and Tony.

Orange pylons scattered as police cars drove into the Downtown Core. Members of the Wings jumped on top of the moving vehicle.

"PARRIS!"

Parris continued to run through it all.

The growing sounds of violence and sirens made Angela's blood run cold, but she couldn't think of anything but that message from the Informant. Angela ran down Elderson, Theo and Jaya still behind her, but gaining distance. She was exhausted, but she had to reach the Pier.

Revenge for Janine was promised there.

"ANGELA, IT'S NOT SAFE!" Theo yelled when he saw gang members stab one another. Jaya screamed when a car caught fire close by.

Ciel City was unrecognizable.

"You kids get inside now!" yelled a construction worker. But the high schoolers continued running through the night.

"ANGELA, PLEASE STOP!"

"ANGELA!"

"PLEASE!"

They continued to follow her, nearing the Pier.

The violence died down as Parris left the Downtown Core. Closing in on the Pier, the sirens and flames quieted down. But she couldn't rest yet. Her feet pounded against the city's streets, Giovanni almost within arm's reach, Tony closing in. Sweat poured from her forehead as she saw the sign for Pier 3. She ran up to the water, turning around in a hurry.

Giovanni stopped running, stalking up to her. His chest heaving in a deep pant.

"You little bitch," he cursed. "You played me, my business, MY GATES!" he thundered. "How dare you, Parris? I made you! You'll regret every lie you told me. I won't kill you, but I'll bring you to death's door over and over again, making you wish for hell's embrace."

Parris didn't flinch at his threats.

Tony arrived at the Pier, also a huffing mess. He held his ribs as he looked between the Informant and his father.

"I usually wouldn't work with him, but for you, I'll make an exception," Tony spat at her, standing next to Giovanni.

Parris pulled out two guns, aiming one at each Moretti.

"It's so nice to see you both get along; after all, I know just how much you hate each other," she mocked.

Tony scoffed as he sauntered up to the Informant. "You won't shoot. You know that without us you're not safe. You're not an Untouchable if the Morettis don't protect you—"

Parris shot a bullet into his kneecap.

Tony fell to the ground in a howl of pain, blood decorating the pier. Giovanni stood still; he knew that she would shoot. He knew his creation. But his son, the utter failure that was his son, would always act first without thinking.

"That felt good!" she gleamed. "I've been meaning to kill you for some time, Tony. But plans change. Killing you wouldn't fix things, I needed to tear down the whole system. Plus, both of us being Untouchables wouldn't guarantee me no repercussions from Daddy

Dearest."

The sound of three figures running down the pier drew Parris's attention.

"Right on time, Angie."

Angela skidded to a stop. Theo called out for her as he and Jaya approached the group. His eyes narrowed at Giovanni. Jaya gasped as she saw Tony on the floor, blood sprouting from his knee.

"What is this?"

"Angie…"

The Informant kept both guns raised at the Morettis.

"Theo, Jaya, so nice to see the two of you again!" Parris called out. "I didn't think you would come, Jaya, so Huifen isn't here. I apologize for that. But we can still make this work."

Parris walked to Angela's side, giving her a gun, the same gun Tony gave her.

The very same one she had tried to kill the Informant with. Angela took the cold steel with steady hands, struggling to control her breath.

"What's happening, Angie?" Theo asked, his eyes never leaving Giovanni. The older man was too busy glaring at Parris, searching for an opening.

"Tell us!" Theo pleaded.

"This is your chance at vengeance," Parris answered as she pointed her lone gun at Giovanni. "But depending on Angie's choice, you may not get to have your go."

"This isn't right!" Theo cried. "This isn't justice! This isn't going to bring back anyone or make up for any of the hurt!"

"Wise at such an age. I did a good job with you, *Cucciolo,*" gloated Giovanni.

Theo saw red. "Shut up, you fucking bastard!"

"Now, now, Giovanni, who said you could speak? Should I shoot your kneecap to shut your bullshit-spouting mouth?" Parris threatened coldly.

"Is this your attempt at an execution, *Bella*? These children don't have the backbone."

"They are no longer children; your kind stole that from them."

Tony laughed from the ground, his face pale. He was losing a lot of blood. He stared at Angela, his face twisting into a sick shape.

"She blames us for giving them what they wanted! You wanted answers and I gave them to you! I told you about the Informant. I gave you *that* gun to protect yourself. Was I really all bad, Angela? It's not our fault you and all your friends want to play. They come to our turf, to our dens, and then they act like the victims! FUCKING RICH!"

"That's not true!" Jaya shuddered.

The pier front was cold, the lake's pitch-black surface doubling as a mirror to all of Ciel's sins.

"You lure us in! We're just kids, we don't know any better!" Jaya shouted.

"Don't you?" Giovanni took a step closer to the STK students.

"Giovanni," Parris warned, stepping in front of the children.

"Didn't Patel warn you at the start of the year?"

"Giovanni!"

"Last I recalled, I gave Theo the money he so desperately needed. I helped him free his abusive father. It was his own inexperience to not broker a deal when loaning money from the Gates. I treated you well, Theo, loved you like my child."

"Giovanni, I am warning you!" Parris yelled, gun aimed at his head. Theo's lips trembled, but he met Giovanni's eyes.

"You all truly didn't know any better?" Giovanni crept closer. His stare landed on Angela. "Mommy and Daddy never warned you about the monsters of the night?"

Parris fired the gun.

The sound silenced the older man. The ground before him was now sporting a bullet hole. Jaya covered her ears, tears speeding down her face from the sound. Giovanni smirked. He held his hands up in mock defeat.

"Angela."

The voice of Parris pierced her soul.

"Take your pick now; if you can't do it, then Theo will get his chance. If both of you choose to leave now, then I'll do it. It's been a long time coming."

"The fuck I do to her?" cried Tony as he struggled to sit up. "I didn't even touch her!"

Parris kept the gun raised at Giovanni, not bothering to look at him.

"Tony Moretti, meet Angela Johnston."

"Johnston… like Janine Johnston?"

Like a ghost from his past, Tony shivered as he noticed the same features of Janine on her younger sister—the same full lips, the same coily hair.

Parris spoke over the quiet lake.

"Take your pick, Angie. You can kill the scumbag who forced her to that ledge, or the devil who made this whole system."

Angela pointed the gun at the ground, trying to decide which one to kill. The reason or the cause? The father or the son? The abuser or the abuser?

"Don't I get to say what happened?" Tony yelled from his position on the ground. Parris sighed, keeping her gun focused on the real threat, Giovanni.

"You don't get to say anything—"

"Don't you want to know why Janine jumped, Angela?" Tony asked, cradling his leg. His piercing blue eyes locked onto Angela. Angela gasped despite herself. Tony continued.

"I loved her! I loved Janine Johnston with all my heart—!"

"You lying scumbag!" Parris yelled, her eyes furious with the man. But Angela pointed the gun at the Informant without a second's thought.

"What are you doing?!" Theo yelled in disbelief.

"I-I want to hear him out!" Angela exclaimed, her eyes refusing to meet the Informant, instead trained on Tony.

Parris looked between the gun pointed at her and her best friend's sister. Parris studied Angie's face. She sighed.

"He's just going to tell you what you want to hear, Angie," Parris replied. "He'll say everything that will convince you that I was the reason."

"Or I'll finally tell her the truth!" Tony exclaimed. "Don't be tricked, Angela. She just wants you to think she is right. She was with us when I spoke to Janine, when I told Janine that I would leave the mafia for her, that I loved Janine!"

"You fucking liar!" Parris screamed, her dark eyes livid. Angela's hand trembled as she listened.

"Parris must have convinced her that the mafia would go after her if we were together. I loved her, Angela! I was the one who bought her her homecoming dress. I took care of her when she was stressed about exams. I always took care of her!" Tony exclaimed in his own puddle of blood. Angela's eyes darted between Tony and Parris.

"Parris was there. She knew about me this whole time! If I am to blame for Janine, then why the fuck am I still alive? If Parris truly cared for her like she claims, then she would have killed me a long time ago. She just wants you to do the dirty work, Angela."

"Enough!" Parris yelled, her gun still trained on Giovanni, who was waiting for Parris to make a mistake, to jump her and take the weapon for himself.

"Angie, I've already told you the truth about your sister. I've already told you that no matter what I do, you'll never forgive me. But please, please for the love of God, look past his lies just for tonight. You're young, I don't expect you to trust me or understand what I'm trying to do. But please."

Parris looked Angela dead in the eyes: no mask or games, just her.

"Please believe me, Angie."

Angela's eyes betrayed her. Hot tears streaked down her face.

The sirens in the distance didn't matter anymore. The Big Three didn't matter. All that mattered was this group of mismatched puzzle pieces by the pier.

Angela raised the gun.

A single gunshot rang across the pier on the blackest of nights.

CHAPTER TWENTY

Me and the Devil

*N*ine Years Ago.

A pair of dark eyes stalked the expensive black car. She had watched him for a while, keeping logs in her mind of where the car went, the type of people he met, and when it would return to the Ciel Construction Company. Her eyes followed his smart suit like a hawk as he entered the homey restaurant. She knew he preferred the inside corner table, sitting against the wall.

In the command position.

Another man entered the restaurant in a hurry from his own car, brushing his thinning blonde hair out of his eyes. This one was more timid-looking.

The mayor of Ciel City.

The men greeted one another with a kiss on each cheek. The mayor seemed intimidated by the other man, his face shiny under the restaurant light. They took a seat at the inside corner table.

The restaurant was empty. Even the staff refused to enter when he would visit. They knew not to interrupt, to only bring out the food, to lower their heads and avert their eyes.

To not catch the attention of the Head of the Gates.

"Congratulations on winning the elections, Robert," Giovanni cheered as he took a sip of his wine.

"All thanks to your support, Mr. Moretti!" Mayor Robert gulped. "Without your donations, I wouldn't have been able to even put up a billboard!"

He raised his glass for a toast, and Giovanni indulged the newly-elected mayor. Their glasses clinked.

"You know, Mr. Moretti, I heard a new syndicate is catching ground."

Giovanni raised an eyebrow. "Is that so? Please tell me more."

"Well," Robert grinned, pleased with himself, "they're calling themselves the 'Wings'—"

"Who ordered the *moussaka*?"

The men snapped their heads to the young waitress. She was holding a plate of food, but she looked out of place in the restaurant. She was dressed in a leather jacket and her face looked young. Robert's eyes darted between the obnoxious girl and the mafia boss, breaking out into a cold sweat. She had a sweet smile as she waited for an answer.

"You're holding a lasagna," replied Giovanni.

"Oh, is that what this is? I knew the kitchen got the order wrong!" she groaned in a childlike way. Giovanni's chestnut eyes studied her, seeming amused. She placed the plate in front of Robert and held her hand out to Giovanni.

"While I have your attention, my name is Parris, and I would love to offer you my services!"

Robert choked at her attitude. "What the hell is this? Do you know who we are? Who I am?!"

Giovanni shook her hand, a sly smile cut onto his face as he pulled his arm back, dragging the girl onto the table. Robert shot out of his seat. Parris giggled, her other hand holding onto the table for support.

"If you want to make a quick buck, I'm not opposed."

"Giovanni!" Robert panicked. "I'm right here!"

"Then leave," he growled back, his eyes locked on his new prey.

Robert grumbled as he excused himself to the restroom. Parris held Giovanni's gaze the whole time, as though she were challenging him to something.

"And what services do you offer, Parris?"

"Information on an unlisted weapon shipment happening tonight."

Giovanni barked out a cold laugh.

"Now I wasn't expecting that! Usually, girls would provide *other* services."

"I don't offer that," she spat out, her friendly demeanour gone in an instant. Giovanni hummed as his thumb drew shapes into the back of her hand. He watched the way she glanced down at her hand before the saccharine smile resumed on her face.

She's new to this. She could be fun, he thought.

He released her hand, leaning back into his seat, sipping his wine.

"How did you come by this information? My syndicate is unaware of any shipment today."

"Oh, silly, the whole point was to hide it from the Gates to begin with!"

"So how do you know about it?"

She stroked her chin in thought. He could see gears turning behind her dark eyes.

"The problem is, if I tell you now, I won't get what I want."

He leaned forward, ready to play this game.

"What is it that you want, *Bella*?"

"I want to be an Informant!" Parris smiled.

"Would you be any good at it?" Giovanni asked.

"I have no need for a kid who wants to play with the grown-ups."

Parris pouted, her childlike behaviour stirring Giovanni's interest in her.

"I mean, it doesn't take a genius to know that you come to this restaurant every first Tuesday of the month." Giovanni lowered his glass, taking her seriously for the first time since she appeared. "You often bring public officials here, so the meeting doesn't seem shady. But the real business deals happen at the Ciel Construction Company, where the Gates have operated for over twenty years unhindered."

"But that's not where the scandalous stuff happens, either! The Gates have thirty-one underground clubs littered throughout the city, along with seventeen brothels, twenty-two ports for trafficking goods, seven warehouses for weapons and drugs, and that's not accounting for all the businesses that the Gates use to hide their laundered money… should I go on?"

The restaurant was silent. Parris stood there wide-eyed, waiting for a response with a tilt of her head. Giovanni's fist shook. The little minx had listed his operations and assets without so much as blinking.

"Who are you?" he asked again.

Groaning, she took a seat across from the Head. "I've already introduced myself! Are you ready to make a deal for tonight's shipment or should I take my services elsewhere?"

Giovanni considered her proposal, his mind racing with calculations. He studied her dark eyes, curious about the way they studied him back, as though he were looking in a mirror of sorts.

"Come to the CCC in a half-hour. If you're a minute late, then I will not consider your deal."

The wink he received told Giovanni that he had made the right choice.

That she really was going to be a fun time.

True to her word, half an hour later, Giovanni watched his men bring in the girl. She ooh-ed and aah-ed at his office as she was led in, noticing the thick oak desk, the roaring fireplace, and the brown leather couch. Parris took a seat in front of him in the plush armchair. He made himself a drink at the bar cart.

"Pick your poison."

"Coffee, please!"

He gave her a look as he nodded at a guard, the guard rushing out to grab the girl a cup of coffee.

"Usually teenagers jump at the opportunity for free booze," he remarked as he leaned on his desk in front of her.

"I'm not a teenager."

"How old are you then, *Bella*?"

"Age is a social construct. Today I am thirty-five years old, tomorrow I'll be eight."

The Head took a deep sip of his bourbon. The girl was growing more and more interesting. It took a lot for the Head to be this interested in another person, let alone someone this eccentric.

"Do your parents know where you are?"

"Ugh, what are you, a social worker?" she grumbled, crossing her arms as she sat in the chair. "Listen, I'm here to make a deal. If you have an issue with my age, then I will take my business elsewhere."

Giovanni held his hand up in false surrender. He chuckled as she pouted, her lower lip jutting out.

He watched her like a hunter.

The guard returned promptly with a piping hot cup of coffee, a pitcher of milk, and a few sugar cubes. Giovanni dismissed the guards, wanting to be alone with the girl. She poured the milk until the coffee matched the colour of her skin. She did not touch the sugar.

They drank in silence.

The tension in the office was growing. The girl sipped her coffee leisurely as she waited for Giovanni to ask her for the information. She wasn't just auditioning for the role of Informant, after all; she had bigger goals in mind.

"About tonight's shipment," Giovanni started. Parris gave him a dazzling smile. "What deal are you proposing, Parris?"

"I will give you the location, the amount of shipment, and the names of the parties involved."

"In exchange…?"

"In exchange for becoming an independent Informant of Ciel!"

His eyebrows drew in. Her request was unusual. Her age showed her lack of foresight. Usually, people would ask to become an informant on behalf of the Gates or of the Halos, but not to work independently. They had to have protection when they operated.

"You can't hop around clients, *Bella*. That's how you end up dead," Giovanni advised. Parris shook her head as she explained, setting down her cup.

"No, not independent… ugh, what's the word you people use? Oh right! I want to become an *Untouchable*!"

Giovanni slammed the glass against his desk. The girl did not jump at the sudden expression of anger. She just tilted her head to the side, waiting for the man to verbalize his outburst.

"Where did you hear that word, *Bella*?"

"Why do you call me '*Bella*'?" she asked right back, not missing a beat.

His hand shot out like a bullet, grabbing her by her hair, yanking her into a standing position. He peered into her dark eyes, starting to notice her mind games.

"I asked you a question, Parris. Answer before I send you to one of my 'stores'."

The hand in her hair grew rougher the longer it took her to answer, as though she were picking which lie to choose for this exact moment.

"I heard it being said in one of the clubs I snuck into one time. Something about Moretti losing his Untouchable."

"You're lying."

"I am."

He pushed her back, and she landed heavily in the chair, her body like a ragdoll compared to his monstrous strength. He leaned on the arms of the chair, his large frame boxing her in.

"You should know that I am quick to anger, Parris."

"I know!" she answered back, not showing any fear at all. "That's why I know better than to beat around the bush with you. I have vital information and I want to become an Untouchable. Up to you to take my deal!"

Taking one final long look into her eyes, he pulled back, finishing his glass in one swig. He took a heavy seat in his own chair.

If the information about tonight is correct, then she had managed to find out about the competition's shipment before the Gates' own informants, not to mention she numbered off all the assets. How did she find out? Giovanni pondered.

"Hate to interrupt!" Parris sang as she finished her coffee "But we need to strike a deal. The shipment will be arriving soon."

His mind was racing through every possible scenario, every single possibility of this girl in front of him: what her potential could bring to the Gates, what she could do for him. Calculations and risk assessments of her information and potential flashed across his mind.

He came to a conclusion.

"Parris," Giovanni decided, "if you provide correct information about tonight's shipment. If your information is valuable and accurate, then… then I will consider making you into an Untouchable."

The young girl beamed at him. "Amazing! Yes, that's all I want!"

"But."

"But?"

"But if the information you provide me tonight is incorrect in even the slightest." He pulled out a gun from the desk drawer. Parris watched the weapon, her excitement vanishing.

"You must kill yourself in front of me."

"And, what if I don't want to shoot myself?" she asked, testing the waters with the intimidating man.

"Then you will live. My stores could always use fresh meat; the johns like a pretty young thing."

The office grew colder despite the roaring fireplace.

"Do we have a deal, *Bella*?"

He held out his hand, just as she had done earlier that day. She reached across the desk, shaking his hand, sealing the deal.

"We have a deal, Boss."

Waiting wasn't an easy game to play when your life hung in the balance. Parris remained seated in the chair, staring at the oak desk. Her smile was gone, her entire demeanour shifted. Her life and freedom were on the line after all. Giovanni watched her from the corner of his eyes as they waited.

She had said that two shipping containers full of weapons were scheduled to arrive at Port 23, a port that was out of the Gates' control. Giovanni had sent a group of his men, led by an executive no less, to investigate her claim.

"For your sake, I hope this isn't like the boy who cried wolf," Giovanni had warned as he made the phone call.

They sat in silence, waiting for confirmation from the executive about whether this would be her last day in this cruel world or the start of her new job.

The ringing of the phone startled the girl. Giovanni answered, "Yes?"

There were too many uncertainties. Parris watched, not able to listen to the executive on the other side. She couldn't read the expression on Giovanni's face either.

"Is that so?" he asked, his eyes landing on the girl, his eyebrows raised high.

Giovanni hung up the phone, standing up. He pulled out the gun, and placed it in front of her.

"They only found one container."

"That's not true, there's two containers," she hissed back.

Giovanni shook the phone in his hand. "That's not what they found."

The gun gleamed on the desk. She tried to even her breathing as she considered her choices: shoot herself or be taken by the Gates.

There's always the third option, Giovanni thought as he watched her reach for the gun. *She could always shoot me and try to escape.*

Parris took the gun; she seemed unsure of how to hold the weapon. Her eyebrows drew in concentration as she thought. Giovanni analyzed her every movement and expression, wanting to understand the girl, wanting to know exactly what she was thinking at that moment.

Wanting control over her.

"I know that there are two containers on that shipment," she brought the gun to the side of her temple.

"As an Informant, I will die with my integrity. Sorry about the mess I am about to make in your fancy office. It was a pleasure working for you, however briefly."

Giovanni crept closer, watching the steady gun press into her head. She wasn't afraid. She took in a deep breath.

Parris pulled the trigger.

She blinked.

Nothing happened.

The sound of sharp clapping drew her attention. Giovanni applauded her, a devious smile on his face.

"Well done, Parris. Truly, bravo!"

"It was empty," she stated, placing the gun on the desk, clasping her hands together. Giovanni patted her shoulder, his heavy hand resting there.

Whether she had been willing to die or if she knew that the gun wasn't loaded didn't matter to him. A perfect obedient child had just been gift-wrapped for him, and Giovanni wasn't one to look a gift horse in the mouth.

"So there were two containers?"

His hand travelled to her chin, tipping her head upwards.

"Yes, *Bella*. A job very well done. You've gifted me a heavy blow to my competition."

Her smile resumed. "I'm so glad I could be of service!" she giggled, her frown from earlier just as quickly disappearing, as though her pleasant expression had never left her face.

"Now, about becoming an Untouchable?"

The air in the office changed.

Giovanni smiled warmly at her, his hand travelling over her neck, then lower. Parris grabbed his wrist, stopping him.

"I already said I don't offer *those* services."

He chuckled as his other hand went to play with her hair. "Do you know how an Untouchable is made, *Bella*?"

She tried to get up, but he slammed her into the desk. She cried out as her back hit the strong oak.

A few office supplies scattered as he pinned her there. Parris stopped struggling, looking up at the older man, a pained smile on her young face.

"Giovanni Moretti claims something as Untouchable. In exchange, the Halos and other small gangs abide by that rule in order to have access to his territories.”

A hand glided under her shirt.

“You’re only partially right, *Bella,*” Giovanni corrected, his hand resting on the left side of her stomach. Parris tensed her body. “But that’s not what I asked. I asked how an Untouchable is *made*, not why an Untouchable is allowed.”

He cherished the look in her eyes, the way she tried to compose herself. Her inexperience made him delighted. She was ready to be moulded into something great.

“An Untouchable is made when I own a piece of it.”

Grabbing the skin over her side, pinching roughly, he pulled and twisted it.

“What the hell!” Parris yelled, trying to push him off of her. Her dark eyes pricked with pain.

“What are you doing?”

Releasing his hold on her, she lifted her shirt to look at the damage. There on the left side of her stomach, her tanned skin was an angry red.

“What was that?” she called out, her pain merging into anger and confusion.

The older man ignored her as he took a poker from the mantle, and placed it into the flames.

“You asked to become an Untouchable. You should have done your research about how you can become one. I own the trustee board of STK and Tony Moretti’s leg. I’ll own your left side.”

He cherished the way her eyes widened in realization.

“Leave if you want, *Bella,*” Giovanni called over his shoulder, “but know that this is your one opportunity to become an Untouchable.”

“You’re going to make me into an Untouchable tonight?” she panicked.

I've pulled the rug out from under her feet, Giovanni thought, watching her struggle to control her emotions. *Whatever her plans were, I've moved them along faster than she's ever anticipated. She must have been ready to work under me for months, maybe even years, until she earned that title.*

Piercing chestnut eyes stabbed into her.

"Is that a problem?" he asked innocently as he inspected the glowing poker. He could hear the way her heart was racing, the smoking machine in her mind trying to produce a response.

To manipulate the situation into a different outcome.

The surge of power that coursed through his veins was heavenly as he appeared before her, the poker a shade of red.

"Well, is it?"

'What if this wasn't the way an Untouchable was made? What if Giovanni was branding me for himself?' Giovanni thought, hiding his snicker. *So easy to read,* Bella.

"Why make me into an Untouchable so soon? Don't you know that I can do whatever I want once news spreads?" Parris tried to buy herself time to think.

Giovanni wouldn't allow that.

Taking a step back, she found herself trapped against the desk, Giovanni relentlessly not giving her space to breathe, space to think.

"Because I know your type. You're like me—hungry for something, hungry enough to do *whatever* to achieve it." He spoke into her ear. "I see myself in the way you think. I can practically hear the gears turn in your delicate head. Whatever your motive was to become an Untouchable doesn't matter. You'll learn soon enough that my will is everything. It is this city. It is your life. My will is your will, Parris. This is a gamble on my part, but it's a calculated risk. You'll be my new Untouchable, an Informant who can operate without restrictions. I want to give you that space to grow, to flourish. Once I've seen you grow before my eyes, I'll bring you back to me."

"Back to you?"

"Back to me," he repeated. "You'll never stray too far. Hell, I'll even respect your wishes and not force myself on you. But you'll be mine— my newest child, my prodigy, *my* Untouchable."

Her chest trembled as she listened, trying to read between the lines. His presence was all-encompassing.

Perhaps God has gifted me with another child with potential, just when Tony became a lost cause, Giovanni pondered.

"Do we have a deal, *Bella*?"

He pulled back, the poker a darker red now. She looked up at him, seeming to have come to her conclusion. Her smile resumed.

"You've got yourself a new Untouchable, Boss!"

It was dark in Ciel City, darker than usual, as though the stars and moon were mourning for her. Parris hugged her side as she slugged down the sidewalk. She knew that she shouldn't be out on her own, especially not after what Giovanni had done to her.

Shaking violently since leaving the red brick building, she couldn't control her body anymore. The vessel betrayed her. The pain in her side was unbearable.

"Is this my Achilles' Heel?" she asked the night. "The River Styx is a river of flames!" she laughed loudly, causing a few pedestrians to hurry past her.

Wiping her eyes roughly, she continued her march into Downtown. She couldn't afford to cry, not when she had achieved so much tonight. The year of planning paid off. The year of gathering information and erasing her past had worked. Her status as an Untouchable would travel fast. She could begin phase two.

"Owl... Owl would want to treat me," she mumbled to the night.

The doctor would be surprised she had really done it, despite her best efforts to deter Parris from actively pursuing her goal. The clinic had been a gold mine of information. All Parris had to do was continue to pull on the threads, following them into the docks, nightclubs, and pawn shops.

To every blackened corner of Ciel.

The light from *Jim's* beckoned her like a lighthouse in a storm. Her body physically relaxed as she ventured closer to the store. Her mind needed caffeine and food, her one safe haven left.

"You."

Came a gentle sound from behind her. Parris stopped. She didn't have the energy for him, not after tonight, not after a year, not after becoming an Untouchable.

"Where have you been?" Logan asked desperately as he rushed to her side.

Parris pushed him away, slugging through an alleyway, trying to escape him. Logan followed. His puppy dog eyes pleaded with her.

"I thought you left Ciel! I tried calling you! I thought your parents pulled you out of school. Where have you been?" he asked, stopping in front of her.

Parris sighed. Her side protested every second standing up.

"I don't know you. You're a stranger to me," she was not able to meet his eyes. She couldn't look up at him. The pained look she envisioned would be there.

"What are you saying?" he asked, desperation in his voice.

"I'm saying that you need to back up! Leave me alone!" she yelled back, fire sparking in her. She looked at him with a disgusted expression. His hair was longer than she last saw him; he was also taller. The biggest difference however was the sunken look in his eyes, as though he hadn't slept in the year since she left either.

"You don't know me. My name is Parris and I am an Informant. Do you understand? You don't know me anymore! The old me is dead."

"Parris? Don't say stuff like that, this isn't funny."

"Then take the hint, Logan O'Brien. You mean nothing to me, never have and never will."

"You're lying."

Parris shoved him, her side exploding at the action. But she had to get him away from her. She had to make him stay away. She had to protect him. She had promised Janine.

He called her name. Her real name. Not Parris, or even Achilles. The name made bile rise in her throat. She hadn't heard her name in a long time. Not since Janine had last said it. Not in a year.

"I told you my name is Parris!"

"No, it's not! Please just tell me why you left. I-I was so alone. I don't understand what happened with Janine, she didn't even leave a note! Did she tell you anything? Were there any signs that something was wrong? I spoke with her family, they were devastated, especially Angie. She couldn't stop crying the whole time…"

Parris dug her nails into her palm. She didn't need to hear any of that. She was there. She saw the way Janine's mother had fallen to the ground in shrieks, how her father stood there in disbelief as they buried their daughter. She saw the way Aunty Kim held Angie. She saw everything. She felt everything. She was Janine's note.

It was her cross to bear.

"Please just talk with me! You've been gone for a whole year. I want to know where you've been—why are you holding your side?" Logan asked, finally taking notice of her hunched posture, the sweat beading down her face, her pained expression.

"What happened?!"

Parris spat at him. Logan stumbled back, wiping his face.

"What the hell?!" he yelled.

"God, there was a reason your dad always hit you, you're fucking annoying!" Parris sneered. Logan's eye twitched. She had hit a delicate nerve. She had to make him leave her. She had to make him angry.

"No wonder you didn't have many friends in school, you're a clingy loser! I don't want to be around you. I want you gone."

"You don't mean that!"

"Don't I?" she yelled back. "I am telling it to your face. I don't want anything to do with a loser like you! No wonder Janine jumped! She was embarrassed to be friends with scum like y—"

Logan punched her across her face.

Parris fell backwards into a pile of trash. Logan panted as he stared at his fist. He had never hit anyone before. He wasn't violent. He never wanted to be like his dad when he drank too much. He snapped his head up when he heard her howl with laughter.

Tears fell down her face.

"Just like Daddy after all!" Parris cried as she laughed, as though she couldn't choose which emotion to feel at the moment. She chose to feel all of them, her face now a mess.

"You… you fucking Parrasite!" Logan yelled at her, tears streaming down his own face now.

Parris flinched at the name.

The trash hurt. Her side burned. Her heart shattered.

"Fuck you," Logan spat. His shoulders shook violently as he left her there.

Their friendship.

Their youth.

Ended at that moment.

Present Day.

"Angela Johnston is transferring to STK this fall," Patel announced as he took a seat across from the Informant. "Or rather, Angela Williams."

"Is she, now? That's her mother's maiden name," Parris commented, tapping away at her phone.

They sat inside his office on a stuffy summer morning. Patel rubbed his eyes; he had not aged well in the past ten years. The stress of the job and dealing with the Gates was not kind to him. Gray hair, deep frown lines, and perhaps chronic anxiety discoloured the composed man.

"I'm thinking of declining her transfer. God knows why she would want to come here, especially after what happened to J—"

"I say let her come. She must have a reason for coming to this septic tank."

"Are you sure, Parris?" he asked hesitantly, looking up at her.

His former student was more than unique. The day after Janine had jumped, she appeared at his house, knocking on his door in the middle of the night. She had asked him to remove her from the school's enrollment, to remove all traces of her from STK. He had been concerned. He knew that they were close friends, that Parris's parents called the school when their daughter didn't call them back, that she had disappeared. But Parris had told him that she *had* to disappear. He had threatened to call the police if she didn't go back home. She smiled as she threatened him back, witnessing Janine Johnston enter the car of Tony Moretti and not doing anything about it. He had breached his duty to protect his students. Patel was compelled to listen to her wishes.

Her dark eyes met his tired ones.

"I'm sure. But assign Jaya Sharma as her welcome buddy. Have her give Angela the orientation."

The principal sighed as he made a note. Rubbing his temple, he groaned, "Anything you can tell me about the trustee board's meeting before senior orientation? They mentioned something about the increase of gang activity in and around the school."

Parris headed to the door. "Since Rafael Gomez's involvement with the Halos and his expulsion, the city council is bringing heat down on the school to make sure the students don't involve themselves with the gangs. The media is on their ass, and if the national news starts investigating, then shit will hit the fan. The city already gave the Gates shit for the increase of drug activity in the school. But Giovanni said he spoke with Huifen about it. Shit if she'll actually listen this time."

"The Big Three aren't cooperating?" he asked, afraid. Parris smiled at her former principal.

A smile that was genuine.

"We're nearing the end, Principal Patel."

Parris wandered the streets of her city. The occasional update from Jaya, a message to Amir, the meetings with the Big Three: she filled her time. Her contact with the Army Reserve confirmed that the Ciel Re-Pavement Project was ready. That their federal guards would be in place for when the time comes. Her plans were coming to fruition.

She stayed strong, but she was exhausted.

She followed the two girls as they ventured into Chinatown, catching up to the alley that Angela and Jaya were trapped in.

Would you be proud of me, Janine?

CHAPTER TWENTY-ONE

Burning Sky

*V*engeance *is at Pier 3, come now! – Angela*

Logan re-read the message over and over again. He left the airport parking lot in a hurry, speeding back into the Downtown core.

He knew he should have left Ciel, to escape while he still had the chance to, but he couldn't say no to Janine's little sister. He drove past fires, bloodied bodies, and violent fights.

This is why she wanted me to leave!

This wasn't Ciel anymore. It was a battleground. He honked at a few Gates who tried to jump on top of his truck. He swerved, knocking them off with the momentum. He continued to drive through the chaos, abandoning his truck once he saw the police barricade.

Continuing on foot towards Pier 3, he prayed that he wasn't late for whatever 'vengeance' was.

The gunshot echoed across the dark pier.

Parris froze. Looking over her shoulder, she saw Angela, gun raised.

Aimed at the sky.

"My revenge won't change anything. Let them pay for their crimes," Angela announced. She lowered her arm; the gun pointed at the ground. "I'm not the only person they've hurt."

Parris continued looking at Angela, a proud look on her face. She was proud of her decision, a choice she couldn't make herself.

"Angie, I'm—" Parris started, but Giovanni pounced on Parris.

His moment came: a crack in Parris's concentration. His hand wrapped around her wrist with the gun, while his other hand grabbed her throat.

"Parris!" Angela called out.

The gun in Parris's hand went off wildly. Theo and Jaya dropped to the ground, covering their heads. Parris tried to claw the hand off, choking, trying to point the gun at Giovanni. Tony watched the scene unfold, his eyes glued to his father and the Informant in disbelief.

Angela pointed the gun at the pair.

"LET HER GO!" Angela yelled. She tried to point the gun at Giovanni, but there was no clear shot.

They danced around one another. There was no way she would hit only Giovanni. Parris couldn't break Giovanni's hold. It was futile. He was too strong. His finger jammed around the gun's trigger, wrapped around Parris's.

"Now then," Giovanni began. He pointed the gun at Tony. "First order of business. I'll need to start over."

"Dad?" Tony whispered.

"My biggest disappointment."

Giovanni pulled the trigger. Theo cried as Tony's brains sprayed the pier. Tony's body dropped heavily with a thud, surrounded by a pool of blood.

The Head of the Wings was dead.

Giovanni shifted his hold on Parris, holding her back against his chest. The gun now pointed towards the children. Parris's eyes widened, fear taking hold of her.

"Who should be next, *Bella*?" he whispered into her ear, delighted that he would win. That he could still be in charge.

"Angela, shoot him!" Parris yelled. She struggled against Giovanni's hold on the gun, trying to point it anywhere besides the kids. Angela didn't know what to do. Theo was still on the ground, and Jaya was starting to stand again.

"Shoot!" Parris begged.

"I can't!" Angela cried. "I don't want to hit you!"

"He'll kill you, Angie!" Parris yelled.

"I'll do it!" Jaya reached for the gun in Angela's hand.

Another gunshot rang across the pier. Jaya screeched as the bullet sailed through her palm. Giovanni grinned, successfully shooting her hand clean. Parris doubled her efforts to point the gun away. Jaya fell to the pier, blood everywhere. Her palm was shredded, the nerves and bones exposed. Theo rushed to her side, wrapping her hand in his varsity jacket, trying to stop the bleeding.

"SHOOT THE BASTARD!" Jaya cried.

"ANGIE!" Theo yelled.

"SHOOT NOW!" Parris pleaded.

Angela pulled the trigger.

She wasn't ready for the recoil, or for the sound, or the tremor that shot through her arm as the bullet sailed through the air. The bullet hit Parris in her side. But it didn't go through.

It didn't hit Giovanni.

"NO!" Angela cried brokenly. She fell to the ground. Blood poured from Parris's left side. Angela stared at the Informant wide-eyed. The ringing of the gun was the only sound she could hear.

"Parris!"

Parris looked down at the wound, then back up at Angela. Parris slumped against Giovanni heavily. Angela screamed. Giovanni tsked as he threw Parris away, the gun now in his hand. He stepped up to Angela, kicking her hand. The gun flew into the water, their one means of protection gone. Angela peered up, finding murder in his chestnut eyes.

"If not for your whore sister, none of this would have happened," Giovanni spat.

The gun was raised again, aimed at Angela. Fear coursed through her veins in an icy river. She was going to die. She was going to die on this pier on the cold night. Jaya and Theo wouldn't get far if they started to run in their state.

It was hopeless.

"NO!" Theo yelled. He jumped in front of Angela, putting himself between Giovanni and her. He met Giovanni's predatory eyes.

"Should I start with you, Theo? I can still salvage you, rebuild my Gates with fresh blood. Make you into my Untouchable." A dark chuckle from Giovanni sent shivers down their spines.

"Giovanni!" Parris groaned into the ground, pain lacing her voice.

Immediately, the Head followed the sound of her voice. He marched up to her, kicking her onto her back. Blood pooled around her, growing with every passing second.

"Of course, you would still be alive."

Parris coughed up blood as Giovanni dragged her to lean against the pier post. She panted, her breath coming in short gasps. Her face was deathly pale compared to its usual tan. She needed to keep his attention on her.

"What now, Boss?" Parris asked in a quiet voice.

Giovanni looked at his city. Parts of it were on fire and spreading. The sound of sirens was almost deafening. But that wasn't what hurt; it was her deception, her utter lack of gratitude. He kicked her across the face. She spat blood as her head snapped to the side.

"Your death will be painful, Parris. Bleeding out all of your lies and sins. This is your atonement for betraying me," Giovanni's hand trembled.

"And you, Boss?" she sang as her eyes stared into the night sky. "Your need for control will be gone once the feds take you in, your freedom gone as you rot in a cell for the rest of your life, nothing but the warden's bitch."

"What did you give them?" his face morphed into a look of desperation. His empire, his Gates were crumbled around him.

"Pictures, videos, recordings, bank accounts, your companies, the CCPD officers. Everything…"

She cried as he stomped on the bullet wound. Her pain turned into laughter as she looked up at him.

"You're nothing now," Parris sang, her voice growing quieter.

"All this for that girl?" Giovanni asked in disbelief, the gun lowered. There was no point in shooting her. It would only grant her a swift death.

"All this for her?!"

"ANGELA!" Logan roared as he ran to the Pier. His voice carried across the cold night. Giovanni watched him grow closer. He opened the chamber of the gun.

Only one bullet left.

The night had finally caught up to him, to his sins. It contracted around his chest like a barbed wire, shortening his breaths. His chest heaved against the concrete. His treasured city was ruined by his most prized creation. His eyes wildly scanned the chaos. Chestnut eyes jumped from burning buildings to the flashing blue and red lights from police cars.

His fist clenched like a vice; his fingernails dug deep into his palm, drawing blood.

All the pain he inflicted so readily did not mould her into his image. He wasn't her god. She wasn't his to control. She had deceived him. Her betrayal stung like a thousand knives lodged into his back. Into his heart.

She had done this to him.

"Not just for her," Parris breathed.

The sound of a police siren speeding towards the Pier caught

Giovanni's attention. He didn't have enough bullets. He didn't have his men or his weapons. He didn't have time to think! His mind searched for an answer in the Informant's fading dark eyes. He found only one scenario where he could remain in control.

She knew it, too.

Of course, she knew. He had made her, after all. He stared at his creation for the final time. She had been perfect. She was everything he had wanted in a child. The sound of the man running drew closer.

"I'll see you in hell, *Bella*."

Giovanni brought the gun to his temple, firing the only bullet left. Theo watched the body of the Head of the Gates crumple to the Pier. Parris coughed blood, smiling with a grimace at the sky.

Logan reached the pier panting. His eyes took in the kids: Theo shaking as he stared at Giovanni's dead body, Jaya whimpering as she wrapped her hand tightly with a jacket, Angela's shocked face as she stared at Parris. His eyes landed on Parris.

On the disturbing pool of blood that surrounded her.

"No!" he yelled as he slid next to her. Looking at her stomach, he added pressure to the bullet wound.

"No please, God, please no!" he wept as her eyes stared into the night sky.

"Parris!" he called out. "Parris, please stay with me, please!"

"Logan?" she asked weakly.

Her intense dark eyes were paler. Their gears finally halted to a stop, their time finally up.

"Yes! Yes, I'm here!" Logan cried as he held her. Her head nestled in his arm.

"Logan, I've missed you," Parris whispered. "The sky's so pretty."

Logan shook violently, but it wasn't from the cold. His chest quivered as he held his dying friend. This wasn't fair.

It wasn't fair.

"Why?" he sobbed. "Why put yourself through all of this? We could have left together! We could have at least had each other."

She smiled, and her eyes finally met his.

"I was afraid. I wasn't brave like Janine. I couldn't kill myself like she did. I had decided that I would kill myself a little each day until there was nothing left."

The sound of the police car screeching to a stop nearby didn't matter. Nothing else mattered but the two of them. Logan gripped her tighter.

"I missed our graduation trip. I'm sorry… I was busy," her mumbling filling the silent night.

Even the sounds of violence quieted down for her. The lake patiently listened to her. The sky watched her final act. Amir rushed to the Pier. She smiled as she looked past Logan, her dark eyes meeting Angela's one last time.

"It wasn't fair to you."

Her head dipped slightly in his arms. Logan screamed as he hugged her to his chest.

Amir was too late. He watched as screams filled the night. He went to the high school kids: checking on Theo, calling in an ambulance for Jaya, and wrapping Angela in his uniform jacket. She was whispering.

"Fair… wasn't fair…"

The girl watched the grieving man and the Informant with vacant eyes.

"Officer Hafiz?" Theo mumbled, his eyes still stuck on the dead body of Giovanni.

"Yes?"

"Please, no more… no more."

Theo shook with tremors; he couldn't be strong anymore. Amir took the pain away, holding him. He was there now. The kids didn't need to be strong anymore. He looked at Parris, upset that he had arrived too late.

But he had already said his goodbye to her.

Weightless. That was the only word Angela could use to describe what she was feeling. She felt like she was floating outside of her body. Her mind and body were not in agreement, opposed to cooperating with one another.

The flurry of blue and red lights, sirens, construction jackets, and noise made it hard to focus.

Angela dragged her eyes to watch Jaya's tear-stained face from her spot on the Pier. She hadn't moved since she fired the gun. Distraught was written over Jaya's small features as she cradled her hand.

I did that to her.

"We need a stretcher here!" a paramedic called out, wrapping Jaya's hand. Her hand was mummified in heavy bandages that formed a ball of sorts. The paramedics called out to one another before lifting Jaya into the back of the ambulance. Angela saw Jaya force one eye open before they slammed the doors shut.

The girls met one another.

With a screech, the ambulance rushed off.

A blanket was placed on Angela's shoulders. Officer Hafiz's jacket alone wasn't enough. The weight was good. She needed to be grounded.

Grounded to the reality she had created.

She couldn't move her head anymore. It required more energy than she had. She felt Theo shake next to her. From the corner of her vision, she could see him fist the blanket given to him. His eyes trained on the black bag that covered Giovanni Moretti.

An officer wearing a construction jacket spoke to her, but she couldn't hear anything anymore.

"NO!"

A yell came from the pier post. Angela already knew who that voice belonged to. Using every last ounce of willpower she had left, she turned her head to watch.

Logan held on to Parris, refusing to let go. Some officers tried to take her from him, a stretcher ready, but he refused to let go.

He couldn't let go.

Logan.

"You need to let go of her now," Amir reasoned. Logan shook his head, rocking himself and Parris. His blue eyes were red-rimmed.

"If she can still be saved, she'll need to go to the hospital now," Amir explained, placing a comforting hand on his shoulder.

"Please, Logan," Amir urged.

"No one else touch her..." Logan sobbed. Amir nodded in understanding, stooping down to pick her up. Logan's scarlet hands shook around the air.

Around nothing.

Amir held Parris gently as he walked to the back of another ambulance. The only telling sign that this was also difficult for him was his jaw clenching shut.

Parris's head lulled back and forth, her mesmerizing eyes closed, the world undeserving to look into them.

Angela sank further into the ground as she watched. That's all she could do. She could only watch the ambulance zoom away with Parris, Janine's best friend.

The woman she had shot.

Her eyes followed Amir as he returned to Logan. Crouching next to him, he whispered something in his ear, hand on his shoulder again.

"Why did it have to end this way?"

She had to look at him. She had to answer.

Facing him was hard, especially with Logan wailing just out of reach, with Jaya injured and gone, with Amir trying to collect the broken pieces left behind, with Parris…

They looked at each other, the children who found comfort from the cruel world together looked at each other—her friend, maybe her only friend left.

"Theo." Finding her voice was like catching a trail of smoke.

Theo's eyes were broken; he had seen enough to fill several lifetimes. His voice was coarse. She had remembered someone screaming earlier. It must have been him.

"You… you shot her," he said brokenly.

"I-I thought I could stop Giovanni. Everyone was yelling at me."

His lips trembled.

"I'm sorry, Theo," Angela whispered.

The feeling of weightlessness was gone as Theo embraced her. Angela croaked, her mind and body deciding to reunite. His hold grounded her. Theo held her tightly, and she felt his quivering heartbeat despite the layers. He always wore his heart on his sleeves after all. She raised her dead arms to wrap around him in return.

"Angie." Her name spilled over his lips.

"I'm sorry, Theo."

The hug was too tight, but who knew what would happen after tonight—if they would ever see one another again, if Angela would be locked away forever, if Theo would be taken away from her again.

They broke apart, her hands dropped to her side. She had used too much energy, all of her energy that was left. The adrenaline from earlier had long passed through her system.

Theo cradled Angela's head with gentle hands.

"Stay strong, Angie. This isn't the end of your story. You protected us. You had to shoot. Once this blows over, I'll find you."

An officer was pulling him up by the elbow. Angela hadn't noticed them.

"Promise you'll stay strong, Angie."

How could I promise that? After everything I've done, how could he ask that of me?

The warmth of his hands left her face. Angela slumped forward without him. He was leaving her, too. His eyes pleaded with her. His eyebrows pulled into a determined look.

"Promise me!"

He was out of reach.

"P-promise."

The word left her mouth before she could realize it. Despite the pain and sorrow, Theo's face broke into a sad smile of sorts.

"You promised, Angie! I'll see you soon!" He disappeared into the back of a police cruiser. The car noisily rushed off.

The night was darker without Theo.

"Angela, are you with me?"

A tanned face and green eyes appeared before her. She was grateful she didn't have to move anymore; her back was aching, legs asleep.

Amir re-adjusted the blanket on her, making sure it was keeping her warm.

Right, I'm wearing his jacket.

"What you're experiencing right now is shock from the trauma you've just witnessed. I know that this is difficult and you would rather not speak at all, but please, try to talk to me," Amir probed tenderly.

He looked over her shoulder briefly.

No one else was around. The people she cared for were whisked away. She had destroyed a part of them. She truly had nothing left.

"Who shot her?"

Whatever was left of her heart shattered into fragments.

"Logan," Amir reprimanded, and his hand pulled Angela closer, away from Logan, away from the man's rage.

Whether Amir did it instinctively or not, she couldn't tell. Her mind reeled with the realization she had forgotten someone, arguably the most important person.

The one impacted by this whole mess since the start like her. Scruffy beard and blue eyes appeared to her right.

"Who shot her, Angie?" Logan asked again. The sobbing and wailing from before was gone, replaced with a heart that was steeped in sorrow and coldness.

"Logan," Amir chided. "She's been through enough. She doesn't need to be questioned right now. I'll get a statement from her and the other kids later."

It was hard to tell if Logan was angry or upset. His face painted the picture of loss and fury so easily. But pain won. His shoulders fell the longer it took her to answer.

Did he look like this when Janine jumped?

"Logan," Angela whispered.

She had to tell him the truth. He deserved the truth. She had to atone.

Maybe if I tell him, he'll kill me. That would make up for it. If Logan kills me then this whole thing can end. Logan would get his vengeance.

"I… I shot her."

Amir's eyes widened at the confession. Logan gasped.

"It was me," Angela cried. "I shot Parris. I thought I could protect Jaya and Theo. Everyone was screaming at me. Giovanni's gun was pointed at us. He had just shot Jaya. Jaya got shot! I had to protect my friends… But the bullet only hit Parris. I killed her.”

Logan's hand shot out, grabbing at Angela. Angela sobbed as he snatched her, her body too numb to move.

“Logan!” Amir yelled, but it was too late.

I deserve this!

Amir's hand shot out to grab her but Logan was faster. Angela looked into Logan's dark eyes. Her chest heaved against concrete.

Angela's face was pushed into Logan's chest. She held her breath. Strong arms wrapped around her head. She felt his erratic heartbeat.

It matched her own.

“No, Angie. You didn't kill her,” Logan mumbled into her hair.

“I did. I had the gun!”

“No. No, you were asked to make a choice. You had to protect yourself and your friends. What happened after wasn't your fault.”

“BUT I SHOT HER!” Angela yelled, not realizing that she was wetting his shirt with her tears.

The cold air slapped her face as Logan pulled back, holding her by the shoulders. Amir grabbed Logan's wrist, watching the tragedy unfold.

“I shot her!” Angela confessed to the quiet night. There were no more ambulances or construction workers left. There was only Logan, Amir, and her left on this cursed pier.

“I tried to kill Giovanni and instead I shot my sister's best friend! How could I? How am I not at fault?”

The metallic smell of blood from Logan's hand flooded her senses.

Parris's blood.

“I shot Parris. I killed her! I thought I was protecting my friends but only she got hit! Why aren't you angry at me?!” she yelled, energy returning to her body. She slammed her arms against Logan's chest.

“Be angry, Lo! Hate me! Hate me!”

"I could never hate you, Angela," Logan asserted.

She grabbed a hold of his arms. Her nails dug into the material of his jacket. Angela wept loudly. Why Logan chose to gather the fractured pieces of her heart, Angela couldn't understand.

"You're just a product of this cycle. Just like me," Logan uttered. "I was always angry at myself for not doing anything to save Janine. You're angry that you thought you could avenge your sister, that you could protect your friends."

A comforting hand rubbed her shoulder. Amir spoke gently.

"Giovanni manipulated the entire situation. He is responsible for what happened tonight. I'll speak with Jaya and Theo and figure it out from there."

"Why?" Angela cried. "Why help me?! I killed her! I shot her even after everything!"

"Because," Amir replied, a knowing look in his green eyes. "This bloody cycle could have only ended like this."

CHAPTER TWENTY-TWO

Graduation Trip

The soft flurry of snow falling would cover Ciel City in a white blanket soon enough.

The soft hum of the medical devices became nonexistent background noise the longer Angela spent in the hospital room. The blinding surgical lights no longer seared her eyes. She could see parts of the city through her window; she often found herself passing the time by looking out. The needle-like building was in clear view.

I never did go up the Stairway Tower before.

A gentle knock came from the door. The giant window in the door spoiled the secret of who was knocking. There was no privacy afforded to her anymore, not after what had happened.

"Good morning, Angela."

Her nurse greeted her, holding a tray of cups filled with medication. He placed the tray on the bedside table, noisily taking down her readings and temperature.

"Your parents are outside waiting for you to wake up. Want me to let them in?"

She shook her head.

The nurse watched her with disinterest. He was accustomed to seeing the detached look on her face. He was here when she was admitted. A police officer brought her in just as the sun was starting to rise. He couldn't hear the hushed whispers of the officer and the department's doctor, but from the safety measures taken around the girl, he figured she was someone important.

Or, she had done something significant.

"Your behaviour has been very well-mannered." The nurse tried to make conversation. "The other nurses and I think you're an angel for being so cooperative."

His voice faded into static. Angela watched the snowflakes kiss the window, the little shapes they drew.

Since that night on the pier, she had been in this room. Her parents came in crying once they arrived in the hospital. Her mother held her too tight, afraid that if she let go, Angela would slip away again. Her father held her hand as he stood tall, praying quietly under his breath.

Thankful that he didn't lose another child.

They came every day once visiting hours were open to family. Someone must have spoken to them before they sat with her. They never mentioned the gun or the pier. Her mother would talk about the newest book she was reading while her father silently responded to work emails in the corner.

They were told to not speak about that night.

It would make sense. Angela barely spoke a word to her counsellor whenever he would pop in. She didn't want to speak with a stranger about what had happened.

They wouldn't understand.

Officer Hafiz would come every other day. He brought her donuts, placing them on the hospital table before taking a seat. He would update Angela on the investigation, assuring her that she wouldn't be charged with anything. He said that he was working closely with the prosecution. Angela nodded silently.

He understood.

The one time she did speak, it was to Officer Hafiz. Just as he said his goodbye and turned his back to her.

"How are Jaya and Theo?"

Turning around, Amir met her sunken eyes.

"Excited to see you, Angela."

She held on to those words for the coming days. Day in and out was a routine: the nurses took her readings; the counsellor would come in, attempting conversation; her parents would try to give her a sense of normalcy; Officer Hafiz brought donuts.

This was her life.

"All done; if you need anything just push the button!" the nurse instructed as he left, leaving the door open.

Soon enough her parents would flock into the room again, acting like their daughter didn't kill someone. Her mother would speak in hushed whispers on the phone with her therapist. Her father would pat her head before diving into his work.

"I think your room is nicer than the one I got."

That voice. She knew that voice. Angela's head snapped towards the door.

"It's got a view and everything. Maybe I can ask them to transfer me to this floor."

Jaya appeared in the doorway, dressed in her own baby blue hospital gown. Her hair was braided into two uneven braids, yellow and orange ribbons mixed in with her black hair.

"Do you like my hair? My sister likes to braid."

It suited her.

"Jaya—"

Angela's eyes wandered down to her right hand. There wrapped in bandages and in a brace was the hand that was shot.

"Jaya, I am so sorry."

Her friend sat on the corner of her bed. Her left hand held Angela's in a soft hold.

"I'm the reason your hand got shot. I didn't stop him!" Angela's throat was dry; she hadn't spoken in days.

"Hey."

Jaya's hand wiped the tears that collected on Angela's face. Angela pinched her eyes shut. She didn't deserve the gentle touch.

"I'm surprised you could still cry after everything. Personally, I've cried about six years' worth."

"Why aren't you angry at me?" Angela asked, sniffling. "You should hate me. I was too weak to shoot the gun sooner. If I had just shot Giovanni, we wouldn't be here."

Jaya continued wiping the tears away, her own face tired: heavy eye bags, prominent cheekbones, chapped lips. She was putting on a mask in front of Angela. Jaya sighed, her eyes watching her own hand move, her right one laying in her lap useless.

"I kind of blame myself, to be honest."

Angela stopped her, holding her by the wrist. Her eyebrows scowled.

"Blame yourself? What did you do? I was the one who went to the pier and brought you with me. You got fucking shot, Jaya!"

They sat in silence as Jaya collected her thoughts, deciding on what to say and how to say it.

"I spoke with Theo about it. He doesn't blame you, either, just so you know."

Angela's lip trembled.

"We both decided that we had followed you willingly to the pier. We both came over even though we knew something was going to happen. We didn't know *exactly* what, but you get the point. We could have left. We could have turned back and left you to decide what to do. We decided to stay with you. You didn't make that decision for us. We did. So please don't take our agency from us, Angie, not after everything do you get to decide that we were being manipulated by you, too."

Anger surged through Angela. She didn't understand. She *couldn't* understand.

"Jaya, I shot her!"

"You protected us! You tried your best, Angie. Not many people can move when a gun is pointed at them! I thought I could take the gun and shoot him for you. He was the one who should be blamed, not you. I don't blame you for not shooting him sooner. I tried to take the gun because I didn't want to lose you, too, Angie. I couldn't lose you," Jaya confessed.

Angela took deep breaths to calm her erratic nerves. She had imagined meeting Jaya after that night, that she would yell or curse her for what she had done. She didn't imagine this.

"I'm here because I need to say goodbye, Angie."

Jaya's eyes rested on her lap, on her injured hand.

"Goodbye?" Angela asked, swallowing around cotton. Jaya took a deep breath, trying to control her own emotions as well. She had lied earlier. Her own eyes were glazing over.

"My family is sending me to the West Coast. After that night, they decided that Ciel City was too dangerous for me. I have some family there and I've already been admitted to a medical rehab program. I hear the weather is nicer than here!"

Jaya tried to joke, but her eyes betrayed her.

"Jaya."

"Principal Patel will see if I can still complete my diploma at STK, which is nice of him considering I was the reason the Halos shot him in the first place."

"Jaya, you're crying."

Jaya's hand wiped at her cheek, laughing at the tears.

"Shit, I am."

"Fuck," Angela whispered, a sad smile tugging at her lips. Jaya chuckled as she continued wiping her face.

"Why are you crying too?!" Jaya yelled with a smile.

Both girls were at a loss as to what was happening. Angela laughed for the first time in days, despite her own tears. Jaya was mumbling about how they had done this before. Her laughter was infectious. Angela cried tears of sadness and love, beyond herself how the hurtful goodbye had turned into this.

"Say, Angie, whenever I come back to Ciel, would you give me a tour sometime?"

The girls looked at each other, not knowing when they would meet again—*if* they would ever meet again.

All they knew was that they would try.

The moment was bittersweet, but Angela responded with more confidence than she had felt.

"Of course, Jaya."

The Ciel City Police Department 97th Division was different. Amir entered through the glass green doors, no longer soul-sucking as he once thought.

Into his new home.

He greeted the federal guards, now dressed in their own uniforms of black, as he made his way upstairs. To room 201.

To Captain Chan's old office.

The office was still as quaint as ever, filled with the same chipped wooden desk and stained walls. The only difference was where he was sitting this time. A knock came on the door.

"Captain Hafiz."

Amir nodded at the federal guard as they gave him more files and USB sticks. They left promptly.

Getting used to the name will take some time.

The prosecution's office had thanked him for the copious amount of evidence he had gathered against the CCPD under Chan's command. His old comrades were now held in pre-trial custody, no bail given.

It wasn't him who gathered all of that evidence. He just showed up at the end and took credit for the whole Re-Pavement Project. There were constant rounds of applause when he would enter the room with the federal agents, or when he entered city hall to arrest the corrupt counsellors.

It was never his doing.

He opened a video from a USB stick, titled '*Angela Williams Johnston.*' His eyes drank in the pixelated image of her.

Of her dark eyes.

"My name is Parris; I am known as the Informant and I am an Untouchable."

Parris spoke to the camera mounted on her marble desk with her signature smile, her office in the background of the video. If Amir focused hard enough, he felt like he was in the room with her as she spoke, as though she were only speaking to him.

"I am of sound body and mind when I am making this recording. This recording is for Officer Amir Adel Hafiz, the only member of the CCPD who has not been bought by one of the Syndicates. He had successfully found a Wings trafficking hotel, a feat I had not accomplished. I expect the federal agents to keep Officer Hafiz on this investigation. The subject of this recording is Angela Williams Johnston, a seventeen-year-old senior student attending St. Katherine's High School."

Amir held his breath as he listened.

"I have been manipulating Angela to comply with my wishes. I have coerced and threatened her, and two of her friends, Jaya Sharma and Theo Grayson, into conducting criminal acts for me. These minors have been under my influence for some time and I take full responsibility for any and all of their actions. If you are watching this video, that means the Re-

Pavement Project was a success."

The federal guards had found the videos and documents when they searched through *Clueless*. Boxes of USB sticks mounted high on the white marble desk with a sticky note that read.

To: Officer Amir Hafiz.

They documented Parris through the years, her telling the camera what she had done to orchestrate the Re-Pavement Project.

Exonerating countless people.

Amir clicked through the files, finding recordings for Logan O'Brien, Lorenzo Cruz, Jaya Sharma, and Theo Grayson.

If he was upset that he didn't find a video titled for him, he didn't admit it. She would have just teased him for it, anyways.

The days started to seem a little different now after Jaya had spoken to Angela. Her parents beamed as Angela started to speak more, asking which day of the week it was, and if they would pick up some food that was actually edible instead of the hospital's attempt at meals.

They happily agreed.

Officer Amir had wanted to keep her at the hospital, close to Jaya, a space where he could position a federal agent on the door to keep an eye on her in case of anything. She was a vital witness to the night on the Pier.

"That's when the door to the other world was ripped open." Her mother's soft voice read her favourite fantasy book aloud. Angela leaned back, her hand wrapped around a warming cup of hot chocolate. She knew what happened next, but she still held the cup tighter. She closed her eyes, letting the words pull her into the book.

Heaven Williams glanced up at her daughter, a fond look in her eyes. She continued reading: "What was before her wasn't the entrance to any magical world she had thought—"

"It was a mirror into her very soul."

Angela's eyes flashed open. There at the door was Theo, reciting the book, snow in his hair, his nose red from the cold. Dressed in a new white and blue varsity jacket. Angela continued where he left off.

"Perhaps her greatest challenge yet."

Heaven welcomed him, fussing about how he'd catch a cold, shaking the snow off him. Theo blushed at the motherly affection. She muttered about making him a cup of hot chocolate before leaving them alone, a small smile hidden on her lips.

"Your mom's delightful," Theo stood by the door. He looked better than the last time she saw him, however long ago it was.

"Hey, Angie."

He was here in front of her. He was safe and here. Angela smiled at him.

"Hey, Theo."

The bed dipped slightly under his weight as he sat next to her.

"You kept your promise," he quipped, his eyes roaming her face and frame. She was healthy.

"I'm trying."

"That's all I ask of you."

Angela nodded; she had missed him. She had been wondering what happened to him after he was taken, if his dad had been released yet, and how he was coping after the death of the older man.

"Did Officer Hafiz say if you're in trouble?" Theo asked.

"I'm… I'm not sure yet. He said I was acting in self-defence."

Heaven entered the room again, giving Theo the piping hot chocolate. She scolded him gently about not introducing himself sooner. Theo sheepishly rubbed the back of his neck, trying to appease the woman.

"It's not everyday we get to meet Angie's friend," Heaven stated, looking between the two and smirking at Angela's blush, only faint enough that her mother would notice. "Especially one so cute!"

"Mom!" Angela groaned. Theo chuckled, his own ears burning.

The room hummed with a pleasant energy as the trio spoke. Heaven's teasing was easier with Theo on her mother's side, poking fun at Angie. Angela rolled her eyes weakly at the pair, a smile plastered on her face.

"You need to visit again, Theo. I'm sure it would boost Angie's morale," Heaven called out.

The hot chocolate was gone now. Theo made his way towards the door, ready for the cold again. He met Angela's eyes.

"I promise, Mrs. Johnston."

It had stopped snowing sometime during the night. Angela watched the city from the sterile room. She pressed her forehead against the cold glass. She watched the ambulance bring someone in on a stretcher, the old man hurrying to the subway with his bag of books, the police officer entering the hospital.

Ciel City. The city she had begged her parents to return to. The city she grew up in. The city that took her sister from her. Ciel was its own being. It wasn't just buildings and busyness. Its presence required something from its inhabitants.

The city constantly took.

It took Jaya away. It took Theo's dad. It took Logan's friends. It took her parents' happiness. It took away her childhood—her innocence, her dreams, her beloved sister.

It also took *her*.

Ciel City was a cruel beast. It demanded for Parris's blood to be spilt, even when Angela didn't want to anymore.

"Busy?" Amir asked as he lingered by the door. She had seen him in the reflection of the glass.

I wonder what Ciel took from you.

Angela shook her head. Amir entered, placing the bag of donuts on the table. He took his chair near the bed. Angela liked it when Amir visited. He reminded her of Janine, of the same gentle presence.

It was a welcomed routine.

"I heard that Jaya and Theo stopped by to visit." He removed his hat, placing it on his knee. "I'm glad you got to see your friends, Angela."

"Congratulations on making Captain," Angela spoke quietly. Amir chuckled fondly.

"Thank you, I wish I could say I earned it."

She turned to the man. Perhaps Ciel didn't take anything from him. Maybe he was the exception to the rule.

He was given something.

"Sometimes I regret not calling you sooner, Captain Hafiz," Angela shared, taking a seat on the bed. Amir watched carefully; it was her first time having a conversation with him.

"Amir is fine, Angela."

"I regret not calling you after Tony attacked us, Amir. I can't stop myself from thinking how different things could have been if I just told you everything there and then."

Amir nodded as he listened to her.

"You could have helped, right? This whole thing could have been avoided if I told you just how involved we were, and what Parris was planning to do. You would have helped us, right?"

"You had to protect your friends, yourself, on that pier." Amir understood. "Angela, it does no good to dwell on the past and the things we could have done differently. What we can do is reflect and learn from our mistakes."

"What is there for me to learn from all this?" Angela desperately pleaded.

Amir stared at his hat. Angela waited patiently; she needed to hear his answer. She knew that the nurses told him that she hadn't spoken with the counsellor yet. Only Amir understood her. He could help.

"When I first came to Ciel City, I came with a goal in mind: to lead the Anti-Gang Task Force," Amir recounted, a distant look in his green eyes. "I came with such vigour, ready to make that dream happen, only, I didn't know what to do. I was naive. I had… a guide of sorts. I followed leads, got into trouble, faced challenge after challenge, betrayal, and a spectacular chase scene in the end."

Angela held on to every word.

"Now that I've accomplished my initial goal, it's hard to refocus. My story should be over. I've defeated the villain. But, I'm still alive. I'm alive and kicking. So my new goal is to serve Ciel in this new role. In a way, that's just my original goal repackaged as something different."

Amir looked at Angela; a kind look entered his eyes as he saw how focused she was.

"You're still alive and kicking, Angela. You've accomplished your original goal."

He held his hand up to stop Angela's interruption. She closed her mouth.

"Whatever that original goal was, it's over. You've done it. What came next is now over. Move forward, Angela. I'm not a therapist, so please take my words with a grain of salt. In a way, you're still in that car waiting to give your sister her lunch. You need to leave that car. Get out. What do you want now? What will you live for? You've already lived for revenge and your sister. You've finished that chapter of your life. Think, what comes next, Angela?"

"Angie."

"Sorry?" Amir asked.

"You can call me Angie. That's what my friends and family call me."

Amir sighed softly. Angela was finally warming up to him.

"Angie," he corrected himself. "Learn from the past and move forward. I know you can."

Angela was right, he was an older sibling. She couldn't help but feel a little jealous of whoever Amir's sibling was.

"Think about it and have a donut; I bought some new flavours for you. And yes, I brought your mom her favourite."

The crinkling sound of the bag filled the room. Angela handed Amir a maple donut, helping herself to an allspice one.

"Now, that's a stereotypical image of a cop! The only thing missing is a coffee."

Angela wasn't fast enough to stop her giggle. Amir raised an eyebrow playfully at Theo, who stood by the door.

"You're lucky I bought enough." Amir shook his head smiling. "Help yourself, kid."

Theo sat next to Angela as he dug through the bag, satisfied with a blueberry donut.

"You're taking good care of Angie, Theo?" Amir asked after a moment of studying the kids.

"Sir, yes, Sir."

"And taking good care of yourself?"

Theo nodded as he took a bite of the donut. Amir, seemingly satisfied with the answer, finished his own before standing up.

"I came by to tell you something, Angie. You can stay, Theo," Amir instructed. Angela swallowed, her hands turning clammy at his tone.

The police hat was re-equipped. Amir was gone and now replaced with Captain Hafiz.

"The funeral service is today. I wanted to be the one to tell you."

A funeral was the natural progression of a dead body. Angela knew this. They had one for Janine. She knew that death was final. She knew this was coming. But knowing and being prepared were two different things.

"So… so she's dead?"

Angela reprimanded herself for asking such a stupid question. She had shot her. There was blood and a body. Of course, she was dead. But when she had been pried from Logan's arms and rushed to a hospital, Angela couldn't stop herself from hoping, hoping that by some miracle Parris was saved.

That she was alive and kicking.

"I'll be on my way now." Amir readjusted his hat, hiding his eyes. He bumped into Angela's parents by the door. He tipped his hat towards them as he pushed past into the hallway.

Angela watched him disappear.

The bed shifted. Her parents asked her why Theo was running after Officer Hafiz, and if he had bought her mother's favourite flavour today.

Move forward. I need to move forward.

"Captain Hafiz!" Theo called out as he ran after the man. Amir continued his march into the elevator, upset when Theo's hand jammed between the door, forcing his way inside.

"Go back upstairs, Theo."

"Captain Hafiz, please take me with you to the funeral," Theo panted.

The elevator announced the first floor. Amir got out. Theo followed him.

"I'd rather not."

"Please!" Theo begged. "She's done a lot for me… I want to pay my respect."

Amir stopped, giving him his full attention. She had mentioned Theo briefly during their meetings, but she never elaborated as she had with Angela and Jaya.

Still keeping secrets, Amir thought as he saw the expression on Theo's face, the earnest look of waiting for approval.

"Fine, you can ride with me."

From the few times Amir had interacted with Theo, the kid was usually in good spirits, but during the entire car ride to the cemetery, Theo had been quiet. Amir welcomed the silence as he shifted through his own thoughts.

Grass peeked between bundles of snow. The tombstones were still in plain view. Amir saw the few cars parked ahead. A group of people scattered around a grave.

Everyone was here.

"Come on," Amir told Theo as he left the car, taking the flowers he had bought from the back. Walking towards the grave and plain coffin, he spotted a familiar black car parked close by.

"Go on, Theo. I'm right behind you."

Theo continued his march, hands in his varsity jacket's pockets as he approached the grave.

Amir knocked on the black glass of the driver's seat.

"Not coming out?" Amir asked once the glass was lowered. Lorenzo sat in the driver's seat defiantly. His usually composed face was gone, replaced with a contorted look of grief.

"It's an empty coffin," Lorenzo answered dumbly.

Amir looked back at the grave, "Yes, it is."

The voice of the funeral director called for Amir with a raised hand. He was the one to organize this. It was time.

"I'm not burying an empty coffin."

"Lorenzo—"

"Where's her body? I want the body so the staff of *Clueless* can have a proper funeral."

"I've already told you, Lorenzo. Forensics has it."

"You're Captain!" Lorenzo spat, tears shimmering in his eyes. "Get it back!"

Amir sighed. He understood the kid. He really did. But he couldn't give Lorenzo what he wanted, no matter how much sense it made.

"Please come out for the burial; you'll regret it if you don't. Now, please excuse me."

Amir continued his march to the grave. He didn't hear the sound of a car door opening.

I've done what I can.

Amir nodded as he passed by an older woman. He walked up to the director and pallbearers.

"Is this everyone?" the director asked with a look.

"Yes," Amir answered respectfully.

The director nodded as they instructed the pallbearers to get into position.

"You would think more people would show."

Amir turned around to face Logan. Amir greeted him with a handshake.

"I saw your car but didn't see you."

"I was visiting another friend."

Amir nodded; he knew which other friend he was referring to. The grave of Janine Johnston was nearby. Logan patted Theo's shoulder.

"Keeping out of trouble, kid?" Logan asked, a soft look on his face.

"Yes, Sir," Theo mumbled, his eyes glued to the tombstone. It didn't have a name or any dates. Nothing to indicate who was buried here. Just a phrase in Latin was engraved on its gray stone.

Acta est fabula, plaudite.

"'The play is over, applaud'," Logan deciphered the headstone.

"Captain Hafiz, we will begin to lower the coffin now. If anyone has any last words they would like to say, now is the time to do so," the director instructed the group. Amir nodded as he looked around.

"Ma'am," Amir offered.

A tall woman with sharp features took a step forward towards the grave.

"That's Owl," Amir whispered to Theo. Owl's piercing eyes burned into the coffin, as though she were scolding Parris now.

"She was a pain in my ass," Owl announced.

Sad smiles painted everyone's face. Owl continued.

"She was a nuisance and a brat. She never listened to anything I said. Always arguing back. Never caring about her own well-being. She would mock me when I would try to give her a talking-to. But… I never had any children of my own…"

Owl looked at the sky, pursing her trembling lips.

"I will forever be haunted that I couldn't stop you. That I couldn't heal you." She stepped back, away from the grave.

All eyes travelled to Logan. He stood next to Owl, so it was his turn. They waited for him to say something. He shook his head, his jaw clenched.

"I'll go," Theo offered quietly. "I don't really know you like everyone else here. But thank you for everything you've done. For helping me when I was in trouble. For giving me a second chance."

Taking a look around the group, Amir took in a deep breath.

"Words cannot express my gratitude. Without you, I don't know where I would be."

The coffin was lowered. Amir threw in the flowers.

"Goodbye."

The sound of dirt covering the coffin was difficult to hear. The group stood there silently.

A car door snapped in the distance. Amir watched Lorenzo race to the group, holding something in his hands.

"She wanted you to have this." Lorenzo's cheeks were red as he held out a familiar jacket and a yellow folder for Logan.

"Lorenzo?" Logan whispered.

"Take it!" he cried. Logan took the items, confused about why he was being given the jacket.

Once the items were taken, Lorenzo ran back to the car. Amir and Logan called out after him, but he was gone, speeding through the cemetery.

Away from her grave.

"Why?" Logan asked, coughing to clear his voice. Amir watched Logan bring the jacket to his face, taking a deep breath.

"You should open it, Logan," Owl suggested. Logan nodded as he handed the doctor the jacket, pulling out a wad of paper and a USB stick from the folder.

"Shit," Logan spat, tears spilled down his face.

"What is it?" Theo asked.

"It's her will," Owl answered. Logan's hands shook. "She's left everything to Logan. There's a few other instructions."

"She thinks I want this?!" Logan yelled.

"Logan, please, calm down," Amir comforted. Logan sank to the ground, a few feet away from the grave. He shook violently as a tremor ran through his body. Owl pried the will from his hands as she read over the document. Logan's fist slammed the ground over and over as he yelled.

"Hey," Amir caught Logan's arms. "Hey, it's okay, Logan. Why are you upset? Tell us, we can help. Please let us in."

"She's been paying for my therapy!" Logan exploded. "She's been taking care of me for all these years! She's been here for me and I've been cursing her!"

Amir hugged Logan. The man shook. It was his first hug in years. Logan held on tightly.

"I wish she really did hate me, then I wouldn't feel like I've wasted my life without her," Logan wailed.

The grave was filled.

The funeral director whispered to Owl, and the staff took their leave. Amir held Logan. Owl smacked Logan's head for being dramatic.

Theo watched, his eyes scanning across the cemetery, pausing on a person visiting another grave in the nearby distance. His gaze came back to Logan.

Theo rubbed away the few tears that escaped.

The deep musk of coffee beans roasting was a welcomed smell. Amir placed a cup in front of Theo as he took a seat across from him.

The inside of *Jim's* had been a getaway Amir found himself frequenting more often. The warm lighting and comfortable chairs had been his refuge since the Ciel Re-Pavement Project. Especially after the funeral and calming Logan down, Amir was emotionally exhausted.

But his job wasn't done yet.

Theo thanked him as he held his cup, his eyes wandering over the café. Theo had asked if he could speak to him after the funeral when Amir asked where to drop him off.

"Thank you for taking me to the funeral, Captain Hafiz," Theo made conversation. "What are you drinking?"

"A Ciel latte," Amir replied.

"Is it good?"

Amir looked inside the cup for an answer, a fond look in his eyes as he replied.

"I'm not a fan, but I will be."

Theo nodded as he took a swing of his hot chocolate. "You got the donuts from here? They were pretty good. I'll have to start coming when I'm in the area."

"Yeah," Amir took a sip, "a friend recommended this place. I can't seem to get my coffee and donuts elsewhere now."

They sipped their drinks in silence. Soft music played over the speakers as the baristas quietly made drinks.

"Are you ready to tell me what's on your mind, Theo?" Amir asked. He could see the way Theo fidgeted. "I hope you're not going to try to negotiate your dad's charges."

"No," Theo responded quickly. "I'm done trying to help him. I think the justice system will decide what happens to him next."

"Good man."

"Maybe I could shadow you for a day? It would be cool to see how the new CCPD protects the city now."

"You're thinking of going into criminal justice?" Amir asked as he sipped the latte.

"At first I wasn't. I wanted to help people by being a doctor and my grades would get me there... but recently I want to help people in a different way. I want to keep Ciel safe."

Amir nodded, his respect for the boy growing the more time they spent together.

"So then what did you want to speak with me about?"

Amir wasn't prepared for the story that Theo told him over the course of the next few hours, how he had gone to the Gates for money. Theo told Amir, tears flowing as the different horrors were recounted. Amir's eyebrows furrowed the longer the story was told.

The more traumatic it became.

"I've gotten rid of all of his gifts, but I still have a handkerchief he gave me. I want to get rid of it, too, but I can't… just not yet."

"I'm sorry, Theo," Amir broke his silence, his first words in hours. "I'm sorry you had to endure so much and are dealing with the effects 'till now."

"Angie said to speak with you since you understand. I'm sorry for bombarding you but I just needed to tell someone. I needed to tell an adult who wouldn't use that information against me," Theo mumbled, rubbing his eyes red.

"Never apologize," Amir assured. "You can always come to me."

Theo sniffled. Amir watched him, thinking of everything he had just been told. How he could realistically help the boy. An idea came to mind.

"Theo, I remember you mentioned you play volleyball?"

"Yes?"

"Why don't we play sometime? The CCPD has a gym in the division we can use. Free up your Saturday mornings. We'll play for a bit, then come here for a catch-up session. How does that sound to you?" Amir offered.

His heart was warmed by the expression of relief on Theo's face. Amir couldn't save Nour, he couldn't save countless others. But for the few he could save, he had to give it his all.

"Sounds perfect, Captain Hafiz."

The white truck cruised past mountains and plush white-covered forests. Logan drove past the welcome sign he had dreamed of reading one day:

Welcome to Banff.

Logan's ears popped from the increase in elevation, the road winding up a mountain. The GPS announced his arrival as he pulled into a beautiful stone cottage covered under a blanket of snow. The home was tucked away in the trees.

Logan left the car, his ears perking at the sound of a nearby river. He fished through the yellow folder given to him at the funeral. He pulled out a key as he walked to the front door.

The door unlocked.

Logan entered the cozy cottage, turning on the lights as he looked around. Wooden beams, flannel blankets, maple leaf-shaped pillows. He gasped when he saw the hot tub outside facing the mountains.

It was perfect.

He entered the heart of the home, the living room where he planned to steal back all the time he had spent in the city.

"Hey," he answered his phone. "I just arrived."

"The drive was okay?" Amir asked on the other side.

"Pretty smooth. The cottage is really nice."

"She did have good taste."

Logan huffed, "She did."

"Well, I have to go. Just wanted to check in on you, Lo. Looking forward to welcoming you to the CCPD's community services department when you're back in town."

"I'll grab some beers for us to celebrate," Logan suggested, walking deeper into the cottage. He hung up the phone, happy that Amir called.

Stopping in front of the fireplace, his eyes travelled to the mantle. There in a frame was his homecoming picture. Logan smiled at the picture. Janine and Parris smiled back at him.

He could heal here.

Aunty Kim's apartment was filled with a pleasant hum. The home felt full and alive with Angela's parents there. Her father replied to emails in the bedroom. Her mother made dinner in the kitchen. They had decided to remain in the city with Angela until Christmas break, to support Angela's return to STK, to graduate high school and apply for university.

"We should have moved back with you," Heaven cried into Angela's lap the first time they saw her in the hospital.

Angela knelt in front of the T.V. cabinet, retrieving the framed photo of her riding Janine's shoulders. She placed it right on the centre of the console, along with her own Halloween picture with Jaya and Theo.

One last thing, Angela thought, holding a dry eraser. She wiped down the hung map of Ciel. The circles and markings Jaya had made all that time ago disappeared with a swipe.

"I'm heading out for a run now!" Angela announced.

"Be back before dark!" Angela's mother's voice called out.

"Wear your jacket, Angel!" her father shouted.

Racing down the stairs, Angela passed the kids playing in the hall. The ball rolled past her.

"Over here!" one of them screamed. Angela kicked it back to them. An echo of 'thank you' rang. Zipping her puffer jacket, Angela stepped onto the streets of Ciel City.

Her breath fogged in front of her. A thin layer of snow covered the buildings but the sidewalks and streets were clear. Her feet beat against the concrete.

The symphony continued. The orchestra of cars honking, neighbours chatting, and construction played in unison. Each section was right on cue. The song would never end. So long as Ciel waved its conductor's baton, the melody would never cease.

Angela panted as she ran into the Downtown Core, through the Entertainment District, not sparing a second glance at the black building as she sped past it.

Clueless no longer taunted her.

My first day went pretty well! Can we call later? I can't wait to tell you about the rehab program here. – Jaya

Angela smiled as she set a time to call Jaya. Her pace didn't falter as she crossed the road into the crimson-lined street with dragons encircling large pillars. The alleyways were no longer as shadowy and dark as she remembered them.

Chinatown had lost its edge on her.

If you and your friends want to come to the cottage for your graduation trip, I can make you an extra set of keys. Also, which souvenir do you prefer, a beaver or bear plush? – Logan

Ciel City wasn't only cruel. There was a gentler side to the city. She just hadn't noticed 'till now. Logan was always checking in on her. He admitted that he had waited to play the big brother role to her, and that losing another loved one pushed him to do what he wanted. Her parents had been overjoyed to see him after so long. Angela asked for the beaver.

I need another statement from you. Why don't you come to the CCPD on Saturday with Theo? – Amir

She finally came to a stop on the pier, hands on her hips as she stared at the lake, warning her that running season would soon be over. Panting, she walked to Pier 3. The blood had been cleaned.

Only a bullet hole in the ground served as a memento of that night.

"I'm sorry I shot you," she confessed to the lake. "I'm sorry I didn't choose revenge. If I had, you might still be here, avoiding me, or hitting me over the head for following you."

A sad smile pulled at her lips.

"I was jealous that you were friends with Nini, that you and Nini and Logan got to be friends. You three spent so much time together. I wanted that for myself. I wanted Nini to spend more time with me. I wanted friends of my own."

Angie! I have to take you to this awesome café called Jim's. *Let's go for a study session together tomorrow?* – Theo

"I guess I never realized that I had Jaya and Theo. Even Logan! I had them, despite looking for you; I should have been focused on them."

The pier didn't respond.

"We both lived our lives for Janine. We were both sides of the same coin. You never left that rooftop, Parris. I love Janine more than anyone. But I want to live for myself, discover what I want to do, who I will become."

The sun began to dip behind the horizon.

"I'm sorry you never got to heal, Parris."

Another message from Theo, Jaya sent a picture of the ocean, her parents let her know dinner was almost ready, a picture of the beaver plushie from Logan.

"I'm ready to heal."